Christmas at
CLARIDGE'S
KAREN SWAN

PAN BOOKS

First published 2013 by Pan Books
an imprint of Pan Macmillan, a division of Macmillan Publishers Limited
Pan Macmillan, 20 New Wharf Road, London N1 9RR
Basingstoke and Oxford
Associated companies throughout the world
www.panmacmillan.com

ISBN 978-1-4472-1969-9

3 5 7 9 8 6 4 2

A CIP catalogue record for this book is available from the British Library.

Typeset by Ellipsis Digital Limited, Glasgow
Printed and bound by CPI Group (UK) Ltd, Croydon, CR0 4YY

For Andrew and Eilidh,

who will no doubt read this book out loud all the way up the M6.

Prologue

April 2003

She awoke with a start. Her dream had been greedy, sucking her into a deep, motionless sleep, and her heart pounded heavily within her chest at the sudden fright. Above her head, the thin blue paisley curtain fluttered wildly like a trapped bird at the open window, the room falling into sporadic darkness as battle-fresh storm clouds surged across the sky, blocking the moon's earthly gaze. She blinked and lay perfectly still, watching the curtain flap and flail and listening to the ghostly sounds outside as the gusting wind skimmed the sea's skin and sprayed droplets through the air, misting the sheet so that it clung to her body like a shroud.

The bang came again and she jumped – not because it was particularly loud, but because it was out of place. The storm had been forecast and everything was tethered. That gate had been locked. She had done it herself.

In one move she was up on her knees, her face scrunched against the wind as it found her in the narrow window and whipped her long dark hair around her like Medusa's snakes. She saw the dark green trellised gate bang against its metal post again before sweeping back on its hinges, ready for the next attack. Her eyes lifted to the frothing surf behind it as rearing white horses stampeded the inlet, throwing themselves against the basalt rocks, while the gate crashed closed again and again and again – the drummer boy to the sea's cavalry charge. If she was going to get any sleep . . .

Her bare feet touched the cold tiled floor as she pulled on the white dotted cotton nightdress it had been too muggy to wear before the storm had broken. She opened her door soundlessly and looked down the long hall. Shadows played in silence, interrupted only by the caprices of the clouds, and downstairs a Viennese wall clock ticked. She ran lightly, the pads of her feet making a tiny sticky patter only the mice could hear.

She moved like a ghost through the kitchen, automatically reaching high for the back door keys that were stored safely on a hook. But they weren't there. Tentatively she put her hand to the handle and pushed down. It was unlocked.

She hesitated, listening for further sounds that would indicate activity or reasons to be outside in the storm, but everything around her seemingly slept on. But . . . she looked at the handle again; someone was up. With a deep breath, she stepped outside, immediately hunching herself into a stoop as the hot wind lunged at her in snappy gusts. Her hair flew across her face, and she had to release one hand from clutching her nightie to pin her hair back behind her ear as she looked across the gardens for signs of life. She was alone. The chickens were nestled together in the furthest corner of their coop, the tree branches empty and there was no sign of the black and white stray cat with ginger tail and eyebrows either. She hobbled over the cobbled-mosaic path, as above her, the olive and cypress trees bent low as if in greeting, the wild daisies in the stone walls nodding their heads in frantic unison.

She reached the gate mid-swing, only just stopping it from slamming again. Replacing it on the catch, she reached down to re-attach the chain that she knew she had secured earlier. Padlocks didn't just unlock themselves and there certainly wasn't enough power – even in these winds – for the gate to force it. To open it required a key that was left on the same hook with the back door keys. Who was out here?

She looked across the small, narrow road that divided the property from the rocky shore, searching for an untethered boat on the savage swell or an uprooted tree – anything that might explain why anyone would come out in this weather. But the moon was eclipsed by buffeting clouds suddenly and the garden plunged into darkness. Shadows were swallowed whole and the wind howled as it victory-lapped the lone villa.

That was why she saw it, the barest flicker of a candle further down the shore path, the only light out there. Her eyes focused with pinpoint accuracy as she keened into the headwind, trying to see the dot of light in the distance. No one would willingly choose to step outdoors during a storm like this. Something had to be wrong.

Letting the chain drop heavily from her hand, she opened the gate again and crossed the narrow road, darting straight into the protection of the fig-tree-lined tunnel on the other side that would take her down to the stepped terraces and the bar area, and then beyond that, swirling down in a vortex of cobble steps towards the beach and boat stores.

The ground was wet beneath her feet as spray – all that was left of the waves pounding the rocks and tors and walls – fell like mist, making her hair and nightie cling defiantly to her skin in spite of the wind's assaults. Her hands smacked against the jagged walls for blind guidance as she headed towards the solitary flicker that she could see now was coming from the tall, round folly on the small bay's furthest promontory. With relief, she knew the dark path she was on would lead directly to steps that descended to the headland; the door was only locked at the bottom, where it opened onto a small concrete bathing platform a metre above the sea.

Disorientated by the dancing, whirling darkness, she reached the first steps before she expected to, almost falling headlong down them and having to grapple with the wall for support, grazing the skin on her forearms. She closed her eyes as the sting smarted, her hands clasping the cuts as her heart pounded from the near miss. A shiver shot over her skin; she was shielded from the warmth of the Saharan-sourced wind here and the chill of her damp hair and skin began to creep.

A sudden noise – a sob? – beneath her made her catch her breath. She strained to hear more and made out the dull sweep of skin on stone, as if something or someone was being dragged, and then a sharp scraping as though furniture was being moved. She waited, her breath held, one hand slapped over her mouth as an insurance policy. There came the sounds of hurried breathing, of panting.

She froze, suddenly certain that whoever was down there, and whatever they were doing, it had nothing to do with the storm. Although the small windows on the stair-well were open to the elements, with only iron bars at them, the steps themselves ran down a central spine, blocking the floor below from sight and protecting everything in there from the weather. Whatever was happening down there, in the dead of night, amidst the storm, it was happening in secret.

She looked behind her into the enveloping blackness, knowing she should turn back; knowing that whatever was going on, it had nothing to do with her; she wasn't supposed to see this. She was eighteen. Her whole life was spread before her like a beautifully laid picnic.

The breathing around the next corner grew more ragged and desperate, building . . . She turned to go. She had to get out.

'Help . . . me.' The whisper reached out to her – only her – in the darkness.

She spun round, her eyes wide and black with fright. Had they heard her? Had she heard correctly? Above the wind, she didn't know if she could trust her ears. But she could trust her eyes. Every instinct was telling her to turn and run, to leap over the steps three at a time and escape back to the safety of the storm. There was fear here. She could feel it reaching up the stairs like ivy and entwining her.

She was unseen, but already a part of this. Even as her head screamed at her to run, her feet began to move, spiriting her forwards and downwards in silence as the storm raged above. Shaking palpably, instinctively sensing that each step she took was a step away from her own path, she turned the corner.

Two pairs of eyes met hers. And she stepped out of the shadows.

NEW YEAR'S EVE, 2013

Chapter One

The red leather-clad phone on the table buzzed waspishly, jolting Clem out of her meditation on the rain. She read it with a sigh.

> *'Where ARE you? If you're not here in five minutes, I'm coming to get you.'*

The sender hadn't signed off, but then, she didn't need to. Stella and she practically maintained an open line to each other. Her hand fell back onto the silk pouch resting on her lap and she looked out into the slippery, gleaming night. It was just gone nine thirty and she'd made a solemn pinky-promise to get there soon after eight, but for all her hard-partying reputation, she loathed New Year's Eve. It was the second worst night of the year in her book.

'Wardrobe crisis,' she texted back.

The reply was instantaneous. *'Bollocks! We decided on the sequin skirt and mohair jumper. Move it!'*

Clem's eyes fell down to her copper sequinned mini skirt – which flashed her extra-long still-brown legs – and the winter-white sweater that slipped off one still-brown shoulder. Stella always knew when she was lying.

'Shoe crisis,' she half-heartedly tried again whilst sliding

her feet into the metallic bronze python stilletoes lying abandoned beside the sofa and pushing herself to standing. At 5 foot 9 inches in socks, the shoes took her above 6 foot and her gaze drifted out the windows onto the reflections in the puddles on the pavements outside. It really was raining very hard she noticed for the first time. Stella's flat was only a couple of streets away, but she'd be soaked if she walked there, and what were the chances of catching a cab on the Portobello Road on New Year's Eve?

The phone buzzed again. *'Pythons. And FYFI Josh just arrived and been ambushed by bosomy blonde in red.'*

'What?' Clem screeched to the empty room. With sudden focus and impressive speed, she raced into her bedroom, digging beneath the piles of dirty clothes for her bag and a coat. Her hands found the rabbit-fur jacket (or *'lapin'* as Stella insisted on saying, making it sound like an exotic tea) and she held it up questioningly. She'd bought it on a whim in the market last week and worn it home in the rain so that now the fur looked like it came from a rabbit that had died of myxomatosis. Hmm.

It was still chucking it down, so she ran back into the sitting room and grabbed the tobacco unlined leather jacket off the hook on the back of the door. It had cost a bomb and she couldn't quite remember whether she'd actually got round to waterproofing it yet, but there wasn't time to worry about that now. Josh was at the party. He was there and she was not, and a woman with a bosom was making a move – Clem was damned if she was going to let that wench undo her two months and nineteen days of hard graft getting him to believe that there really was more to her than just a good-time girl.

Grabbing her keys and phone, she dashed out of the door, slamming it behind her. A minute later, she was letting herself back in again and running – she was surprisingly fast in 4-inch heels – to the fridge. The Billecart-Salmon was nicely chilled. At least the bitter night air temperatures were going to work with her on that. Shame the rain would make her mascara run, her jumper pill and her hair flat.

Ooh. Hair flat. Hat! She bolted into Tom's room and grabbed the Akubra hat he kept on top of his wardrobe, her eyes falling on the bike in the far corner as she checked herself in the mirror. She stopped and stared at it, her mind racing with the sudden possibility. No. She couldn't. It was a spectacularly bad idea, even by her standards. And Tom would kill her. Completely hang her up by her earrings and . . .

'. . . *Hair flick followed by bosom thrust.*'

Clem gave another small scream that made Shambles, their pet parrot, fall off her perch, and crossed the room in record time. To hell with Tom. This was an emergency.

The streets were quiet, the shops and cafés long since shut and all the residents safely ensconced in raucous house parties or the pubs, out of the rain. The roads gleamed in their wet skins beneath the street lights and Clem allowed herself a laugh of delight as she sliced through a deep puddle, her feet off the pedals as the spray dived cleanly to her left and right.

The bike – even though it was a man's model – fitted her well, her famously long legs stretched fully on the downward rotations, and it felt responsive and light to manoeuvre, even riding one-handed. She'd have to see whether she could get herself one of these. It'd be a dream for getting through the market, and she could be in Hyde Park in minutes. Maybe she should give up running and take up cycling instead?

Turning right onto Ladbroke Grove and third left into Oxford Gardens, she mounted the pavement, almost taking out a man striding towards her. He began swearing at her in French, but Clem didn't have time to stop and even less inclination to apologize. '*And* you nearly made me drop my bottle!' she hollered indignantly over her shoulder. 'What you doing out here anyway? Got no mates?'

She pulled up at Stella's flat minutes later, swinging her leg off the bike as if she was dismounting a horse, and grabbed the mirror from her bag to check herself over. Her cheeks were flushed from the cold night air and her eyeliner had smudged a little in the damp, but she decided she rather liked that. She always preferred to look a little 'undone', and anyway, it picked out the aquamarine tints in her blue-green eyes, which usually only appeared when she cried. And she wasn't going to be crying tonight. Oh no.

The door was on the latch, but she had to push it with some force to get past the revellers drinking, dancing and talking in the hall. There wasn't enough room to lean the bike against the wall, but she noticed the looped metal demi-chandelier wall-lights . . .

'Hey!' she shouted over the music to a guy in a gunmetal-grey shirt, allowing her signature husky voice to become even more gravelled. 'Would you mind . . .?' She indicated from the bike to the wall light. From the look on his face, just the sight of her with her jumper slowly slipping off her shoulder, would have made him lift a tractor up there had she asked.

Clem flashed him a teasingly grateful smile and pushed

her way past the bodies to the party's hub in the long, tall living room. It was so crowded that there wasn't enough room to swing her hair, much less a cat, but people moved aside for her anyway, their stares slow and interested at the sight of her looking soggy and dripping raindrops from the brim of her hat, while still somehow managing to be the most arresting woman in the room. Stella was standing near the fireplace, drunkenly pouring vodka into a row of shot glasses.

'Where is he?' Clem asked, grabbing one of the vodka shots and downing it.

Stella, unperturbed, did the same and they each picked up a fresh glass, ready to go again. 'Kitchen. You took your time.' Concern posing as suspicion danced in her glass-green eyes.

Clem ignored her. 'Any idea who the dolly is?'

'Nope, but she dances like she's been tranquillized and she's got all the subtlety of a claw hammer.' They clinked glasses and dispatched them without missing a beat.

'Hmm. How do I look?'

Stella gave her the quick once-over – she was, after all, the designer of Clem's outfit that evening. As the two of them always said, she was the one with the eye, Clem was the one with the legs.

'Hatefully gorgeous, and keep the hat. Bonus points for styling,' she replied, arranging Clem's nut-brown hair so it curled softly like sleeping kittens around her shoulders. Clem let her gaze drift around the room. She knew most of the faces there. Fifteen feet away she could see Tom and Clover chatting to his rugby mates, Tom leaning against the back of the sofa, a beer on the go and his ever-ready grin plastered all over his handsome face, as Clover winsomely stroked the back of his neck with her hand. Clem slunk down a little. It was usually Clover she avoided, but she really didn't want to deal with her big brother right now.

Stella handed her another shot of Grey Goose. 'You've got to play catch-up,' she ordered bossily, as Clem wiped her mouth with the back of her hand and watched a silky brunette move in for the kill on Freddie Haywood, her ex, three times removed.

'Regrets?' Stella asked, watching as Freddie's eyes flickered towards Clem.

'Who? Freddie? Don't be daft,' Clem murmured, looking away.

'I still don't get why you two broke up. You made a great couple.'

Clem threw her an annoyed look. 'Uh, because we'd been together for three weeks past my official relationship expiry date, he texts with his middle finger and he wears the same pants three days running.'

'So do you most of the time,' Stella said.

'Tch, do not,' Clem replied, even though she was famous for either going commando or wearing the first pair of knickers she could find in the mess on the floor that passed for her laundry basket. Tom kept muttering that he'd never be able to move out until she worked out how to work the washing machine.

'Well I think it's a shame, that's all.' Stella shrugged, reaching down into a bowl of Pringles. 'You seemed happy with him and he's obviously still mad about you.'

'Moving on,' Clem snapped, closing the conversation down once and for all. 'Josh is much more my thing now: mature, considerate, *enlightened*. He could teach me things. Make me a better person.'

Stella choked on her crisp. 'Bollocks. You're only going after him because he's the first man you've ever met who hasn't fallen at your feet.'

'Not true.'

'Bang on, more like. Yes, he's good-looking, but quite frankly I don't trust any man who jacks in a good career in Private Equity to man the phones for The Samaritans. And as for giving up booze to compete in triathlons every week-end, well . . . you should be very, very wary, that's all I'm saying.'

'But I could grow with him.'

A pulse of disbelief followed this statement and Clem was forced to give a tiny shrug in acknowledgement of the ridiculous words coming from her mouth.

'Grow bored more like. You might be able to convince him that you volunteered at the cat sanctuary in your gap year, and that you only listen to chamber music on your iPod, but you and I both know that "danger" is your middle name. You're pretending to be someone you're not when you're with him. It won't last.'

'It doesn't have to,' Clem replied, flashing her friend a sarcastic smile. 'I'm not looking for a husband.'

'Well then, you're the only single twenty-nine-year-old female in London who isn't,' Stella said, pouring herself another drink, her eyes tracking someone over Clem's bare shoulder. 'Anyway, I don't have time to stand here chatting about your self-imposed problems. I still haven't got myself a date for midnight, so if you're so convinced Josh is your Mr Right Now, then go get him, Tiger,' Stella said, slapping her hard on the bottom and wandering off in pursuit of a guy in skinny jeans and a trilby.

Clem watched her go. If *she* had the legs and eyes combo

to take out most men, her diminutive firecracker friend had the E-cup cleavage and handspan waist. Clem smiled as she watched Stella almost immediately hypnotize the guy into stunned submission, his mouth falling open like a guppy – she knew one of them was sorted for the night. It was time to get her groove on: the first buzz of vodka was mixing with her bloodstream and there was a code red in the kitchen.

The party was ascending to a riotous peak, the floorboards vibrating to the pounding dance-floor beat, as she turned into the crowd, began to sway and let herself go. If there was one thing she could do – really do – it was party. No W11 party was complete without her. She moved deeper into the melee of smiling mouths and loud laughs, the glassy eyes and lecherous stares, the flushed cheeks and glossy hair tosses that she called 'home', everyone dancing and swaying around her, singing drunkenly and punching the air. Except for one.

His stillness jarred against the throb of the crowd and she lifted her chin fractionally to get a better look at him from under her hat while flashing him a glimpse of her stunning eyes. He was leaning against the wall, watching her with notably glacial-blue eyes of his own. He was a predator, like her. Her gaze didn't move from his but she peripherally registered the pale blue shirt worn over Swimmer's shoulders, the offbeat grey marled jacket with black revers that was classic, yet subversive too – and clearly expensive. She noted heavy straight brows, a square chin, dark blond hair that would look brown when wet, planed cheekbones that would stretch the skin thin when – if – he smiled.

And then everything went black.

'Hey! Who said you could wear that? It's an heirloom remember?' a distinctive male voice boomed next to her.

Clem pushed the hat back up off her eyes hurriedly. Talk about ruining the mystique! 'Just because it was Dad's doesn't make it valuable, Tom,' she said irritably, looking past her brother to find the stranger still staring, but with less heat and more laughter in his expression now. Something about him was familiar . . .

'The concept of emotional significance really is lost on you, isn't it?' Her brother tutted as Clover drifted over – obvs – looking clean and meadowy amidst the gritty urban party animals seeing out another year in Notting Hill. She gave Clem a tight smile.

'Sentimental tosh more like. A hat is a hat is a hat. And it's raining out there, you know.'

'And God forbid Josh should see you looking anything other than perfect, right?' Tom teased.

'That's right.'

'Well, he should be *doubly* pleased tonight then,' Tom said meaningfully, unable to keep the laughter out of his voice.

Clem shifted her weight uneasily. 'What does that mean?'

'Only that your intended tucked into the punch with some gusto when he got here.'

'The punch?' Clem echoed. Stella's Bacardi-vodka-tequila punch was the stuff of legend.

'Yep. Someone might have told him it was a non-alcoholic option.'

Clem felt a kernel of dread harden in the pit of her stomach. 'But there's no such thing at Stella's place. She's never drunk juice in her life. Not without vodka in it.'

'Well, *we* know that . . .' Tom grinned, his twinkly eyes glassy with booze. 'Oh, talk of the devil! Josh, how's it going, mate?'

Clem watched in horror as Josh bowled towards her,

holding onto walls, sofas and nearby shoulders for support. He stopped in front of Clem, standing on her toes and swaying with a rhythm that had nothing to do with the music.

'Ah shit, Clem . . .' he slurred, his eyes running up and down her like scales. 'I've had enough of this. You've been messing with my head too bloody long,' he said, swooping down to kiss her, unfortunately forgetting to account for the rigid brim of her hat, so that his lips were kept, pursed, away from hers for several, agonizing moments before the hat suddenly bowed under the pressure and his mouth quite literally fell upon hers in a clash of teeth.

Clem staggered back under his weight, aware of Tom and Clover's laughter as Josh stumbled to remain joined to her. Talk about bad to worse. First her brother humiliates her in front of the stranger and now—

But a sudden intake of breath, horrified and aghast, stopped her short. She pushed Josh off and looked up at Tom in panic. He had gone sheet-white and his generous smile completely vanished. He was holding his breath, his knuckles white around the beer bottle in his hand, so that Clem worried it would shatter from the force of his fist.

'What have you done?' he managed, his voice choked.

Clem didn't need to follow his line of sight to know that he was looking at the bike hanging on the wall.

'It was raining,' she whispered. She'd known he'd be cross, but the devastation in his face was more cutting than the fiercest anger. Her eyes followed the track of his like a cursor as they ran over the bicycle's rosy, twinkling, caramel leather-clad frame, now soaked dark with rain, stained with beer, graffiti'd with biro and speckled grey with cigarette ash that was smouldering slowly through to the glossy golden skeleton beneath.

A turgid silence ballooned between them and when he finally spoke, his voice was more of a rumble, like a bomb going off several miles away. 'I suppose it completely passed over your head that that prototype cost a hundred and thirty-five grand to make.'

Clem's jaw dropped open.

'One hundred – and thirty – five – thousand,' Tom repeated. 'It's plated in rose gold and has real fucking *diamonds* studded in it! It was never designed to be used! I left it in the flat in order to protect it over the holidays because our insurers won't cover it in the studio without . . . without a bloody security guard. And you're telling me you brought it to a mosh-pit party because it was *raining*?'

'I panicked. Josh was chatting up another girl.'

Tom's usually benevolent gaze drifted from her to the husk of a man leaning on her, so far gone he couldn't even focus, much less keep up with the conversation.

'And was it worth it?' His contempt was withering, though whether it was reserved for her or Josh wasn't clear.

Clem shook her head. 'I'm so sorry, Tom. I didn't know it was that mu . . . I'll make it up to you. I promise.'

'How, exactly?'

She shrank back from the disdain in his voice. They both knew there was no rescue remedy to this, her latest, disaster.

'We're supposed to unveil it at the Expo in Berlin next week. It's the lead exhibit. There are companies coming from China just to see it. '

'I'll work without pay,' she offered desperately.

'That'll simply mean I have to pay your rent and food for you, too.' His hand reached out for Clover's and she grasped it keenly, her thumb rubbing reassuringly –

proprietorially – over the back of his hand. He shook his head. 'I don't know what it is with you, Clem. You've got it all going for you, and yet for some reason, everything you touch turns to shit. I'm up to here with you acting like a spoilt child and never thinking about anyone but yourself. When are you going to get your act together and just grow up?'

'Tom, I . . .' she faltered, but he thrust his half-drunk beer roughly into her hand and stormed off, pulling Clover behind him like a kite.

Clem bit her lip, tears stinging her eyes as she watched him stride over to the hall, pushing people out of the way and unhooking the priceless bike from the wall sconces. Beside her, Josh fell over his own feet and landed face first on a Moroccan pouffe. Clem looked down at him in despair before remembering the enigmatic stranger, the Swimmer. But, like her brother and the prospect of ringing in a happy new year, he was long gone.

Chapter Two

The rain had fallen even harder on the way home. Not that Clem remembered this. Finishing off the bottle of Grey Goose had been so effective at staunching the hurt of Tom's contempt, it was almost as if their fight hadn't happened at all. Rather, it was the sodden leather jacket – untreated, as it turned out – bleeding tannin into the pale maple floor that showed just how wild the weather had become. That, or she'd had a bath in it, which frankly couldn't be discounted as an option either. She'd done worse in her time.

She groaned as the room moved around her prostrate form on the sofa, her hands automatically stroking the curly tufts of the sheepskin sofa that soothed her like a teddy bear. The silk envelope had fallen to the floor, its precious contents still pristine, thankfully, and she knew she had to hide it again before Tom came back. It had been reckless to—

Tom. She swivelled one mascara-clotted eye around, looking for him. Usually he woke her nose-first, cooking up one of his famous fried-egg sandwiches, which always settled her stomach and enabled her to move to a vertical position. But the flat was quiet and still, yesterday's dirty dishes were where she'd left them on the worktop and the eggs were keeping their healing properties a secret in the fridge.

It was too early for him to come back from Clover's, she

reasoned. It was still dark outside. She should go back to sleep and try to slumber through the worst of this. But water. She needed water.

Shambles, watching from her perch in Tom's room, squawked loudly at the sight of Clem's jerky, hesitant movements. 'Sexanddrugsandrocknrollsexanddrugsandrocknroll.'

Clem nodded feebly in acknowledgement and slowly sat up, smoothing a hand through her matted hair and seeing, with damped horror, Tom's flattened Akubra hat, which she'd used as a pillow.

'Oh, Shambles,' she mumbled, trying to punch it back into shape. 'Why didn't you warn me?'

'*Where's* the remote?' the parrot squawked.

'Mmmgh.'

Grabbing a handful of seeds from the bowl on the small round kitchen table, she opened the door to Shambles' cage and scattered them in. She left the door open so that Shambles could come out to stretch her wings, and staggered over to the sink.

The sound of keys in the door made her turn apprehensively, but the first glimpse of giant blue Ikea bags told her it was Stella following after, not Tom. She was over so often, she had honorary housemate status with her own set of keys.

'Hey!' Stella panted, throwing the bags ahead of her like a ball at skittles, and stopping short at the sight of Clem standing dazed and confused in just last night's jumper and knickers. At least she was wearing knickers. 'Oh dear. You look *baaaad*.'

'I *feeeel* bad,' Clem groaned, sagging against the worktop. 'Thank God you're here. You can do that egg thing that makes me feel better.'

'What, eggnog?'

Clem retched. 'God no. That always makes me throw up.'

'Oh, Tom's hangover special, you mean?'

'That's the one,' Clem sighed, giving up the fight against gravity and collapsing onto a kitchen chair. 'How come you're up so bright and early anyway?' Clem moaned, her head in her hands, as Stella crossed the room and got busy in the kitchen. She was wearing an outfit only an official designer could get away with – a vintage kimono coat over silk pyjama bottoms and a metre-long scarf – and looked dispiritingly healthy, even though she had drunk Clem and most of Tom's rugby club under the table. Quite where she put the alcohol in her 5-foot-2-inch frame, no one knew.

'It's hardly early, babes. It's almost five.'

'In the afternoon?'

Stella grinned at her, delighted. 'It was a great party, wasn't it?' Stella always gauged the success of her parties by the severity of Clem's hangovers and the number of bodies unconscious in her flat the morning after. 'There were seven still sleeping it off at mine this morning. Last one only just left, although he had rather more reason to stay than the others.' She winked joyously as she cracked the eggs, accounting for the flush in her cheeks and the brightness in her green eyes.

'Well at least one of us got lucky.' Clem frowned. 'What . . . what happened with Josh?'

'He passed out at ten and slept in the bath. I got Tom's mates to move him out of the way for me. He was hogging the sofa. Gone by the time I surfaced this morning, though. He's no doubt cycling up Snowdon as we speak.' She pulled a sympathetic face. 'Hate to say it, but I did tell you not to trust a man who doesn't drink.'

The eggs hissed as they splashed into the hot oil.

'From now on I shall stick to married men and public school boys with recreational drug habits. At least you know where you are with them.'

Shambles flew out of the cage and swooped above Stella in the kitchen, enjoying the hot thermal current coming off the frying pan, before settling on the windowsill. Clem watched despondently, distracted. Five o'clock? Tom would definitely be back by now ordinarily. This was no mere spat.

'What's wrong with me, Stell? Why do I always mess things up? I'm a one-woman disaster zone.'

'No you're not. You're just one of life's energy force fields. You attract everything to you and sometimes things just spin a little bit out of control, that's all,' Stella murmured, her hands moving quickly so that in a few moments more, she placed a steaming, oozing toasted sandwich in front of her beleaguered friend. 'Now get that down you. I need your body.'

Clem sighed appreciatively and tucked in. Stella always knew how to rally her. A shoot-from-the-hip Finchley girl, she'd been raised by her father after her mother died when she was four, and she had a bustling, maternal nature that soothed Clem and brought her down from her more outrageous antics. Their friendship had been instantaneous and intense since the day they'd met at St Martin's College, where Stella was studying Fashion Design and Clem was doing the Fashion Journalism and Marketing course. Clem had been hired as a model by one of the more pretentious design students, Taylor Dart, who had put on a still-life fashion installation in a mechanics' workshop. Stella had been helping Taylor with the fittings as he had all the technical dressmaking ability of a goat, and she and Clem had bonded for life over the armless dress he had reserved for her.

Unlike Taylor, Stella had an unerring instinct for what women wanted to wear – and more importantly how they wanted to feel – and her graduation show had been one of the standout presentations that year, with editors and buyers keeping close tabs on her as she apprenticed with Topshop and then the Burberry Brit division. But Stella had quickly grown restless with giving her best ideas to others so they could profit from them, and when Clem mentioned in passing that her florist friend Katy had told her a stall on Portobello was coming up, the deal had been done. It might not be the glossy shop front she dreamed of on Westbourne Grove, but at least everything had her name on the label, and as one of the most famous markets in the world, it was a fashion mecca.

Stella wandered over to the capacious bags she had bundled in with, and pulled out various bolts of fabric. She was genuinely gifted and her stall in the market was always thronging at the weekends. Clem had worked on the stall for her for a while, but after the third successive theft, in which half of Stella's collection was lifted while Clem either flirted with the guys in the betting shop or slept behind the changing-room curtain, they had agreed it was better if she simply donated her body to fashion and left it at that.

Clem stood up and took off her jumper, standing in the middle of her flat in just her knickers, as Stella began to wind a length of dusky pink butterfly-print silk-chiffon around her lean frame.

'Ooh, I like that,' Clem murmured, looking down as Stella moved nimbly round her, pleating, tucking and folding. 'What are you going to make with it?'

'Not sure yet. Let's see,' Stella mumbled with pins clenched between her teeth, lifting up Clem's arms.

Clem looked out and into the flats opposite. Old Mrs Crouch, who'd lived in Portbello all her life, so for well over seventy years, was picking some basil from her window box. Clem gave her a wave. The old lady was used to seeing Clem half-dressed and didn't bat an eyelid at the goings-on over the road.

'Do you think we should have some resolutions this year?' Clem asked as Stella pinned a dart and the fabric moulded beneath her bust.

'What for? Our lives are perfect the way they are.'

'Mmm.'

Stella rotated her ninety degrees so that she was looking at the wall and the series of framed black and white photos Clem had taken of her and Tom during the phase when she'd fancied being a photographer. She studied her brother's floppy brown hair, which always fell over his left eye, and the slight gap between his teeth, which gave him the endearing, scampish look girls fells for time and again. Not that he ever noticed. He had been with Clover for five years now and was as loyal as a puppy. The only reason he hadn't proposed to Clover yet, Clem knew, was because he worried about her and wanted to see her more settled first.

'I'm just wondering whether I need to make some changes. Tom's really pissed off this time. I messed up big style.'

'He'll have forgiven you already, you know he will. He hasn't got a resentful bone in his body, that one.'

'He says I have to grow up.'

'But you are grown up,' Stella pouted prettily, as though the slight was as directed at her as at Clem. 'You live in this great flat—'

'With him – which he bought off Mum and Dad. Paying him rent is like giving back my pocket money.'

'You have a cracking job.'

'At his company.'

Stella pulled back from her position on the floor and looked up at her, as though she was trying to be difficult.

'See what I mean? I can't cook. You and Tom make everything or else I get a take-out.'

'Or go without,' Stella reproved, knowing that Clem's lack of interest in food was one of the reasons for her spectacular figure.

'And I can't drive. I get buses and cabs everywhere.'

'Yeah, but what d'you need to drive for in London? Parking's a nightmare and we both know your car would be permanently clamped. Or you'd forget where you left it.'

'But what if I want to go into the countryside?'

Stella shot her such a pained look that for a moment Clem wondered whether she'd accidentally swallowed a pin.

'Yeah OK, so not that. But you know, I might want to go to . . . Clapham, one day.'

'You never go south of Hyde Park, east of Ladbroke Grove, west of Westbourne Grove or North of North Ken. This is your patch. Why go anywhere else?'

Clem sighed. 'I just think I should have some resolutions this year. For Tom's sake. Be a better sister, flatmate, em--ployee, person.'

'Like what then?'

'I dunno.' Clem stared across into Mrs Crouch's cluttered flat, where the lampshades were draped with fringed scarves and her china figurine collection adorned every surface. 'I could promise to clean the flat once a week.' Her eyes scanned the stacked up dirty dishes, the fashion and gossip magazines thrown like scatter cushions across the sofa, the leather jacket still weeping quietly in the middle of the floor, her clothes overflowing from her bedroom . . .

'Well, get a cleaner at least,' Stella grimaced. 'No need to go overboard.'

'Yes, you're right,' Clem agreed gratefully. 'I'll hire a cleaner. And I'll learn to cook.'

Stella arched one finely plucked eyebrow.

Clem held up her index finger. 'One thing. I'll learn to cook one thing really well.' An idea came to her. 'Like lasagne. That's Tom's favourite, and besides, I'm fed up of people talking about béchamel like it's a private club.'

'All right. I'll join you in that if you can find a hot Italian to teach you. What else?'

'And I'll learn to drive. I should have done it years ago.'

Stella pulled a face, as if she was sucking on a lemon. 'Well, if it'll make you happy.'

'I just want to make it up to him, that's all. I'm fed up with being everyone's favourite disappointment.'

'Hey!' Stella protested, flicking a length of material against her leg. 'Enough of that. You are deeply lovable and we wouldn't have you any other way. Tom most of all. He's a total softie where you're concerned.'

'I know, but he shouldn't have to be. I should be making him proud and helping him, not holding him back. I'm the pelican around his neck.'

'Albatross,' Stella murmured, going back to her pinning.

'Yeah, yeah, that's what I said.'

Chapter Three

Clem stood on the doorstep and rang again. The bell sounded deep into the shadows of the tall magnolia house and presently she heard the sound of her father's slippered footsteps on the other side of the imposing black door.

She readied herself with a smile as she heard the sound of the deadbolts being pushed back, and knew that meant she was the first to arrive – for once. The break with tradition didn't thrill her as perhaps it should have done. Tom hadn't come home at all yesterday and her sense of dread for when she did next see him was growing deeper with every passing hour.

'Bunny,' her father smiled down at her, still determined to call her by her baby name, even though she had a maxed-out credit card and a freezer stocked with vodka. At sixty-six, he was still an imposingly tall man of 6 foot 3 inches. She had inherited his height, wry sense of humour and languid demeanour. Everything else was her mother's fault.

'Hi Daddyo.' She reached forward to kiss him on the cheek, her fingertips burrowing softly into the holey, patched cranberry cashmere sweater that he had worn all her life and possibly a significant portion of his life before that, too. 'Happy New Year and all that jazz.'

'Indeed.' He shut the door and looked down at her fondly for a moment, resting one hand on the top of her head, like he used to when she was little. He was one of the very few people she remained 'little' to. 'And how is the year treating my girl so far?'

Clem nodded brightly, wondering whether Tom had rung ahead and ratted on her. 'Well, I've decided to break my resolution never to have any resolutions.'

'Oh?' A flash of hope raced across his gentle features, which Tom had inherited, his florid cheeks clashing with the smooth snowy-white hair that had once been raven black.

'Don't get your hopes up! It's nothing earth-shattering. Just the normal self-improvement ones that most people make. Thought I'd give them a go.'

'You're not going on some ridiculous diet, I hope? That's what most of you young'uns bang on about nowadays and you're like a wire hanger as it is.'

'Thanks! And no, that isn't one of them. I'm going to learn to drive, cook . . . that kind of thing.' The hope that had skittered over his face a moment before was chased now by what she thought was mild disappointment. 'I figure I have to keep it realistic or I'll never do it,' she added quickly. 'And I'm not getting any younger.'

'Quite so,' he nodded, staring at her with a wistful look. 'Well, come through. Your mother's in the conservatory, waiting to see you.'

Clem knew it wasn't *her* that her mother was waiting to see, but she followed after him anyway, automatically smoothing her hair – which she'd conditioned especially – and checking her appearance in the tall gilded mirror: pale grey jeans and heeled camel ankle boots, a dusty pink silk shirt Stella had made her and a thin leather strap she'd picked up in the workshop and wound around her neck several times like a lariat. The Akubra hat would have been the perfect finishing touch, but it hadn't recovered from the other night and she'd hidden it at the bottom of her wardrobe, hoping that what was out of Tom's sight would be out of his mind, too.

'Mother,' she said, crossing the glass room to where her mother was sitting reading *The Economist*, her seated form as erect as a ballerina's, half-moon spectacles perched on the end of her aquiline nose, and her grey bobbed hair already immaculately styled by her hairdresser, who gave her a blow-dry every morning on his way to the salon. 'Happy New Year.'

'And to you, Clementine.' Her mother's distinctive turquoise eyes – which had in part singled her out as one of the notable beauties of her generation and were extending the same compliment to Clem – skimmed over her smart appearance. 'Are you going into the office today?' The question was posted as though she couldn't be quite sure. Outfit fail.

'Yeah, worst luck.'

But her mother wasn't listening. She was looking beyond her to the hall. 'Where's Tom? Isn't he with you?'

'No. He stayed at Clover's yesterday.'

'All day?'

Clem nodded casually, but she saw the understanding shift into her mother's sharp eyes immediately. The siblings had always been close and Tom was a stickler for the family being together on high days and holidays, even if being with Clem on New Year's Day usually involved holding her hair back.

'I know, that's what I thought. And then I thought maybe he's proposed or something,' Clem said quickly, trying to throw her off the scent. 'I mean, it has been five years now, and I suppose New Year's Eve is one of the traditional times to ask.'

'Good God, I hope not,' her mother grimaced, appalled. 'What a horrid cliché. I would hope we brought you both up to have rather more imagination than that.'

Clem smiled as her mother sidetracked into disappointment – mission accomplished – then sank into the orange velvet sofa that had faded along the back where the sun caught it in the late afternoon. A giant fern obscured her mother's face from view, but she made no effort to move it, throwing her long legs over the tapestried scatter cushions and checking texts, just as Lulu, her parents' caramel-coloured cockerpoo, bounded into the room like a hairbrush on springs and jumped onto her lap. She was crazily cute, even though she was so small, spoilt and fluffy she had no business calling herself a dog. There were cats on the street that could bark more convincingly.

'Don't put your feet on the sofa, Clementine,' her mother admonished quietly as Clem tickled the dog's tummy. 'And put Lulu down. You're encouraging her to jump up.'

Reluctantly, Clem put the dog down on the floor and pocketed her phone. *Where* was Tom?

'So, what did you and Daddy do for New Year?' she asked, swinging her leg metronomically in the full knowledge that it would drive her mother mad.

There was only the slightest pause before her mother answered. 'We did our usual safari supper – drinks and canapés at the Bennetts', dinner at the Wilson-Hopes', pudding and Bridge here.' She dropped her voice fractionally. 'As we have done for the past twenty-six years.'

'Nice,' Clem nodded automatically.

'And you?'

'Stella threw a party.'

'Of course she did.'

Clem peered through the fern at her mother, who had a smile on her lips but none in her eyes, just as her father walked through, carrying steaming plates of grilled kippers, poached eggs in hollandaise sauce and ribbons of smoked salmon twisted into appealing heaps. Since retiring as CEO of music publishers Haycock & Gibson twenty years earlier, he had fallen into a passionate secondary love affair with food, and was so often to be found chatting to the deli owners and fruit and veg market stallholders about black garlic or how to cook with lavender salt, or the merits of pecorino over parmigiana, that for the first year of his retirement, Clem's mother had been quite convinced that he had not just another woman, but an entire other family on the go.

'Well, we can't wait for your brother any longer I'm afraid,' he said, putting the plates down on the oval table, which was painted in a grey limed wash and set with olive-embroidered linen napkins and bone-handled cutlery. 'I'm running a tight ship here and I calculated my cooking times according to you both needing to be in the office by ten so . . .'

Just then, the doorbell rang.

'Ah, his ears must have been burning. Tuck in!' Her father waved his arms around eagerly like a conductor. 'Don't let it get cold. Nothing worse than congealed hollandaise.' He pulled a face to indicate there really was *nothing* worse and marched out into the hall.

Clem let her mother sit down first and watched out of the

corner of her eye as she made a fuss of opening out her napkin and draping it elaborately across her lap. Clem displayed no such delicacy and had forked a piece of muffin before she'd even sat down. She had just pierced the delicate skin of her poached egg and was watching the golden yolk ooze over the plate when Tom followed in after their father.

Both women's jaws dropped at the sight of him. His usually clean-shaven face was covered with a dense undergrowth of stubble that looked like it would bloom into a full forest within twenty-four hours, and deep purple moons lay cradled beneath his eyes – Clem had seen more pigment in one of Lulu's marrow bones. He hadn't slept since the party, that much was clear.

'Tom!' Mrs Alderton cried, jumping to her feet and forgetting all about the napkin she'd been so precious about moments before. She cupped his face in her hands. 'Oh, darling, what has she done to you?'

Puzzlement crowded his eyes before they slid over to Clem's. She saw understanding gather and knew he could guess what she'd told their mother – and why. She saw the resignation dawn on her big brother's features.

'I didn't propose to her, Mother,' he said, gently taking his mother's hands off his cheeks. 'But as and when I do, it'll be at a rather more inspired time and place than that.'

'Oh darling,' Portia Alderton beamed back at him happily. So long as the proposal wasn't clichéd, she could clearly work with the rest. 'Well, thank heavens for that.' She laughed, fluttering a delicate hand above her heart.

'The hollandaise is congealing,' Edmund Alderton muttered sadly from his seat at the opposite end of the table.

'Do come and sit, darling,' Portia urged her son. 'We

were waiting for you. Ignore your sister, she couldn't wait, *naturellement.*'

Clem sighed and silently passed her brother the kippers instead.

'So what are we supposed to make of your appearance this morning then, Tom?' Edmund asked. 'I assume you aren't going into the office today after all.'

'Actually, I've just come from there.'

'What? At this time of the day?' Portia asked, appalled, realizing he must have worked through the night. 'Thomas, you need your sleep.'

'Remember Berlin's coming up, dear,' Edmund said soothingly to his wife. 'Things always get hectic in the run-up to that. It's where they have to strut their stuff. Isn't that right, Tom?'

Tom took a deep breath. 'Actually, we're not going this year.'

Clem's fork dropped to the plate with a clatter.

'We're too busy with the Perignard launch. We go into production the week after next. It's not the time to be away from the office,' he said, keeping his eyes on his plate, spearing almost half a poached egg and ramming it into his mouth ravenously. He clearly hadn't eaten since the party either. He looked so tired that Clem thought he might fall asleep in his plate.

Clem knew he was using the Perignard account as a cover to divert his parents' concern, but cancelling Berlin altogether was . . . catastrophic. She looked back down at her plate and twiddled a salmon ribbon with her fork, her appetite completely gone and alarm bells sounding in her head. She was beginning to realize that things were even worse than she'd feared.

'Perignard, yes, I walked past the premises last week. It's a good-sized space,' Edmund said chattily, completely buying the alibi.

'Mmm,' Tom agreed.

'I still can't fathom how you're going to line the walls with leather that's been studded with diamonds.'

Tom swallowed. 'No one can, that's what's so special about it. We've spent the last year developing the technology, Dad.'

'Well, I can't wait to see it,' Portia exclaimed, delight and pride in her eyes. 'I hope we'll be invited to the launch party?'

'Of course.'

'And the coming year? How's that looking for the leather trade overall?' their father asked. 'Tough times all round, I should say.'

'Well, obviously the building trade's been hit by the downturn – it's always one of the first industries hit; new builds alone are down forty per cent from two years ago – but it has begun trickling through to us now. A lot of clients are stalling on projects they'd intended to green light this year, even just the refurbs.'

'So what does that mean for Alderton Hide?' Portia asked, her fork poised mid-air, keenly aware that her son was leading up to something.

Tom took a deep breath. 'I may need to make some redundancies at the factory in the mid-term. As for the immediate future, I'm going to have to pass on the new premises in Blenheim Crescent.'

His mother looked aghast, pressing her hand onto his arm. 'But you spent months looking for the right space. You're absolutely boxed in where you are now. You can't possibly be expected to run the headquarters of such a prestigious brand from those cramped offices.' The way she talked about them, Alderton Hide sounded like the next Louis Vuitton.

'I don't have a choice, Mum. We'll just have to put up with it for a bit longer.'

'But Tom—'

'Look! The economy's a mess, the banks aren't lending and I can't take the risk, OK?' he said in a fierce tone that shut the conversation down.

There was an awkward silence and Clem realized she had stopped eating, her eyes pinned to her brother, who resolutely refused to look at her.

'I'm sorry, darling,' Mrs Alderton said, laying a hand over her son's and squeezing it. 'I know you always say there isn't, but if there is ever anything we can do . . .'

'I know, Mum. Thanks,' Tom nodded and a small muscle flickered in his left cheek. At the sight of his childhood tic, Clem's stomach contracted. Tom was on the verge of losing it, and she couldn't bear to see him cry. She'd always been able to bear anything but the sight of her big brother crying.

'*Amazing* eggs, Daddy,' Clem exclaimed, desperately trying to move the conversation on to safer ground for him, but earning a roll of her mother's eyes in the process.

'Goose,' her father replied delightedly. 'Pink-footed genus from Iceland that winters here, so you can only get them at this time of year. I found a chap from Worcestershire who travels over every week, so I've struck a deal with him for a regular order. Pricey, but worth it I'd say.'

'Oh yes, definitely,' Clem said eagerly.

Mrs Alderton took a deep breath and smiled, her eyes still on Tom. 'Well, Daddy and I have something for you that might cheer you up.'

Clem felt a pinch at the bottom of her lungs as her mother got up and took two wrapped packages off the side table, which Clem had spotted the moment she'd entered the room. It was why this breakfast was happening: the New Year Alderton tradition – at least, since Tom had turned twenty-one and Clem nineteen – where their parents 'gifted' them each a possession with significant emotional value on New Year's Day (although this had had to be shifted to the day after once it became apparent that Clem was rarely ever home in time for breakfast on New Year's Day, and even if she was her hangover precluded eating or socializing in any form). Tom insisted it was a sweet bonding exercise that created heirlooms and knitted the generations of their family together. Clem argued that it was a way for them to divest their estate, piecemeal, without having to pay inheritance tax. She dreaded this annual event, not least because she knew that coming her way, one day, would be the evil-eyed mink tippet that had belonged to her great-grandmother.

Her mother placed this year's package on the table in front of her. Clem accepted it with a nod and a half-smile – the best she could manage. The parcel was large and firm, but with give in it, and as her hands moved slowly over the tapered, boxy shape, her brain automatically trying to guess the contents, her heart gave a little defiant skip as a thought came to her. Surely not. There was no way her mother would give this up . . .

Breath held, she broke the wax seal – always imprinted with the crest on her father's signet ring, one of his foibles – and pulled apart the brown packing paper. The vivid orange dust bag glowed like an orb of sunlight in her hands.

Clem gasped involuntarily as she pulled out the Hermès

bag, the deep jet colour enriched with age, the brass-tipped straps fastened and secured in defiance of the accepted norm to leave them hanging.

'Your Birkin?' Clem croaked, her hands running softly over the crocodile leather. She had coveted the bag since childhood – ever since she had used it as a bed for her Sindy doll and long before she had known about its value or the years-long waiting lists to buy one. Listening to the love story that accompanied it had been one of her favourite childhood rituals – she would sit on her mother's lap, her small hands playing with the clasps as Portia told her how her father had met one of the master craftsmen at Hermès whilst they were honeymooning and bought the bag from him. But it wasn't just any old Birkin. Aside from the ultra-rare leather and colour combinations, it was a Shooting Star Birkin, identifiable by the shooting star motif embossed below the logo; only the top artisan in each year is allowed to make one, and only one per year is made, driving up the rarity value and rendering them collectors' pieces. Naturally, most of the craftsmen give them to their wives. But being a widower of long-standing, this craftsman had made it purely as a personal challenge in the pursuit of perfection, and when Edmund Alderton had crossed his path, he had bartered it for an untitled symphony – which happened to be gloved in Edmund's briefcase at the time – to be named after his wife instead. It was little wonder that Tom and Clem had inherited a love of all things leather.

Clem would have her mother repeat the story to her at bedtime each night, as they stroked and smelled the leather, and Clem had honed her fine motor skills fastening the clasps. The bag had become not just an emblem of her parents' love but also hers and her mother's. But things had changed since then. 'I . . . I don't know what to say.'

Her mother shifted position, a slightly frozen expression on her face. 'Yes, well, before you get carried away, it was your father's idea.' Her hand fluttered tenderly over the bag, not quite daring to make contact with it, as though it was a sleeping baby. 'I'm sure I don't need to remind you that your father bought this for me on our honeymoon. It's not just any bag.'

Clem nodded in silence, wounded that her mother had clearly forgotten how beloved their ritual had once been. Anger began to surge through her, the precious bag tainted now that it was being given here, like this. It was her mother's insidious way of trying to make amends for what she had done, papering over the devastation she had caused, throwing money at the problem.

Clem swallowed the feelings down, as she always did, and rose to kiss her mother, her lips meeting one velvet-smooth, perfumed cheek before settling back in her chair, her polite movements belying the fact that her heart was drilling like a jackhammer in her chest.

It was Tom's turn now, so all eyes were off her for the moment, and she took several deep breaths as their father handed over a small parcel the size of a matchbox. Tom opened it, his eyes lighting up with their familiar sparkle at the sight of the car keys lying there.

'Your MGB GT? But Dad you can't! You love that thing!' The flash of old Tom – lively and happy – made Clem relax a little. It freaked her out to see her big brother so subdued and diminished.

Edmund Alderton smiled sadly. 'Pah. It's too much of a beggar for me to park now without power steering. Besides, it's a young man's car. No one wants to see an old duffer like me haring around in one of those things.'

'I don't know what to say,' Tom said, handling the keys. 'It just seems too much. That car's your most treasured possession.'

'No, you two are our most treasured possessions,' Edmund Alderton corrected. 'Family's all that matters in the end. Your mother and I don't need anything but you two, and for you both to be happy.'

Clem felt her pulse skyrocket again at his words – his eyes were on her – and she looked out into the bald, damp grey garden, blinking hard. It was no good, though. Tom could buy into this, but she never would. Talk was cheap, these gifts a joke. She pushed her chair back roughly so that it grated harshly across the floor. 'I've got to go,' she managed.

'Clemen—' her mother started, annoyed.

'A meeting I forgot about—' Clem pointlessly dabbed at her mouth with her napkin, trying to make her excuse look genuine.

'What meeting?' Tom interjected suspiciously; it was the first time he'd looked at her all morning.

'Thanks for breakfast,' Clem continued, placing her napkin with forced care across her plate. 'No, stay sitting, Dad. I can see myself out. I'll call you soon, OK? Laters.'

Astonished silence followed her all the way down the hall, but she was no stranger to that in this house. She slammed the door behind her and stumbled down the steps, her hand gripping the wrought-iron handrail so tightly her knuckles glowed white. Her breath was coming fast and heavy as she marched blindly down the street towards the market, which was already filling up. It was all a lie, all of it, and she was the only one who would face it. She pushed herself amongst the bodies, letting herself be jostled and carried along by the current, gradually feeling herself relax as she was swept into anonymity down the road, getting lost in a crowd where even Tom couldn't find her.

Chapter Four

'Happy New Year, Clem!' trilled Pixie, the diminutive pink-haired receptionist Clem had suggested Tom fire on more than one occasion, not just because of her name but also on account of her relentlessly chirrupy demeanour, which only ever escalated Clem's hangovers.

'Oh, has it brightened up now then?' she asked chirpily, clocking Clem's Tom Ford blackout glasses and leaning across her desk to peer out at the sky, which was hanging as low as an overloaded washing line, bruised clouds buffeting the London rooftops like dirty sheets. 'Oh.'

Clem sloped mutely past, wearing yesterday's clothes and bumping straight into the corner of a desk. She swore under her breath, and not just from the pain – Tom was already in.

'Morning,' she muttered, straightening up abruptly at the sight of the Birkin bag sitting in the middle of her desk.

'You forgot that yesterday,' Tom said in a quietly accusing voice, his eyes fixed on his computer screen.

'I . . . was in a hurry,' she murmured, scarcely able to tolerate the sound of her own voice, much less his. Her hangover was epic, even by her standards. She collapsed into a slump in her chair, her fingers massaging her temples, her eyes anywhere but on the bag.

Tom glanced over at her as he picked up his coffee. 'Mum's gutted; she was almost in tears after you left. She thinks you don't want it.'

Clem managed a shrug. 'It's just . . . fake.' Her voice trailed off to a whisper.

Tom spluttered on his flat white. '*Fake?* Are you bloody mad? Do you know what Dad—'

'No, I don't mean the bag. I mean that whole . . . rigmarole.'

'It's a tradition, Clem, nothing more! Why do you always have to make such a thing about it?' Tom was almost shouting, a tremble of barely controlled rage in his voice.

Clem squeezed her eyes shut, grateful for the shield of her sunglasses, and nodded in silence. There was no point in arguing with him. She waited for the shouting to continue, but everything fell into a taut silence, and after a couple of moments, she opened her eyes and looked across at him. He was sitting behind his desk, staring at her, a devastated, lost expression on his usually happy-go-lucky face.

'What *is* it, Clem? What's the story?' he asked quietly, aware that Pixie had gone into overdrive licking envelopes by the door, trying her best not to look like she was listening. She wasn't very good at it, just like she wasn't very good at pretending she wasn't in love with her happy-go-lucky boss.

Even if Clem had had an answer to give him, she couldn't have replied. Simon, their production bod – a Scottish red-haired numbers genius with a penchant for sideburns and practical jokes, particularly at Pixie's expense – sauntered in, a coffee in his hand.

'Oh, is this a domestic?' he asked delightedly at the sight

of them. 'Because I can make myself scarce.' Clem and Tom both knew his definition of 'scarce' meant hiding behind the photocopier.

Tom sighed. 'No, it's fine.' He sat up straighter, cricked his neck and looked back at his computer. Clem could see the tension hard-wired through his shoulders and wondered how long he'd been here for. Had he pulled another all-nighter? He looked even worse than he had at breakfast yesterday, and from the looks of things, she wasn't the only one in stale clothes.

Simon threw his bag across the back of his chair and sat down, his eyes lingering on Clem across the way. He spotted the Birkin. It was quite hard not to. 'Is that . . .?'

'No,' Clem replied quickly, shooting a warning look at Tom. 'Fake.' Hermès in this office was like the Holy Grail.

'Shame.' A sly grin crossed his pale face. 'So what happened to you yesterday?'

'Me?' Clem echoed innocently. 'I had the day off.' Dammit. She remembered too late that she'd told Tom she had a meeting. She could tell by the way he stopped typing that he'd heard.

'Make the most of it, did you?' Simon chuckled, taking in her enormous sunglasses.

'You know me. Seeing in the new year is a three-day event,' she quipped.

'What *did* you get up to last night?' Tom asked casually from across the way. 'Stella popped by for a drink.'

'Oh, did she?' Clem asked innocently. That was that alibi blown.

'Yeah,' Tom said levelly. 'So where were you?'

She tapped her shades. 'The pub, *obvs*.' She flashed him a fake grin.

'With?' Tom wouldn't be deterred.

Clem looked at her computer screen officiously, even though it was still turned off, aware that everything had gone quiet. She could sense Simon's eyes swivelling left to right and left again as he listened to the verbal volleys between brother and sister.

'Josh.' Even from across the room she felt the tension stiffen like a flexed board. 'And before you say anything, he's a lot better now. He's officially back on the wagon.'

'If you say so.' Tom spat the words out as if they were nails.

'I do . . . and it's not like I need your permission anyway,' she muttered.

'Children, children,' Simon interrupted, as amused as ever by their squabbling. 'As much as I do love a good bitch fight, if I'm to officiate you're going to have to clue me in. I thought Josh was the do-gooding teetotaller?'

'He is,' Tom sneered.

'Then why the long face?'

'Said the bartender to the horse, boom, boom,' Clem finished in a low voice.

'It's a long story,' Tom said, opening a drawer and pretending to look for something.

'Must be,' Simon shrugged. 'I mean, I'd come to accept that Clem was incapable of finding a functional, committed, virile man like myself irresistible. You weren't supposed to like her boyfriends; that was the point. But now she's dating Mr Perfect and you hate him? What's with you people?'

Clem and Tom each cracked reluctant smiles at the twisted logic, just as Tom's phone rang. Simon wagged his finger at Clem, as if to say 'behave', but Clem just stuck her tongue out at him.

The doorbell buzzed – the first of the deliveries for the new year – and Pixie jumped up as if she was on springs. Clem rolled her eyes at the sheer *bounce* in her body.

'I'll help you,' Simon said, getting up and holding the door open for her. Clem watched him, bored.

Tom had taken his call into the conference room – in reality, a tiny box room with a skylight and a plug socket for a laptop – and Clem sat in the office, alone and silent until her eyes found an anomalous shape resting on the wall behind Tom's desk. It was shrouded with a white sheet, but she knew what it was.

Getting up, she pulled off the cover and gasped to see – in the harsh light of day – exactly how wounded and diminished the bike was. Contrary to her daydreams of owning a bike like this, she saw clearly now that this was not a bike that could ever have been chained to a lamppost outside the pub; this bike was for people who wanted to cruise round their vast country estates when the Bentley was too big and the Ducati too fast. And she had trashed it at a party.

One hundred and thirty five thousand pounds? Once maybe, but not like this and not in this condition. They'd struggle to sell it at a car boot sale now, and Clem felt a wave of nausea grip her as she took in the full scale of the damage. The caramel and baby pink woven leather handle grips had come loose and untucked in several places where cigarette burns had caused the leather to fray and pull apart; the diamond-studded leather casings on the top and upright tubes looked like they had been tie-dyed with red wine; and the rare, peachy hide they'd used for the saddles – the foreskin of a blue whale was it? Or was that just the punchline of a joke she'd heard in the pub? – had been defaced with an obscene cartoon in red biro. Only the gold bell inset with a pink diamond and surrounded by hundreds of yellow pave diamonds shaped into petals had escaped unscathed – probably because the revellers had assumed it was fake. She opened up the leather panier, which had been whip-stitched by elves (or by hand, same difference) and opened out, tailgate-style, to reveal a Fortnum's-stocked picnic – only someone had popped the bottle of Tattinger and the tin of foie gras was missing altogether, a crushed packet of Marlboro Lights having been popped in its place.

Covering the bike again, she turned away, depressed, and her headache getting worse – the two ailments possibly weren't unrelated – and stepped towards the window to stare down into the street below. The Christmas lights were still strung up between the lampposts, criss-crossing the street, but they looked sad rather than festive now and Clem hoped the council would take them down quickly, along with the Christmas trees lying upended outside every house or flat, littering the pavements and making it difficult for residents with hangovers to get to work. She just wanted Christmas and New Year to hurry up and be forgotten for another eleven months, so that life could go back to just drifting along again, without this overbearing need to mark time.

Below her she saw the flashing hazard lights of the white delivery truck as Simon signed for the shipment, saying something that made Pixie laugh, and Clem grudgingly admired her shoes – shiny raspberry-pink ballet flats with the bow fashioned to look like Minnie Mouse ears.

She watched as elderly residents came out early to do their shopping with tartan trolleys, dogs being walked on short leads by owners holding small black bags; office workers standing by doorways smoking, a cup of coffee in hand. It wasn't the glitzy, razzmatazz image people conjured when they thought of Notting Hill and the famous Portobello Road market. It was greyer, damper, messier than that, and still in the kind of morose hibernation that comes from three days of solid rain. It only really looked the way the tourists imagined in the summer, when the pastel-painted houses baked like cookies in the sun and the faded shop awnings were rolled out to throw shadows on the ground, when the pub gardens overflowed with revellers and geraniums, when men – old and young alike – wore panamas and shorts, and girls cycled the streets on rattling boneshakers wearing vintage petticoats.

She watched as an elderly Jamaican man bought a hand of green bananas from Bob Ashley, the grocer – her father's most trusted fig supplier; a troop of teenage girls, not back at school for another week and all identically dressed in a junior version of her own outfit – bleached skinny jeans, swing jumpers and studded ankle boots – slunk past on their way to Trudie's café, where the coffee still only cost a pound and you got a bourbon biscuit for free. She smiled as she saw Katy, her florist friend, put together a beautiful spray of ranunculus roses and pussy willow, tying a blowsy hemp bow expertly around the stems as she chatted and laughed with relaxed familiarity to the customer, a well-dressed lady with white hair and a tweed coat and gloves. An orange-clad street sweeper was making slow progress down the road, pushing his cart in front of him and clearing chip wrappers and blue-striped polythene bags with his long-handled grabber, meaning he never had to so much as bend his knees – which was just as well since he was sixty-four and had been sweeping Portobello for forty-seven years. His name was Bert, and Clem had known him her entire life.

She pressed her hand to the glass as the old, familiar ache seeped through her. This was her home, her manor. She belonged here; she was a true local, born and bred in the tall, gracious villa her parents still lived in, two streets away on Elgin Crescent; she and Tom had been educated at La Scuola Italiana a Londra in Holland Park Avenue half a mile away – her parents were big believers in raising children to be bilingual, although Clem was becoming more and more convinced that her father just wanted them as interpreters on his long and involved annual gastronomy tours through Italy. In fact, the two years she'd managed at St Martin's in Covent Garden – it was supposed to have been three – were the longest she'd ever been away.

Even now she was all grown up – supposedly – she lived and worked in buildings only 500 yards from each other. If Clem pressed her face to the window and looked to the right, she could see her flat above the hardware store, op-- posite the Punky Fish clothes shop. She loved it here, she belonged here. And yet . . .

She wandered back to her desk, her eyes coming to rest upon the bag still sitting there, like a silent accusation. She stared at it for several long moments, knowing it was a bribe not a gift, before hurriedly lobbing it out of sight under her desk as the others came back into the room.

Simon and Pixie were still laughing. Tom . . . Tom looked like death. He seemed to have greyed just in the time he'd been on the phone.

'Tom, what is it? What's happened?' Clem asked urgently, unable to keep the alarm out of her voice.

Simon and Pixie fell silent, and Tom looked up at them all with bloodshot eyes.

'Tom?' Clem's voice wavered to see her brother look so broken, and she pushed her glasses onto the top of her head to get a better look at him.

Silence cloaked them all, and only the intermittent ping of incoming emails and a truck reversing in the road provided any soundtrack.

'That was Perignard.' His voice had flatlined. 'They're pulling the project.'

Clem's hands flew to her mouth and Simon had to steady himself by grabbing the nearest desk.

'But we're going into production in twelve days,' Simon said, almost laughing at the preposterousness of Tom's words.

'Not any more we're not,' Tom said, shaking his head.

'But we've been working exclusively on this for the past year,' Simon argued, his Celtic colour beginning to rise. 'We've ploughed everything into getting the new machines manufactured. We've got a contract.'

'They would argue that we're in breach of that contract.'

'How?' Simon asked, growing redder in the face. 'Everything's ordered and being shipped as we speak. We're bang on schedule and cost. I don't understand.'

Tom drew his lips into a thin line, his eyes unable to meet Clem's, and she saw the tic quiver in his cheek. It was because of her, she realized. What she'd done.

'Could someone please tell me what's going on?' Simon demanded into the vacuum.

Without saying a word, Clem crossed the room and pulled the sheet off the bike. Simon almost howled as he caught sight of it. 'It's my fault,' she said quietly, meeting all their eyes.

'What did you do?' Pixie whispered, walking over practically in a trance.

'I fucked up.' *As usual*, she didn't need to add.

An appalled silence followed.

'You all know that this was the showpiece for the new Dover Street store,' Tom said quietly.

'It's the window display; Perignard's had state-of-the-art glass fitted especially so that anything short of a tank couldn't get past,' Pixie said proudly, her eavesdropping having paid off. 'With all the passing traffic, it's an invaluable branding opportunity for us.'

'Was,' Tom corrected quietly.

'No, no, hang on!' Simon interjected agitatedly, his quick mind racing. 'This doesn't just affect Perignard. What about Berlin? We were going to unveil it to the trade in Berlin next week! It's supposed to showcase the new technologies we've invested in. How can we do that now when the bike's . . .?' Words failed him as he looked at it, visibly paling as he took in the scale of destruction.

'It's clearly unuseable in this condition,' Tom said quietly. 'Or, to quote Perignard, "not fit for purpose". And they're right.'

'But surely we can repair it before next week?' Pixie squeaked, looking at the bent spokes on the front wheel, where someone had squeezed in some bottles of Stoli, as though it was an obscure bottle rack.

Simon gave her a withering stare. 'The bike is vintage, so everything on it is made to bespoke dimensions. We've had it plated in *rose gold*. And if I told you that I was practically standing over the calf at birth, that would still be making light of the lengths I went to, to source the slink saddle leather.'

'Oh.'

They all stared at the trashed bike despondently.

'Do they want the diamonds back?' Pixie asked.

'Obviously,' Simon snapped.

Clem could see Tom stretching his lips thin, trying to keep control of his emotions.

'Can't we just, y'know, regroup and get everything ready for Berlin *next* year?' Pixie suggested, relentlessly optimistic.

Tom inhaled deeply and slowly. 'For one thing, our competitors will have caught up with us by then. At the moment we have the patent on the technology, but it's already an arms race and I know for a fact that Hermès is maybe only two months behind us. This is our USP, and we banked on it being our springboard into the next tier, offering a deluxe product that no one else could bring to the table. It was what made us stand out for the Bugatti contract.'

Clem's head snapped up. She hadn't heard anything about Bugatti before now.

'Bugatti? What? Like the cars?' Pixie chirruped.

'Exactly like that,' Simon muttered sarcastically.

'I didn't know there was a contract with them up for grabs,' she said to Tom.

'It was highly confidential. Si and I had to sign non-disclosure agreements; we couldn't tell even you,' Tom replied, looking at her feet. 'But with Russia, China and the Middle East as their biggest markets now, offering a diamond-studded interior is exactly the edge they're looking for.'

Clem thought she was going to be sick.

'And now there's nothing to show them,' Simon mumbled, folding his arms across his body and dropping his chin to his chest. 'Any reputation we had for professionalism will be scuppered once this gets out. There's no way we can get something else done for Berlin in the timeframe and ... Fuck! We can hardly come clean about why we're not showing the bike. We're just going to have to say the technology's not finessed yet and hope to God that Perignard keeps quiet.'

'I'm so sorry,' Clem said quietly. 'I really, really, really am.'

Her words were directed at them all, but her eyes were on Tom. No one would look at her.

'Simon, let's go into the meeting room,' he said, ignoring her again. 'We need to review where we are on invoices and new business.'

'Sure thing,' Simon said, grabbing his iPad and coffee from his desk, and shooting Clem a look that for once wasn't suffused with repressed yearning.

Clem's heart beat double-time as she watched them walk off together, Simon's hand slapping Tom's shoulder in commiseration, their voices already low in consultation. *She* was always the one who made Tom smile when things were bad; now he could barely look at her, and when they did talk, it was practically with a snarl.

Pixie, realizing she was alone with Clem, widened her eyes excitedly, clearly about to suggest a sympathy cupcake at the Hummingbird, but one look at Clem's expression and she scooted quickly back to her desk.

Clem stood stock still, resisting the urge to barge in to the meeting and demand to be allowed to help. This was her doing! She ought to be given the chance to fix it! That was what she wanted to say, but deep down, she knew a low profile was all Tom wanted from her at the moment.

He had built the company from nothing, but in eight years it had come to be seen as the successor to prestigious

British leather houses like Connolly and Bill Amberg. Tom wasn't happy stopping there, though. He was going after the big guns – Hermès, Gucci, Prada and Louis Vuitton – he wanted *his* leathers wrapping the luxury world. He'd been just one bike away from taking that first step, and he'd done all that with the £10,000 their parents had given each of them when they'd graduated – or in Clem's case, dropped out. Like the prodigal son, he'd used it as seed money to buy twenty hides, a specialist sewing machine and a six-month lease on this office.

He had asked her at the time if she wanted to join forces – what they could do with a £20,000 start-up would bring forward his five-year plan by at least three years – but after the disaster of failing her second-year exams (although turning up would have helped, she admitted afterwards) Clem had been adamant that what she needed was to 'get away' and see the world and had promptly bought a one-way business-class ticket to Bali and sat on the beach for eight months, until she ran out of money and had to ask their father to sub the flight home.

If Tom had been disappointed by her decision, he'd never said. He'd even ridden to her rescue when she'd been fired from her last and latest job as a sales manager at a chichi lingerie boutique on Westbourne Park Road. He had thrown her the lifeline of working for him, even though there was no real role to cover and her job was more display than anything else.

Tom covered the corporate and trade accounts, and was the only point of contact for hotels, high-end architects, investment banks and car manufacturers etc., whether they wanted leather walls, floors, desks, tables, chairs, rugs, sofas, beds or steering wheels. Simon, on the other hand, dealt with the less sexy accounts, invoices, sourcing and production functions.

She, by comparison, was called the Press and Marketing Manager, but it wasn't lost on anyone that Alderton Hide didn't advertise, they weren't in retail or wholesale, and in the five months she'd been taking up office space, she'd managed only two one-line mentions in *World of Interiors* magazine. If she was honest, she mainly just answered the phone and flirted with the clients when they were examining the colour wheels.

Her phone bleeped in her bag and she groaned as she reached down to retrieve it.

'Where you been? Keep missing you. Electric tonight? New Scorsese on.'

She tapped back in the affirmative, feeling her spirits lift slightly. Stella would have some words of wisdom to impart; she always gave sound advice – not including the time she said necking vodka shots through your eyeballs was the low-cal way to get drunk. Tom might not want her help, but surely there had to be something she could do. Stella always said she was charmed, born lucky. Something would come up to make everything right again. It always did – in the end.

Chapter Five

'Wassup?' Stella demanded, shrugging off her khaki parka and collapsing into the seat Clem had reserved for her as Clem poured her an enormous glass of red wine from the carafe on the antique-mirrored table between them.

'Bike-gate's gone to a whole new level,' Clem grimaced, handing the glass over. 'Perignard's pulled the account.'

'No!' Stella breathed dramatically.

'Yep. No bike equals no lovely leather-clad, diamond-twinkly showroom.'

'Shit.' Stella's eyes were wide over the rim of her glass.

'Oh but no! That's *nothing*! Apparently the bike was also the big *raison d'être* for Berlin, which is where we get all our new business, and an "I-could-tell-you-but-then-I'd-have-to-kill-you" confidential pitch to Bugatti, which was the big prize all along. Over three hundred thousand in projected revenue, gone. Just like that.' She took a big glug of her wine. She'd almost fallen over when Simon had told her the figure after his meeting. He hadn't even looked angry, just scared.

'Holy mutha.' Stella tried stretching her legs out on the footstool, but it was too far away, perched as it was, comfortably under Clem's ankles. She reached inside the stool and pulled out the black cashmere blanket instead, wrapping it around her legs. 'You'd better drink up.'

Clem did as she was told and scanned the room absently, looking for familiar faces in the queue for the bar. She had bagged seats towards the back as usual. The Electric was one of her favourite haunts. At the front, the heavy red velvet curtains were still closed, and smug couples were lying stretched out on the signature velvet beds. Almost all the leather club chairs were filled with couples or groups, laughing and dipping flatbreads into hummus before the lights went down.

'Well, I had thought this might impress you,' Stella said, rummaging in her jeans pocket and pulling out a crumpled piece of paper. 'But after hearing that, probably not.'

'What is it?'

'An ad I saw in Ajeep's. Cleaner looking for work.'

'Oh right, great,' Clem said, taking it from her lethargically.

'Give her a ring,' Stella insisted. 'Remember what we talked about? That could be one way of making things up to Tom at least.'

Clem shot her a look. 'He's just lost three hundred grand because of me; you really think he's gonna care if I hire a cleaner?'

'You know what they say,' Stella tutted. 'A tidy house equals a tidy mind.'

'Who says that?' Clem frowned as the lights began to drop.

'Just ring her. And make sure you check the references,' Stella hissed as blackness fell like a sheet from the rafters, and everyone swivelled around in their chairs to face the bright screen. A few latecomers darted into the last remaining seats and Clem stared, annoyed, into the playfully tossed-up hair of the girl who sat down right in front of her.

Stella jiggled the box of popcorn loudly and Clem thrust her hand in, florets of popcorn spilling out of the cone all over the floor. They laughed at their messiness, prompting a few curt shushes from anonymous members of the audience. Clem pulled a face at them in the dark and lobbed a single floret into the crowd.

To her astonishment, a moment later, it came back.

Stella gasped, lobbing a fresh couple of her own in the same direction. Sure enough, several moments later, they were back in her lap. Both girls leaned forward, trying to see their combatants. A pair of cocky grins, almost blue-tinted in the cinematic glare, shone back at them.

Not bad, Clem mused. That was certainly her favoured way of shrugging off a bad day. She poured herself and Stella a fresh glass each and sat back in her seat, deciding to let them stew for a bit and refusing to make further contact of either the eye or popcorn kind, even though several more florets were expertly thrown into hers and Stella's laps.

She tried to concentrate on the film, but the girl in front's hair was in the way and she had to angle herself diagonally in her chair to see round her. Matters weren't helped by the fact that the girl constantly fidgeted away from her boyfriend's affections as he tried to caress her slender neck. Clem sighed. That was all she needed right now, a lover's tiff right in front of her.

The person on the far side of the girl appeared to say something to her and she leaned in to listen. Then she took something and turned around. 'For you,' she murmured, holding out a scrap of paper towards Clem and Stella.

Oh.

Clem took it with a surprised nod. 'Thanks.' Then she opened it up to read it, Stella's chin resting on her shoulder curiously.

Wanna get out of here?

'Cheeky beggars!' Stella giggled, clearly delighted and straining to get a better look at their admirers. 'What do you think?'

Clem looked over, too, wondering which one she'd choose. From what she could make out, they looked a couple of years younger than her and Stella, but that had its own advantages as far as she was concerned. 'Yeah, why not?' she said in a low voice. 'If I'm going to spend a night in the dark, I may as well spend it doing something other than brooding.'

'What about Josh?'

'What about him?'

'I thought you two were getting a regular thing going.'

'Listen, I still like that he's different to the other guys I usually go for but . . .' she shrugged. 'Every time I look at him now I'm reminded of what I did.' She rolled her eyes. 'And he *so* wasn't worth it. It's not his fault but . . . we're not going to get past it. Come on,' she whispered, checking her make-up in the mirrored table before standing up and bending down low to collect her bag, accidentally knocking the contents onto the floor as she did so.

'Shit!' she hissed, crouching down and hurriedly sweeping her purse, hairbrush, keys and spare 'get lucky' knickers back into her bag. The boyfriend in front turned at the sounds of the kerfuffle and Clem felt herself go limp as she met the glacial blue eyes that had held hers once before.

The Swimmer.

Her knees wanted to buckle, to force her to sit back down again so that she could spend the rest of the evening staring at the back of his head in the dark. How could she not have noticed him before?

But it was too late. The cocky strangers had seen the girls get up and had themselves left their seats and were now making their way up to the doors to wait for them.

Stella hissed at her in the dark. 'Move it, Clem! I'm not bloody going on my own.'

Painfully, tearing her eyes away from his, Clem walked towards the aisle, aware of his gaze upon her back. Why had she thrown that damned piece of popcorn? Why couldn't she just have sat quietly in the cinema like a normal person instead of starting a food fight with strangers across the room?

'All right? I'm Jake, he's Oscar,' the taller one said to her as she approached, appraising her with lively hazel eyes; she could tell it was his grin she'd seen in the dark. Stella was already in full flirt mode with his friend – a Matt Damon lookalike but with a goatee and thighs like thunder.

'Clem,' she muttered as Jake reached for her hand and gallantly kissed it.

'Well, Clem, let's go and find some real fun, shall we?'

He held the door open for her and Clem hesitated for a moment. She looked back at the Swimmer. He was holding his beautiful girlfriend's face in his hands, cupping her like a flower, as if she was the only woman on the planet, much less in this room. Then his lips were upon hers, the door swung shut and once again Clem found herself spun out of his orbit.

The following morning it was so cold that Clem's breath hung like bridges in the air, leaving a trail of ghostly suspensions behind her as she ran, soft-footed, through the sand paths of Hyde Park. To her right, the No.12 bus was pacing her along the Bayswater Road, and she was gradually gaining on the Queen's Household Cavalry, who were out for their early morning drills, the red-plumes from their helmets bouncing bonnily, their brassware clattering and steam rising from the flanks of their mighty horses.

She reached the path that turned right towards the Serpentine and accelerated, feeling last night's alcohol dissipate like spirits in the mist. Stella had long since given up trying to stay abreast of her. They did everything together but this. Where Stella ran to lose weight, Clem ran to . . . well, she didn't really have a reason for it. It was a physical need. She just did it because she could. This was the one thing she was truly good at. And for the record, she didn't jog, she ran – hard and fast, as though, if she felt like it, she might not stop.

Jake had still been sleeping when she'd left, but she knew he'd be grateful to her for slipping out early and discreetly. He'd been fun. They'd ended up drinking cocktails and chaser shots at the Portobello Star, as he'd determinedly jollied her out of her sulk. Her parting image of the Swimmer kissing his girlfriend had messed with her, and she'd spent much of the first hour wondering whether the charge that surged between them was a figment of her imagination. Then the alcohol had kicked in and everything had settled down into that familiar, dreamy blur that she knew so well and she'd stopped thinking about anything much at all, other than dealing with what was in front of her.

She sped around the Serpentine and back towards the Italian Gardens, hurdling athletically over a buggy that suddenly appeared from behind the café wall, and overtaking a posse of women in orange BMF bibs being shouted out by a commando. By the time she caught sight of Stella ahead of her, fifty minutes later, she'd run three times as far as her friend on half the breath.

Clem laughed as she watched her jogging alongside the cavalry on their way back to the barracks, talking in vain to one of the soldiers atop an 18-hand horse who, in spite of his raging desire to talk to the bosomy brunette, was gloomily bound to regimental silence.

'Give it up, Stell!' she called, sitting on the back of a park bench, and motioning for her to come over. 'He'll have to clean the loos with a toothbrush for a month if he even looks at you.'

Stella jogged over slowly, holding an overflowing bosom in each hand. 'Shame. He looked good in brass,' she panted as she got closer.

Clem chuckled, wiping her hair away from her face and drinking greedily from her water bottle.

'You were off like a rocket today,' Stella remarked once she'd got her breath back, instantly reaching into the waistband of her leggings and pulling out a packet of Marlboro.

'Yeah, I felt like I had some puff today.'

'You usually only run like that when you're wound up about something,' Stella murmured into a cupped hand as she lit up.

'Me? No.' Clem slapped the water bottle from hand to hand as if it was a ball.

There was a suspicious silence as Stella inhaled deeply before blowing out smoke slowly. 'Come on, out with it. I can always tell when you're hiding something from me. You're being far too virtuous – running, water. Get you, angel girl.'

Clem sighed. 'It's this bloke.'

'Of *course* it is!' Stella cried triumphantly, sliding down the bench until she was lying on her back as if she was on a shrink's couch. 'Tell me everything.'

'There's nothing to tell, that's the problem. I was hoping you could tell me.'

'Me?'

'I've got no idea who he is. I first saw him at yours on New Year's Eve.'

'Describe,' Stella ordered, waving her cigarette around as if it was a wand and closing her eyes in concentration. One of her strongest skills was her photographic fashion memory. She was a nightmare with faces, a disaster with names, but Stella could remember people and places by outfits. There was precious little point in Clem saying '6 foot 3 inches, dark blond, angular, big shoulders, blue eyes.'

'Charcoal jacket with black revers, pale blue shirt, jeans.'

There was a short silence as Stella mentally catalogued the night's outfits before firmly shaking her head. 'Nope. Must have been another party.'

'No, it was definitely New Year's Eve.'

'Uh-uh.'

'I promise you, Stell, it was. I saw him just before Tom pushed the hat down over my eyes and Josh face-planted me.'

'Ooh, class act.' Stella giggled. 'Nah, sorry babes. I'd remember someone in that get-up. The jacket sounds cool.'

Clem rolled her eyes and watched a black cab chunter past on West Carriage Drive. 'Well anyway, I saw him again last night. He was sitting in front of us at the Electric. Came in late with his girlfriend.'

'Oh yes – tie-dye Marant jeans and orange pash. She was gorgeous.'

'Yeah, I know,' Clem replied dejectedly.

'Oh dear,' Stella said, tipping her head back and taking in her friend's lacklustre demeanour. 'You have got it bad.'

'No I haven't. I'm just hungover. Anyway, it doesn't matter. I'll probably never see him again anyway. I just wondered if you knew him, that was all.' She took another swig of her bottle.

There was a short silence. 'Jake was sweet, though.'

'Yeah, he was funny. I liked him.'

'Going to see him again then?'

'Nah.' Clem watched a young couple chasing after their toddler, who was staggering like a drunk across the grass.

'Yeah, me neither. I mean, Oscar was cute but a bit young. I have a horrid suspicion he might've thought it was more than just a fling – he kept talking about getting tickets to see Florence + the Machine at the Roundhouse. I mean, who said anything about *dates*? Got to make a swift exit from guys like that, I'm telling you.'

'No good can come of it,' Clem muttered.

'Ain't that the truth.'

They sat in silence for a few minutes, with just the slap of tumbling water and wobbly smoke rings for company.

'Fancy a sausage bap?' Stella asked after a while. 'I've got evil munchies.'

'Yeah, great.' Clem stood up, kicking her feet out to shake her thigh muscles, throwing her arms above her head and sinking into some half-hearted side bends.

'My treat, you need cheering up,' Stella said, squeezing her arm fondly and propelling her along the park towards Notting Hill Gate.

'Honestly, I'm fine.'

'My father always said, "What's meant for you won't go past you." Just you remember that,' Stella continued solemnly.

'Anything else your father said that I should know about?'

'Never trust Sagittarians or men with long nails.'

There was a short silence. 'Interesting man your father,' Clem said finally.

'I know! Right?' Stella laughed, waving her arms so wildly that she inadvertently flagged down a cab. A look of pure longing crossing her face.

'Oh, get in, then!' Clem grinned, opening the door and smacking her on the bum. 'This can be *my* treat.'

Chapter Six

The low winter sun skated through the sitting-room window at a sharp angle, and at first Clem thought she was home alone as she opened the doors to the flat and blinked into the light-drenched room. But the honeyed aroma of white jasmine wood-scented sticks told her Clover was in the house. She kept them on a high shelf in Tom's wardrobe, knowing that neither Tom nor Clem would ever bother to retrieve them for themselves, even though they both agreed they smelled heavenly and added a layer not just of sophistication but comfort to the flat. Their message was clear: Clover could make a home for Tom, more so than his slatternly sister.

'I'm back!' Clem shouted, feeling cheerier after hers and Stella's carb-loading at the greasy spoon caff on the corner of Lonsdale Road.

'So we hear,' Clover's soft voice replied from the far corner. Clem peered through the slanting light to find Clover standing by the worktop in one of Tom's rugby shirts, boxers and hooped socks. 'Lapsang?'

Clem pulled a face and tried not to retch. 'Hell no. Where's Tom?'

'In bed, trying to catch up on his sleep. Leave him. He's not slept for more than a few hours a night all week, poor thing.' Her voice was so soft Clem half-wondered whether she had meditated herself into a trance.

Clem pulled her muddy trainers off her feet and crossed the room, wondering why Clover always made her brother sound so fragile, as though he were some delicate creature that needed protecting (from her, doubtless).

'I'm bloody well awake now,' Tom croaked from the bedroom. 'I'd need dopamine to sleep through that foghorn voice.'

Clem loped through to the bedroom. 'Hey, bro! Why so lazy?'

Tom groaned as she did a flying leap through the air and landed on the bed so heavily that it rolled several inches across the room on its castors. 'Some of us have already been up and running, you know,' she said virtuously, throwing herself widthways across the bed. 'My body is a temple.'

'Temple of doom, maybe,' Tom muttered, pulling the duvet up to his waist and folding his arms behind his head, watching her. 'Where were you last night? Josh's again?'

'Not exactly,' she grinned, overjoyed that he was talking to her again.

Tom's eyes narrowed. 'Don't say . . .'

'*I'm* not saying anything, big brother. I'm the very soul of discretion.' She gave a cheeky wink.

Clover wafted into the room carrying a tray of lapsang souchong tea and freshly toasted waffles, topped with chopped bananas, hazelnuts and maple syrup. Both Clem and Tom's eyes widened at the sight and smell as she gracefully pushed the bed back into the wall with her legs.

'I'd have made one for you, but you've already eaten so . . .' Clover sat lightly on the bed and fed Tom a bite of waffle.

'No I haven't,' Clem protested, watching as her brother's eyes closed happily.

Clover tipped her head to the side. 'So then, the ketchup on your chin . . .?'

Tom chuckled quietly as Clem put a finger to her face and it came back red. She jumped up and peered at her reflection in the mirror. Excellent. A huge gob of ketchup was smeared from lip to jaw.

'Shamblesshambles,' Shambles squawked loudly in her ear from the cage beside her.

'Thanks, Sham,' Clem moaned. 'Cos *you've* got such great table manners.'

'Shamblesshamblesshambles.'

'Am not.'

'How many times have I told you not to argue with the parrot?' Tom asked with a full mouth from the bed. 'It makes you sound properly mad.'

'And besides, you know she'll always win,' Clover jibed.

Clem wordlessly opened the cage door to let Shambles fly around the room, knowing that Clover had an irrational, but unarticulated, fear of the parrot landing on her head and getting a claw tangled in her hair. Clem came and sat back down on the bed, watching as Clover moved closer to Tom, her eyes never leaving the parrot.

Revenge. Just like that.

'So, what are you lovebirds up to today, then?' Clem asked, tucking her legs beneath her and stealing the last bite of waffle left on Tom's plate while he took a sip of tea.

'Oi!' he protested.

'Cos I'm up for a lazy afternoon at the Electric if you are. I still haven't seen the new Scorsese yet. I started to last night but . . .' she shrugged.

Tom's eyes narrowed again.

'Well, as much as an afternoon sitting in the dark sounds exciting, we've made some appointments to view a couple of flats later,' Clover smiled.

Clem looked at Tom in alarm. '*What?*'

'Jesus, Clo! You said you'd let me handle it!' Tom muttered, visibly annoyed, pulling himself up further into a sitting position. He looked back at his sister, his most placatory expression on his face. 'It's only some viewings, Clem. We'll probably hate them.'

But he was missing the point. 'You want to move out and leave me?'

'Not leave *you*, sis,' Tom replied urgently. 'Just . . . here. Maybe.'

Clem blinked at him, speechless, which had the effect on Tom that his tic had on her.

'Look, it was pretty clear after going through the numbers with Simon yesterday that I have to get some capital into the business. Fast. We've used up all our credit with the bank investing in the new machinery, and they won't extend any more.'

'But why does that mean you have to move out?' Clem whined. 'I pay my rent on time.'

Clover gave the patient smile of the victor. 'With the company in such trouble, it would be foolish for Tom not to look at downsizing. We've talked about it and Tom agrees the best option would be to release his equity in this place and reinvest it in the company instead.'

Equity? Clem felt like she'd been shot with a tranquillizer gun. Their voices seemed hollow and distant, as if they were in a tunnel. 'You mean you want to *sell*?' Clem asked her brother, resolutely ignoring Clover. Talk about going from bad to worse! He was wiping imaginary crumbs off the bed onto the floor and keeping his eyes well away from hers. She saw the now-familiar tension tighten in the corner of his mouth again.

'Like I said, it'll probably come to nothing. These flats we're looking at are all the way out in West Kilburn,' he replied flatly.

'Kilburn?' Clem screeched, as though he'd said Dark Side of the Moon.

'Yes, Clem. It may not have the fancy Portobello address, but a one-bed out there is almost half what you'd get for this,' Clover said firmly. 'It would solve all Tom's problems in one fell swoop.'

And yours, Clem thought bitterly, glaring at her. She'd been angling for Tom to move in with her for years. This way she was going to get Tom alone at last and herself on the mortgage deeds. 'But what about me?'

Clover smiled. 'That's the beauty of it. You can stay here and just buy the flat off Tom.'

'Just buy? *Just buy?*' Clem hollered, jumping to her feet so that she was standing on the mattress, her head brushing the bottom of the light, which had a top hat as a shade, making for quite a ridiculous image. 'You know perfectly well I don't have half a mill to just shell out whenever I want!'

'No, but your parents have always made it perfectly clear they'd give you financial assistance if you needed it. All you have to do is ask,' Clover said smugly.

'The bloody nerve!' Clem stormed at her brother. 'Telling us what our parents can or cannot do with their own money. Are you really going to let her get away with that, Tom?'

Tom looked away, his open face horribly closed, pinched and grey. He did look angry, although whether it was due to Clover's bold assertions or the fact that his sister and girlfriend were at each other's throats again, she couldn't be sure. 'Clem, I . . . we're just looking. Nothing's set in stone yet. It's just one option that I'm looking into, that's all. If it means I can keep the company going and we can all keep our jobs, then I have an obligation to look into it properly.'

'But either way, *I'm* shafted. Whichever way you look at it, I'm going to lose either my job or my home, right?' Clem sank dramatically back down onto the bed, her head in her hands.

There was a long pause before Tom could find his voice. 'As things stand at the moment, yes, that's pretty much the sum of it,' he said quietly. His eyes met hers, and Clem almost burst into tears at the sorrow she saw in them. She immediately wanted to throw her arms around his neck and tell him it was all going to be OK, that they'd get through it together, just like they always had. If they could survive being locked in old Mrs Gantry's shed for three hours that time when they'd climbed over the wall to retrieve a football, then they could survive anything. But she couldn't, not with Clover lying in the bed next to him, her skinny ankle casually hooked around his leg.

Clover allowed herself a long sip of tea. 'I don't know why you're so surprised, Clem,' she said calmly and intrusively. 'You surely must have understood better than anyone that there would have to be some hard decisions taken after the Perignard and Bugatti deals were lost.'

Clem felt the pain of Clover's words hit home. Clover was a bitch to say it, but it didn't stop her being right.

Shambles gave a loud and sudden squawk that made the

others jump, and Clover dived for cover under the duvet as the parrot swooped off the bamboo ladder that doubled up as Tom's clothes horse, and came to perch on Clem's shoulder, rubbing her beak like she was polishing it in Clem's hair, before taking a loving nip of Clem's earlobe.

Clem didn't holler in response like she usually did, though. She barely even registered it. Instead, she slowly climbed off the bed and lowered her shoulder to the open door of Shambles' cage, whereupon the bird walked in with particular dignity, her long red tail feathers sweeping behind her like taffeta ballgown skirts.

Clem tried to do the same as she turned on her heel, but it was a hard look to pull off with ketchup on her chin, and she'd only just rounded the corner when the tears blinded her way and she had to hold the wall for support.

'Shit, Clem . . .' Tom called after her, and Clem heard the bed creak as he moved to follow her. 'What did you have to say that for, Clo? It's not like she doesn't know . . .'

'No, Tom,' she heard Clover say to him in a low voice. 'I've told her the truth, that's all. She's just sulking because she wants to be a Portobello Girl all her life. She's spoilt, that's her problem. You and your parents have indulged her for too long. You're the one who's got to leave the area altogether to release enough money to plough straight back into the company, keeping her job going when this whole sorry mess has come about because of *her* recklessness.'

'That's not strictly true, Clo. I should never have invested so much before we signed contracts—'

'If she hadn't ruined the bike, you would have headlined Berlin and won the Bugatti account. True or false?'

There was a reluctant silence. 'I suppose you're right,' Tom muttered eventually, although his voice sounded strange.

'I am, Tom-Tom, you know I am. And who knows, maybe this will be the best thing that ever happened to her? You're not doing her any favours shielding her from the consequences of her own actions, you know. It's high time she started taking responsibility for her behaviour. She's only got away with playing the wild child for so long because you've enabled her to.'

'I just worry about her, Clo, that's all. She's not as tough as she makes out.'

'No, she's nowhere near as fragile as you think, Tom,' Clover contradicted. 'And the sooner you accept that, my darling, the better life will be – for all three of us.' There was a heavy pause, and when Clover spoke again, her voice was lower, different. 'And you know I can't wait for ever, Tom. Please don't force me into a decision I don't want to take just because you won't make the one you know is right.'

Clem realized she was holding her breath as the bedroom fell silent. There it was, the ultimatum Clem had known was floating between them all in the ether: Tom had to choose between them. Clover had played her card at last.

Clem rested her cheek against the wall, willing him to choose her, to look after her, just like he'd always done, ever since they'd been little, before everything had fallen apart.

And as the silence grew, she felt her hopes lift. He wasn't saying it. He wasn't giving Clover the answer she wanted. She'd come on too strong; played it wrong. Clem knew her brother better than Clover, better than anyone. He was easygoing and amiable, everybody's buddy, an honest, fair and good man, but he was no walkover. Clover had sorely misjudged him if she thought she could divide and conquer *them*. Clem and Tom shared a bond that nobody could break.

But then she heard a low groan and the creak of the mattress springs as weight was shifted. Her centre of gravity dropped a foot as she realized what she was hearing, and a moment later a shoe, thrown across the room, slammed the door shut like a slam-dunk. Clem closed her eyes and sagged against the wall – the end of her world as she knew it had just begun.

Chapter Seven

Clem wandered down the road, getting in everyone's way. Being a Saturday, all the stallholders were in the throes of the busiest day of their week, calling out to each other for small change and shared mirrors as punters moved between them at a tortoise-like pace, their purposeful marches when they'd emerged at Notting Hill Gate tube dissipating as the stalls stretched out before them like the yellow brick road.

The day was bright and approaching a shade of warm in the sunlight, but Clem felt cold, even in the destroyed leather jacket she'd grabbed from the sofa on her way out. She was still in the sweaty harem-style sweatpants and over-sized tee she'd worn running, and although they'd almost dried, her skin felt damp and chilled in them. Her hair was up in a scruffy, unbrushed ponytail, exposing her bare neck to the elements, and she wished she'd had the presence of mind to grab a beanie before she left. But she couldn't go back to the flat now. She couldn't bear to see the silent triumph in Clover's eyes, or worse, the shame and disappointment in Tom's.

She knew Stella would be up to her eyes on the stall by now, but where else could she go?

'Hey, Clem!' a raspy voice called out. She looked up to see Katy grinning at her from her flower stall, swaddled in her signature WWII army officer's overcoat, Doc Marten boots and a mothballed pompom hat that had seen better days. 'You look like I feel. Good night was it?'

Clem felt the smile climb across her face automatically as she wandered over. 'Fake it till you make it' was her motto, and she was the queen of faking it. 'Yeah! Top.'

A tired-looking woman with a baby in a papoose strapped to her chest drifted over to the stall and started looking at the calla lilies, one of Katy's priciest items at £8 a stem. Katy widened her eyes fractionally – hopefully – at Clem, and Clem shuffled further out of the way so as not to dissuade the lady from browsing.

'Let me know if I can 'elp you at all.' Katy smiled at the woman, blowing into her hands which, as ever, boasted raw pink fingers. Clem found herself thinking how much warmer Katy would be with a wrap of sheepskin around her hands – maybe done up as wrist warmers or fingerless gloves, so that she could still keep her fingers free? 'So, what was it last night then? Or rather, who?' She winked.

'Just some bloke I met. Drinks in the Star,' Clem smiled, zipping up her jacket as the nip in the shadows began to bite.

'The Star? Heavy on the tequila then.'

'Is there any other way?'

'I don't know how you do it. Out partying all night and looking fresh as a daisy next morning.'

'You deal with daisies and we both know they bear no resemblance to me first thing in the morning. How's Scott? Anything come up for him yet?'

Scott was Katy's live-in boyfriend. He'd been made redundant from his job at a printers' in Queen's Park, and Katy needed to sell a lot of calla lilies to make their rent each week. Stella had told him to buy a job lot of T-shirts, print them up and she'd sell them on the market for him, but Katy kept saying, unless they found a cache dumped in one of the bins, they couldn't afford the upfront costs.

'Nah, although Pip in Bee Me thought they needed someone on rounds at the post office, so I've just texted him to get out of bed and get down there sharpish.'

The woman browsing wandered off and Katy let out a weary sigh. 'Shit.'

'Still quiet for you?' Clem asked, looking at the tourists and day-trippers thronging around them, picking up mismatched silver spoons, crumbly books and polyester lace dresses. She looked back at Katy. Clem always thought she was so pretty – tall and fine-boned with clear blue eyes and an elegant nose; her mouse-blonde hair was stringy and always hung limply, tucked behind one ear, but rather than diminishing her in any way, it just lent her a natural, un-made up air. She always looked like she needed a good hot meal, though, and today she looked not just cold, but drained too, boasting the same pinched expression Tom was currently wearing.

'Yeah, but it ain't so bad,' Katy managed with the convincing brightness she was known for locally. 'The Christmas wreaths did so well they've given me some breathing space. And I reckon everyone'll cheer up once the daffs start coming in.'

'Of course they will. Everyone loves daffs.'

'Did you see Portobello House has planted their boxes with my snowdrops? They look dead pretty. So there should be a bit of interest from that.'

'Totally,' Clem nodded. 'And once Mum and Dad are back from St Lucia, they'll want something bright and colourful for the hall – you know what my mum's like.'

'I do indeed,' Katy grinned, winking at her. 'Caribbean, hey? How the other half live. I could do with a bit of sun on my bones. I feel like it's been raining for months.'

'And yet you never get ill. It's amazing. You're out here in all weathers, day after day, whilst I'm practically sitting on the radiator in the office. Simon thinks I'm nesting eggs.'

'Bet *he'd* like to keep you warm,' Katy cackled, blowing into her hands again and shuffling her feet to keep the blood moving.

'Nah, he's over it now. He's been at close quarters for too long now. He's seen just how dysfunctional I am.'

'Maybe he'd like to be your personal salvation.'

Clem rolled her eyes, closing the topic down. 'Anyway, I was just off to see Stella and get some lunch. Wanna join us?'

'I'd love to, but I daren't leave. Ron's flat out today.' Katy jerked her head towards the neighbouring stallholder, who was selling tights, socks and scarves like they were going out of fashion – the weather forecasters had predicted a cold snap. 'He won't be able to deal with any customers I might get, too. Although there's not much hope of that on the strength of things so far! But I'd better stay here, just in case.'

Clem rubbed Katy's arm reassuringly. 'Well, I'll bring you a treat on my way back, OK?'

'You're a doll. Thanks, babe.'

'Oh, and before I forget, it's Tom's birthday next Thursday. Can you get me in some of those orangey flowers he liked last year?'

Katy thought for a moment. 'Freesias, weren't they?'

'If you say so.'

'Great, no probs. How many d'you want?'

Clem shrugged. 'Put something gorgeous together for me. And don't spare the horses.'

Katy pointed at her and gave another wink. 'I owe you.'

'No. You really don't.'

Clem let the sluggish current eddy her along, raising a hand or nodding her head as familiar faces called out in greeting, but she stopped short of chatting again. Her problems might not be as pressing as Katy's – sleeping on the street wasn't the threat hanging over her; it was *not* sleeping on *this* street that had her running scared – but the fragile happiness she knew was at shatter-point. Tom was giving up on her, she could feel it, and that meant she was truly alone now.

As she headed north past Elgin Crescent, a guy with dreds was standing in one of the traffic islands playing the metal drums and bringing the Caribbean to North London. Clem's thoughts wandered to her parents and what they might be doing at that moment. They had jetted out yesterday for their annual winter sojourn in St Lucia; her mother couldn't stand the cold.

Clover had been right, of course. Clem knew her parents would fall over themselves to help out, no doubt stumping up the cash for her to put a deposit down on a flat, or giving Tom the money directly to invest in the company. But Tom's pride meant he would never take it, and although Clem had long since given up the notion of having any pride in herself, she wouldn't take her parents' money either.

The vintage fashion stalls under the railway bridge and canvases in Portobello Green were mobbed, as usual, as teenagers, stylists and students considered Norwegian jumpers, Edwardian tea dresses, Mod parkas and every trend, epoch and era in between.

Clem stopped at the French bakery stall and bought three chocolate-filled crêpes and hot chocolates, paying a pound extra for one of the girls to run down with one for Katy on her stall.

Skirting the crowd altogether, Clem climbed over the generator wires and stray chairs that lay between the stalls at the back, pushing through the black Spanish lace curtains that marked the 'walls' of Stella's domain.

'What's wrong?' Stella asked immediately, handing over change to another satisfied customer and making eye contact with the next. 'Sixty, love.'

Clem handed Stella her lunch and sat dejectedly on the upturned bucket, taking a half-hearted bite of her crêpe.

'Clover finally did it. She did the "her or me" thing. Tom's moving in with her.'

'No!' Stella gasped in horror, startling a Japanese student who almost leapt across the road in fright. 'Sorry, not you, duck. That top's forty quid.' She looked back down at Clem, who was absently squidging the chocolate filling of the crêpe as if it were toothpaste in a tube. A thought occurred to her. 'Does that mean *I* can move in, then?'

Clem hoiked up her eyebrows. 'Yeah. If you can buy the flat off Tom.'

'He's *selling*? That's a bit bloody drastic, isn't it? Why can't he just rent out his room? That flat's the best investment ever.'

'Because he needs to release the equity to refinance Alderton Hide. Things are even worse than I'd thought. The company's on the brink of collapse.' She sighed.

'Shit. What are you going to do?'

'What can I do? I'll have to get a place on my own.'

'Crap.'

'Yeah. It is.' Clem noticed a chunky woollen sleeve hanging down the back of the trestle table. 'I'm frozen; this jacket's useless. Have you got anything I can put on? I left the flat in a bit of a hurry. Clover's celebratory sex noises were more than I could take.'

'Ugh, rolling in Clover . . .' Stella murmured, rummaging in one of her giant Ikea bags under the table and pulling out a copper-coloured cable-knit floppy beret. 'Here, try that.'

Clem rammed her ponytail in it and pulled it down over her ears. 'Ooh, that's better.'

Stella regarded her for a moment before tipping the beret fractionally to the right. 'Perfect.'

'How much?' The Japanese girl was pointing at Clem's head.

Stella looked down at her. 'Thirty for the beret. It's hand-knitted.'

The Japanese girl nodded and opened her purse again. Meanwhile, Stella whipped the hat off Clem's head.

'Oi!' Clem protested.

'Shurrup,' Stella murmured. 'I've got another one in the bag.'

Clem sighed and waited for her ears to be covered again. This time the beret was silver grey. 'Thank you,' she said pointedly, making her own little adjustments, just as she heard Stella say, 'Thirty.'

She looked up, but too late, the beret was whisked straight off her head.

'Hey!' she protested again as the hat was bagged up and handed over.

'Sorry 'bout that.' Stella reached back down into the bag and pulled out a fake-fur deerstalker. 'Here you go. You'll be safe in that. Can't sell these for love nor money.'

'Finally,' Clem pouted, giving the hat an extra tug down and returning to her crêpe, which was now as cold as her nose. 'So what d'you think I should do? I could try and get Clover off the scene. I reckon I'd be good at revenge.'

The hat was whisked off her head before she'd even finished the sentence.

'Oh you've *got* to be kidding me!' Clem scowled, standing up and staring down at the customers, who were all eyeballing the furry deerstalker in the lucky punter's hands.

'Holy cow, you're my lucky talisman.' Stella giggled. 'Here, put this on.' She was holding out an olive green parka with a fake-fur lining and matching-trimmed hood.

'No. I don't want to,' Clem retorted, crossing her arms belligerently. 'I'm freezing. I'm still sweaty from running earlier.'

'Which is why you should put it on.'

'Why? You'll only take it off me again.'

'It's not my fault if people want to look like you. Put it on, you daft nana.'

Looking at everyone suspiciously, Clem shrugged on the coat. She'd barely tipped up the hood before Stella casually said, 'A hundred and forty.'

Instantly, arms shot forward with bank notes clutched tightly in their hands.

'I'll give you one fifty,' cried one of the girls further back in the crowd.

Stella looked across at her – eyes wide with surprise – and Clem burst out laughing. She had to. It was ridiculous. *Beyond* ridiculous.

After that, they had some fun with it, running the stall as a fashion show auction. Clem put something on, Stella gave an opening number and the customers vied and bid until almost everything on the stall had gone.

'My God!' Stella wheezed with laughter as she packed up several hours later – not that there was much left to pack. 'What *was* that?'

'Some kind of fashion flash mob?' Clem groaned. She was exhausted, although no longer cold, and the crowd's adoring attention had restored her spirits after Tom's rejection.

Stella plonked herself down on the spare bucket and looked across at her friend, as though seeing her for the first time.

'What?' Clem asked nervously, as Stella scrutinized her. 'Don't say I've got chocolate on my face now?'

'No. I'm just trying to pinpoint exactly what it is about you that attracts people.'

'Oh thanks.' Clem laughed nervously.

'I don't mean it like that, you numpty. I'm your biggest fan, you know that. But what one thing is it, do you think? Is it your eyes? Your hair? The fact that you've got legs as long as ladders?'

'I think it's girls just having some fun and getting carried away,' Clem replied dismissively.

'No, no, there's something else, Clem. I made more money showing my designs on you today than I usually do in a month of markets.'

'Drinks are on you, then.'

'I'm serious. Other women admire and envy you. If you've got it, other women want it.' Stella patted her knee. 'You can be my own personal cash cow.' She grinned. 'From now on, I'm not just going to pin my designs on you, I'm going to photograph them on you, too. Make a look book showing how everything should be worn and pin them up here.'

'If you like,' Clem shrugged, finding a last, stray deer-stalker underneath the trestle table. She spun it on her hand. 'But your designs wouldn't sell if they weren't any good, Stell, not even if Kate Moss wore them. You're a brilliant designer. I mean, look at this hat. It's a really flattering style. It looked good on everyone who tried it.'

'Mmm, shame about the fabric, though. I never did like that faux fur.' She shrugged. 'But what you gonna do? I can't afford anything pricier.'

Clem stopped suddenly and looked at the hat more closely. 'Could this be made in shearling?'

Stella frowned. 'Of course. That—' She saw that conspira-torial look she knew only too well shining in Clem's eyes. 'Wait! Stop right there, lady. When I approached Tom about doing some small bits for the stall, he made no bones about the fact that he doesn't want to do fashion.'

'But it doesn't have to be fashion. It could be *lifestyle*.'

'That's just a play on words. A hat is a hat.'

'But lifestyle is what Alderton Hide's all about,' Clem argued, her beautiful eyes beginning to shine. 'I mean, if you're going to commission the curly sheepskin sofa, the shearling beanbag or the suede wardrobe, wouldn't it make sense that you'd want to wear a bit of that luxury, too? Can't you see it? Ski lodge, log fire, fur throw, cashmere socks . . .' She pulled the deerstalker on, tipped her head back and let her hands frame her face, her eyes faraway as she envisaged a glamorous life far removed from the grimy streets of London. 'Shearling deerstalker all fluffy around your hot-oil-conditioned glossy hair. I'm thinking chocolate brown and really shaggy – you know, Toscana shearling –

so that it's extra-luxuriant around the face. Like Julie Christie in *Dr Zhivago*.' Clem looked back at her and planted her hands on her narrow hips. 'I'd wear it.'

'And we'd all copy you, babes.'

Clem leaned in to her friend excitedly, her mind beginning to race. 'I really think I'm on to something, Stell! A capsule collection that gives women a taste of the Alderton Hide lifestyle. So what if you can't afford the leather walls? Buy the hat instead. Or . . . or the gilet. D'you remember that time I put a big belt over my Temperley one?'

'Shit, yeah, I loved how that looked.'

'Me, too! And we can't be the only ones.'

'After today, we *know* we aren't! But Tom'll still never let you do it.'

Clem shot Stella a look her friend knew only too well. 'So we won't tell him.'

Stella raised one over-plucked eyebrow. 'And how do we hide from him the fact that we're running a lifestyle collection in his name, based on his materials? It's not just Tom you'd have to get past; it's Simon, too.'

Clem considered this for a minute, her mind racing. 'Leave that to me. I know how to handle *him*. In the meantime, I want you to start doing some drawings, get some ideas together. But they have to be things that don't require big cuts, OK?' Stella narrowed her eyes but Clem shook her head. 'Just trust me. If you can come up with the designs, I'll come up with the rest.'

'I really don't know, Clem. I don't want to drop Tom in it any further. Things are bad enough for him as it is.'

'Stell, we could print money if today was anything to go by. This could give the company a lifeline.' She clutched Stella's arm beseechingly. 'We've just got to scale up a bit and think big. What Tom doesn't know won't hurt him. I *am* doing this to save his hide.'

Stella paused at the pun. 'Tell me you didn't just say that.'

Clem gave a wicked laugh that resonated throughout her body. 'Work on the sketches tonight, yeah? I'll swing by yours tomorrow lunchtime.' She grinned, turning to go.

'Where are you going now? I thought we could get a drink at the Duke.'

'I need to buy us some time and that means I've got some bridges to mend, babes. If Clover thought I was a nightmare before, just wait till she sees my angelic side. She's not getting rid of me that easily.'

'Huh?'

'I'll explain later. Can't stop.' She winked, pulling the hat down on her head. 'Things to see, people to do.'

Chapter Eight

Tom was stirring a freshly made pot of chicken soup when Clem got back to the flat, and a single charged beat pulsed between them as Clem's eyes and ears strained to detect Clover's whereabouts.

'She's gone home,' Tom said, putting down the wooden spoon and leaning against the counter. 'I told her I wanted to spend the evening with you. I haven't seen you properly for days.'

'Well, you've been working so hard.'

'And you've been partying so hard,' he replied softly. 'Which always worries me.'

'I'm a big girl, Tom, I can look after myself,' she said brightly, pulling off her trainers and hanging her jacket on the hook behind the door, prompting a pleasingly surprised look from Tom. 'It's you who needs looking after at the moment,' she said, walking over and grabbing the bottle of red that was sitting on the counter. She poured them both a glass and clinked his with a heartiness more suited to plastic than crystal.

Tom took a deep breath. 'I'm not selling because I want to leave you, you know. And I'm not moving in with her because I *don't* want to live with you. It's just how events have unravelled, Clem. Suddenly it seems to be the solution to all our problems.'

Clem looked up at him, seeing all the sadness and worry in his eyes. Poor Tom. He really was in the thick of it, stuck between her and Clover. 'I get it, Tom. Really I do.' She nodded, resting a hand on his chest, as though that alone could steady his heartbeat. 'Just promise me one thing, OK?'

'Anything, you know that.'

'Just don't rush into anything immediately. You never know what the next few weeks could bring.'

'Clem it's highly unlikely—'

'That the dream commission will come in, in time? I know. But just hold out a little hope, yeah? Don't sign anything just yet. Only for a few weeks. For me?'

A sudden laugh broke through him. 'You know I can never say no to you when you give me that butter-wouldn't-melt look.'

'So is that a yes?'

'I promise not to rush things along,' he replied dutifully, kissing the top of her head before ruffling her hair like their father did and making it stand up with static.

'Good. So then, in turn, *I* promise to make more effort with Clover. It's not fair us being at each other's throats all the time and you being piggy in the middle.'

'Seriously?' Tom looked choked.

'I know I've never really given her a chance.' She gave a rueful smile. 'Guess I was maybe a bit jealous. Thought she was going to take you away from me.'

Tom swallowed more nervously. 'That'll never happen, Clem. Even if . . . well, *when*, I suppose, we get married. Nothing will change between you and me.'

Clem nodded. She wanted to tell him that if he really wanted to marry Clover, he would have asked her by now – regardless of how chaotic his little sister's life was – but he had enough things to worry about, without scrutinizing the fears in his subconscious too.

She gave a wicked grin instead. 'Well, you never know. I may even get married before you, and then you'll have no excuses not to ask her. I can't be your fall guy for ever, you know,' she said, earning herself a punch on the arm from him. 'What? There's nothing to say you'll beat me to it just because you're in a happy, stable and committed relationship.'

'No, nothing at all,' Tom replied, bursting out laughing. 'Things are that serious between you and Josh then, are they?'

'Not even close! But I could still surprise you. My Mr Right could be just round the corner. I might meet him tomorrow.' An image of the Swimmer drifted in front of her eyes. 'I could even have met him already.'

'True,' Tom nodded, thoroughly amused as he returned to stirring the soup. 'Hungry? I made your favourite.'

'Starved. I've eaten nothing but junk today.'

Tom rolled his eyes. 'It's a wonder you don't have scurvy. Can you get the bowls down?'

Clem reached behind her into the cupboard and passed him two bowls.

'Dad rang, by the way. The weather's lovely there – obviously,' Tom said as he ladled the soup in and she quickly buttered the rolls he'd left out on the breadboard. 'He was asking after you and whether you were using the bag.'

'Oh yeah?' She thought about the bag, untouched in her bedroom, hidden away at the back of the wardrobe.

'Said they're having a good time. They went sailing on the Bridgestocks' boat today.'

Clem gave a small snort. 'Another ambition fulfilled

then.' She caught sight of Tom's enquiring glance. 'Oh come on! Mum's been angling for that invitation for years. It's the only reason she hosts that ghastly charity fair at the house each Easter. Octavia Bridgestock is one of the chairs of the committee.'

'Oh.' Tom frowned, unhappy and bewildered to hear Clem talk about their mother in that way. Clem knew that he saw her as an effortlessly gracious and elegant being – little did he know how much discreet posturing and positioning went on below-radar to maintain that illusion.

They carried their supper over to the table and sat down, Clem taking chunks off her roll and dipping it in her soup.

'So, d'you fancy a film tonight?' Tom asked as they ate noisily together.

'I so do.' She groaned at the welcome prospect of a night stretched out on the sofa. 'But I need a bath first. I haven't changed since my run this morning.'

'Grim,' Tom said, pulling a face at her. 'It really is a constant source of wonder to me that anyone finds you attractive.' He was teasing her again, which was a good sign.

Clem giggled and swatted his arm with the tube of kitchen roll there for mopping their chins. 'By the way, I've hired a cleaner,' she said. That wasn't strictly true. She hadn't rung her yet, but she wanted to keep the good news coming and undo some of Clover's earlier manipulations.

'Really?' If she'd told him she'd entered herself for a bodybuilding competition, he couldn't have looked more surprised.

'Yeah. Her name's Mercy something and she's forty quid for the morning.'

'Great. I'm fed up with this place looking such a dump

all the time. Mum's always on my back about it. When's she starting?'

'Uh . . . Tuesday. Nine a.m.'

'How did you find her?'

'Ad in Ajeep's,' she replied, lifting the bowl and draining the last drops of soup like a toddler.

'And you've checked her references and everything?' Tom asked, watching her with a look akin to disbelief.

'Course,' Clem lied.

Tom pulled an expression that showed he was impressed. Clem grinned and stood up, feeling the momentum going with her. Clover who? 'And for my next trick, I'm going to clear the dishes.' She carried the bowls and plates across the room, tongue sticking out between her teeth in concentration, as if she was spinning them on poles.

'Little sis,' he chuckled at the vision of clumsy domesticity. 'I never thought I'd say this, but there may be hope for you yet.'

It was early when Clem knocked on the shabby front door the next morning – earlier than she usually saw anyway. A night spent on the sofa with nothing more indulgent than Tom squeezing her feet as they watched *Goodfellas* (his favourite film) meant she had slept soundly and woken up easily. Her grand plan had taken root in the night and, unencumbered by her usual hangover, her mind had started firing off ideas left, right and centre, leaving her utterly incapable of lying around in bed.

Clem knocked on the door again, wondering what on earth the occupant could be doing other than sleeping at 8.23 a.m. on a Sunday morning, unable to resist fiddling with the flaky maroon paint that was peeling away. She pulled one bit, which was sticking out like a hangnail, and it ripped slowly up the grain of the door, exposing the bare wood beneath like a vivid scar.

She gasped, appalled by her thoughtless act of . . . well, hooliganism. The two-foot-long timber strip hung limply from her hands just as a groan rumbled from somewhere deep inside the flat.

The rattle of a chain on the other side of the door made her throw the offending paint strip down the stairwell, so that she was standing to attention with her hands behind her back when the denuded door opened and Simon's pale, bleary face appeared around it.

'What is it?' he muttered grouchily, before focusing and seeing Clem standing before him like one of his visions. 'Shit, Clem! What are you doing here?' His hands were off the door and crossed in front of his genitals in an instant, before he realized he was wearing a pair of cream boxers with brown stripes on and that a modicum of modesty, if not of style, was preserved.

'I need to talk to you,' she said, smiling serenely and really getting off on her new-found sobriety. It felt great to see someone else looking shocking for once.

He gaped at her in amazement and Clem had a feeling that of the many times he had rehearsed this moment – finding her on his doorstep – in his head, it had never gone quite like this. 'What, *now?*'

'It can't wait. And I can't discuss it in the office anyway.'

Simon blinked at her. 'Why not?'

Clem leaned in and waited for him to lean in to her, too. Which, after a hesitation, he did. 'It's a secret,' she whispered. 'Let me in.'

Simon looked behind him, back into the flat. 'It's uh . . . not really a good time,' he protested weakly.

'Oh, Si, don't be such a chump,' Clem sighed, losing patience and pushing past him anyway. 'As if *I* care about how messy your flat is.'

It was just as well she didn't. Last night's pizza boxes, a case of beers and a bong still sat on the sitting-room table; the huge plasma TV was flickering snow and the Xbox was humming loudly with thick black wires hanging out of it.

'Shall I play Mother while you get dressed?' Clem asked brightly – it was more of an order than a question – locating a kettle in the far corner and opening a window.

'Uh, uh . . .' Words defeated him and Simon ducked into the bedroom, falling over furniture from the sounds of things, as he tried to catch up with the dream sequence that was happening in the next room.

He emerged a few minutes later in his jeans and a red-checked shirt, looking quite the lumberjack with his ginger stubble and wild hair. He ran a hand through it casually, and Clem had to stifle a giggle as she found it standing on end and quickly licked his palm to pat it down again.

'So.' She smiled, letting him clear a space for her on the armchair – actually it was a gaming chair, ergonomic and rocking, and so low she may as well have lain on the floor. She could see straight under the sofa opposite. 'Good night last night?'

'Uh yeah, yeah. Quiet, nothing special.'

'Did you watch the game?' The words tripped off her tongue easily, although she had no idea whether there'd even been a match last night, much less his team's.

'No, I . . . No.'

There was an awkward pause.

'Good, are you?' Clem nodded towards the Xbox.

'I can hold my own,' Simon replied, sitting down facing

her, his bare feet inches from her. Clem tried not to look. His toenails looked pre-fungal and there was an alarming sprout of hair from his big toe. 'Actually, I'm in an international tournament if you really want to know. It's pretty major league.'

'Are you playing for money?'

'I wish! No, prestige. It's a pretty tight community, even though it's international.'

'Have you never met these people then?'

'Not face to face,' he said, with a tone that suggested personal contact was highly over-rated. 'But in some ways these guys know me better than my mates. We know all each other's strengths and weaknesses.'

Clem nodded. 'Cool,' she murmured, with her distinct way of saying the word that made it sound like she was conferring the honour rather than acknowledging the fact. She sat back in the chair, letting it rock slightly. 'I like it here,' she nodded, looking up at a framed poster of a Banksy mural. 'I like what you've done with the place. Been here long?'

'Six years.'

'I didn't realize you were so nearby. I walked here in ten minutes.'

'Yeah?' Simon asked brightly, clearly hoping this might become a familiar and well-trodden path. 'How did you know where I live?'

'I've been stalking you for months, Si,' she deadpanned.

'*Yeah?*' he asked, even more brightly, before realizing her joke. 'Oh. Tom.'

There it was – her cue. 'No, and actually it's massively important that he doesn't know I was here,' she said, crossing her ankle over her knee.

'Why not?' Simon asked, his eyes helplessly following her movements.

'Well, he thinks he might have to sell the flat to find the money to keep the company going, which obviously is a disaster. He loves living in Portobello.' She leaned forwards and put her hand on his knee. 'We have to stop him, Si.'

'We? How? It's his company. You know he'll do whatever it takes to keep it going.'

'Well, I've had an idea. Me and Stella hit pay dirt yesterday. Everything I put on at her stall, she sold.'

'That's hardly a surprise. I've been telling Tom for ages that you could be an ambassador for the brand. You're the girl everyone wants to be – or be with.'

'So then you agree that it'd be logical for me to set up a lifestyle collection for Alderton Hide?'

'Well now, hang on a second, I didn't quite—'

'I know retail's not something he's been prepared to look at before,' Clem interrupted, too distracted by her own sales pitch. 'But you know what? Times change, and we need to adapt to survive. It's all very well being a niche, high-end bespoke business, but hello? The economy's in the shit and what we really need right now is a fast cash injection. I'm convinced a capsule collection's the way to get it.'

Simon sighed. 'Even if Tom gave it the OK – and I can tell you now, he won't – but even if he did, that kind of branch-off would take investment, and ready money's precisely what we don't have at the moment.'

'But that's the beauty of it, Si. We wouldn't need to buy in any new materials. It wouldn't cost anything at all. We'd make the collection using all the spare off-cuts that normally get thrown. Stella's doing some drawings for me of hats and gilets, wrist-warmers, snoods and that kind of thing, and none of them requires big cuts. *And* she'll do all the technical stuff for free.'

Simon looked at her suspiciously. 'I don't understand why you're here. What do you need me for? You know I don't have the authority to OK this,' he asked warily.

'I just need you to tell the factory to keep all the off-cuts – they won't listen to me. They'll only take your word or Tom's, and he mustn't find out. Not yet.'

Simon blew out through his cheeks unhappily. 'There is no way you can keep this a secret from him. It's *his* company, Clem,' he said. 'And my job will be on the line if Tom found out I'd helped you.'

'But your job's already on the line. All our jobs are! We're going to sink if we don't do this. What have we got to lose?'

'I know where you're coming from with this, Clem, really I do. You don't want him to sell the flat, but it really is the best solution to the problem.'

'I disagree.'

'Why? Because it means you have to find a new place to live? Because it means he'll finally move in with Clover?'

'No! Because it's the wrong thing for *him*.'

'You know he can't keep looking after you for ever, Clem. At some point you're going to have to let him go.'

'This is not about me,' she insisted. 'I'm thinking as much about the future of Alderton Hide as I am the present. He's been too narrow-minded, refusing to branch into retail. I've always said it, you know I have.'

'I do. But I don't think you realize exactly what it would entail.'

Clem straightened up. 'Like what?'

'Well, even if we do as you suggest and stockpile the materials and Stella does the designing and patterns, there's still the matter of promotion and marketing, not to mention sales presence. I mean, how are people going to know about it without Tom knowing? And where are you intending to sell this stuff?' He held up a hand, his eyes closed piously. 'And please don't say on Stella's stall. I know you're not *that* reckless.'

She sighed irritably. 'You've heard of the "flash fashion" hashtag, yeah?'

'On Twitter? Yes. So?'

'I'm going to set up a pop-up shop for one day only. Just make it a real party, a guerrilla brand attack – we're there one day, gone the next – and we'll make a small fortune in the meantime. Honestly, we would. Stella quadrupled her take-home yesterday and Tom wouldn't need to find out until afterwards, when we hand him the great big fat cheque.' Clem looked across at him hopefully, squeezing her hands together in excitement.

But Simon wouldn't play ball. 'It wouldn't be enough, Clem. The Bugatti account was megabucks.'

'The projected *profit* from it was, yes. But in terms of liquidity, you said yourself yesterday that we only need £100k to keep the wheels turning for another four months, which is plenty of time for us to land another commission.'

Simon sighed. 'Look, Clem, I want to make this work as much as you do. Believe me. I love what Tom's created with Alderton Hide and I really believe in his vision, but this just isn't going to work. There's simply no way you'll get this past Tom. There'd be talk, rumours. There's no way you could keep it quiet. He's like hawk-eye. He knows every last thing that goes on in that company.'

Clem felt the frustration burst out into sudden anger. 'Does he, though?' she asked archly, throwing herself back

in the chair so that it rocked, her eyes glittering dangerously.

Simon took a step back, aware of the change of energy in
the room. 'What do you mean?'

Clem reached down and picked up the fuchsia-coloured
patent Marc Jacobs ballerina shoe with 'mouse ear' bow
that was peeping out from under the sofa. His expression
curdled at the sight of it.

'You know what a stickler Tom is for keeping all relation-
ships strictly professional in the office,' she said mildly,
admiring the tiny size-4 shoe in her hand, knowing full well
Tom had been directing the 'professional conduct' rule at
her and her alone. He knew his sister well enough to know
she'd eat Simon for breakfast and he couldn't risk losing his
Second in Command.

'I . . . That's not what you think.'

'Oh. Is it not a shoe then?' she asked. 'Morning, Pixie!'
she called through to the bedroom.

'Jesus! I . . . shit!' Simon muttered, raking his hands
through his hair and making it stand up on end again.

'Chill, Si,' Clem said loquaciously, throwing the shoe
down and picking up her bag. 'It's no biggy; I don't care.
I'm not here to hurt anyone. On the contrary, I'm just trying
to help. But the way I see it is this, if you can find a way of
keeping my secret, I can find a way of keeping yours. Yeah?'

Simon looked at the floor, angry but boxed in, as Pixie
stumbled to the bedroom door wrapped in a Spiderman
duvet. 'Clem!' she cried excitedly, greeting her like a best
friend. 'What are *you* doing here? Can you stay for breakfast?'

Clem flashed her a dazzling smile. 'Sadly, no. I'm meeting someone. I was passing and just popped in to say hello.'

She crossed the room and opened the door, smiling back at the happy couple. 'See you in the morning, though, yeah?'

'Look forward to it!' Pixie trilled like a demented canary. 'Can't wait.'

'All right then,' Clem chuckled, shaking her head as she pulled the door to, behind her. She gave a silent punch in the air that the first obstacle had been tackled, before texting Stella to wake her up. It was time to get down to business.

Chapter Nine

Clem blinked her eyes open and stared at the small bare patch of floor that wasn't strewn with clothes. Something had pulled her from an especially nice dream about Bradley Cooper, but she didn't know what.

The knock at the door came again and she pushed herself up onto her elbows, peering blearily at the clock on her phone. Eight thirty-six.

She frowned. The postman?

Pulling on her fleecy onesie, she got up and answered the door. 'Yeah?'

'Hey!' A woman – all of 5 foot 4 inches and with as much going on behind her as in front – stepped forward, black eyes shining. 'I'm Mercy.' She spoke in a dramatically lilting Jamaican accent that would be just about decipherable so long as she didn't get excited or break rhythm.

Dammit. The cleaner. She'd forgotten all about the text she'd hurriedly sent her on Saturday night.

'Hi! Hi! I'm Clem, hi,' Clem replied, straightening up and trying to look impressively awake. 'It's so nice to meet you. Come in.'

'Thanks.'

Mercy quite literally shuffled in – she was wearing white towelling hotel-style slippers over black socks. Mercy caught her staring and said, 'My cleaning shoes. Some customers, they get funny 'bout the floors.'

'Oh sure, I can imagine.' Clem put a sincere hand to her chest. '*We're* not like that. We're very relaxed.'

'I can see that,' Mercy replied, taking in the messy flat.

Clem looked around, taking in the disaster zone that passed as her home with fresh eyes. 'Well, I never get it when people tidy up before their cleaner gets there. I mean, what's that about?' she chirruped, walking over to the kitchen, taking the hairband that was perpetually around her wrist and tying her hair up in a messy topknot. 'My mother's guilty of it. She actually scrubs the bathrooms before the housekeeper arrives. Coffee?'

'Sure.' Mercy walked slowly around the flat, her eyes scrunched up in scrutiny, as if she was assessing it for damp or settlement cracks, rather than cobwebs and grime. She peeked her head into Tom's bedroom, retracting it instantly as though a sulphur bomb had gone off in it – his socks – and slapped a hand across her gargantuan bosom, which wobbled like jelly in reply. 'There's a bird in there.'

Clem looked back. 'Oh, that's Shambles, our parrot, she's very tame and sweet. She's great company. She talks to you, but try not to swear. She picks up on everything and really drops me in it with my mother. D'you like birds?' Clem said, calling slightly as she filled the kettle.

Mercy shook her head.

'Oh.' Bother. 'Well we can make sure she's locked in the cage when you come over.'

'That would be . . . preferable.'

Clem held up the Nespresso tray of multi-coloured foil capsules. 'Which coffee d'you like?'

Mercy hitched up an eyebrow, sucking on her lower lip

and waving an index finger around in circles as she decided which colour – rather than blend – she liked best. 'Purple.'

'My favourite, too,' Clem said, popping it into the machine and hoisting herself up onto the worktop. 'So, have you had far to come?'

'No. I live in the Hallfield Estate, Paddington, fifteen minutes from here.'

'Cool. Good commute.'

Mercy nodded, her eyes still roaming the flat. 'So, I'm guessing you've never had a cleaner before?'

'What gave it away?' Clem grinned, reaching up and hooking a cobweb with her finger.

'D'you live here on your own?'

'Officially, I share it with my brother, Tom, although he hasn't been around much lately.' She wrinkled her nose as Mercy's met hers curiously. 'Pushy girlfriend.'

Mercy nodded. 'I met some of those in my time. Lived here long?'

'In this area all my life. My parents live on Elgin Crescent. We got this flat seven years ago.'

'Nice.'

'Thanks.'

'So there's two bedrooms, one bathroom and this room?'

'That's right. Nice and compact. We don't need anything major doing – just hoovering, cleaning the bathroom . . . uh, stuff like that.' Clem waved her hands in the air in a vague manner, unsure what else counted.

'Dusting, cleaning the windows,' Mercy opened the oven door and peered in. 'Scouring the oven, lifting the rugs. You want me to strip the beds and launder them, too?'

Clem's eyes widened as though she was a fairy god-mother, here out of benevolence alone. 'Would you?'

'If you pay me to I will,' Mercy chuckled, a deep, heaving sound more akin to dredging. 'The ironing, too?'

'Oh God, please!' Clem said, hopping off the counter and pouring the coffees. Her life was changing before her very eyes. Outsourcing! Why had she never done it before? Wait till Tom saw how she'd streamlined everything for them. Now when they came home after work, they wouldn't have to fight over who did the ironing and who made dinner (him and him, usually). And Tom wouldn't complain about there being no room on the sofa, or of the towels smelling musty. And their Mother would be silenced – finally – when she did one of her impromptu drop-ins and spent the whole time looking disappointedly at Clem for not being better at 'keeping house'.

'Do take a seat,' Clem said, motioning to the sofa as she came over with the coffees.

'I like this sofa,' Mercy said, stroking it as if it was a pet.

'Thanks, it's a prototype. My brother's company made it. Alderton Hide, have you heard of them?'

Mercy shook her head, her fingers gently winding around the curly tufts of sheepskin.

'No, most people haven't. They're a bespoke business-to-business company, supplying all different types of leathers and suedes – shearling, reindeer, crocodile, ponyskin – to clients, mainly hotel groups and city banks.'

'Sounds expensive.'

'Yes,' Clem sighed. 'It is.' She sat down next to Mercy and looked at her properly. It was hard to get a handle on her age: Thirty? A bit older maybe? Her face was round and deep, like a pillow, with cheeks you wanted to pinch and a mouth that seemed to triple in size when she smiled. Her skin was two shades from ebony and her big black doe-eyes radiated constant mirth.

'How old are you?' Clem asked, curiosity getting the better of her.

'Forty-six.'

'Forty-six!' Clem spluttered. 'But I thought you were the same age as me! And I'm twenty-nine!'

Mercy winked. 'Ah, plump skin. The fat girl's revenge,' she chuckled, making Clem splutter even more.

'Have you got kids?'

'Five. All between twenty-five and eight.'

Clem shook her head. 'Five kids? And I can't even look after myself.'

'I can see.' Mercy chuckled again, looking down into her coffee. 'But that's why you called me. My past boss used to call me "Angel".' She shrugged. 'Angel of Mercy.'

'Did you work for them long?'

'Three years. I was nanny to them kids, too, not just the cleaner.'

'Why did you leave?'

'The baby was starting at school and they didn't need me for so many hours.'

Clem nodded just as a door slammed downstairs. Footsteps travelled up the stairs and stopped outside in the hallway; there was a jangling of keys and then a perky laugh – a laugh Clem knew only too well.

The door opened and Clover practically skipped through. 'So this is *it*,' she purred over her shoulder, arms opened wide and half-raised in a happy shrug – until she turned and saw Clem and Mercy sitting on the sofa. Then her arms dropped as if they were broken. 'Oh! What are *you* doing here?'

A young guy in a shiny too-blue suit followed after her and, for a split second, Clem thought she was cheating on Tom. But then she saw the digital tape measure in his hand and understood exactly what was happening.

'It's *my* flat,' Clem retorted indignantly. 'Why wouldn't I be here?'

Clover tried to regroup, looking embarrassed and awkward. 'I meant . . . I thought you'd be at work.'

'Hoped, more like.'

Clover looked away. 'If it's not a good time . . .'

'No. It's not. I'm having a meeting,' Clem spat, stretching herself taller at the words, to give them added importance, and clearly totally oblivious to the fact that she was wearing an owl onesie. With *ears*.

Mercy sipped her coffee, one hand still twirling the sheepskin, her eyes swivelling right to left between the two women as if it was a posh version of *The Jeremy Kyle Show*.

The estate agent, whilst keeping one ear trained on their spat, was more concerned with doing a visual recce of the flat, taking in which direction it faced, the imposing ceiling heights, the original feature cornicing and fireplace, working sash windows, the wide planked maple floor . . .

Clem felt her blood begin to boil as she watched him. How *dare* Clover sell Clem's flat! 'Like what you see, do you?' Clem sneered at him, making the poor man – boy – jump. 'Well, think again, mate. It's not for sale.'

'We discussed this the other day,' Clover said in a tone that implied she was being reasonable (and therefore Clem was not).

Clem stood up, willowy and proud like the white queen (albeit dressed as an owl), a move that made both Clover and the estate agent take a step back. 'I don't suppose Tom's told *you* that he agreed to wait for a while?' The surprise on Clover's face was confirmation enough. 'No, I thought not . . . You know, I almost feel sorry for you, Clover, not losing a second on this. I mean, you just can't wait to get him out of here, so that you can hook your claws into him. You're so desperate it's embarrassing.'

Her words hit their mark and this time it was Clover who advanced, the black queen drawn into battle, her face pinched with anger. 'You want to know who's embarrassing, Clem?' she half whispered, half hissed. 'It's you. Poor lost you who can't hold on to a job, a man or any semblance of adult life. You need Tom to do everything for you, and you can't bear it that he wants to be with me. He's only still here with you out of some sort of misplaced loyalty or pity. When are you going to get it? Whether he does it this month or next Christmas, he *will* choose me over you.'

'You're wrong. If he was sure about his feelings for you, he'd be with you in a shot. There'd be nothing I could – or would – do. He stays with me because I'm his best friend, not because I'm his sister.'

Clover gave a short, joyless laugh. 'If it makes you feel better to think that . . .' she sneered. 'Come on, Joe. We'll come back another time.' Clover turned and headed for the door.

'No you won't!' Clem shouted after them. 'I already told you, this flat's not for sale!'

Clover stopped at the door and gave a half-smile, her own set of door keys laid out like a taunt in the palm of her hand. 'We'll see about that.'

The cushion hit the back of the closed door, but without any power and certainly lacking in the fierce 'smashing' sound a cup would have achieved. Clem sank back into the sofa, shaking as the adrenaline subsided.

Mercy was silent for a moment. 'I see what you mean . . . Pushy.'

Clem slid her eyes over to her, a smile breaking the tension in her face. 'When can you start?'

Chapter Ten

'D'you think we can smoke in here?' Stella whispered as the congregation sat back down again.

'No!' Clem retorted, her fingers stroking the capacious suede pouch she had slung across her body. It was ivory with a ruby-red silk cord drawstring, and she'd already clocked several women checking it out; she'd put money on them coming up to her after the service and asking where she'd got it.

She'd be ready for them when they did: flyers with details of the Twitter account to follow to get the time, place and date for the pop-up shop were in the bag. She and Stella had been working tirelessly for seven weeks now, forsaking pubs and pretty boys for evenings in, eating bowls of noodles as they sorted the irregular cuts of leather, suede, sheepskin and shearling into bundles of similar sized patches and worked out what to do with them. So far, they'd done the shearling deerstalkers and wrist warmers (Clem had almost sprinted down the road with the proto-type to give to Katy), some Toscana shearling beanbags that were as long-haired as Afghan hounds, some croc-embossed buckled leather phone covers that looked especially lovely in saturated jewel colours, and furry tags that had been dyed in a range of colours and attached to rings to accessorize handbags. But it was this suede bag that was the hot pick, thanks to the model Laura Bailey – a regular at Katy's stall – agreeing to carry it to a film premiere, where a frenzy of flashbulbs popped as usual. The fashion pack had been on the phone to her stylist within hours, and bloggers and trend spotters had been trying to identify it, but all anyone could get hold of was the Twitter account and hashtag to follow, building a growing buzz for the as-yet-unidentified label, while Clem and Stella frantically worked through the nights.

The church filled with cries as the vicar poured cold water over the baby's head at the font, and Clem felt her phone buzz in the bag. She took it out and checked.

Josh. Again.

He hadn't taken the break-up well, looking stunned as Clem launched into her usual patter, even though she'd been so busy with her new evangelical mission that she'd forgotten to call him for three weeks beforehand. She couldn't understand how he hadn't seen the writing on the wall when they'd failed to move past booty-calls to dates.

Unmoved, she let Josh's plea go to messages and looked around the congregation instead as the baby's cries grew louder. Everyone was young, in couples and hats. Quite a few of them had babies, too. Christenings, she grimaced, were the new marriages, heralding the fact that life was grinding relentlessly forward, whether she chose to keep up or not.

Towards the front, Tom was sitting with Clover. She was wearing a hat that looked more like roadkill and a smile that suggested the next time she stepped inside this church, she'd be in white and wearing a tiara. Things hadn't improved between the two of them since their argument in the flat, although if Tom knew about it, he didn't admit to it, and Clem was determined not to be the one seen to be breaking the peace. She had explicitly promised Tom she would try harder with Clover, in return for Tom delaying any drastic decisions, but Clover was playing the same game and the two of them were embroiled in a stand-off – an agony of polite, sisterly consideration, which only just concealed the visceral antipathy that existed between them.

Today was part of that game. The baby being wetted and now attempting to shake the church from its foundations, was Clover's sister's child, and it was for Tom's sake only that she was here in the name of bonding with Clover's family. It was bad enough for him that the sister, Peony, was several years younger than Clover and already living her big sister's dream; Tom didn't need any extra hassle on that score.

The service drew to an abrupt close as the baby's cries gathered in volume and speed, and Stella and Clem stayed in their seats at the back as the guests shuffled slowly up the aisle.

'Guess we should go out and show *this* baby off,' Stella murmured, stroking the sheepskin bag. 'It's certainly a lot prettier.'

'Just make sure Tom doesn't see you handing out the flyers, OK? That'd be the last thing we need.'

'Right, boss.'

They slunk outside, leaning like stroppy teenagers against the pillars by the church door and watching the photographer group the guests together for the official photos. Clem checked her watch impatiently, desperate to escape and work on some more ideas. Now that she had started thinking in a creative vein, she couldn't stop, and ideas were coming to her in the middle of the night, during her shower, her runs – she had to keep a notebook on her at all times to jot them down. She reckoned an hour back at the house for drinks, tops, and then they could reasonably leave.

'Miss?' She looked up. The photographer and the eyes of the crowd were upon her. 'Could you come and stand here?' He was gesturing to a space in the heart of the family circle.

'Oh . . . no, I'm not family,' she demurred as an assistant took her by the elbow and wheeled her into position.

'Nonsense,' Clover beamed insincerely at her. 'You soon will be.'

'But . . .'

A hand behind her settled on her waist and gently pulled her back a little, the fingers spreading and applying a gentle pressure that was almost ticklish, almost . . .

'That's better,' murmured a quiet voice. Foreign, male, gorgeous as hell. She went to turn to see who the voice belonged to but—

'Everyone smile!'

The flash popped, the baby cried and everyone dispersed again, eager to get away from the ear-splitting bawls. Clem looked around as strangers swarmed, all looking for their partners, children and cars.

'What's wrong?' Stella asked, looking up from her phone with pink, excited cheeks. Oscar – the rogue from the Electric – was resolutely ignoring all her protestations that theirs had been just a one-night thing and kept belligerently calling her or turning up at her stall with food and flowers and cruelly making her laugh. The fact that neither she nor Clem had been seen in their usual haunts for the past couple of months had made his job a lot harder, but he hadn't given up, and Clem wasn't sure whether to admire or worry about his persistence.

'Nothing. I . . .' She turned a circle one more time but there was no way to identify the stranger. 'Oh God, I just had an erotic moment with a disembodied voice,' she groaned, rolling her eyes. 'I *so* need to get out more.'

'Yeah, me too,' Stella sighed, pocketing the phone.

Clem watched her. 'Stell, if you like him, see him again.'

But Stella simply pulled an unflattering 'As If!' expression and hooked her arm through Clem's. Tom and Clover were coming over.

'Wasn't that wonderful?' Clover sighed. 'I just love christenings.'

'I prefer funerals; more peaceful and better clothes usually,' Stella quipped, lighting up again and loyally blowing a smoke ring in Clover's face. 'Better for pulling, too.'

'D'you guys want to come back in our car? I've got space in the MG for two little ones, if you sit on the back,' Tom said. 'It isn't far to go.'

'Lead on,' Stella commanded, flicking her cigarette butt to the kerb.

The reception was being held in a tiny but very 'done' taupe house just off Ledbury Road. The front of the house was screened from the road by high horizontal wooden-slatted screens and an electric gate that seemed *de trop* for such a small house. There was nowhere to park, of course, and Tom dropped the girls off, driving away in a sulk to spend 'the next forty minutes trying to find a meter'.

Clover immediately peeled away to an upstairs bedroom to 'fix her face', whilst Clem and Stella made a beeline for the drinks table, which had been set up in the navy blue dining room.

'If I don't get a drink in my hand quickly, I'm not sure I'll be able to cope with this scene,' Stella said, perching her round red Dolce & Gabbana glasses atop her head. 'Christ, it's dark in here.'

'It's not so bad,' Clem said in an uncharacteristically nervy voice as she necked a vodka tonic. 'I mean, it's not like they're all complete strangers – I recognize half of them from school.'

Stella grunted. 'Yeah. And there's a reason why you didn't stay in touch.'

Clem tried to keep her face neutral as she took in the gaggles of laughing women, all accessorized with babies and bumps. They looked like an army in their stretchy wrap dresses, layered hair and low-key manicures; Clem's turquoise silver-striped semi-sheer Isabel Marant shirtdress, slouchy boots and black nail polish were by comparison . . .

The two of them stood in silence for several minutes, taking in the vast gulf between themselves and the other women.

'Honestly, look at them all – everyone acting so proper and pleased with themselves, so *madly* in love with their new husbands and pushing out their bellies and boobs in the hope that no one will notice how completely *huge* their arses are. Well, I do,' Stella scowled, jabbing her thumb into her chest. '*I* do.'

Clem, recognizing the change of tone in her friend's voice, patted her gently on the arm. 'Hold your breath and count to ten,' she said soothingly.

'You always say that.'

'Because it works. Best thing I know for stopping the tears. Do it.'

Stella held her breath as Clem rubbed her arm consolingly.

This kind of aggression – a defence mechanism – usually only came out at the tail end of weddings, when the DJ started playing ABBA.

'You OK?'

Stella shrugged and necked her drink. 'Yeah sure, it's just . . . I mean, when did all this *happen*? Do you know? 'Cos last time I looked we were all just enjoying being young and living in London – working hard, playing hard. I never really noticed that people were actually doing all this shit: getting married and having kids and stuff . . .'

Clem was silent for a minute. 'Well, I reckon there's something to be said for freedom. I feel kind of sorry for them all actually,' she said finally. 'I mean, it really speaks of a lack of imagination on their part, don't you think?'

Stella's drink went down the wrong way and she started coughing noisily. 'OMG, you just sounded so like your mother!' she guffawed once she'd recovered, slapping her hand over her mighty chest.

Clem shuddered. 'Don't even joke about it.'

They stood in silence again, still transfixed by the parade of domestic happiness as the christened baby was handed from one woman to another.

'Well, for all that this isn't our kind of party, it's still a cracking marketing opportunity. We need to get these flyers out before Tom gets back,' Clem said in a brisk tone, finishing her drink. 'Come on. Then we can get the hell out of here.'

Posting her most dynamic smile, Clem strode into the cliques – the odd one out among them: a peacock amidst a battery of hens.

'Clemmie!' one particularly annoying woman whom she distantly remembered from school, trilled at her, holding out the baby like a bag of groceries. 'Your turn.'

'God, no!' The words were out of her mouth before she'd even had time to plaster a smile on her face. 'Babies, uh, they totally hate me. I'm really not good with kids.'

There was an amazed silence – what kind of woman *wouldn't* want to hold the baby, after all? – before the annoying woman laughed shrilly, convinced it must be a joke or modesty on Clem's part, and thrust the baby into her arms anyway. Clem had to grab hold of him – her? Who could tell? – or else she'd drop him.

'There's no need to be shy. Just because you don't have any of your own yet, we all have to learn somehow, don't we? The more exposure you get before having your own babies, the better. Trust me. I wish someone had done the same for me. I was a dis-*ah*-ster when little London was born.'

Clem arched an eyebrow. London? She'd called her child London?

Clem caught Stella's eye, wanting to laugh, but she was too awkward, standing there with a random baby, and she wasn't sure exactly how to hold it.

'Support her head,' someone offered.

'They love being bounced.'

'Let her see your eyes.'

Clem swallowed and tried to jiggle the baby, who had begun to squirm and go red in the face. Something was building up and she didn't want to be on the receiving end of it.

'OK, well, there we go – that's enough for one day,' she said quickly, passing the baby to the nearest woman to her, as if it was a game of Pass the Parcel. On cue, the baby began to bawl. Again.

'Not your thing?' one woman asked her pityingly.

'No.'

'Not *yet* anyway,' another said, as if consolingly.

'No. Just not my thing.'

That shut the conversation down, and out of the corner of her eye, Clem could see Stella stifling a laugh. 'I prefer bags to babies.'

'Talking of . . . I so *love* yours,' one of the women said, leaning in to stroke it. 'Divine.'

The floodgates opened.

'Yes! I saw it the moment you came into church!'

'Me, too! I'm sure I saw one just like it in Grazia.'

'You did.' Clem preened.

'Where's it from?'

Clem smiled, back in her comfort zone, and slipped her hand inside her bag, her fingers closing around the Twitter flyers. 'Well . . . she lowered her voice and gave a conspiratorial smile. 'Can you keep a secret?'

'You're being watched,' Stella murmured, sidling up to her twenty minutes later and planting a fresh drink in her hand.

'Hmm?' Clem murmured distractedly, counting how many flyers she had left. Twelve from one hundred. A lot of the women had taken several for their friends and to distribute at the school gates.

'Ten o'clock,' Stella said without moving her lips, just in case the watcher was trained in lip-reading.

Clem looked up to her left and felt the same sudden stillness she felt every time her eyes met his. She opened her mouth to tell Stella that it was him, the Swimmer, the one she'd been trying to get her to identify from the party, but her voice failed. He was coming over.

'I think a little bit of wee just came out,' Stella squeaked beside her, finally breaking the spell just as the Swimmer stopped in front of them.

'Hi.' It was the voice. The one from outside the church. So, he had a voice as well as eyes.

'Hey,' Clem replied, her eyes steady upon his with the surety that came from this not being their first meeting. There wasn't just chemistry going on here; they had history together, too. That night in the Electric, as she'd flirted with a stranger in the dark, he had kissed his girlfriend deliberately – she knew it now, standing in the heat of his gaze. He played her games too.

'You know my friend Stella, of course,' she said calmly.

Basic courtesy demanded that he acknowledge Stella at this point, but he wouldn't look away from her.

'N–no, we haven't actually met,' Stella stammered, five inches below both of them and out of peripheral vision.

Clem arched an eyebrow ever so slightly at the fact that he was going to snub her friend.

'Of course. It was a fun party, New Year's Eve,' he replied, finally breaking the gaze to look at Stella, who visibly wilted beneath him.

'You were there?'

'Only for a bit. I just . . . looked in.' His eyes, dancing, pinned Clem back up again, and suddenly she knew why Stella hadn't clocked him. He hadn't been invited. He'd been the guy on the street she'd almost knocked over on the bike (that blasted bike). He'd *followed* her.

'I think I'm just gonna er . . . go,' Stella muttered as they continued to stare at each other, a thousand words passing between them unsaid.

'Do you know my name?' Clem asked, once they were alone.

He nodded.

'Where I live?'

He gave a small smile and nodded again. 'I'm afraid so.'

She jerked her chin in the air. 'Do you usually follow women around London?'

'Never.' His accent was delicious, tumbling and melodic, as if he was bouncing it off the walls. What was it? Italian? Spanish? He shifted position, stuffing his hands into his trouser pockets. Settling in. 'I sense you would like to know my name, but that you will not ask,' he said slowly, and she could have sworn he was smiling with his voice. She thought he could probably do many things with that voice.

Clem didn't reply, she simply raised an eyebrow, as if interested in this hypothesis.

'So I shall tell you, because I really want you to know it.' He took a step closer towards her, his hand resting lightly against her cheek, his thumb hovering tantalizingly above her bottom lip, as though they were already intimate with each other's bodies. 'And because I really want to hear how you say it in that distinctive voice of yours.'

His proximity made her head spin and Clem swallowed, waiting, waiting for the touch, the revelation. What was it? What was his name? The thought of going another minute without knowing it seemed suddenly unbearable. It was all she could do not to rub her cheek against his palm like a cat, not to close her eyes in sweet surrender.

'But no.' He straightened up and took a half step back, so that she could feel the air between them again. 'You must ask.'

Clem blinked at him in surprise, her composure blown.

'I have chased you up till now. You know what I want,'

he said, his eyes openly exploring her mouth. 'Now you have to show me that you want it, too.'

'You can't just tell me your name?'

'No.'

'So, what you actually want me to do is beg to find out your name?' Clem said slowly, dazzled and disoriented by his game.

'Exactly so,' he replied, the only laughter on his chiselled face to be found in his eyes now.

The effect upon her was immediate and she felt the heat in her cheeks at his power play. She had met her match.

'What is . . .' she began, raising her sparkling aquamarine eyes to his, offering him the surrender he wanted in return. 'What is it that you do?'

His reply was a barely perceptible tilt back of his head and an amused smile. 'Take that and chew on it,' Clem messaged with flashing eyes, and for a moment they stood locked in silent, motionless combat as the room buzzed around them in a carousel of social manners.

His eyes roamed her face as if it was a painting and she wondered why they were even bothering to talk. Why not just cut to the chase and kiss? It was obvious what they both wanted. She had Stella and Tom for conversation.

'*A prochaine*, Clementine,' he murmured in a voice that vibrated through her entire body. Then he turned and left the room, leaving her to admire the athletic torso and long legs that could have been hers that night if she'd just done what he asked.

'Tell me everything, *instantly*,' Stella hissed, running over from the spot where she'd been hiding behind the sofa. 'That was the sexiest fucking thing I ever saw. When are you hooking up?'

Clem, distracted, kept her eyes on the spot where the Swimmer had been, and now wasn't. 'We're not.'

The glass fell from Stella's hand onto the velvet ottoman. Luckily, and unsurprisingly, it was empty. 'What the . . .? Why *not*?'

'He wanted me to beg.'

'For what? Sex? Because I'd have done it. I practically was anyway. He's gorgeo—'

'For his name.'

Stella walked around and positioned herself in Clem's line of sight. 'Let me get this right. You're telling me you let *that* walk out of here, because you wouldn't . . . ask his name?'

Clem looked down at her, as if waking out of the trance, and nodded. She blinked nervously, waiting for Stella's response. But Stella was mute with shock, lost for words for the first time in her life.

'Where are you going?' Clem asked as Stella turned on her heel, shaking her head and muttering to herself.

'To ring Oscar. You won't ask a bloke his name? Jeez, no wonder I'm not married!'

'Stell!'

But Stella just stuck her nose in the air and got on the phone. 'It's the blind leading the bloody blind with you.'

Chapter Eleven

Clem lay on the bed staring up at the ceiling, her arms folded behind her head as Shambles put on an aeronautical display for her, as though sensing her low mood. But even her party trick of dodging her head up and down, and side to side at breakneck speed wasn't working.

Tom was out again – either working late or staying at Clover's – and she was all alone in the quiet flat. The evenings were getting longer now that they were in the middle of March, but the light was still fading, and she knew she ought to get up and switch some lights on. Lying alone in the dark with an eager-to-please parrot really was depressing.

Her eyes swivelled slowly around her bedroom, taking in the chocolate brown walls of her kingdom, with exposed brick on the chimney breast; a black and white poster of Joni Mitchell blu-tacked to the wall; wedged in the corner of the mirror some photos of her and Stella – legs dangling out of the sitting-room window, a beer in each hand and Union Jack bunting strung up between their flat and Mrs Crouch's at last year's Notting Hill Carnival – a jumble of necklaces looped over a silver candelabra (one of a pair she'd received from her parents a few New Year's Days ago), a vintage wooden champagne case that had boots spilling out of it . . . She was twenty-nine years old and this was what she had to show for her life. Not for her a smart sports car or ball-breaking career, a besotted husband or a tall townhouse with a live-in nanny and a playroom. She still lived like a student, stuck in time, unable to move forwards.

Maybe Stella had been right; maybe she had played it wrong. The Swimmer had gone to ground. It had been almost two weeks since the christening, and although she'd scanned every crowd and café for his triangular torso and angular face, she hadn't seen him once.

'*A prochaine.*' The way he'd said it, she thought he'd pop up in front of her flat the next evening, with a bottle of wine in his hand and a rueful smile on his lips. 'Touché,' he would have said and they'd have both capitulated, falling into each other's arms and finally getting it on.

But the days had slipped past, apologetically empty. Even Josh had finally got the message and stopped calling; and Simon had resolutely refused to flirt with her ever since she'd ever-so-nicely blackmailed him in his own living room. She could scarcely believe it, but there was an awful truth staring her in the face: she'd lost her touch.

The scratch of keys in the lock alerted her to Tom's arrival and she jumped off the bed eagerly. She padded into the sitting room and turned on the floor lamp, just as the door opened and Tom fell in, laughing, followed immediately afterwards by Clover. Drat.

'Oh, you *are* in,' he said, throwing down his bag and giving her a smacker on her forehead. 'It looked dark from the street.'

'I was, uh, napping,' she mumbled, wandering to the window and looking down the road – just in case. Across the way, she could see Mrs Crouch in her flat, pouring some gin into a rose-painted teacup and sipping it slowly, with her tabby cat Esme sitting on her lap whilst they watched *Coronation Street*.

'D'you fancy an Indian tonight? I'm happy to get it,' Clem said, perching on the windowsill and watching as the two of them moved busily about the flat.

'Are you *sure*?' Clover asked, her eyes raking briefly up and down Clem in her Topshop playsuit, man's cardigan, thick grey, ribbed tights and snood twisted in her hair.

Tom was oblivious to the slight. 'Would have loved to, but we're meeting the boys in the Duke in ten. I've just popped back to get a clean shirt for tomorrow.'

'Oh.'

Tom slammed one drawer shut and hastily tore open another. 'I don't suppose you know where my bone cuff-links are?'

'The ones Dad gave you?'

'Yeah, I can't find them anywhere. I've searched Clo's, and they're not in the obvious places here . . .'

Clem shrugged. 'Cufflinks aren't much use to me,' she murmured, leaning against the sofa and watching as Clover neatly folded a pink shirt into an overnight bag for him. He was staying at Clover's five nights out of seven, and Clem wondered whether he was acclimatizing to living with her full time. Even though he'd been as good as his word and held back from putting the flat on the market, she felt sure he now saw selling it as the answer to all his problems. No big commissions had come in for Alderton Hide, the phone barely ever rang – Simon was of the view that Perignard had leaked what had happened – and the only remaining project was due to be completed next month.

And, in spite of her very best efforts to pull a rabbit out

of the proverbial hat, things weren't quite going to plan with the collection either. Yes, they now had nearly 400 followers on their Twitter page, thanks to a stealth word-of-mouth campaign, and her, Katy and Stella surreptitiously scouting potential customers in the market, but quite where the pop-up shop could actually be, or when, they still didn't know. She didn't know anyone with a big enough house to host who didn't also know Tom, none of the landlords were prepared to rent out their vacant properties for just one day and the market inspectors wouldn't budge on respecting the years-long waiting lists for stalls. It was a maddening situation: they had the beginnings of a collection, but nowhere to sell it.

'Stella coming over later?' Tom asked, stopping by her on his way back out and resting a warm, calloused hand on her shoulder.

Clem nodded convincingly. ''Course.'

'Well, give the old trollop my love. I haven't seen her much lately.'

Clem nodded. Nor had she. 'Sure.'

The door closed with a click and Clem fell back onto the sheepskin sofa, her legs dangling over the arm, the rest of the evening stretching out, long and shapeless before her.

She had some options, of course: her parents were finally back from their holiday now; she could be over at theirs, tucking into a bowl of Scottish mussels with her father within twenty minutes, but that would involve seeing her mother. There was also a good chance Katy and Scott would be having a quiet drink in the Duke, but that would involve being sociable. She could fix herself some dinner and watch TV, but that would involve moving.

She was so absorbed in the utter nothingness of her

evening that at first she didn't hear the knock at the door, but when it came again – more loudly – she sat up and stared at the door accusingly, her heart accelerating instantly to a gallop. She knew who it wasn't. It wasn't Stella: she was with Oscar again tonight. And Tom and Clover had their own keys . . .

Had he been waiting and watching after all, hidden in the shadows? Had he seen the light go on and Tom and Clover leave? Did he know that she was here, and that she was here alone?

Her mouth felt dry and she spun in a circle three times, not sure whether to wet her face and swallow some tooth-paste in the bathroom, or hide her dirty clothes on the floor in the bedroom. Shambles, picking up on her sudden agitation, went into an even greater frenzy, speeding up the head slides alarmingly.

But before Clem could decide what to do first, the knock came again and she knew she had to answer it. He wouldn't knock a fourth time, she knew that. He'd called her bluff once before. Whipping the snood off her hair and fluffing it up in the mirror, she slapped her cheeks hard several times, hoisted her breasts up in her bra and took a deep breath. This was it.

She opened the door.

Simon shrugged back at her. Clem knew that the expression on her face when she found it was him on her doorstep was the exact opposite to his when he'd found her on his doorstep.

'Oh.'

'Only me, I'm afraid. Were you expecting someone?' Simon asked, taking in her flushed cheeks, parted mouth and cleavage.

'No, no, don't be ridiculous,' she exclaimed in a voice that tremored with disappointment. 'Come in.'

He shut the door behind him and hung his coat on the peg with relaxed familiarity. Tom had held plenty of meetings here over supper. 'Tom's not in, I'm afraid. Just li'l old me,' she said, padding over to the fridge and grabbing a bottle of Chablis and two glasses. 'Thirsty?'

He nodded. 'Good. Because it's not Tom I'm here to see. It's you.'

'Oh shit, what have I done now?'

'You mean apart from blackmail me?'

There was a small silence before Clem caught the twinkle in his eye and they both laughed.

'It was the only card I had left to play, Si,' she said, pouring them a glass each and flopping down on the sofa next to him. 'And I did do it as nicely as I could.'

'It's true, you are the nicest blackmailer I've ever done business with,' Simon grinned, clinking her glass. 'I forgive you.'

'How are things with Pixie anyway?'

'Oh, uh, so-so.'

Clem frowned. 'Are you still nailing her or not?'

He tutted. 'You are such a bloke sometimes.'

'Answer me. Is that why you're here? To say you've dumped her and I no longer have a hold on you and you're going to dob me in to my big brother?'

'You'll always have a hold over me, Clem,' he replied with a grin.

'Glad to hear it. My ego could do with the boost right now,' she quipped.

His eyes flicked up at her before he leaned down and reached into his bag. 'Actually, the reason I'm here is because we took delivery of a large shipment today. The pieces that had been sourced for Perignard.' He pulled out his iPad.

'Oh shit. We'd already ordered materials?' Clem curled her legs up, resting her chin on her knees.

'The entire showroom was designed around this,' he said, bringing up some architect's drawings and showing them to her. 'They were going to line the walls with this. Dappled with pink diamonds of course.'

'Of course.'

He showed her a close-up of rose-pink suede that even from here looked as supple as silk.

'Gorgeous!' Clem gasped, getting up onto her knees. 'That pink is amazing.'

'It's nubuck, a full-grain leather. Took two months to source enough hides of sufficient size and quality before we could even start tanning and splitting.'

'I'm gobsmacked.'

'I know! Can't you just imagine the glow it would have given off? Everyone looks good in a pinky light, and the jewels would have looked really lustrous.' He flicked onto another image, showing the palest green and ivory mottled shagreen leathers. 'And these were intended for the cabinets. Again, incredibly rare and it took months to source.'

A small groan escaped Clem. How could one reckless moment have endangered so much?

'No point in dwelling on it,' Simon said, reading her thoughts. 'What's done is done. We can't change it and it's their loss as far as I'm concerned. My point is, we now have a consignment of finest top-end leather that's all but useless. We obviously can't return it, and if the company does go into receivership, it'll simply be sold on at cost, which would frankly be criminal.'

Clem gasped. It was hideous even hearing the word 'receivership'. 'So then what are you going to do with it?'

He looked directly at her. 'Give it to you.'

Clem's mouth dropped open in surprise.

'I've been thinking about what you said, and the more time goes by without any help on the horizon, the more I think what you're doing is right. Bespoke is fucked right now, the banks won't even table any more meetings and the VCs who were circling last summer aren't interested when they see our orders book. I'm trying to bring forward invoicing, but legally no one's obliged to pay yet, and they're all in the same boat as us, waiting for someone else to pay *them*. We've got to do something else, something new. The way I see it now, we can either continue to sink slowly or go down in a ball of flames.'

'Simes, I can't believe it!' Clem gasped emotionally. 'Wait till I tell Stella! She'll go nuts with this leather. She'll be able to do something really amazing with it.'

'How have things progressed with your plans?'

'A bit like you and Pixie: so-so. I've got a target customer base poised and ready to shop. Stella and I have trawled the market and a couple of events, handing out flyers to women we reckon would like what we're doing. I've set up a Twitter account @clemportobello. It's got over four hundred followers already and I've only done one tweet so far.'

Clem brought it up on her phone and showed him the screen: '*@clemportobello Watch this space . . .*'

'When everything's ready, I'm going to tweet the date, time and location of the sale. And there'll be no paper trail for Tom to find out.'

'You realize how badly this has to work? The company's reputation might be all he has left. If you trash it—'

'I never would. I know what it means to him. But doing a collection doesn't downgrade the brand; it just opens it up to a new audience.'

'I agree,' Simon shrugged, taking the bottle from the table and refilling both their glasses. 'I just wish he saw it that way. Who'd have taken Tom for a snob? He's the most liberal, egalitarian bloke I know, and yet . . .'

Clem shrugged. 'He's just become blinkered on this issue, that's all. He'll come round when he sees what we've done. Talking of which, do you want to see one of the bags?'

Simon nodded eagerly and Clem jumped up, wandering into her bedroom to find the bag she'd hidden at the back of her wardrobe. Simon drained his drink and followed after.

'I've only got this one bag here. I'm having to keep everything at Stella's obviously; I can't risk Tom finding things here.' She handed him the ivory suede pouch with the ruby-red silk cord. Had it not been for the outsize scale, it would have looked like something a Tsarina would have carried. 'Like it?'

Simon nodded. 'I love it,' he murmured, inspecting it closely for quality. He nodded, impressed by the welted seams. 'And you made this with an *off-cut*?'

'Yeah! Do you remember the suede we had for making the benches in Barclays' head offices?'

'This is from that?'

'What was left of it. We only had enough to make three, but I reckon that just means we can charge more for them. Rarity value. I'd like to hold on to one myself, but I'm going to have to be selfless for once.' She sighed longingly.

'I wish I'd seen this earlier. I'd have seen the light imme-diately.'

Clem shrugged. 'I felt bad enough coercing you into it, I

didn't want to make you any more complicit than you had to be.'

Simon gazed at her steadily. 'You know, if everything else is as strong as this, you might just have something here. You could do it.'

'Well, especially now that there are some complete hides, we could. It's been really hard working with such small, irregular pieces. We're only going to earn so much selling purses, hats and wrist-warmers. Some big statement pieces could really stamp an overall personality on the collection, plus a lot more profit margin.'

'Listen to you with your business jargon. You're a revelation,' Simon smiled, handing the bag back to her, his fingers brushing hers as she took it.

'Well, I wouldn't go that far,' Clem said, clocking a look she knew all too well in Simon's eyes. 'It is, after all, because of me that we're all in this mess.'

She went to move past him back into the sitting room, but in one swift move, he caught her by the elbow, his lips finding hers with an ease that had been practised in his dreams. He tasted of toothpaste and wine, and his stubble grated against her skin.

'Simon,' she protested, struggling to get out of his grip whilst trying to bring a light-hearted laugh to her throat. 'Bugger off.'

But his hands were on her, gripping and squeezing her, ramming her to him as his mouth covered hers.

'Simon!' she managed. 'Please stop.'

'Come on, Clem,' he said urgently, holding her hard by the arms. 'Why not? You know how crazy I am about you.'

'Because I don't think of you like that,' she said, trying to lean back.

'But you're a party girl. You've slept with guys just because they bought you a drink.'

With a burst of anger, she pulled away and slapped him hard around the face. The sound of it resounded between them, like a vibration pushing them apart.

'Oh my God!' she whispered, her hands rushing up to her cheeks. 'Simon, I'm so sorry.'

He stepped away from her, his head lowered, his hand to his cheek. He shook his head, his face scarlet, and a long silence stretched between them in which Clem didn't dare move or speak.

Eventually, he looked up at her. 'I'm sorry, Clem. I should never have . . . tried,' he began. 'I don't know why I thought you'd go for it . . .' He sniffed. 'Don't worry, it won't happen again.'

He turned and walked quickly out of the room, picking up his jacket from the sofa, then he walked to the door.

Clem stayed by the doorway of the bedroom, desperate for him to go, but not as an enemy. 'Simon, we are still friends, aren't we?'

Her words stopped him, but he didn't turn back. 'I'll see you tomorrow, Clem.'

He closed the door softly and Clem ebbed against the doorframe, feeling relief, humiliation and shame flood through her. A party girl. An easy lay. A sure thing – predictable and disposable. Why wouldn't he think that?

She sank into a ball on the floor and began to cry.

Chapter Twelve

Clem blinked sleepily as she stepped out of the front door and into the first March day where the sun actually had any heat in it. She tipped the brim of her fedora down a bit to hide her red, swollen eyes, and undid the single button of her leopard-print pony-skin blazer. It was only nine o'clock, but the road was already in full swing with stallholders setting up.

'Hey, Clem, looking foxy today!' Jimmy the fishmonger called out to her as he hoisted up a crate of crayfish sitting on crushed ice.

'Back at you,' she drawled, even though he was wearing white overalls, a hair net, blue plastic bootees and smelled of kippers.

Striding off the pavement, she walked down the centre of the road at a fast march. Their father had asked to meet her for breakfast and she was already late.

'Morning!' Katy called out as she approached the stall.

'Hi! Can't stop, I'm late!' Clem waved as she stalked past.

'Drinks later? We're meeting up at the Duke.'

'Sounds good,' Clem replied. 'You haven't seen my dad have you?'

'Yeah, 'bout five minutes ago. He went that way,' she said, pointing with a sheepskin-muffled hand that looked rosy with warmth.

'Thanks,' Clem replied, walking a bit faster.

She strode down the road with the practised eye of a local, knowing exactly where the potholes were and dodging the bikes that came round corners too fast. Ahead on the right, she could already see the distinctive dark pink and brown awnings of the Hummingbird Bakery, rolled out to save the rainbow-iced confections in the windows from the glare of the early spring sun. But it wasn't there that she was headed for today – she had to embargo herself from ever going there before 11 a.m., else she'd have Red Velvet cake for breakfast – instead, she was stopping just shy on the opposite side of the road at Gail's, the large, bright deli-café where all the yummy mummies congregated after the school run, sitting out at the tables in the sun.

Her father, she could see, had bagged a small, round table on the pavement, and she smiled to see him sitting there, looking so incongruous in his mustard cords and loden cashmere sweater, staring into space, a copy of *National Geographic* magazine unopened before him.

'Hey, Daddyo!' She called her usual greeting as she approached the table.

He looked up at her distractedly, and the expression in his eyes stunned her to a complete stop. It was gone in the blink of an eye, his familiar twinkle coming back at the sight of her, but Clem felt like she'd been tasered.

'Daddy, what is it?' she asked, dismayed, sinking into the chair he'd left ready for her, her hands immediately clasping his.

'What?'

'You looked so . . . so *sad*.'

'Me?' He made the suggestion sound ridiculous. He was, after all, the man who ate Icelandic goose eggs for breakfast

133

and had just holidayed in the Caribbean. 'I was just day-dreaming. Can't an old man stare wistfully into space any more?'

Clem shrugged. Was it wistfulness she'd seen?

'Tea?'

'I'll get it,' she said.

'I insist,' he said, rising from the table. 'Will you have anything with it? See if we can't feed you up a bit.'

She shrugged again. 'I'm not that hungry. But I'll share something of yours if you like.'

He shook his head, tutting. 'Just like your mother,' he mumbled, disappearing into the bakery. He came back out several minutes later with a pot of Earl Grey and a flapjack. Clem broke a third off the end of the flapjack and nibbled on it, watching her father pour the milk.

'So, what's up?' she asked, although she already had an inkling why he'd asked to see her. 'Is it Tom?'

Edmund Alderton replaced the teapot with care and inhaled deeply. His usually jocular features – so full of colour and animation – seemed bloodless and limp today and he seemed older than she thought him.

'Tom, yes. How is he? I was hoping he'd be here, too, today.'

Clem shrugged. 'Frantic at work.' Clem was amazed how busy he could be doing nothing.

Edmund tutted. 'Always working, that boy. He never calls any more, and he's cancelled our weekly lunch for the last four weeks on the trot. Whenever we call him, he always seems to be either working late or rushing out of the office. He says he'll call back but he never does.'

Clem bit her lip. So it wasn't just her feeling abandoned then? Clover was tightening her grip, pulling Tom away from all of them, not just her.

'Well, I've not seen much of him myself, if that's any consolation. He stays at Clover's practically every night now,
and if he's in the office he's always on the phone, or else
he's off-site at the factory or trying to schmooze potential
clients.'

'Hmm, has any new business come in?'

Clem shook her head. 'No. It's really quiet. We've had a
few speculative calls and some follow-up meetings, but
nothing seems to be coming of them. I've tried telling him I
think we should diversify into other business models but
. . . well, he doesn't really take me seriously.'

Edmund patted her hand. 'Don't take it to heart. It's his
baby. He's always been dogged like that. He'll listen only to
the voice in his head when all's said and done.'

Clem sighed, pleased at least that her father's words confirmed her own instincts to keep her plans a closely guarded
secret. She couldn't risk widening the circle of confidence
any further.

'It's a shame he's away so much,' Clem said, stirring a
sugar into her tea. 'I've got a new cleaner coming in twice a
week. She's lovely, and the flat's never looked so good, but
Tom's hardly around to notice.'

Edmund gave a rumbling sound of disapproval. She
knew her father had never taken to Clover either. 'Is he getting ready to propose, do you think?'

Clem sighed heavily. 'Who knows? It's hardly the time if
the business is really on the skids.' She didn't dare mention
that it was a lot more likely if Tom went ahead with the idea
of selling the flat and moving in with Clover anyway – and
she didn't see how he wouldn't, with things so bad at work.
He'd done as he promised and given her some time; everything had gone quiet on that front since Clem had thrown

out Clover and the estate agent in front of Mercy, but it wouldn't last for ever. Spring was here and the road was beginning to burst into colour once more. If he was going to sell, it would be soon.

She bit her lip anxiously at the thought of moving and resolved to get Stella round tonight, no matter what; they *had* to get the collection finished. Simon's gift, last night, of the rose-pink suede and shagreens was a blessing from heaven, but it was going to mean a lot more work, and it was already getting harder to separate Stella from Oscar in the evenings. If that flash sale didn't happen in the next few weeks it was going to be too late.

'It's not just Tom we're worried about,' Edmund said, staring at her with concerned eyes. Her face was puffy from another night spent in tears. 'You seem to have become even more distant recently.'

'Me?' Clem asked innocently.

'We live two streets away and yet it may as well be the other end of the country for the amount of times we see you.'

'We're doing this, aren't we?' She gestured around them.

'You never pop in. And you seem to be going out of your way to avoid your mother. She's very deeply hurt by it, Clemmie.'

'We clash, that's all. It's just easier . . . not to.' Clem looked away, watching as two skinny teenagers, who probably should have been at school, lit up behind a bin. 'Besides, it's not me she's interested in. Tom's always been her favourite.'

'That is categorically not true,' Edmund said sternly. 'She loves you very much. You must know that?'

Clem looked at him side on, before looking away again.

She didn't reply. Last night's tears weren't quite spent and she felt dangerously emotional.

'I know you're very different creatures and that your mother can be . . . particular, at times, but I wish you'd try to get on a bit better,' her father said, gently stroking her fingers whilst she watched the truanting teenagers. 'Bear in mind that we're none of us getting any younger, Clemmie. Your mother and I aren't going to be around for ever. We want to see you both happy and settled.' His voice had a tremor to it that made her look back at him.

'I am happy and settled.'

'You know what we mean.'

Yes, she did know what they meant: married with kids. Clem stared into her tea just as a solitary tear dropped into it with a splash. She categorically did not want to have this conversation.

'I like my life the way it is, Dad,' she mumbled. Is this what today was about? Not Tom at all? She had been ambushed into a discussion about the ruins that passed as her life? Why did everyone think you had to be married with kids to be happy?

'I wish I could believe that, darling. But if I'm honest, when I look at you, I see a lost little girl who somewhere along the line took a wrong turn. You put on a very good show, but you don't fool me, Clemmie. I'm your father.'

Clem drew her hands in sharply. 'You're wrong. There's nothing I would change about my life. Nothing,' she said with a defiance that was the only barrier keeping all the other tears in check.

Her father stared at her for a long moment, before bowing his head and nodding. 'Well, your mother and I miss you, that's all, and we'd both dearly like to be more a part of your lives.'

It was all Clem could do not to laugh at the statement. Her mother, wanting to be more involved with her life? As if.

She rose to go. 'I have to get to the office, Dad.'

He looked hurt. 'Because it's so busy there?'

'Because I'm paid to be there, whether it's busy or not. Tom needs me.'

Edmund nodded reluctantly. 'Just think about what I've said. Your mother's the only one you've got, and you're losing time with each other by pursuing this silent war. She loves you very much.'

Clem kissed him quickly on the cheek and left without saying another word. She couldn't. Her poor father didn't know that his words were false, that they'd already been found to be untrue. He was merely doing his wife's bidding, saying the words that would choke her if she tried. But it was too late for olive branches now. Clem wouldn't tolerate it. What her mother had done, Clem could neither forgive, nor forget.

Everyone was busy trying to look busy when she walked into the office six minutes later. Pixie was collapsing cardboard boxes in the store cupboard, Simon was feeding paper documents into the shredder and Tom was on the phone.

Clem dumped her battered vintage satchel disconsolately on the desk and slumped in her chair. Her father's words – kind, loving, concerned – had rung in her ears like insults all the way back up the road, and she felt nervy and unsure of herself.

She noticed a Post-it on her desk, written in Simon's distinctive too-neat hand: 'Delivery, 5 p.m. today.' She looked up at him – well, at his back. He was standing with his back to her, manually forcing sheets of paper through the cutting teeth every five seconds. He had to have seen her, he'd been standing side on to her when she'd walked in.

'Thanks for this, Si,' she said quietly. He was only 10 feet away from her, but he acted as though he hadn't heard, widening his stance and pushing fatter wodges of paper through the machine, the revs filling up his silence.

It was his version of a slap back, and she swallowed at the rebuke. Not friends after all, then. A great day this was turning out to be. Just great: a guilt trip from her father, and now a guilt trip from him.

Pulling her phone from her bag, she texted Stella: *'Surprise bounty of complete hides. Will explain later but must meet. Mine, 6 p.m. tonight? It's urgent. Don't blow me out for luvaboy.'*

Tom came off the phone, replacing the handset with something approaching a flourish, and both Simon and Clem looked back at him quizzically as he stared at it intently, lost in thought.

'What?' Clem asked, able to discern that he was trying his best to suppress the kind of warrior yell that had been the hallmark of their childhood. 'Who was that?'

He looked up, as though startled to find them all watching him, and an enigmatic smile flitted across his face like a phantom. 'Possibly . . . only possibly, a new client.'

Clem gasped in excitement.

'Hold it! Don't celebrate! It's just a meeting,' Tom warned her, worried by her instant happiness. 'It'll probably come to nothing.'

'I bet it won't!' Clem gushed excitedly. 'You're Mr Charisma, you are. The bummer's been the phone not ringing. As soon as you get someone face-to-face and start on your spiel, they're goners every time. They love you, big brother.'

'Actually, this might come down to whether or not they love *you*,' Tom said steadily.

'Me?' Clem was stunned. She was never allowed near the clients. Hadn't she proved time and again that she couldn't be trusted to play with the grown-ups?

'They've asked that you come to the meeting, too.'

'Why me?'

Tom shrugged. 'Hopefully because they heard there's a good-looking chick on my staff and they want something pretty to look at whilst they spend vast sums of money.'

Clem tutted and threw a biro lid across the room at him.

'Care to share?' Simon asked, abandoning his position at the shredder and walking past Clem's desk without acknowledging her. 'What's the project?'

'A private house in Italy. Ligurian coastline.'

'Nice!' Simon nodded. 'Big house?'

'Big enough that it's got a boathouse with . . . a boat,' Tom said casually, his lips curling into a smile. 'A sad and bedraggled boat that needs to be completely redesigned and reupholstered.'

'A *boat*?' Simon shouted. 'Say you're not messing with me.'

'I'm not messing with you,' Tom replied, thoroughly amused by Simon's reaction – he knew full well this was Simon's dream commission. Tom's, too, albeit for different reasons: a marine project was up there in the prestige stakes with the supercar market, and would not only save the business, but propel it into the next level, just as they craved. Bugatti might have been lost to them, but they weren't dead in the water yet.

'Obviously, the boat's going to require all manner of technical compliances, so I'd like you to get on it, Si. Research everything. I want to go to them with something innovative. We'll give them navy and white over my dead body.'

'Unless they want navy and white,' Simon said sternly, arching an eyebrow.

'Exactly.' Tom laughed.

Clem smiled to hear the sound – so rare in recent weeks – she could almost see the stress lifting off him like a heat cloud. Would Clover be so happy, she wondered, to learn that the business might be viable after all?

And what about her collection? Was it even going to be needed now? She wondered as she watched Tom and Simon talk earnestly and eagerly, heads bowed together as Tom directed orders and Simon took frantic notes.

Her phone buzzed with a new text and she looked down to see Stella's reply: *'Sure. Intrigued. Laters.'*

Timing!

Clem watched as the boys high-fived each other. So much for not getting carried away!

She felt a kernel of nervousness harden in the pit of her stomach, anxious to see her brother so clearly investing all his hope into this one meeting in spite of himself, even though, as he'd said himself, it could all come to nothing.

She bit her lip thoughtfully. Well, *she* wouldn't take the risk. For once, she'd be the one playing it safe. The hides were being delivered later and Stella was free to come over – things were already in motion anyway. The best thing she could do was to carry on as though their world was falling apart and she alone could save it.

Chapter Thirteen

'You're under my feet, girl,' Mercy said, flinging the Hoover alarmingly towards Clem's bare feet as she painted her nails a deep, glittery shade of plum.

Clem lifted her legs in the air, letting Mercy pass by, the Hoover in one hand, a glass of red wine in the other. Mercy had had to switch her hours because of another, awkward employer who refused to negotiate on either times or wages, and she was now often here in the evenings when Clem got back from the office. It suited them both. With Tom so rarely around, Clem enjoyed the company, and the confrontation with Clover had been a powerful bonding exercise. They chatted easily about anything and everything, and Mercy not only didn't bat an eyelid at Clem wandering around half-clothed, which was the true litmus test of whether they could be friends, half the time she joined her.

Clem admired her glossy, dark-disco toes. 'Like?' she asked.

'They look bruised if you want my honest opinion,' Mercy said, planting a hand on her hip and fixing Clem with a sceptical stare. 'Like a truck ran over them.'

'Good, that was *just* the look I was after.' Clem giggled, delighted to be so contrary, pushing the rolled-up tissue paper further between her toes.

The slam of the street door told them both Stella had arrived, and Clem got up to open the door for her, walking in a peculiar fashion on her heels to keep her nail polish from smudging.

'Good look!' Stella grinned up at her from the stairs as Clem stood by the door in a vest and knickers.

'It's boiling in here, I'm warning you,' Clem said, kissing her friend on the cheeks as Stella unwound her signature metre-long Aran-knitted scarf. 'Fuck knows where the thermostat is. I think Tom's taken it with him. Or Clover's hidden it.'

Stella stopped dead at the sight of Mercy hoovering vigorously in Clem's bedroom. With her spending so much time with Oscar of late, the two women hadn't met yet and Clem couldn't tell if she was stunned by the shocking tidiness of the flat, or the fact that Mercy was wearing just her jeans and a fuchsia-pink bra. Mercy, sensing she was being scrutinized, stopped hoovering and straightened up.

'Stell, this is Mercy. Mercy, this is Stell,' Clem said calmly as the two buxom women quite literally sized each other up. A hug was going to be out of the question: they'd never get near enough.

'I've heard lots about you,' Mercy nodded as she coiled the wire along the back of the Hoover, ignoring the fact that Stella couldn't take her eyes off Mercy's chest. 'All bad.'

The comment jogged Stella out of her trance and she laughed, albeit nervously. 'All right?' Stella nodded in greeting as Clem hobbled back to the sofa to pour her a glass of wine. Stella followed, sporadically looking back at Mercy in amazement. 'Why is your skin brown? Mine looks like porridge.'

Clem shrugged. 'My father's genes; nothing to do with

me. Besides, you're a lot cleaner than me. I don't wash as much as you.'

'Mmm, I guess.'

Stella went to collapse on her usual place on the sofa opposite Clem when she caught sight of the heap of pink and blue-green hides draped across the back of it. 'Holy cow!' she cried.

'Well, quite,' Clem quipped. 'Only the holy ones are pink, you know.'

The three of them laughed.

'Is that what you meant when you said, "bounty"?'

Clem nodded.

'And it bloody is. Is this really for us to use?'

'Mmm hmm.'

'But where did it come from? Can you be sure of the quality? You know we can't scrimp on that.'

'It's top-notch, direct from the Alderton Hide factory. Simon got it for me. It had already been ordered for the Perignard account before everything . . .' She ran out of words.

'Was Clemmed?' Stella offered, gently fingering the leathers. 'God, these are gorgeous.'

'I thought you'd like them. Now we've just got to spend tonight figuring out what to make them into.'

'Isn't it a bit risky doing it here, though?' Stella frowned. 'What if Tom comes back?'

Clem sighed. 'He never comes back mid-week any more. Next time I'll see him here will be Saturday morning, when he comes over for his rugby kit.'

'Has he properly moved out then?'

'Not formally. I think he's been staying with her so much to "acclimatize himself"' – she made quote marks in the air with her fingers – 'for the real thing.'

'How's all that going? Many viewings?'

'Don't be daft! It's not even on the market,' Clem replied indignantly. 'I bared my teeth and Clover ran for cover, didn't she, Mercy?'

Mercy gave a solemn nod, taking a sip of the red wine from her glass on the worktop, a duster in her other hand.

'She won't step out of line again, I can tell you,' Clem said, with a little diva-ish waggle of her head. 'What?'

'You obviously haven't seen this,' Stella murmured, tapping something into her iPad.

'What?' Clem took it, frowning, before jumping up in horror and smudging her toes. 'The devious bitch! I can't believe she's done that!' Clem cried, staring at the estate agents' website, which featured a lovely picture of the very room they were standing in.

Mercy shook her head, tutting away. 'Pushy, that girl.'

'Pushy' had become the dirtiest of all words.

'Sorry, hon. I thought you knew,' Stella said.

'My own home's on the market and I didn't even *know*?' Clem raged. 'That's such a shitty thing for Tom to do! I can't believe he didn't tell me. I thought we'd cleared the air.'

'He's under a lot of pressure, remember,' Stella counselled. 'Don't be too hard on him. It's probably the last thing he wants to talk about.'

'Yeah, because he knew what I'd have to say about it!' Clem stomped off into the bathroom to find some nail polish remover and cotton wool balls. She wanted to be understanding and selfless, she really did, but she couldn't help but wonder whether Tom wasn't deliberately punishing her for what she'd done. This was, after all, entirely her fault. If the meeting did come to nothing and he had to sell up against his will, it was because it was *her* fault. She wiped her toenails clean, but didn't bother reapplying the varnish. It wasn't like they were going to be going out tonight anyway.

She wandered back into the sitting room to find Stella had her top off, too, and was comparing hers and Mercy's industrial-strength bras.

'Blimey!' Clem laughed, forgetting her upset for a moment. 'Mrs Crouch'll think we're having an orgy in here tonight,' she said, making no move to go to the window and close the shutters.

'It's so tropical in here you could grow mangoes,' Stella said distractedly, closely examining Mercy's bra straps. 'Anyway I reckon there's still a gap for seriously gorgeous bras in bigger sizes. It's just a nightmare, isn't it, Mercy?'

'Most of mine look like they could double as hammocks for baby hippos,' Mercy replied seriously.

'We should talk,' Stella said, eyes slitted in deep concentration.

Clem, who, being a B-cup, knew nothing of such woes and most of the time went bra-less, walked over to the heap of hides and dragged the topmost one into the centre of the room. 'Another time maybe. Right now we need to decide what we're going to do with these,' she said, sitting next to the hide cross-legged and lightly stroking the pile.

Stella joined her on the floor and Clem could see from the intensity on her face that her mind was already whirring. 'Well, the first thing I'm thinking is a jumpsuit – you know, biker-style, really tight and sexy, tab closures—'

'Oh! Adore!' Clem interrupted excitedly, clapping her hands. She loved watching Stella at work.

Stella dragged the rest of the hides over and began counting and measuring them, writing down dimensions in a small Orla Kiely notebook. 'And I really love this green. Imagine a pencil skirt in that.'

'I so can,' Clem said dreamily, accessorizing it in her head with her vintage Fifties Roger Vivier stilettoes. There were such great benefits to being Stella's friend.

'Imagine the dry-cleaning bills,' Mercy quipped on her way through to the kitchen, the Hoover trailing behind her. 'And you'll need sharp needles for sewing that or they'll snag.'

'How'd you know that?' Stella called after her.

'Worked in a factory making tents once. I can stitch a straight line like you wouldn't believe,' Mercy cackled.

Stella grinned back, her smile fading as she looked at her notebook. 'The thing is, Clem, this is all gorgeous, but is there going to be enough profit margin in these pieces to make it worthwhile? You can't charge for a pair of trousers what you'd charge for – I dunno – lining a wardrobe with the stuff, even if you end up using less leather and less man hours. It's just a different market, different mark-up. I've done costings for all the other pieces we've made so far, and I reckon that even if we sell everything, we're still only going to pull in twelve grand.'

Clem looked at her, appalled. 'But that's nowhere near enough!'

Stella shrugged. 'It's a tough business.'

'Can't we whack twenty per cent on everything?'

Stella looked at her doubtfully. 'There's a recession going on, remember? If we can get the punters into a bit of a shopping frenzy we can apply a small premium – you know, it's a one-off opportunity, limited edition and whatnot – but they're not fools. People won't pay just anything. These hides will obviously help bump the profits up. We can maybe get up to . . . what, twenty grand?'

Clem visibly deflated. 'Still not enough. How are we

going to really make some proper money?' She leaned against the sofa, her long legs crossed at the ankles, one foot jiggling anxiously. She had to think. There had to be something they could do that would bring in the amount they needed. If the entire collection couldn't do it, then it would need to be one incredible item. One standout, special piece that money couldn't buy—

'Oh my God!' she exclaimed, sitting up so suddenly that the wine in her glass sloshed alarmingly high, threatening to splash the pink suede, and bringing Mercy, who'd started cleaning in the bathroom, running back through, Marigolds now added to her 'look'.

'What's the matter?' she cried.

'I've got it,' Clem whispered.

'What?' Mercy and Stella asked in unison.

Clem dashed into the bedroom and came out several moments later holding the bright orange dust bag. 'This!' She smiled, pulling out the Hermès bag. 'This is our golden ticket.'

Stella paled. 'Your mum's Birkin? What are you gonna do with that?'

'Auction it.'

'No way!' Stella screeched, almost dropping the glass on the precious hide herself.

'Yes, way.'

'But it's priceless. You told me yourself it's one of those rare, money-can't-buy ones.'

'A shooting star, exactly – which'll be why it goes for such a premium. These babies sell for five grand, *entry level*. But this one's got provenance, a contrast lining that's, like, super rare, *and* it's croc. I'll ask for fifty as a reserve bid.'

'Fifty thousand?' Stella spluttered. 'You're mad. No one

would spend that. No one *could* spend that, apart from Victoria Beckham or the Ecclestone sisters.'

'Oh yes they could. It's just a matter of getting the word out. There are international collectors who'd come from all over for this – do you have any idea of what the Asian or Middle Eastern markets would pay to get hold of this? There are plenty of people on the Alderton Hide client list alone who'd qualify.'

Stella put her glass on the ground and clasped her friend by the shoulders. 'Clem, listen to me. I'm deadly serious about this: She – will – kill – you,' Stella said slowly, no mirth in her expression.

Clem's eyes met hers. She knew Stella was right. Her mother would never forgive her for doing this. It was the most precious item her mother could have given her, everyone knew that, but they didn't know it was tainted as if it had been revealed as a fake, that it had been given as a bribe. Consequently, she couldn't look at it and hadn't even opened it; she'd just hidden it at the back of her wardrobe, trying to push it – and everything it now represented – out of her mind.

Clem shrugged. 'She'll thank me one day. It's the only way to bring in enough money to save her darling boy's company.'

'Clem—'

Stella was silenced by a muted slam, followed by a tinkle of laughter floating up the stairs – all three women stared at the door in horror.

'Oh, you have got to be kidding! *Today?*' Clem hissed as the sound of footsteps grew nearer. She looked down at the heap of hides on the floor. There was no way she could explain why they were there. 'Quick, we've got to hide these. Help me get them into my room.'

All three women lifted a corner each of the 9-foot hides, managing only five at a time.

'Damn, they're so heavy,' Stella panted as they dragged the first batch through to the bedroom and threw them over the far side of the bed. They ran back into the room and picked up another batch, but the sound of keys in the door made them freeze in the middle of the room.

'Mercy, quick!' Clem whispered. 'Put the chain on and lean against the door. Don't let them in.'

Mercy gathered her bosom in her arm and ran across the room, just as the door started to open. For a fraction of a second, Clem's eyes met Clover's as she and Stella shuffled with the second batch of hides across the floor, but Mercy got her shoulder to it and, putting her considerable weight behind it, slammed the door shut again.

'Hey! What's going on?' Tom shouted, using his fist on the door. 'Clem, open up!'

'Oh, sweet Jesus! This would happen . . .' Clem giggled as they dumped the hides in her room. There was one batch left to move. 'Just . . . just a minute,' Clem shouted back. 'Just wait a sec.'

'What's happening, Clem? Who's in there?' Tom demanded, pounding the door so hard that Mercy, leaning with her back against the door, bounced to the movement. She crossed her arms and rolled her eyes as Stella and Clem formed a pincer movement towards her bedroom for the third time.

'It's not like this in my other job,' Mercy muttered.

'There,' Clem said, throwing her duvet over the hides and emptying the contents of her wardrobe onto the bed and floor to complete the look – instantly undoing all Mercy's hard work. 'OK, Mercy, let them in,' she whispered.

Mercy undid the chain and opened the door, Tom almost falling in as he prepared to rain down another set of blows. 'What the . . .?' he exploded, before falling mute in the doorway at the sight of Clem and Stella lying on the sofas, drinking wine, Mercy dusting – all three of them in their underwear.

'What?' Clem blinked calmly.

'W–w–why did you chain the door?' he stammered, taking in the large amount of cleavage in the room.

'Mercy was just cleaning behind it.'

'I thought . . . I thought you were being attacked or something,' Tom roared.

'God, Tom, you're so melodramatic. Take a chill pill! Come and have a glass.'

But Tom was too flabbergasted. He looked at Mercy, unsure of where to start.

'Oh, have you met Mercy yet?' Clem asked, seeing his confusion. 'She's our new cleaner. Been with us for almost a couple of months now.'

'Nice to meet you,' Mercy said, nodding gravely in her enormous hot pink bra.

'Does she . . . always do the cleaning half-dressed?' Tom asked, his voice weak and looking bewildered.

Mercy and Clem looked at each other. 'Not always.' They shrugged. 'But you've obviously set the heating to tropical temperatures for Shambles . . .'

'What? And you hadn't thought to turn it down?'

'If only I knew how.' Clem sighed, prompting a muffled squeak of indignation from Clover. 'Anyway, the flat looks good, doesn't it?' Clem said, prompting Tom to tear his eyes away from the décolleté on show and notice the sparkling surfaces and dust-free floor.

'Oh . . . yeah . . .' he said, brightening up, before spotting the carnage in his sister's bedroom. 'Well, apart from your room. Another wardrobe crisis, was it?'

'Obvs!' Clem gave a throaty chuckle as she shared a look with Stella.

Clover, who was looking furious at the clique of loquacious, undressed women – stepped forward. 'You were carrying something,' she said to Clem.

'Me?' Clem repeated, eyes wide.

'Yes. When the door opened, I saw you . . .'

Clem shook her head. 'Not me. I've been charged with emptying this bottle of wine and keeping the sofa warm, and I'm taking my responsibilities *very* seriously.'

Clover's mouth tightened. They both knew perfectly well that Clem was lying, but she didn't say anything further. She couldn't. It was Clem's word against hers.

'Are you staying for supper? We thought we'd get a takeout.' Clem smiled at Tom.

Tom snapped his attention back to her. 'No, I . . . I've just come back to look for my Hermès tie. That meeting's at eleven tomorrow. You haven't forgotten, have you?'

'Tch, hardly! What d'you think the mess in there's all about?' she said as he wandered into his room and began rummaging through the wardrobe.

Stella winked at Clem as their eyes met again. Clem refilled Stella's and Mercy's glasses, but pointedly didn't offer one to Clover, who was still awkwardly standing around them.

'Dammit, where is it?' Tom groaned, coming back out, his hands gripping his hair. 'It's not there. I keep bloody losing everything at the moment.'

'Well, if you are going to insist on living between two

homes,' Clem said lightly. 'And before you ask, no, I haven't worn it.'

'Why don't you wear the one I bought you for Maisie and Finn's wedding? You know, the striped Ralph Lauren one?' Clover suggested.

'Because that's too . . . clubby,' Tom rebuffed. 'It's a morning suit tie; it's not for a lounge suit. Besides, the Hermès one was Dad's. I always wear it to important meetings. It brings me luck.'

'It really doesn't.' Clem sighed.

Clover, who was pinker and more animated than Clem had ever seen her, pinned her overly bright eyes on Clem, and Clem had a feeling that her agitation was less to do with Clem's flippancy than Tom's flat rejection of her suggestion. 'By the way, Clem, did Tom mention that the estate agents are hosting an open day here next Saturday?'

Clem's eyes remained fixed upon Clover's, though she could see Tom stiffen in her peripheral vision. She tilted her head interestedly. 'Oh?'

'Yes. There's been so much interest in the flat, they felt that was the best way to go. So you might want to get your cleaner to work her . . .' Clover's eyes strayed to the carnage in Clem's bedroom '. . . magic here on Friday.'

Clem saw Mercy straighten up menacingly, but Clem just smiled. 'Sure. If that works for you, Mercy?'

Mercy, surprised but taking her cue from Clem's languid demeanour, shrugged. 'No problem.' She nodded.

'All settled, then.' Clem smiled, trying her best to simper. She knew exactly what Clover was trying to do. The news that the flat was being marketed at all had been intended as a body blow, never mind that there was significant interest. Bless Stella for giving her the heads-up first. To be forewarned really was to be forearmed. It gave her an idea. 'But

you guys will have to do the tours. I'm busy,' she added, as
if as an afterthought, sipping her wine.

'Sure,' Tom said eagerly, visibly relieved that she'd taken
the news so well. 'What've you got on?'

'Oh, you know, girl stuff,' Clem replied, winking across
at Stella. They had a collection, a cash cow and now a date
where Tom was guaranteed to be out of the way. It was
almost too perfect. On the very day Clover expected to sell
the flat, Clem would instead gazump her with a cash injection that would bring all her plans crashing around her
feet. Everything she tried to do, Clem would cancel out –
they wouldn't need to sell the flat, Tom wouldn't need to
move out, the business would be saved and everything
would go back to how it had been. She sighed, stretching
out longer on the sofa and shooting Clover a winning smile,
that of the victor. For the first time in a long time, things
were beginning to come together.

Chapter Fourteen

The taxi pulled up outside Claridge's, and Clem hopped out with the daintiness of a ballerina on pointe, even though she was in 5-inch heeled suede ankle boots. She smoothed the wrinkles out of her leather trousers and fluffed her hair in the window's reflection, pleased with the new Pucci jacket she'd bought off eBay: it was buttonless, with clashing ikat and zebra prints, and needed no further accessories than a plain white linen tee and mirrored aviators.

Tom pulled the enormous leather-bound swatch books out of the back of the cab and rested them on the pavement to fiddle with his non-Hermès tie. In spite of yesterday's swagger about being Mr Charisma, he looked flustered and harried. Clem thought he looked nearer forty than thirty today.

'You all right?' she asked, sweeping the shoulders of his jacket, mainly to soothe rather than remove lint or dandruff.

"Course,' he replied gruffly, but as his brown eyes met hers momentarily, she saw everything in them that he didn't want to show. She knew him far too well for secrets.

'Oh, Tom,' she said quietly, squeezing his biceps. 'This is going to be great. They'll love you. Everybody does. They'll take one look at your portfolio and be begging to secure your services. Remember, *they* don't know we're on the ropes. Just play it cool, OK?'

'Cool,' he echoed, his eyes ever so slightly watery before he swallowed hard and blinked them dry. Then he jutted his chin in the air and picked up the portfolios.

The doorman held the glass door open for them, tipping his hat as they passed, and they walked through into the glossy black-and-white floored lobby.

'Reservation in the name of Alderton, eleven o'clock.'

The receptionist smiled. 'Your guests haven't arrived yet, sir. Can I take your bags for you?'

'No thanks,' Tom replied, gripping the cases more tightly. 'We'll go straight through.'

'Of course. Follow me, please.'

They walked through to a lounge which, even at mid-morning, had a darkly sensuous, opulent feel about it. Clem was aware of eyes swivelling in their direction as they passed. They made a dazzling couple, and she knew that if her T-shirt was printed with the words, 'Duh! He's my brother!' there'd be an audible sigh of relief throughout the room: women were as attracted to Tom's boyish good looks and demeanour as men were to Clem's spirited defiance.

The receptionist seated them in a pocketed-leather alcove at the far end of the room. 'Can I get you any drinks?' she asked.

'Just some water for now. A bottle of each please,' Tom said authoritatively, before she could ask 'still or sparkling'. 'Clem, sit opposite me here,' he said, just as bossily to her, ordering her to sit with her back to the room. 'That way I can see when they walk in.'

Clem slid reluctantly into the pillar-box-red leather club chair. 'They're wearing well,' she murmured.

'As they should do. Aniline lambskin,' Tom replied, stroking the arms with a critical eye. It was no coincidence that they'd arranged to hold the meeting here: refurb'ing this bar had been one of Alderton Hide's first big commissions. 'It took sixteen treatments to get the colour right. Christ, I thought Simon was going to resign on me.'

Clem looked down at the mention of Simon's name – he'd managed to get through the entire day yesterday without once looking at, or talking to her, and she knew it wouldn't be long before Tom noticed and started asking questions.

Tom shifted position and cleared his throat, switching his phone to silent, and then shifted position again, his eyes flitting constantly towards the door. He was utterly oblivious to the women staring at him around the room.

'Feeling OK?' she murmured, her crossed leg swinging slightly.

He nodded abruptly, jerking his chin in the air again, and she felt her heart lurch at the sight of his barely concealed vulnerability. They had to land this commission; she didn't know how he'd take it if they didn't. He seemed dangerously on edge. She had to be at her best in this, for his sake.

'OK, this is it. He's coming,' he murmured, fiddling with his tie again and getting up, stepping forward with his hand outstretched before she'd even got out of her seat. 'Mr Beaulieu?' Tom said behind her. 'Tom Alderton, a pleasure.'

Clem took a deep breath and pushed herself to standing. She turned with a smile, a smile that faded as quickly as it had appeared.

'May I introduce my Press and Marketing Director, and also, in her time off, my sister – Clem Alderton.'

The Swimmer's hand clasped hers firmly and she almost jumped at the touch.

'Ms Alderton,' the Swimmer murmured, his head tipped

slightly but his eyes boring into hers. 'A pleasure to meet you again.'

Tom was taken by surprise. 'You know each other?'

'I wouldn't say that,' the Swimmer replied, still holding her limp hand, his eyes raking over her outfit and body like fingers. 'But we've been at the same events a few times.'

Clem was silent. Not a word would come from her throat. She wondered whether he could see the flush creeping up her chest and neck, whether her deeply dilated pupils were giving her away, whether she was actually panting or if it was just the hammering of her heart that she could hear?

'Oh.' Tom shifted warily. 'Well, please take a seat,' he said, interrupting the interlude and motioning for them to sit down.

The Swimmer sat at the end of the table, with brother and sister on either side of him. He was wearing a dark grey suit with a seahorse-print pink Hermès tie – lucky for him too? – his long legs crossed, his fingers pitched together into a steeple, his eyes on Tom, but his mind, Clem knew, on her.

Clem sat back in her chair, trying to look a lot cooler than she felt. She still hadn't uttered a word and she wasn't sure she could. The chemistry between them was almost too much, throwing her off her stride every time, and she didn't like it. She had been tricked into coming here and – given that at the christening he'd mysteriously known her name and address – he probably knew very well that there was too much riding on this meeting for Alderton Hide for her to walk out.

She kept her eyes dead ahead, determined not to let her gaze wander as Tom began his pitch.

'I'd like to begin by saying that in contacting Alderton

Hide to discuss your requirements, you've already made a key decision, and that's a commitment to collaborate not only with an elite team of craftsmen and designers but, crucially, to pursue your vision in an ethical and sustainable way. Many of our competitors have a less, shall we say, "organic" approach to their businesses. Everybody operating in this niche market is working with discerning clients who want only the very best, and we do, too, but we stand alone because we believe we can marry a high-spec aesthetic with good ethical and environmental practice. We source the very best and rarest hides in the world, while insisting upon utmost transparency and integrity throughout our supply chains, from the farmers through to the abattoirs through to the tanneries. We passionately believe that beauty doesn't need to be cruel—'

'*D'accord*,' the Swimmer murmured, his eyes on Tom still, but his words, Clem knew, directed for her alone. This wasn't a meeting, it was a private game – foreplay. She felt a shiver tiptoe up her skin.

'That's our company philosophy in a nutshell and, should you be interested, I can give you more detailed examples of how this works in practice.' Tom reached for the iPad he'd put on the table and Clem noticed his hand trembling slightly. 'But before we look further into your requirements for this project, I thought it might be useful for you to take a look at our portfolio and see in closer detail some of our past projects which, broadly speaking, dovetail with yours.'

He pressed 'play' and handed over the iPad, which showed a smooth sequence of glossy images, most of which Clem had jazzed up with Instagram filters for varying moods.

Clem allowed herself to study his reactions as he watched

the presentation. His profile was really quite magnificent – aquiline, smooth, his jawline close-shaven and tight, the plane of his cheekbones mitred, the slight swell of his lips, the outer edge of his eyes – those eyes, betrayed by one faint laughter line. Did he laugh? He seemed too intense to laugh, and that alone made her long to hear it, to be the one to break the perfection of his face and soften it with a single line.

He looked across at her suddenly, catching her staring directly at him, and she almost gasped at having been caught. She felt her complexion flame and she looked away. What was it with him? He made the most normal, trivial behaviour explode into something more . . . more significant. Looking at him, asking his name became somehow a weakness or, at least, a weakening, and she sensed it was all part of a possession he had of her, the power he wanted over her.

'I'm impressed,' he said to Tom, handing back the iPad and nodding vaguely, thinking in silence for a few moments. 'Let me tell you what it is I'm looking for,' he said quietly, and Clem half-expected him to say, 'Five foot nine brunette with aquamarine eyes and an attitude.' 'The house is an eighteenth-century palazzo with eight bedroom suites, six bathrooms, three receptions, library, two kitchens and a media centre. We're stripping everything back to the bones.'

Clem cast a glance at Tom and could see his ankle jigging furiously beneath the table, a look of smiling calm on his face. He was the proverbial swan, she thought sadly, gliding serenely on the surface, feet paddling furiously beneath. They had to land this.

'As for the boat, it's an Azimut One Hundred Leonardo – thirty metres, two storeys, four cabins, two staff cabins.

The hull has been stripped back and rebuilt, and the decks will be refitted imminently with teak. But the soft interior needs to be done from scratch.'

'So the shell refurb's almost complete?' Tom asked in surprise. 'I would have thought you'd have secured your designs for the interior by now then?'

'I had,' the Swimmer replied. 'But then . . . then I heard about you.'

Tom grew an inch, his handsome face finally beginning to relax. 'Well, we're immensely flattered to hear that,' he beamed, but Clem knew the compliment had been targeted at her. If she'd thought she'd blown it after he'd walked away at the christening, she knew with absolute certainty now that he wasn't going to stop coming after her – not if he was prepared to give Alderton Hide a commission on this scale. Most men just took her for a drink and she didn't ever ask for more than that; she wanted nothing from them other than a short-lived good time. No strings, no rings – that was her rule. And yet this guy was the richest, most gorgeous of the bunch, and she was making him jump through hoops, giving him less than any of the others, refusing even to ask his name. It didn't make sense, not even to her. But then she'd never been big on self-scrutiny.

Clem thought she heard a question mark and looked across abruptly at Tom, who was staring at her. 'Huh?'

'I asked whether you could pass me the book with the aniline leathers in?' Tom said, glaring at her for flirting with the client.

'Oh, yeah, sure,' she mumbled, reaching down for the case and handing it over. The Swimmer covered his smile with his hand.

'So, these leathers are produced by a tannery in Santa

Croce sull'Arno in Tuscany. We've been working closely with them for a couple of years now, and they've developed a technique, which is currently being patented, whereby an aniline, top-grain leather can be made fully waterproof, but retains the suppleness and fluidity of nappa. So far, they're only supplying Hermès and us.' Tom made a clicking sound with his tongue. 'We may be a small and young company, but we're already renowned for our pioneering approaches and heavy investment in driving the industry forwards.'

The Swimmer's expression didn't change, but Clem detected he was amused. 'I'm impressed,' he said again, his soft accent giving the innocuous words a ridiculously sensuous spin.

'And as you can see, the colour range is pretty impressive. Over forty—'

A woman had stopped by their table and rested a slim hand on the Swimmer's significant shoulder. The men immediately stood up, adjusting their ties. Clem followed, but a lot more slowly and uncertainly as she recognized the girl from the cinema.

The Swimmer kissed her lightly on each cheek. 'You are late.'

'I am sorry. Traffic,' she smiled back at him, her voice accented like his. Clem stiffened as the girl lightly stroked his cheek with her finger. It seemed their lovers' tiff was long since forgotten. 'I always forget how bad it is . . .'

He smiled and their eyes locked, before remembering they had company.

'Fleur, I want you to meet Tom and Clem Alderton of Alderton Hide.'

'A pleasure,' Fleur replied, addressing Tom first and giving Clem the lightest, briefest of handshakes.

Tom moved out of his seat and one along so that Fleur could sit beside the Swimmer. Clem returned to sitting, grateful to relieve her legs of the sudden burden of supporting her, and stared at Fleur in open astonishment and dismay. She was demurely dressed today, a socialite to Clem's rock princess, elegant and understated, a khaki silk shirtdress, discreet Cartier tank watch and taupe patent Ferragamo pumps. Clem practically tutted and looked away at the sight of them. Ferragamo?

She wasn't as tall as Clem, but not much shorter, and she was certainly as slim, although probably with more effort. Her skin was lightly tanned from an olive base and she had bright brown eyes that were milk chocolate to Tom's dark. Her mid-brown hair was expensively tinted with caramel highlights and she had a flitting, skittish way of moving, as though she was as fragile as a butterfly. Clem wanted to kick her.

Humiliation rained down upon her and she stared at her hands in quiet fury. Was that what all this was? She'd made a fool out of him and now he was returning the compliment?

'. . . would like to know what Clem thinks.'

Clem snapped to attention. 'What?'

Everyone was looking at her.

Tom's smile was fixed and stiff. 'Mr Beaulieu was interested in hearing your opinion on the anilines.'

Clem looked over at him. The Swimmer was sitting back in his chair, legs outstretched, his fingers still raised in a steeple. To the rest of the room, his pose was languid and unconcerned, but the expression in his eyes told her differently. The earlier heat had gone and he knew what was running through her mind. He knew what was about to happen.

She stood up abruptly. 'I'm sorry,' she croaked, her voice convincingly weak. 'But I don't feel well. I'm afraid I'm going to have to excuse myself.'

Tom, who'd momentarily looked furious, looked concerned in the next instant. 'You are pale, Clem. Are you OK?'

'I will be,' she mumbled, grabbing her bag. 'I'm so sorry,' she mumbled to Fleur, refusing to meet the Swimmer's eyes again. He'd thought he'd trapped her here, but who was trapped now? 'It was a pleasure meeting you.'

She left without another word, determined not to run. She wouldn't run. But she had to move quickly. In three meetings and less than a hundred words, he had managed something no man ever managed: to upset her.

She saw the Ladies' across the lobby on the right and darted inside, ignoring the women standing by the mirrors, who stared at her as she dashed into a cubicle. She leaned against the wall, her eyes squeezed shut.

Stupid! She'd been so stupid! He'd played her for a fool; he'd been waiting for that moment to happen from the second he'd arrived and had watched every flash of surprise, shock, envy and dismay run across her face. She thought of the nights she'd lain awake thinking about him, re-running their smoke-and-mirrors conversation through her head, the look in his eyes the night of the party and again at the Electric, his candid manner at the christening when he'd put it out there that he wanted her. No bones. Just acceptance of what was inevitable between them. Anticipation.

But she'd pushed him away, effectively laughed in his face, and this was his response. She'd won the battle but he'd win the war. He wasn't going to give Tom the business. He had simply needed a forum to humiliate her, push her back, and they were both going to lose out. Tom was going to be penalized because – yet again – of something she'd done.

Flinging open the cubicle door, she stormed to the basin, opening the taps so fully that water sprayed in the sink and the other women making up their faces had to jump away. Clem didn't care. She splashed cold water on her face over and over, before turning off the taps and leaning heavily on her hands. She stared at herself in the mirror, willing the anger to override the upset. This was nothing. Absolutely nothing. Just a shock . . .

With a deep breath, she pushed herself up and raked her wet hands through her hair.   Then she flung the door open and strode out—

Straight into him. He grabbed her by the elbow and marched her to the opposite wall.

The concierge, alerted by their harried movements, looked up, and – seeing they were clearly lovers – discreetly looked away again.

'Don't.' His voice was quiet and low.

Clem's mouth opened but she couldn't reply. Overwhelmed by his sudden nearness again, the tears she had been so determined she'd never show him were falling, just like that, betraying her to him. She wanted to slap her own face, much less his.

'Don't,' he said, his eyes tracing the tear tracks before coming back to her gaze with sorrow.

'Y – you – are – with her,' she half-hissed, half-hiccupped, furiously wiping her eyes with the heels of her hands. She didn't want his pity.

He released her elbow, reassured she wasn't going to run at least, and put his hand in his pocket. 'Yes.'

Clem tried to laugh, but couldn't quite manage it – instead a strange, strangled sound came from her throat. 'Well, that's great. I'm *thrilled* for you,' she said sarcastically, going to step round him.

But he grabbed her by the arm again and stopped her. 'She's everything you're not. Polite, charming, gracious, elegant . . . dull, predictable, compliant. What am I supposed to do? Break it off because I've seen you a couple of times and we've had one conversation where you couldn't even be bothered to ask my name?' *He* was angry now. 'Ask it. Ask me my name and I'll go back in there right now and break it off with her.'

'What?' She looked at him in astonishment.

'Ask me. I'll do it.'

'No!'

He stepped towards her, so close she almost had to put her hand against him to keep him from advancing. 'Ask.' His breath was warm on her skin and she could smell his cologne – subtle, slightly smoky.

'You're crazy,' she whispered as he stared down at her, robbing her of breath and focus.

'Thanks to you? Yes, quite possibly. You're driving me out of my mind.' His voice was low and urgent, his hand on the wall keeping her close. They hadn't even begun and already there was more, here. That first time, in the party, she'd felt it: that he could see right to the heart of her. For all the eyes that had ever lingered on her (and there had been many) she'd only ever been looked at that way once before, and she knew he could see what other people didn't, looking straight through to the wall that had been bricked up inside her, hidden and hard. But if she let him in, he'd try to pull it down. He had proved today that he would keep on trying.

'*Ask* me.'

The tears fell and she raised her hand to his cheek, one lover to another. Her lips formed the word long before her throat could get the sound out.

'No.'

Chapter Fifteen

Clem was dancing on the bed in her underwear when Stella let herself in an hour later, Florence + the Machine blasting through the flat.

'Oh! Right, *really* sick,' she said sarcastically, leaning on the doorframe and watching as Clem performed a gangly leap, the beer in the bottle in her hand flying through the air and spattering the duvet as she landed. 'Nice.'

'Mmm, saving some for later,' Clem giggled drunkenly, taking another swig. Several bottles – some still unopened – were grouped on the bedside table, another on the floor. 'Want one?'

'We're in double figures, right?' Stella shrugged, briefly checking her watch and picking up the nearest one, opening it swiftly by bringing the heel of her hand down on the bottle top, angled against the bedside table. 'So what happened?'

'Don't know what you mean!' Clem shouted above the music, jumping on the bed so hard it creaked.

'Tom texted me!' Stella shouted back. 'Said you had to leave the meeting 'cos you were so sick.'

'Yeah, I didn't feel so great,' Clem shrugged, pausing her frenetic dance to swig more beer. She stumbled on the bed slightly, her head hanging so that her hair swung, before resuming the frenzied gazelle leaps.

Stella watched her for a moment before crossing the room and removing the iPod from the docking station. Silence filled the room like a gunshot.

'Hey!' Clem protested. 'I was—'

'Out with it. What's going on?'

Clem frowned.

'You and I both know how important that meeting was to Tom,' Stella said patiently, settling herself on the pillows. 'And you and I both know you'd eat your own leg before ever willingly doing anything to upset him. So why did you do a runner? The maths too advanced? Someone gave you Chardonnay?'

Clem sighed and sank down onto the end of the bed. 'I left because of *him*.'

'Him? Tom?' Stella looked puzzled for a moment, before she remembered the enigmatic stranger at the christening. 'Oh Christ, *him*? The Swimmer?'

Clem nodded, almost wincing at the name they'd given him. 'He was the client we were meeting today. He set it all up.'

Stella's eyes brightened and her hand gripped Clem's wrist more tightly. 'And?'

'And his girlfriend pitched up. He did it deliberately.'

The light in Stella's eyes darkened. 'Bastard!'

'Yeah, I mean, seriously? All that hassle just because we've flirted a few times and I knocked him back? Jeez, he needs to get a life.'

'Well, to be honest, hon, there was *way* more going on there than mere flirting! A frickin' blind man could see that. You practically had full sex in that sitting room. Even though you had your clothes on and . . . and didn't actually touch.' She circled the beer bottle around frantically. 'You get my point.'

'I really couldn't give a shit,' Clem replied defiantly, swigging from the bottle again.

'Clearly,' Stella quipped. 'That's why you're wàsted at eleven thirty on a Tuesday morning. I mean, he was only the man who was clearly going to give you the best sex of your life, right?'

'Exactly. Good riddance.'

Stella lapsed into silence, watching her friend carefully as she studied the label on the bottle, a devastated expression settling on her face in repose. 'Are you sure this is about his girlfriend? You've been funny about him since the off.'

'No I haven't.'

Stella arched an eyebrow. 'What's his name?'

Dammit. Clem shrugged slightly. 'Something French.'

'You *still* don't know? You've had a meeting with the guy and you don't know his name?'

Clem tutted and began peeling the beer-bottle label, shredding it and rolling the gluey bits between her fingers.

'I thought so.'

Clem raised her eyes to her friend's. 'What?'

'You're scared.'

'I am not!' Clem was indignant.

'Yeah, you are. If you didn't care about him, you'd have asked it the first time and forgotten it the morning after, just like normal. But you like him.' She gasped as the realization hit. 'You're worried about how much you *already* like him, that's why you're being so weird about it all. You're scared shitless of falling for him.'

'Wrong!' Clem intoned the word, eyes shut, as if it were the strike of a bell.

'Not.' Stella swigged her beer and looked at Clem closely. 'I think you're afraid of falling for him and losing control because you're afraid of falling in love and being happy.'

'No!' Clem protested, frowning furiously.

'That's why you dump guys after three months, *no matter what*, and I don't care what you say – Freddie Haywood was good news for you.'

'Bullshit!'

'Yeah,' Stella said, eyes brightening as she warmed to her theory. 'He made you happy, but that made you scared. You like to be the one calling the shots: they do the loving, you do the leaving. You'd choose a hot one-night stand over a steady relationship any day of the week, and that's not normal, Clem. I'm sorry, but it isn't. You really are the only single twenty-nine-year-old in London who genuinely doesn't want to settle down. For some reason, you're actively seeking the chaos—'

'Stop it!' Clem shouted, startling them both. She had jumped up to standing on the bed again, her legs trying to balance, as if she was popping on a surfboard, her beer-free hand balled into a tiny fist. 'You are categorically wrong. You couldn't be more wrong.'

'You don't usually care if they've got a girlfriend, Clem. You never hang around long enough for it to be a problem. So why are you running away from him?'

'I'm not.'

Stella sighed. 'You walked out of the meeting because his girlfriend pitched up, and you refuse to even find out his name,' she said slowly, as though Clem had been drugged or lobotomized. 'That is running away.'

Clem stared down at her, swaying slightly. 'Fine then! Just to show you how totally, completely and utterly wrong you are, I shall bed the boy. Happy? Will that dispel your hyp . . . hypothemus?'

'Hippopotamus?'

'Stop laughing at me!'

Stella giggled, pulling her legs up too late as Clem swiped a kick at them. 'Good, I'm glad.'

'You should be. I'm only doing it to make *you* happy.'

'And *I'm* only making you do it to make *you* happy.' Stella sat back against the headboard, satisfied by her reasoning as Clem – much drunker – tried to keep up with the twisted logic. 'So you promise you'll call him?'

'Uh-huh. That'll call his bluff. He won't be expecting me to call him after today's little show. Ha! And then I'll . . . I'll treat him just like all the others – good time, goodbye. No special treatment.' Clem inhaled sharply.

'Even if he's effectively your boss?'

Clem shook her head sorrowfully. 'That's not gonna happen. The whole thing was just a ruse to restore his male pride. He was never gonna give Tom the job. I sincerely doubt there even *is* a job.' She went to take another swig of beer, but the bottle was empty.

'Come on, give me that. You've had enough. Go and have a bath and I'll get us some food. You can think about what you're gonna say to luvaboy.'

Clem rolled her eyes, but jumped off the bed and grabbed her dressing gown from the hook on the door. 'Fine. But just so we're both clear, I won that argument,' she said, swaying slightly as she looked back at Stella.

Stella nodded magnanimously. 'Yeah. You did.'

Clem lurched across the sitting room towards the bathroom, rankled. They both knew she hadn't.

They were halfway through the boxset of *Borgen*, two empty, slightly soggy pizza boxes by their feet, when the door downstairs slammed and they both jumped. A small group of people were singing very badly – caterwauling, in fact – as a multitude of feet stomped slowly up the stairs. As they got closer, Tom could clearly be heard leading the group in a rendition of 'Chicago' – the rugger bugger version – as he stopped in the hall and attempted, many, *many* times, to get the key in the door.

'Oh shit, this doesn't sound good,' Clem winced, just as Tom finally succeeded in his quest and fell into the flat holding a cardboard box, closely followed by Simon and Pixie. They were each holding an open bottle of Perrier-Jouët in their hands.

'Champagne?' Stella asked, rather incredulously. 'Have you got something to celebrate?'

'You'd better believe it.' Tom grinned, reaching into the box, pulling out a fresh bottle of fizz and handing it to her. 'We're saved! Alderton Hide is back in business!' He frowned and gave a single hiccup. 'Or do I mean, *staying* in business? Because technically we never actually ceased trading. Things just got pretty s – l – o – w there for a while,' he said, moving in slow motion to make his point.

'Oh my God!' Clem gasped, delighted and clapping her hands excitedly. 'I can't believe it! You did it! You actually did it!'

'That's amazing,' Stella exclaimed, thinking how strange it was, for the second time today, to be the sober one. 'So what's the job?'

'Oh, nothing special,' Tom shrugged. 'Just a . . . mansion and yacht in Portofino!'

'*Portofino?* Fucking A!' Stella grinned, looking over at Clem and giving her a conspiratorial wink. 'Can I come and work for you?'

Portofino?

No!

'Yup. An' it's all thanks to my li'l sister doing what she's best at: batting her eyelashes till the poor client can't even see straight.' Tom staggered over to the sofa, sitting down clumsily on the arm and draping a heavy arm around Clem's shoulders.

She looked up at him, as though bewildered to see him there.

'I've got to hand it to you, sis, you did the right thing cutting and running once his girlfriend arrived,' Tom continued. 'I didn't like the way she was looking at you *at all*. Things became a lot more focused once you left. He couldn't wait to hammer out the details.'

'So it's all confirmed, then? It's definitely going ahead?' Stella asked.

'Signed, sealed and delivered!' Pixie yelled, throwing herself at Simon so that he had to catch her.

Tom turned Clem to face him and tried to look sober, which he couldn't. 'Now look, sis, play safe with this one, OK? I can't say I'm happy about it but' – he held his hands out, shaking his head acceptingly – 'it is what it is. We're all depending on you, so don't stuff it up. Do it for me.' He stood up and brought his hands together in prayer, his eyes closing as the room began to spin, a soppy smile on his face.

'Oh? And why's this all dependent upon Clem?' Stella asked, grinning mischievously at her friend. This was all getting better and better as far as she was concerned.

Tom stared at Stella and tried to focus, but she was an exceptionally long way down. And he was *very* drunk. 'Clem's the project manager on this. The client insisted upon it.' His tone betrayed his bewilderment – even now, several hours later. 'In fact, it was his only condition: carte-blanche budget, but he wants Clem to oversee it all. He says she has a distinctive eye. Or . . . did he say she had distinctive eyes? Anyway, whatever!' He burst out laughing at his joke, before looking across at his sister. 'It's going to mean the summer in Portofino. Will you cope?' he teased.

'No,' Clem whispered, looking up at him.

Tom laughed. 'I know! It's a tough job, but someone's got to do it, right?' He took another swig of the bottle. He smacked his lips together and appraised the three-quarters-drunk bottle. 'Christ knows what I'd do if I didn't have a pretty sister, eh, Simon? We'd be *fucked* if I had to rely on your face pulling in the business.'

Both men fell about laughing, Pixie cooing sympathetically over Simon and telling him he was 'very handsome really'.

'Tom—' Clem said.

'Whatever you do—'

'Oh I think we all have a pretty good idea of what it is they're going to do,' Simon interjected waspishly.

Tom tried to wag his finger at him, but the effort was too much and his hand dropped. He looked back at Clem. 'As I was saying, whatever you do, don't dump him before the project's finished. Wait till after it's done, even if it means going past your "three-month rule".' He made quotation marks in the air with his fingers. 'Or better yet, wait for him to dump you. Huh? Huh? Novel idea, I know.'

'Tom—'

'And more importantly than *anything*,' Tom slurred, almost falling over with the force of his own words. 'Don't let the girlfriend catch you at it. I've got a feeling she's fiercer than she looks,' he said with a sage expression.

'Right, well, that's enough big brotherly advice for one day. Who needs another bottle?'

'Me!' Pixie's and Simon's hands shot up in the air as if it was a spelling test.

'I can't do it.'

The words were so quiet and flat that, for a moment, no one responded. A cork popped and Pixie laughed as Simon tried to lick the foam before it reared out of the bottle.

Tom turned, slowly, and looked at her. 'What?'

Clem stood up and met his eyes pleadingly. 'I can't do this job. I'll do anything for you, you know I will, but just . . . not *there*, not Portofino.'

Silence rang like a bell. He straightened up, greying before her. 'Don't be ridiculous.'

'Tom . . . can we go into a room and talk about this privately, please?'

'No!' he replied in an icy tone. 'What do you mean, you can't do it?'

'It's not something I can talk about here,' she said, her voice getting smaller, her eyes darting from one person in the team to the next. Simon particularly, she thought, looked incandescent, angrier even than Tom.

'Why not? What have you done?' Tom demanded with a wild look. 'Have you gone off him already? Bagged him already, is that it?' He raked a hand through his hair. 'No, no, I know it isn't! I saw what the two of you were like together. That only ever comes *before* with you. You lose interest as soon as you've got them.'

Behind Tom, Clem saw Simon's eyes burning.

'You didn't know he had a girlfriend, is that it?'

'Tom, I—'

''Cos it's not like that's ever stopped you before.'

'It's not that. It's not him.'

He stared at her. 'So what is it, then? Is it because . . .' he racked his brains. 'Is it because you feel like you're being hired out? Is that it? You think I'm *pimping* you?'

His laughter was cold and furious, and a hot, angry tear slid down her cheek. How could Tom do this to her, shout at her in a drunken rage, humiliating her like this?

'Leave her alone, Tom!' Stella said furiously, seeing Clem's distress and pushing herself between the two of them. 'You're drunk and behaving like an arse.'

'Oh! Oh, I'm sorry, Stella,' Tom slurred, smacking his hands on his chest. 'Am I not entitled to celebrate the deal that's just saved my company, all these good people's jobs and *her* flat? Am I not entitled to be a little bit angry that she's going to jeopardize all that for . . . well, we still don't know what for.'

'She has her reasons,' Stella replied staunchly, even though she too had no idea what they might be.

'Oh, I'm quite sure she has. My little sister always does. Her *reasons* determine everything in our family. I've stuck up for her all my life. There's never been a time when I haven't had to wade in and rescue her from a disaster of her own making. But now, now when I need her, when the boot's on the other foot and I ask for something in return – and she says *no*! – I'm just supposed to accept it?'

'I get why you're angry. I do. All I'm saying is, sober up, and talk about it rationally and calmly then. You can see she's upset and you're in a state.'

Tom looked over at his sister, his eyes focusing with pinpoint accuracy suddenly. He looked back at Stella, unmoved. 'I don't care. Not this time,' he said coldly. 'Too many people are depending on this deal to happen. It was the one stipulation, the one caveat that will cancel the deal if she doesn't agree.' He looked at Clem. 'You owe me, Clem. You *will* do this.'

'Tom, please,' she pleaded. 'There are other options. This isn't the only way to save the company. There's . . . there's something else.'

Tom blinked, taking a step back, as though she'd pushed him. 'What do you mean? Is there another client? Have you had an approach?'

Simon snorted furiously, turning away. Stella caught Clem's eye, shaking her head furiously.

Clem, looking anxiously between Tom and Stella, faltered. 'I . . . I can't tell you yet. I'm sorry. It's . . . I promise it will work. Just trust me, please.'

'Give me strength,' Simon muttered, raising his hands and face to the ceiling. 'Trust you? You want me to trust *you*? After everything you did, losing us the Perignard account, Bugatti, the new business from Berlin.' He was counting the disasters on his fingers.

'I get it, Tom! I know it's all my fault. I know I'm a fuck-up! But I just need four days, I promise. And then we won't need this account. Everything will be saved again.'

'How? I've got an open budget on a make-or-break commission that can propel us to the next tier and you want me to believe your *secret* can save the company?' He reached into the champagne box and pulled out some typed sheets that had been stapled together. 'This is a hard-and-fast, signed contract. It's a legal document, and an absolute guarantee of our future. There's a dotted line in it that needs your signature and you *are* going to sign it, Clem.'

'No!' she shouted, trembling with anger now. 'I won't! I don't need to. I'll show you in four days.'

Tom took a step towards her, the contract folding beneath the pressure from his fingers. 'You *will* sign it.'

'Or what?' she demanded, and the air in the flat became electrically charged, tension crackling between the two siblings, who knew exactly how to wage war with each other.

He straightened up, his body rigid. 'Or I will never set eyes on you again.'

The words punched through her, pushing into her muscles and bleeding out like bruises. He threw the contract on the table and strode towards the door.

'You don't mean that!' she called to his back in a wobbly voice.

But when Tom stopped at the door and turned back to face her, she saw that his eyes were reddening, their sorrow showing how true his words were. 'Try me.'

Chapter Sixteen

The clock chimed midnight and Mercy yawned in her chair at the kitchen table.

'OK, try this,' Stella said, holding up one of the rose-pink suede jumpsuits.

Clem, who was only in a T-shirt and knickers anyway, was out of her clothes and wriggling into it in an instant, sighing as the inner velvety pile brushed against her skin. She pulled her hair out from under the stand-up collar and pulled on a pair of grey studded ankle-boots that sent her up to ceiling height.

Everyone cooed at the sight of her: the silhouette was second-skin, with epaulettes on the shoulders, a stand-up collar, press-stud fastenings that could be opened as bare as you dared and lightly stitched knee-pads to guard against bagging. It was triumphant – sexy, cool and luxurious all at once.

'It's the most beautiful thing you've ever made!' Clem gasped, holding her hands to her mouth as she caught her reflection in the window. They were all emotional – exhausted and strung out from three solid days of working round the clock trying to get everything finished in time for the flash sale. The tweets flagging up tomorrow's date as D-day had already gone out and there was an army of women on standby for the follow-up tweet revealing the time and place.

Clem nodded silently as her hand brushed the feather-soft hide over her thigh. They were going to do this thing! With hindsight, Tom locking her out of the office on Wednesday morning had been a blessing. Being so clearly and pointedly determined to avoid her, it had meant Stella could move into the flat without fear of him coming back, and they could work on the final hides full time. She realized now that they'd needed to – there was no way it would have been finished otherwise – and that was *with* Mercy's help. They had made a great team: Mercy's sewing skills were even better than she'd let on, and she did all the technical work with Stella, whilst Clem helped with the design ideas, but was mainly the official model and tea girl.

Thank God the end was in sight. Clem felt close to collapse from both the physical and emotional strain of everything that had happened with Tom; she just couldn't put it out of her mind, was constantly twitchy and nervy, her nails bitten to the quick, and sleep had become something that only happened to other people – like happy endings and job promotions. It was only her steadfast belief in the collection they'd created that was keeping her going.

Still, once these jumpsuits were done, everything would be ready to go: the ivory suede pouch bags, Toscana shearling deerstalkers and belted gilets, two-toned nappa plaited scarves, silk-lined shagreen skinny trousers – again with biker stitching details – mannish blazers cut from the cream skins, and knee-length cardi-coats made from blonde shearling on the body, with jumbo-knit wool arms that Stella had ingeniously knitted on two broom handles. Even the colour palette of chocolate, ivory, caramel, frosted sage green and old rose looked considered, rather than opportunistic, and no one would ever have guessed that most of it had been harvested from factory-floor cuttings.

It had cost nothing but time, and the result was a tight, directional collection that spoke to a refined woman with demanding, high-end tastes. There was nothing here that undermined the Alderton Hide brand, in fact it enhanced it, bringing the company's niche aesthetic down to a personal level. Tom didn't know it yet, but Clem, Stella and Mercy had done him proud. Alderton Hide would be able to continue without compromise – to anyone.

Clem slipped the jumpsuit off and handed it to Stella to snip the remaining threads, while Mercy was finishing the stitching on the oval knee-pads.

'Tea anyone?' Clem asked, pulling her T-shirt over her head and trying to suppress a yawn. She was so tired she felt sure she could sleep on a spike.

Stella looked across at her. Clem was pale and had lost a bit of weight – the back-to-back curries hadn't been enough to assuage her anxieties about Tom's threat. 'Go to bed. We're nearly finished here. There's nothing more you can do. We're going to have to get busy again in the morning getting this place straight.'

'Yeah, well, we won't try too hard on that score. It's not like we want it to sell,' Clem said, looking around at the mess – stray cuts of leather and suede, and miles of coloured thread littered the floor, and there were takeaway boxes piled up on the worktop. The flat looked like hell and it was going to take another team effort to get everything straight and cleared out before the open day started the next morning. Tom had texted to say he'd be over at 10.30 a.m. – his meaning being: be gone by then! – and the most important thing was that the collection was ready to ship out: she had already boxed everything that was loose, like the hats, wrist-warmers and phone covers, and had hung the jackets, gilets and trousers in polythene covers on Stella's collapsible market rails.

'You're sure you don't need me?' Clem asked, feeling guilty, but already walking towards the bedroom.

'Be gone,' Mercy murmured. Her own duvet and pillow were stretched over the sofa in readiness. Once Stella had filled her in on the siblings' tearful showdown, she'd stayed over for the rest of the week, getting her sister to look after her youngest son while they made the final push towards completing the collection.

Clem fell into her bed, barely able to muster the strength to pull the duvet around her. Her hand automatically slid under the pillow, feeling as it always did for the small silk envelope that was the closest thing she had to a security blanket. She reached out to turn off the bedside lamp, her eyes falling on the dust-bagged Birkin sitting on the chair by the door, ready for its guest-of-honour appearance at tomorrow's festivities. The room fell into darkness and sleep began to creep up her body from the toes first, but in those few moments before oblivion won, another emotion started to pool in her stomach – something she was too drowsy to articulate clearly, but which felt akin to fear.

It was Shambles who woke them, screeching to be let out of his cage and almost inducing a heart attack in Stella, who'd been sharing Tom's room with her.

'*Jeezus*,' she muttered, leaning against the doorframe, one hand over her heart, as Clem moaned in the next room and

Mercy snored from the sofa. 'I nearly died . . .' Stella mumbled, rubbing her eyes and pushing her crazy hair back from her face. She was wearing one of Tom's shirts which, in spite of it being a strapping 17½ -inch collar, still strained at the chest.

'What time is it?' Clem moaned indistinguishably, her head under the pillow. 'It's too early.'

'It's . . .' Stella faltered.

Silence descended upon the flat once again and, deep in her feather-filled vacuum, Clem wondered whether her friend had fallen asleep standing up. Reluctantly lifting her head, she pushed the pillow off and looked up to find Stella – mouth agape – pointing at the clock on the far wall.

They were late, that much was instantly apparent. Clem jumped out of bed and ran to the door. Ten past ten.

'No!' Clem gasped, looking around at the flat, which looked more like a landfill site at that particular moment. 'Mercy, wake up!' she cried. 'Tom's going to be here in twenty minutes.'

Within seconds, all three women were standing in a frozen panic in the centre of the room.

'There's no way we'll get this cleared in time,' Clem wailed, her fingers tightly bunching the hair by her temples. How could they have overslept, today of all days?

Stella took charge. 'Mercy, you clean up. Hoover first, it'll look a whole lot better when the floor's clear. And stuff all the cuts into a bin bag with the curry boxes. Clem, you and I need to get these clothes outta here.'

'Right,' Clem nodded, grateful for the orders and dashing back into the bedroom to pull on some ribbed leggings and a sloppy joe.

Stella didn't even bother. She just pulled on a pair of

Tom's hooped rugby socks under her Uggs and a parka, and started carrying the boxes down the stairs.

'What are you doing? We can't leave them there,' Clem cried as Stella started piling them up in a perilous tower behind the front door. 'Tom'll see them.'

'Yes, but why would he think they're anything to do with us?' Stella replied calmly. 'They could belong to any of the other flats. He'll just walk straight past them. So long as they're not in your flat, it'll be fine.'

'Yes, yes, you're right, OK,' Clem nodded, adding her own box to the tower and following Stella back up the stairs.

Mercy was hoovering in her bra again – Mrs Crouch had become as accustomed to that as she was to seeing Clem in the buff – whilst spraying some of Tom's deodorant around her head. 'Best I could manage to get rid of the curry smells.' She shrugged.

Clem quickly opened all the windows and turned the oven onto preheat, throwing a par-baked baguette in for good measure, before trotting back downstairs with the other boxes.

'Oh God, Stella, how are we going to get rid of the hanging rails?' Clem asked as they cleared the floorspace of boxes. 'That's not a quick job.'

'It is for me.' Stella winked. 'I'll dismantle them if you put the clothes in that big box there. We'll have to steam everything later if needs be.'

'Right,' Clem nodded, grabbing great armfuls of jumpsuits and coats, jackets and trousers, and stuffing them into a box in the corner. 'Where's the masking tape?' she demanded, panicking, as Mercy crawled around her feet, picking up the irregular snippets of coloured hides.

'Mind my fingers!' Mercy muttered, slapping Clem on the ankles.

A slam downstairs made them all freeze on the spot and the sound of Tom swearing as he walked into one of the boxes drifted under the door. He was early. They were out of time. They were about to be caught red-handed! Clem hurriedly folded down the flaps of the box and hoisted it up in her arms protectively.

'Hi,' Tom said tersely ten seconds later, Clover hanging behind him like a shadow, her hand tightly gripping his.

Stella, who had dismantled the hanging rail but was still holding it, leaned against it casually, pulling her parka closed so that he wouldn't notice she'd slept in his clothes. 'Hey, Tom! How's it going?' she asked, as though it was such a surprise to see him there.

Tom didn't reply. He was transfixed by the sight of Mercy vigorously polishing a side table in just her leopard-print bra. Again. 'Does she ever get dressed?'

Stella shrugged.

Clem swallowed hard as she waited for Tom's eyes to find her. She was all but hidden behind the enormous box in her arms and she felt as though her heart was going to leap out of her chest. She was standing in front of him, carrying a box filled with clothes, made from the leather that should have lined the walls of an upscale jeweller off Bond Street. There was no getting out of this. If he lifted the flap of the box, she was done for.

His eyes, when they met hers, were cold and unresponsive, and she flinched to see his anger still so ready. The contract remained unsigned.

'You said you were going to get this place sorted for today,' he snapped. 'It stinks of curry and . . . cheap aftershave.'

'I'm sorry, I—'

'Had a party?' he finished for her, walking further into the flat, his nose wrinkled in distaste. 'Yeah, tell me something I don't know.'

Clover drifted in serenely, practically floating an inch off the floor. Her day had come. It was a wonder she wasn't wearing a tiara. Without a word, she walked into Tom's room and retrieved the smelly scented sticks, arranging them artfully on the sitting room table before plumping up the cushions on the sofa and refolding the blanket draped across the back. Before everyone's eyes, the flat began to morph from workshop to home again.

'What's that smell?' Tom asked, wrinkling his nose as the distinct aroma of something burning wafted through from the kitchen.

'Oh shit!' Clem cried, dropping the box and running to the oven. She pulled out the baguette, now so carbonized it could hatch a diamond, and pulled a face. 'Dammit. I was trying to make the flat smell of freshly baked bread.'

Tom rolled his eyes in exasperation. 'Quite frankly, the most useful thing you could do would be to get the hell out of here and let us deal with everything. I should have known it would be beyond you to get this sorted. People will start arriving in twenty minutes,' Tom said coldly.

'I did tell you she'd try to jeopardize it for you,' Clover said quietly, taking the duster and can of Pledge from Mercy's hands and throwing her deep cleavage a look of distaste. 'Thank God we got here early.' She began polishing the windowsill.

'That is not what I was trying to do. I was trying to help!' Clem snapped, the blackened, smouldering bread still in her hand.

'Well, Tom's just told you how you can be most helpful.' Clover smiled, nodding over her shoulder towards the door.

Clem considered throwing the baguette at her; it was so hard it might cause concussion, fingers crossed.

'Come on, Clem,' Stella said quickly, reading her thoughts and gathering the dismantled hanging rails, quickly binding them together with the masking tape so that she could carry them in one load. 'We need to get on anyway.' Pinning Clem with a stern look, she gestured with her eyes to the discarded box which was still untaped and had one of the flaps hanging open where Clem had dropped it, a pink suede sleeve clearly visible through the gap.

'Yeah . . . you're right. We're just getting under your feet here,' Clem acquiesced too readily, causing Clover to narrow her eyes suspiciously. Clem picked up the box and hurriedly closed it. 'See you later then,' Clem mumbled, moving towards the door.

'And thanks for tidying your room. Appreciate it,' Tom said sarcastically, seeing her bed unmade, the curtains still drawn, clothes heaped like bonfire piles.

'Oh! God, I almost forgot,' she said, doubling back on herself and squeezing past Tom to grab the Birkin, which was still sitting quietly in its bright orange Hermès dust bag.

'Why are you taking that?' Tom queried as she laid it across the box. He took an interested step towards her, reaching for the bag.

Clem jumped away in alarm. If he so chose, he'd be able to see straight into the box. 'Why wouldn't I take it, Tom? It is my fucking bag! It's supposed to be used.' Attack seemed to be the best form of defence, and it worked – Tom flinched at her words and hung back – but Clover, who'd been leaning against the windowsill, watching them, straightened up suddenly. 'What's in that box?' she asked, as though detecting a plot amidst the burnt offerings and synthetic pheromones. 'And why've you got those rails, Stella?'

Clem and Stella looked at each other in panic. For once, both women were out of ideas and words.

'She was showing Clem the new collection. Is that OK, your highness?' Mercy interjected, coming to their rescue.

'Your high—?' Clover gasped. 'Tom! Are you going to let her talk to me like that?'

'I am not,' Tom replied with impressive indignation. 'Apologize this instant.'

'No.' Mercy folded her arms – just – over her chest and waited.

Tom looked unsure of what to do next. Usually someone of her girth would get rugby tackled, but being a woman . . .

'Well, it doesn't surprise me in the least,' Clover said after a minute, as Tom stammered himself into silence. 'Good manners are the last thing I'd expect from a woman who can't even be bothered to be *clothed*. The mind boggles at what her previous job entailed if she strips off this easily.'

'You just be jealous,' Mercy retorted, but her cheeks had reddened and her bosom was trembling impressively with suppressed rage.

'Hardly,' Clover quipped witheringly.

An explosive silence boomed through the room, emotions crashing against the walls and rebounding in again. Everyone was red-cheeked and edgy, anger and irritation beginning to bubble in a caustic mix.

Clem saw a new expression bloom on Clover's face suddenly as she stared down at Mercy. 'You know, Tom,' she said thoughtfully. 'Don't you think it's odd that things have only started going missing since she started working here? I mean, you never did find that Hermès tie or those bone cufflinks, did you?'

Clem's eyes widened in horror. 'Now hang on a minute!' she roared. 'You can't go round making accusations like that! Tom's always bloody losing things.'

But Tom blinked, looking across at Mercy, and Clem could see the seed had been planted.

'You checked her references, didn't you? You told me you did.'

Clem swallowed. She had meant to, but time had just slipped past and . . . She could see Mercy staring at them all in horror.

'You *didn't*?' he asked; he knew her far too well. 'Jesus, Clem! She could be anyone!'

'But she isn't! I know Mercy, she's a mate now. There's no way she would ever steal from us. Never.'

'You can't be sure of that!' Tom shouted. 'You've opened up our home to a stranger off the street.'

'Well, there's one way to solve this. I'm sure Mercy won't mind showing us the contents of her bag,' Clover said snidely, grabbing for the bag in Mercy's hands.

'Don't you dare!' Clem screamed, dropping the box on the sofa and lunging for the bag herself.

'If she's got nothing to hide—' Clover sneered.

'There's a tie knotted round the headboard in your room – I left it there as I assumed it was some kinky game you played and I didn't want to *embarrass* you by removing it. I don't know if that's the one you talking 'bout.' Mercy's voice was quiet and dignified, causing Clem and Clover to fall still. 'As for them cufflinks, there's a pair at the bottom of the birdcage, but I'm not opening it to get them out. No, I'm not. I don't do birds. I said that from the off.' She folded her hands across her chest.

Tom's mouth fell open and he had the decency to blush. Clem snatched the bag out of Clover's hands once and for all, glaring at her. 'Bitch!' she hissed with deadly fury.

'Let's get out of here,' Stella said authoritatively, grabbing Mercy's blouse and herding her towards the door. Clem followed after, the cardboard box and Birkin back in her arms again. She staggered down the stairs, unable to see her feet, and dropped the box on the floor by the street door just as Mercy burst into tears.

'So damn *pushy* . . .'

'I know, I know, pushy as fuck, she is,' Clem said, giving her a hug and feeling just as exhausted as she had the night before. She looked down at the beautiful clothes they'd made, the stunning collection that was going to save Tom's dreams in the next few hours. But in the wake of all these accusations and slanders, she couldn't help but wonder if it was worth the effort any more.

Chapter Seventeen

'Top right, up a bit,' Stella ordered as Clem reached higher. 'Perfect.'

Clem pushed the blu-tack further into the wall and stood back. The huge black and white image of her wearing the Toscana shearling gilet, her belted waist looking tiny as she playfully swung from the branch of a birch tree, dominated the end wall, the one positioned beneath the roof lantern, which everyone would see as they entered the room. She was pretty pleased with it, with all of the posters actually. Six other images were pinned around the long room, showing her in the different collection pieces – even the shagreen phone covers looked covetable when held in her hands, the wind blowing her hair across her cheeks, her eyes making contact with the lens, reportage-style.

They weren't the best quality obviously. They'd had to squeeze the shoot in with everything else that needed doing – Stella taking the pictures of Clem in Hyde Park quickly yesterday morning, then taking the file into the one-hour-photo place, which could turn around poster-prints in twenty-four hours – but if the images lacked sharpness, they more than succeeded in encapsulating a sensual, luxe mood and a vision of a modern, urban woman. The Alderton Hide woman. Even Clem, who was pretty lacka-daisical about her reflection, thought they were cool.

Clem planted her hands on her hips and scanned the room for the next thing to do – the past week had been spent at 'frantic' level, but it seemed, incredibly, that they were good to go. Music was pumping from the speakers and the staff at Electric House were busy whisking up cocktails behind the long bar. The venue was perfect: discreet and in-the-know only. The idea of using the private members' club had come to Clem in the middle of the night, after weeks of fretting about occupying empty commercial premises. The last thing she needed was to get arrested and for Alderton Hide's name to appear in the press for all the wrong reasons! The fact that she had known the manager since nursery school days meant one phone call had seen her request bumped to the top of the pile, and the second-floor playroom had been cleared for her for three hours over lunch as a 'discretionary favour to a local business'.

'Do you want to do the honours?' Stella asked, holding out her phone, the cursor on the Twitter page blinking at her.

Clem bit her lip and typed: *'Playroom @ Electric House, Portobello Road. Now. #Aldertonhideflashsale #shootingstarbirkinauction.'* She pressed 'send' and blinked up at Stella. 'That easy, huh?'

'That easy.' Stella grinned back.

They came in droves. Within twenty-five minutes, the room was packed and the staff were forced to close the doors, citing fire regulations, leaving a growing swell of women trapped outside.

The music was turned down and Stella took to the mic, standing on a table so that everyone could see her.

'Hey, ladies!' she called out with all the confidence of

someone who spent her days giving patter on a market stall, and the din of excited chatter mellowed to hear her. 'Congratulations! You only beat half of London to be here right now!' A delighted cheer rang out. They were a club within a club. The cachet couldn't have been greater! 'Today, quite possibly for the only time *evah*, we are auctioning a unique capsule collection, crafted from the very finest leathers and suedes that Alderton Hide is renowned for. I'm sure lots of you already have a little Alderton Hide in your life – a wardrobe maybe, or a desk? And even if you don't, you will already know and love the quality, colours, finishes and design, or you wouldn't be here now! But today is all about pieces for *you*. A one-off, one-time only, now-you-see-it-now-you-don't opportunity.' A collective intake of breath betrayed the women's nerves. They weren't just in shopping mode; they were in sale shopping mode – the most dangerous of all shopping forms – it was just as well there wasn't a man in sight. 'And to show you how the collection should be worn, here is none other than the Alderton Hide brand ambassador herself, Clem Alderton.' Another wall of sound rose up, and the talking intensified as some of the women pointed to the images of Clem looking like a Julie Christie redux on the walls. 'Yep, that's her! Isn't she gorgeous?'

Clem stood behind the kitchen door and squeezed her eyes shut as she heard the buzz grow with Stella's commentary. She had changed into the skinny shagreen biker trousers, pairing them with gunmetal-grey ankle boots and a distressed T-shirt, and she rubbed her hands together nervously. What if everyone hated the clothes? What if she and Stella had got it all wrong, become carried away because of one lucky day on the stall? What if she got out there and everyone just . . . laughed? Walked away? Didn't bid?

'. . . it up for Clem!' Stella cried.

Clem stepped out, trying to hide her nerves as she took in the sea of intrigued women staring back at her and clapping excitedly. Mercy, who was manning the iPad, winked at her as Stella held out her hand and pulled Clem up onto the table, so that everyone could see her.

Clem took a deep breath and did a small twirl, feeling faint with nerves and completely ridiculous as 230 pairs of eyes settled upon her like bees to honey. What had they been thinking? They'd been mad to think this would work.

'Thanks, babes,' Stella said, squeezing her shoulder encouragingly as she came to a stop. She, at least, was enjoying herself – her delivery was upbeat and intimate, her energy infectious. Everyone was straining to get a good look at Clem's clothes. 'So, as you can see, girls, these skinny trousers are cut in the shagreen leather, which has a gorgeous iridescent effect – *so* much cooler than python print. They've got front slash pockets to keep a really lean line and we positioned the pockets on the back pointing in slightly' – she turned Clem around by the shoulders – "cos it just makes the bum look smaller, you know? Not that Clem has to worry about that, the skinny bitch!' Stella grinned, swatting her playfully on the behind. Everyone laughed. 'They're fully lined in aqua silk to retain their shape, and the stitch detailing on the knees also helps with that; they're dry clean only, *obvs*, and we've got six pairs – two in small, two in medium, two in large. They come up small, but buy true to size as they're supposed to be tight. And if you like them, there's also a blazer in the same hide coming up later. So . . . that's the boring stuff out of the way.

Let's start shopping! We'll begin with the small size first, who'll start me at £225? That's cost price, girls. Cost.'

A quiver of hands shot into the air and Clem swallowed, wondering whether to do another twirl. Everyone was talking to each other, their eyes on her. She usually didn't mind attention – she was pretty used to it – but this was a different league altogether.

Stella rose the bids in £25 increments and Clem dutifully stood in various poses, sometimes standing with her back to the room so they could examine the rear of the trousers. She quite liked it, even though it meant everyone was scrutinizing her backside, as it gave her a break from all the stares and she could look out the window to the street below. A crowd had begun to gather and people were standing in the market looking up at her standing clearly in the window. She saw Katy, filming her on her phone, and she waved down to her. The crowd cheered in response as if she was a rock star. Word was spreading. A taxi couldn't get through and some cyclists had to dismount to wheel their bikes through the crowd.

The trousers – all six pairs – went for a combined total of £3,140, and Clem climbed off the table to quickly dash back to the 'changing room' and put on the belted blonde gilet with her plum-coloured Mother jeans and a matching thin polo neck.

This time, when she stepped out, there was an audible gasp. Appetites had been whetted and everyone's desire was up. They literally wanted the clothes off Clem's back. She smiled as she did her turns again, beginning to pop her hip a bit and enjoy herself. Bidding was getting faster and more intense, the buzz of chitchat fading away as the women became more focused and competitive. The sale was on!

The five gilets brought in £4,620, the eleven deerstalkers £320 each, the ivory pouch bags practically inciting a riot as they went for £540 each. By the time Clem was zipping up the rose-pink jumpsuit, the finale piece of the collection, they had raised £16,780. There were five jumpsuits, which would surely go for almost a grand a piece, and there was still the Birkin to go . . . Tom needed £100,000 to keep the business going for the next four months. The starting bid for the bag was £50,000, but they'd need to get over £75,000 for it to clear the numbers they needed. She closed her eyes and prayed, psyching herself up for the finale. This had to be big . . .

She stepped round the corner and the crowd screamed – actually screamed – when they caught sight of the lean, rose jumpsuit. Stella and Mercy burst out laughing, giving each other high-fives and doing small rain dances – or money dances – on the spot.

'Now, girls,' Stella crooned once she'd calmed herself down. 'You might not be able to see from where you're standing, but there's a *huge* crowd on the street outside, trying to get into this sale, and we're going to need to wind this up soon if we don't want the police to break us up for causing a public disturbance.' A medley of boos peppered the room. 'I know! Right? We're only shopping . . .' Stella laughed. 'So, you don't need me to break this down too much for you. It speaks for itself: rose-pink jumpsuit made from a suede that's more supple than Madonna – and I reckon the animal it came from had a better skincare regime, too. It's *so* soft. We've got five of these babies, three small, one medium, one large.' She put her hands up. 'Don't shoot the messenger. That was how the patterns broke down off the hides. So, cost price is £580, but we're gonna start at

£700, because owning this beauty is a once-in-a-lifetime opportunity, and you may well never get the chance to wear Alderton Hide on your backs again. Who's in?'

The entire room seemed to move as one. Clem's eyes rode them like waves, giddy with delight. She had been right. She had been right after all and Tom had been wrong. There was an entire market out there, untapped. She knew what women wanted, and she'd given it to them in the most difficult of scenarios. If she could create this kind of clamour with a flash sale and off-cuts, imagine what she could do with a boutique and a budget! When she gave Tom the cheque this afternoon and showed him the film of the sale and the posters that branded the Alderton Hide woman, could he continue to deny the logic? This was where the company's future lay – at least in part.

Her mind wandered as the all-but-last bids of the day hailed in, and she wondered how the open day was going. The thought of legions of people trooping through her flat as Clover literally keened with anticipation made her stomach turn, but it was a necessary evil. It had kept Tom out of the way and facilitated this sale happening.

The final jumpsuit was being bid for now, and Clem tuned back in as shouts accompanied the head nods and hand waves. Everything was reaching fever pitch and numbers ceased to have any monetary meaning as they climbed higher and higher. This was the only thing left, and the bidding seemed to be between two women. Clem tried to track them with her eyes, but it was hard in such a dense, agitated crowd with the bids moving so quickly.

'Sold!' Stella hollered, pointing at a girl towards the back – the girl held her hand up so that one of the Electric House staff could reach her with a sales ticket.

Clem clapped weakly – she hadn't even heard the final sales price, but she knew it was staggering – as the Birkin bag was quickly slipped out of its dust bag and passed to Clem to hold up for everyone to admire.

Stella indicated for calm with her hands. The room fell into an awed silence and suddenly they could hear a commotion outside. Clem wondered whether the police had indeed arrived, or whether that had just been a sales ploy by Stella to unleash riotous spending.

'And now, the final moment of today's event: you can see as clearly as I can that this isn't an Alderton Hide product. But it is the *very item* that inspired Tom Alderton to found his company in the first place. It comes from another prestigious house that shares the same values of quality and integrity, and which inspired Alderton Hide to design, in turn, their own such legacy. Girls, this is no ordinary Birkin . . .'

A murmur of lust rippled over the room and Clem stared at the bag, inviolate now on a velvet cushion, high above the madding crowd. Her mother's cherished gift, given by her father as a token of love . . .

No – she blinked hard – it was just a bag. Passed on to her for the worst of all reasons. The room shifted and she realized she hadn't eaten yet: Shambles' brutal alarm call had led straight on to frenzied activity, and two Mojitos had passed as brunch. She needed some sugar.

'This bag is what we call a Shooting Star bag, identifiable by the said emblem stamped below the logo. What *is* a shooting star bag?' Stella grinned, cupping her ear. 'I'm glad you asked! It's a tradition at Hermès that every year, one top craftsman is allowed to make a bag for his own personal use. In this instance, Tom Alderton's father, who was on honeymoon at the time, happened to meet one such craftsman and negotiated to buy it for his new wife. You cannot buy these on the open market, ladies, that's what makes these such covetable and collectable bags. But be warned, Hermès does not like these bags passing out of the care of the person that made them, and don't even *think* about taking it into an Hermès boutique to be refreshed. They won't do it, so look after it well. Now, I'm sure you all know that to buy a Birkin today, any old, basic entry-level Birkin, would involve a two-year wait and £5,000. *This* flawless specimen, however, this piece of fashion history, is going to sell today, here and now. It's in the 40cm size, and is made in black saltwater crocodile leather, one of the most prized Hermès leathers. It *should* have a matching black goatskin interior – all Birkins match inside and out – but . . . oh! Oh! What's this?' Stella grinned, nodding for Clem to hold the bag open so that everybody could see inside. 'It's got the Hermès orange interior, an individual touch that's the preserve of the Shooting Star bags and alone is worth fifteen grand! It's just another rare nugget that helps to explain why the starting bid, and this isn't the reserve amount but the *starting* bid, is fifty – thousand – pounds.'

A reverential hush fell again. Precious few people in the country, much less this room, could afford to spend those numbers on a bag, even one as rare as this, but Clem couldn't hear anything but the sound of her own blood rushing in torrents through her head. They would understand. When she handed the cheque over, they would all understand. It was for Tom. It was just a bag.

'Thank you. Fifty-five?'

Just patches of crocodile leather sewn together, by hand. Just a bag.

'Sixty?'

Most people were more excited by the orange carrier anyway. That bag.

'Seventy?'

Her palms felt sweaty, and she went to wipe them on her thighs, before remembering – just in time – that she was still wearing a suede jumpsuit that now belonged to *someone else*.

The commotion downstairs had moved up – so quickly? It had to be the police – and was now in the corridor outside. Clem looked over at Stella, urging her to hurry up. If the police walked in before she'd sold the Birkin, everyone would be disbanded and they'd be without the major portion of today's funds. It wouldn't be enough without the bag.

Stella was unruffled. 'Final bid, going for ninety-five thousand : . .' Stella looked calmly round the room, even as the doors began to rattle.

Clem held her breath.

'Sold!' Stella cried, pointing to the winning bidder just as the door at the far end burst open and the seal on their rarefied vacuum was punctured.

'I told you!' Clover cried, pointing at Clem standing on the table at the far end of the room. 'I knew she was up to something. Thank God Peony's friends tweeted me.'

The room fell silent and a pathway naturally opened up as the sea of women took in Stella, Clem and Mercy's stares tethered to the small invading party.

'Look, Tom, didn't I tell you I saw something pink in that box?' Clover continued, pointing at Clem as she led the march up the room.

Tom? Tom Alderton? He was good-looking enough to be

known by a fair few of the women in the room through lavish editorial features and local reputation. There was a murmur of unease and discomfit as they took in his evident displeasure.

Tom didn't move. He was as rooted to the spot as a fifty-year-old oak, his eyes darting between the images of his sister on the walls and the vision of her before him, wearing skins he recognized only too well. Furrowed brows began to knit, as everyone stared with growing comprehension at Clem's illicit pink jumpsuit and Tom's sickened expression.

Stealthily the women began to hug the tissue-wrapped goodies closer to their bodies, slipping silkily from the room one by one.

Clover realized what was happening first. 'Stop! Don't anyone leave until we've ascertained exactly what's been happening here,' she ordered imperiously. 'This is copyright infringement.'

But her words had the opposite effect to what she'd intended and the women suddenly rushed for the doors, the room emptying like an upturned milk bottle, expelling shoppers in pulsing, chugging beats. No one was returning anything.

Tom didn't move. He didn't try to stop them. He wouldn't make a scene. Enough damage had been done.

Without taking her eyes off him, Clem jumped off the table, landing lightly two metres from him.

'*This* was the secret. And it was a success, Tom,' she said quietly, hands held up in appeasement. She gestured lightly towards the posters. 'We didn't damage the brand, we preserved your vision, your quality.'

Silence.

'They *loved* it, Tom. This is a new avenue for the company. If you could just have seen it. We could have sold ten times the amount . . .'

Silence.

Someone – Stella? – cleared their throat. 'The final total was one hundred and thirty-eight thousand, plus some change,' she murmured in the smallest voice Clem had ever heard from her, pushing a list of the total sales into Clem's hand.

'D'you hear that?' Clem whispered. 'It's enough, Tom. Enough to keep going. You don't need to sell the flat now.'

A ripping sound made her break eye contact, and she saw Clover tear one of the posters in half with a look of unconcealed fury.

Clem looked back at her brother, more worried by his calm than Clover's anger. 'Say something. Please.'

'How did you make that much?' he asked finally, his voice a shade of its usual depth.

Relief flooded her. 'The collection – we've been working day and night on it for weeks, months in fact. It's all from off-cuts and . . .' She hesitated, not wanting to drop Simon in it. For everything else he was guilty of, he'd kept her secret at least. '. . . and those Perignard hides that were just s–sitting around in the factory.'

He blinked slowly at her words, as though each one was a stab wound.

'How did you make *that* much?' he repeated, his teeth gritted as though it was taking considerable effort to get the words out and stay still.

Clem felt the world wobble. This wasn't about his name? 'I . . .'

He raised an eyebrow and waited, and she realized he knew. He just wanted to hear her say it.

'It was just a bag,' she whispered. 'The money's all that matters. I thought you'd be pleased.'

He turned his face away.

'I did it for you, Tom,' she pleaded, moving towards him. 'You have to believe that. Look.' She held out the sales tally towards him. 'It's all yours.'

Tom stopped and looked at it, the large number written in vivid black looping script, written with joy and happiness. He reached for it slowly and Clem felt herself inhale again. OK then.

He ripped the sheet of paper twice, letting it fall to the ground like confetti.

'You disgust me,' he said. 'It was never just a bag, and you know it.'

He walked back towards the door and Clem saw, for the first time, the tall couple standing in the doorway, heads bowed but shoulders back. Her mother was holding her father for support and her skin looked grey and slack.

'Mum,' Clem faltered, feeling the walls of her world begin to fold in on her. 'I can explain . . .'

Her mother's eyes, usually like liquid fire, met hers, and the depth of betrayal reflected in them was like a fathomless blue pool. Her father – beloved Daddy – wouldn't even look at her. Clem felt the words leave her as the door swung shut on them and they left her behind.

Stella came up and threw her arms around her. 'You were just trying to do the right thing,' Stella soothed her, squeezing her hands vigorously.

'But I've made it even *worse*.'

'They'll calm down.' Stella hushed her. 'Give them time; they'll see your motives were pure.'

Clem shook her head, panic beginning to over-ride her.

'No. He'll never talk to me again. You saw him that night. You *know* he meant it. He's going to cut me out for good.' Her breathing was shallow and rapid, her shoulders pulled up, trying to get more air into her lungs. 'Wh–wh–what am I going to do?'

Stella bit her lip, looking pained by her friend's distress. 'I don't know, babes.'

A terrified sob escaped Clem – Stella always knew! Stella always had a plan! – and she hid her face in her hands as the tears wracked her exhausted, nervous frame. It had been her winning hand. There was nothing after this.

Another hand – warmer, plumper – settled on her shoulder like a dove bringing peace, and Clem looked into Mercy's big, sympathetic eyes.

'I do,' Mercy murmured. 'But you're not going to like it.'

PORTOFINO

Chapter Eighteen

'Tell me it's raining.'

Clem looked out of the car window and tapped back:

'Resolutely not raining. Sky like topaz.'

'Ever occurred to you to lie? Chucking it down here. Sky like bin.'

'Fine. Can't wait to get there.'

'Now you're getting the hang of it.'

'Feeling buoyant and perky.'

'Bravo, there you go. For my part, I'm delighted to see the back of you.' Clem gave a small smile at that. Stella had wept at the airport like the mother of a gapper going backpacking in Iran. *'Where are you now?'*

'In the knee of Italy with the sea on my right.'

'Gotcha. It's lovely there.'

'The water is bright green.'

'Algae problem? Abort mission. Repeat abort.'

'Aquamarine green. Stunning.'

'We've talked about this. Lie dammit.'

'Miss you already.'

'Me neither. Laters.'

Clem smiled and stared out of the window as they drove into yet another mountain tunnel. It was just as well Tom wasn't here. He couldn't – literally couldn't – drive through a tunnel without holding his breath; he'd be hypoxic by now.

Not that there'd been any chance of him coming with her. He and her parents were stonewalling Clem, on top of him having moved out of the flat and firing her outright. She had managed to reverse that decision when she'd shown him her signature on the contract's precious dotted line, but he'd still banned her from the office, and she wasn't fooling herself that her employment was anything other than a technicality. He needed her to do this commission, because he needed this commission to save the company, but once that contract was fulfilled . . . He had finally done what she feared most and turned his back on her, and as much as she didn't want to be anywhere near Portofino, without Tom or her father there was actually no reason to stay in Portobello. Her roots had been wrenched up through the familiar concrete pavements and cast adrift to the gentle Mediterranean bob, with only Stella in her pocket for company.

The car came to a smooth stop and was opened a moment later by Luigi, the uniformed driver.

'Signorina Alderton, welcome to Italy,' a man said as she emerged. 'I am Stefano. I work for Signor Beaulieu.' He was the same height as her, with a stocky build, mariner's tan and the uniform of the staff of the rich: a pale blue polo shirt, tan chino shorts and deck shoes.

'Hi,' Clem nodded, shaking his hand lightly, her eyes scanning the marina. Massive gin palaces, some four storeys high, cast them in shadow, as crew slopped water over teak decks and hosed down fibre-glass walls.

Where were they? They had passed the sign to Portofino, pointing right, several miles back, but had driven on to this large town that sheltered a wide, shallow bay. 'I thought we were going to Portofino?'

'We are,' Stefano smiled. Luigi walked past them demonstrating admirable strength as he transferred her many bags from the car. She was never one to pack light, much less in these circumstances. 'But Signor Beaulieu's house is not accessible by land with luggage. This is the town of Rapallo. We will travel the rest of the way by boat,' he said, gesturing to a mahogany motorboat moored behind him.

A Riva? Oh, Tom!

'This is Alberto,' Stefano said, motioning to a similarly clad man holding the wheel as he held out his hand to help her step down into the boat. It was breathtakingly beautiful, with a sunbathing area on the back and seats upholstered in the palest Tiffany-blue leather.

'Is this a new model?' she asked, embarrassed to see her bags took up the entire back row of seats.

'It's a 1964 Super Aquarama. One of only two hundred and three made.'

'Huh.' Of course it was. She settled down on the seat and fished in her bag for her aviators, tightening the grey scarf at her neck. It was always colder on the water, even on a day such as this, with a deepening blue sky and spreading sun. Stefano cast the mooring ropes and hopped onto the boat as it pulled away from the jetty, the boat pivoting as smoothly as a train on a turning circle.

'You might want to hold on to your hat, signorina,' Alberto said, pulling back slowly on the throttle. 'She can get up to fifty-two knots.'

Clem took her panama off and held it tightly between her knees. A few people had stopped to watch, looking on enviously as the boat purred into deeper waters and pointed her nose to the small, craggy, tree-topped promontory of Portofino.

They sped over the water as if it were glass, and Clem angled her face to feel the sun on her skin, trying not to overthink or overfeel. She had spent the entire plane journey formulating her action plan for getting through this, and it was a simple one: she would just live in *this* moment, the present one, with no thought of what was before or behind her. No Tom, no Swimmer, no . . . So right now, she was determined to be conscious only of the wind, the sun, gentle bumps beneath them as they sliced through other boats' wakes.

Gulls wheeled and cried overhead, blotting her with their pinprick shadows, and she opened her eyes as they moved deeper into the bay; the headland that Portofino tipped beginning to hook around them like an arm, drawing them closer. Her eyes skimmed the old towns and villages that had embedded themselves in the cliffs like fossils, the buildings all painted in an undulating, sun-baked palette of ombre, melba pink and taupe. As they drew closer to land, she could see that many of the buildings – villas, churches – were striped, some in thin spaghetti strips, others with wide blocks of colour, like layered ice cream. Most of the roofs were tiled with classic terracotta peg, but the grander ones had bleached grey slate tiles, intricately laid like overlapping fish scales and topped with statuary pineapples.

As they sped closer still, the vista sharpened into deeper clarity and she began to see the lives being lived there – a market was stretched along the promenade of one town and she could make out busy shoppers, tall dotted orange trees, sheets hanging over balconies, rows of scooters. Mediterranean life. Her life, for a summer. A summer she was determined to live just one moment at a time. Determined to.

She scanned the coastline with barely suppressed desperation. He was in there somewhere. Where was he?

Clem looked up at the cliffs that rose in jagged tusks on three sides around them as Alberto cut the engine and the boat drifted into the tiny bay on its forward momentum. Stefano jumped on to a slab of rock that had been concreted flat and secured the mooring ropes. Clem reached over and stared down into the still-cool water that lapped gently against the boat. Several feet below, domed rocks glowed bright white, and combined with the speckled shadows thrown down by the umbrella canopies of the cypress trees, the inlet was mottled with vibrant patches of turquoise, cerulean, peacock blue and bone.

She looked around the enchanting cove. It seemed to be the only access to the small shingled beach, just a few feet wide, with a jetty and the steps beyond it that must lead to the house. It was privately owned, clearly, with nothing on it but the wide double doors of a boat shed that looked neglected – the dark green paint was flaking and one of the small glass panes was cracked.

Stefano offered her his hand again and Clem stepped onto the platform as Alberto began the unfortunate task of unloading her bags.

'Follow me, please,' Stefano said, leading her up the stretch of steep but wide steps that curled away and out of sight from the private beach. Clem planted her hat back on her head and followed, trying to compose herself. This was the moment to think of Tom. She was doing this for him.

Her heart rate climbed along with her as they moved up

and away from the water, but she was young and fit and kept going until the steps fed into a wide path. It wasn't exhaustion that stopped her but the sight of the house: tall with narrow, balconied windows, it had round-topped towers at each corner that would have made it seem more castle than villa had it not been for the pale pink and peach stripes still faintly rendered on the plasterwork. It was grand but tired, long past its glory days, and she felt a pinch of anxiety at the scale of the work that lay ahead. She and the Swimmer both knew he was using this project as a lure, but the job still needed to be done. If she was going to make things up to Tom, she had to pull this project off. It was high profile and every visitor would be a judge. Alderton Hide needed her to do a good job.

A movement at one of the windows caught her eye and she dropped her head down quickly, hiding her face with the brim of her hat, just as she had on the first night they'd met. Was he in there watching her?

Stefano led her through the gardens, which were gathered in concentric-stepped lawns and terraces, the beds as wildly coloured as if they'd been painted; they walked past stumpy olive trees with gnarled trunks and feathery-leafed heads into the long shadows of the house.

A door opened as they approached and Clem braced herself for that devastating moment when her eyes rested on his again. But it wasn't him. A stout woman in a black dress and white apron stepped out. Clem guessed she was around her mother's age, early sixties, with long, still-dark hair looped beneath a discreet hairnet.

'Signorina Alderton, welcome to Villa ai Cedri. I am Signora Benuto, Signor Beaulieu's housekeeper.'

'Hi,' Clem replied, barely managing a smile and fiddling with her hat. She felt jumpy and nervous.

'Signorina, I shall leave you now,' Stefano said, tipping his head.

'Oh, right. Thanks, Stefano,' she said, nodding back at him. She turned back to Signora Benuto just as the woman's eyes were on their way back up her. Disapproval sang through them – Clem supposed most people here didn't wear a blazer, T-shirt, leather mini and heeled ankle boots for travelling – but in the next instant, she had blinked the look away.

'We have everything ready for you, signorina. Would you like to follow me?'

Clem nodded, moving as if to step into the house, but to her surprise, Signora Benuto stepped out instead, and started along a path that ran across one of the top lawns. Clem turned right and followed in bafflement as they walked further around the estate. A green swimming pool gleamed beneath them on one level, with a trio of cushionless steamer chairs arranged to face the sun, and on the level above, she saw the canes and netting of a kitchen garden and vines being trained along a pergola.

Signora Benuto stopped at a steep flight of steps just before a stone wall and turned to check Clem was still with her – she had set a swift pace in her white soft-soled shoes – before climbing up. Clem followed and was amazed to find they were on a small, humped bridge, traversing a narrow public footpath below. Beyond the wall on the other side was yet more garden, but it was wilder and uncultivated here, just a tangled olive grove with a compost heap on one side and an upturned wheelbarrow. After a few more minutes of silent marching on the winding path, the wind suddenly picked up and a flash of pinks to Clem's left made her catch her breath – her first glimpse! They had come to a short round stone building, also painted in pink and peach stripes, like a matching pepper pot to the house. A key was already in the door and Signora Benuto led the way in.

'These are your rooms,' the housekeeper said, standing back so that Clem could pass.

Clem, who'd been straining to peer at the port through the trees, reluctantly stepped inside. It took a moment for her eyes to adjust to the dim light. The room was round, maybe four metres in diameter, the floor was stone, the white walls thickly plastered, and large circular windows like outsized portholes were spaced evenly all around. A small comma-shaped sofa in dusty pink linen was pressed back against the wall to the left, with a round glass-topped coffee table before it, and a lemon-coloured squashy armchair positioned to the near side, with its back to the door. A television sat upon a bookcase, and a wood-burning stove was set into the right-hand-side wall. 'Bijou' was the best way to describe it.

'Alberto has already left your bags in the bedroom upstairs, signorina,' Signora Benuto said, indicating the dark wood winding staircase next to where they were standing. 'Would you like me to unpack for you?'

'No, that's OK. I'll do it myself,' Clem mumbled, her eyes scanning the small, rough oil paintings on the walls, mainly depicting Mediterranean scenes. She was practically itching with agitation.

'I shall leave you to settle in then. Would you like to take dinner in the house tonight or here?'

Clem thought of the Swimmer waiting for her in the big house. She could just imagine him standing by the windows, barefoot, one hand in his pocket as he'd watched the boat speed her towards him, waiting for her to appear in his Italianate garden in her Portobello clothes, caught at last. Well, in spite of her promise to Stella, she had no intention of surrendering to him. The rules of the game had changed since their bet on the bed and it was terrifying enough that she was out here at all. She couldn't cope with his manipulations, too.

'I'll eat in here tonight. I'm tired from the journey.' It was a petty victory but a clear signal to the Swimmer to think again if he thought that her being here was any kind of indication that things between them were going to go the way he planned. She was determined to show him that 'no' in Portobello meant 'no' in Portofino too.

'Of course, signorina,' Signora Benuto nodded. 'It shall be with you at nine o'clock.'

'Thanks,' Clem replied briskly.

She waited for the door to close before breaking into a run and sprinting up the stairs. The ceiling was vaulted with rafters and a huge round bed, which was encircled by white gauze that hung from a central corona that dominated the room. But it wasn't that which she was interested in. Clem dashed to the farthest window and opened it hurriedly, feeling the wind zip round her immediately, as though it had been waiting for her on the other side of the glass. As she thought, the folly was on the rocks, on the opposite side of the private beach to which she'd arrived, and ahead of her lay the empty horizon as the Mediterranean stretched out like a rumpled silk sheet.

She ran to the next window to the left and saw the Ligurian coast, hazy on the opposite side of the bay, but tightening into clarity as her eyes tracked nearer. She moved across to the next window and the smooth indistinct coastline began to crumple and jut with inlets and headlands. Another round striped folly, this one yellow and beige, stood perched on an outcrop lower than hers; it was so close to the water it was as if it had been built as a dare.

She ran to the last window. The private beach was 270 degrees behind her now and she finally glimpsed what she'd been looking for: the tiny, pinky rectangular notch that had become a global watchword for sophistication.

The buildings were shabbier than a newcomer might expect, the piazzetta even smaller than they might anticipate, the small fishing boats that bobbed lightly in tethered rows, disappointingly humble compared to the shoals of super yachts that clustered in other premier destinations like St Tropez or Capri. But Clem wasn't a newcomer. She'd been here once before and every last detail was as highly nuanced in her memory as if she'd grown up here, or visited last week. This was where her dreams drifted to if she didn't blot her nights out with drink, this was where her thoughts settled if she didn't fill her days with chat. She remembered this tiny, remote, foreign village on a molecular level, and the sight of it soaked into her like water into sand because this was where her old life had ended and her new one had begun. She closed her eyes as the tears slid and her soul trembled. She didn't want it to be true, she always resisted the fact with every conscious fibre in her body, but there was no getting away from it: her heart was here and this was home.

Chapter Nineteen

She slept with the window open, wanting to feel the warm, salty wind brush her, even in her sleep, but she awoke damp and early, thanks to the sound of the waves breaking on the rocks below. She lay in bed for an hour, her fingers stroking the comforting silk pouch beneath her pillow, every part of her reconnecting with the sounds, sights and smells she'd denied for so long. The urge to drink or go for a run was overwhelming.

Running seemed the most cautious option. The most sensible. She should do that. She'd run all the way back to Genoa if she had any sense at all.

A familiar bleep on her phone drew her out of herself. It was Stella, checking in.

'*How goes it?*'

'*Not seen him yet. Cast out in a clifftop folly.*'

'*Seriously?*'

'*Seriously.*' Clem took a couple of pictures – one of the bedroom and one of the view back to Portofino – and sent them over.

'*They probably heard about your table manners.*'

'*Xpect so.*'

'*Can we call it your Ivory Tower?*'

'*No. It's stripy and looks more like a stick of Brighton rock.*'

'Are you going to grow your hair long?'

Clem got the Rapunzel association immediately and burst out laughing. *'ROFL'.*

'Good. Laters then! Xxx'

Clem sighed, feeling cheered up, and wandered downstairs in The Killers tour T-shirt Tom had missed when clearing out his wardrobe. To her astonishment, a tray was sitting on the table filled with a coffee pot, cup and saucer, and a basket of cornetti wrapped in linen. The coffee was still steaming. She hadn't heard a sound.

An envelope was propped against the side of the cup and she opened it curiously.

'Please come to the house at 10 a.m.'

Her summons. She poured herself some coffee and slumped on the arm of the sofa. The games were about to begin.

Clem knocked at the door and stepped back, wondering whether today's outfit – her black leather trousers, black ankle boots and sloppy grey marl sweatshirt – would pass muster with Signora Benuto.

The door opened and the housekeeper motioned for Clem to enter.

'Buongiorno,' Clem said, instantly taking in the vast ceiling height first, the hammer-beam timbers second. Her eyes swept over the reticulated staircase, two large hunting-scene tapestries that were suspended on poles on the walls, an antique oak blanket box that was adorned with ornate silver candlesticks, and taffeta curtains at the window.

She resisted the urge to blow out through her cheeks. Everything was expensive and befitting of a house of this stature, but it clearly hadn't been touched in thirty years. If it was grand, it also felt musty and unappealing. Why would a man like the Swimmer – no slouch sartorially – want to live in this?

Her pulse quickened at the thought of him as they walked through a long room with windows on one side, an enormous fireplace on the other and bald velvet chairs arranged in groupings in between. More tapestries, Clem noted.

'In here,' Signora Benuto said, stopping at the doorway to a room that was more fully furnished, with a Prussian blue and red rug, tatty red silk curtains and a pale gold velvet sofa. There were floor-to-ceiling windows on two sides and an antique desk was positioned in front of the set that looked out to sea.

Clem took a deep breath and stepped through, feeling her pulse accelerate as she braced herself, yet again, for that moment that always seemed to take so much from her. It would get easier, she reassured herself, looking around the room for him.

She turned a full circle.

'Where is he?' she asked Signora Benuto.

'Where is who?' the housekeeper replied, looking equally puzzled.

'Signor Beaulieu.'

'He is not here, signorina. We are not expecting him.'

'But . . .' Not expected? 'But then why am I here? I can't get on until he's briefed me.'

'This is your office now. He has said you are to have free rein.'

A chuckle escaped her. 'Well, there's having free rein and then there's having free rein, if you see what I mean.'

The housekeeper shook her head. 'No.'

God, sense of humour failure, Clem thought to herself. 'Well, is there a spec I can look at until he does deign to arrive? At least I can get up to speed with the floor layouts, colour charts, fabric swatches and stuff. Who's the interior designer?'

'There isn't one. Signor Beaulieu was very clear that you must make it look like you would like it to look.'

He wouldn't say that if he'd seen my flat, Clem thought, laughing, before realizing what the housekeeper had just said. No interior designer? She shifted weight, more nervous now. 'You . . . don't mean he wants me to do the . . . the whole thing?'

The housekeeper nodded solemnly, but her pursed lips revealed her private feelings about the directive. 'Would you like some coffee?'

Clem blinked. This couldn't be happening. 'Look, there's obviously been a misunderstanding. I am *not* an interior designer. Our company doesn't do *entire houses*,' Clem said, waving her arms in the air at the words. 'We do leather finishes and furniture.'

'Yes.'

'So . . . so then you'll realize that I cannot wrap this entire house in leather. I mean, I *could*. It's theoretically possible and God only knows we need the work!' she muttered, before realizing she was being indiscreet and clearing her throat. 'What I'm saying is, I have to get a brief from him on exactly which walls or floors he wants done, what furniture – such as whether he wants a leather wardrobe in the master suite or a sling log basket in here. I mean, we do the accents, not the whole thing.'

'Yes,' the housekeeper repeated.

Clem sighed. She obviously wasn't making herself clear. She tried speaking more slowly. 'You have to ring him, you have to explain this to him. I can work carte blanche, if that's what he would like, within an interior designer's overall scheme, but I'll need to see that scheme and collaborate with *them*. They design, we supply. Capiche? Will you call him please and tell him that?'

The housekeeper nodded. 'And I shall bring you some coffee. Please feel free to look around the house.'

Clem rolled her eyes as the older woman walked away.

There was another set of doors at the far end of the room, on the same side as the doors she'd just come through, and she walked through them into what had clearly once been the library. The walls were lined on both sides with floor-to-ceiling shelves, though they were dusty and bare of books now; just a Meissen chandelier and a chair on castors remained. She clocked a door on the right and peered through – it opened into the long room she had passed through moments earlier. Exiting at the far end, she found herself back in the imposing entrance hall, at the foot of the stairs.

She walked up them slowly, checking for creaks, but its construction was sound and she stood at the top, with corridors flanking her on both sides. She took the left wing first and studied the three bedrooms dispassionately, making mental notes about the dimensions, original features, and directions they faced, the condition of the plaster walls and the wooden floors. They had only beds in them, no further furniture, and the two bathrooms had been ripped out so that only exposed, capped-off pipes remained.

She did the same in the opposite wing, sketching with her back to the windows so that she could concentrate on the job in hand and formulate a strong initial impression of the tone of the house. The final two bedrooms were upstairs in the attic but still boasted impressive ceiling heights and proportions that could comfortably swallow her London flat.

By the time she wandered back downstairs, Signora Benuto was laying out the coffee.

'Did you speak to him?' Clem asked without any gracious preamble.

'He says you are to proceed as though it was your house,' the housekeeper nodded, repeating her earlier words.

'But it's *not* my house,' Clem protested in exasperation. She should have spoken to him herself, except that . . . the thought of his voice in her ear . . .

'He wants you to think of it as though it were.'

Clem and the housekeeper stared at each other, mutually aghast at the very clear message being spelled out between them. This was Fleur's role, not hers.

'The boat, too,' the housekeeper murmured.

Clem shook her head as panic began to assail her: eight bedrooms, a library, a drawing room, a long room, the entrance hall – all needing redecorating and refurbishing from scratch. And she hadn't even seen the kitchen or other downstairs rooms yet. And as for the boat . . .

'I'm not qualified for this,' she said, her voice quailing.

'He says he trusts your instincts,' Signora Benuto said, repeating his words obediently.

'But we didn't sign up for this. I mean, I don't know any suppliers out here for . . . for paint or wallpapers or . . .'

'Signor Beaulieu is sending someone through who has contacts with all these people and will liaise with them on your behalf.'

Clem bit her lip. 'But then that person is the interior designer surely.'

'Signor Beaulieu wants your vision for the house, not theirs.'

So he was sub-contracting a designer to implement her vision, as opposed to the other way round? Clem sighed. She was supposed to be the professional, not the client, but the boundary was already blurred.

'I wouldn't know where to start with the plumbing or electrics,' she said, frustrated, throwing her hands in the air and beginning to pace. What the hell was this guy trying to do to her? They barely knew each other and he'd thrown her entire world into disarray.

'That has all been upgraded over the spring, signorina. Everything is in the correct position ready for fitting.'

'So I just have to choose the fittings? Basically act like this is my house and do it up however I want?' Clem blinked at her.

Signora Benuto winced back. 'Yes.'

The entire situation was ridiculous, overwhelming. She began pacing. 'This is completely unacceptable . . . I mean, you should know there's nothing . . . you know, going on between . . . us.'

Signora Benuto remained impassive.

Clem stared back at her, knowing this woman was not her ally. 'I need to make a phone call.'

'Of course.' The housekeeper left the room and Clem grabbed her phone from her bag, speed-dialling Stella.

'You are not going to believe what's just happened to me!' she hissed before Stella could say a word.

'He hasn't jumped you already! The randy sod!' Stella half gasped, half laughed.

'He's not even here. I'm here alone.'

'Oh.' She sounded disappointed. Stella was still firmly of the conviction that the chemistry between them was too strong to deny and would lead to a happy-ever-after ending, whether Clem liked it or not.

'He wants me to do the house however I like. I mean, like, everything. Baths, taps, curtains, carpets – way, way beyond anything to do with leather. The whole bloody thing, Stell!'

'Noooo,' Stella gasped enviously.

'Yes!'

'Fuck, that's romantic!'

'No it's not!'

'Babes, he's clearly telling you that he wants this house to be yours. It's a grand statement of intent,' she said slowly, as though this had completely passed Clem by.

'Stell, I don't even know the guy's name.'

'Technicality, babe. That's just you playing silly buggers. Meanwhile, he's moved on to the next level. He's moved you in and now he's got you playing lady of the manor.'

'I won't do it.'

'You have to. Unless you want your family to never speak to you again. If Alderton Hide goes under, it'll be you they blame. And let's not even talk about the bag.'

'It was just a bag,' Clem hissed furiously.

'Not to them.'

They fell silent until another thought struck Stella.

'Look at it this way: if you're working that much outside the brief, you can charge way higher fees and you'll be helping Alderton Hide even *more* than you'd intended. Tom will have no choice but to love you again.' She was joking, but the words still cut through Clem like steel through flesh.

'I suppose the fact that he's not here will make it tolerable,' Clem muttered, although in truth that had thrown her more than anything. If he was making grand statements of intent, why wasn't he here making them himself? Their last meeting at Claridge's had clearly bruised them both.

'That's the spirit!' Stella chuckled. 'Now stop being a diva and go and spend the man's money. If you like, you can fly me out and I'll knit him a carpet!'

Clem had to laugh. 'I'll call you later then.'

'You'd better!'

The line clicked dead and Clem noticed Signora Benuto standing discreetly by the door.

'Stefano is ready to take you when you are ready.'

'Take me where?' Clem enquired, puzzled, as she pocketed the phone and hurriedly downed the coffee.

'To the boatyard in Viareggio.'

Oh God. 'Is that far?'

'One hour across the bay. The interior designer will meet you back here this afternoon at four o'clock.'

'Right,' Clem sighed, raking her hands through her hair and feeling exhausted already.

'I shall have coffee prepared.'

More coffee. 'Well, in that case, would you mind making mine with milk?'

Signora Benuto looked pained.

'I know I know, you think our coffee's like dirty water. But I'm English, that's how we like it.' Clem shrugged. If they were going to live and work together, they may as well set some ground rules.

Chapter Twenty

'Tom? It's me.'

There was a pause – angry, defiant. 'Hi.'

'H–how's it going?' she asked, hoping it wouldn't lead to a conversation about the weather. It was doubtless raining there, still sunny here, and she didn't want to come across as boasting. She knew full well he'd have given his eye teeth to be summering in Portofino working on this commission. Instead, he'd been locked out, forced to watch from the sidelines as his disastrous sister flirted with the client and carried the entire weight, hopes and fortunes of his company on her slender shoulders.

'Fine. Quiet.'

She nodded, wishing he meant the flat without her, but knowing he was referring to the office and it's not-ringing phones. She looked out to the horizon. It was in sharp focus now.

'So, I've got good news for you and bad news for me,' she said, envisaging him sitting there with his eyes closed, his rugby-muscled body braced for the next blow. 'It turns out this project isn't just about Alderton Hide finishes. It's much, much bigger than that. Did you know? Did he tell *you*? He wants us to do everything – I mean, second fix onwards: paint colours, doorknobs, lights, taps.'

Still nothing.

'Obviously, we can't do it *all* in leather. I mean, it would look ridiculous to clothe the entire house in hides. But I'll use it wherever I can, don't worry about that. I won't miss an opportunity. I just . . .'

The resounding silence on the other end of the line was distracting.

'Well, I just wanted you to know that I'll obviously be billing him for far more than the agreed contract – it'll be my time he's paying for, too, not just our products. So . . . so that's the good news, it's all money back in the A. H. coffers. I mean, I know we're not interior designers, but there's a really good opportunity here to showcase our vision – I mean, *your* vision – from start to finish. Usually we only get to add the accents, but this . . . this is a unique chance to do it the other way around and base the entire scheme around us.'

There was a long pause. 'Great.'

Great? That was all he had to say? She had come out here; she'd just told him she'd be invoicing for more than double, that this villa was in effect going to be an Alderton Hide show home, and all he had to say was 'great'?

They fell silent – her out of words, him refusing to try – and she felt a flash of anger spark inside her. What was it going to take? 'Right, then. So, I'll keep you posted.'

She hung up, exasperated tears begrudgingly falling down her face. She'd wanted to ask his advice, get his help, lean on him for guidance. This was too big for her. If the house hadn't been intimidating enough, the boat alone would have been – 30 metres long with a massive salon, four bedrooms, four bathrooms, a kitchen. And that wasn't even touching the staff quarters.

Clem had wanted to cry at the sight of it. It was massive out of the water, with its deep-water keel clad in scaffolding, the hull still rusty red and rough as it waited for its state-of-the-art paintwork. Tarted up, that boat was going to cost millions, and she had proved she couldn't even be trusted with a bike!

Why was the Swimmer doing this to her? She was out here, all alone, with no support network to rely on, and realizing the full and final magnitude of the job had ramped up the pressure. It had been bad enough thinking she was simply out there for him to seduce and win. But this, too? She literally didn't know where to begin.

'Signorina?'

She looked back and saw the housekeeper standing in the doorway.

'Signor Fox is here.'

Clem glanced at her watch. Four o'clock. The interior designer. Dammit. She'd been non-stop all day and now she was going to have to meet the person whose commission she'd stolen. This was going to be fun.

'Thank you. Please show him in,' Clem replied wearily, dipping her head and wiping the tears from her cheeks. She rose from the desk she'd thrown her bag under and walked over the faded blue and red carpet.

'Hi.' The Antipodean twang made her jerk her head up. A man, early to mid thirties, was standing there, smiling at her. His blond hair was long and shaggy, with a fringe that hung over his eyes so that all she could see were teeth and muscles. He was wearing, incongruously, a slim pair of dark red trousers rolled up at the ankles, a sailor-striped T-shirt and a pale blue sleeveless tank, and he had an iPad tucked under his arm.

Her jaw dropped. *Not* what she was expecting. 'Hi.'

'You're Miss Alderton?'

'Clem, call me Clem,' she replied, walking towards him and shaking his hand.

'Chad Fox.'

'You're Australian,' she said vacuously.

'Fair dinkum.' He grinned, laughing as her eyes widened further at the proof. 'Don't worry, I'm just kidding. That's not actually part of my vernacular.'

Her eyes widened further still. Vernacular? He looked like a surf bum.

'I . . . I'm sorry,' she said, gathering her wits. 'It's just it's been a long day and—'

'I wasn't what you were expecting? No worries. I get that a lot.'

'Won't you sit down?' she asked.

'I will.' He grinned again, emphasizing 'will' as though they'd been arguing about it and gently puncturing her mother's formality.

They sat, knees angled towards the other, on the sad, barely gold velvet sofa. It creaked a little under their weight and Clem cracked a wry smile, too tired not to. Two weeks ago she'd been eating curry in her flat with Stella and Mercy as they made a secret collection; now she was sitting in a crumbling palazzo in Portofino with an Aussie surf dude who talked wallpaper?

Signora Benuto set down the coffee – along with a small jug of steamed milk for Clem – and left them.

'Nice trousers by the way.'

Clem smoothed them self-consciously. 'Thanks. One of the perks of working for a leather company,' she shrugged. 'I'm practically contracted to wear leather on a daily basis.'

'Hot out here, though. At least it will be soon. The temperature ramps up quickly once May hits.'

Clem nodded, wringing her hands nervously. 'Yeah.'

'So, I'm really excited about working with you,' Chad said, watching her as he sipped his coffee. He took it black, like the locals. 'I've admired Alderton Hide's work for a long time. Adding you to my contacts and suppliers is going to be great for my book.'

'Thanks,' Clem said nervously, wondering whether he knew he wasn't the principal designer here, and that she wasn't simply a supplier. 'Have you uh . . . I mean, what've you been told about this project?'

Chad looked at her carefully. 'It's all right, I'm up to speed if that's what you're worried about. This is your gig. Your ideas, my contacts. It's all cool. I'm here as backup, the facilitator who'll get the right people implementing your vision.'

Clem smiled at him gratefully, instantly reassured by his professional largesse. 'Well, that's the problem,' she confided. 'I don't have one.'

Chad frowned. 'Really?'

'I'm not a designer and I don't pretend to be. I've only walked into this scenario today, and to be honest' – her shoulders sagged – 'it's freaking me out.'

Chad looked at her consideringly. 'Well, I'm not surprised. You did only get here today; it's bound to be a shock. But you've clearly got great style. You're a very cool chick. No wonder Beaulieu's given you a free hand.'

Clem looked up at his words. She could tell from his tone that he was rapidly decoding the subtext to her commission, even if nothing had been explicitly said. 'Do you know him well?'

Chad shrugged. 'Not on a personal level. He's not often here and I work all over Italy. But we'd obviously worked quite closely together on the initial spec.'

'Initial . . .?' Clem swallowed. 'You mean you'd already done designs for this place?'

Chad hesitated before nodding. 'Yeah. We were a month off from starting when the call came that he was going in a "different direction".' He made quote marks with his fingers in the air, a bemused smile on his lips. Clem wished she could see his eyes more clearly. He must *hate* her. 'Don't worry. It happens. And he forfeited a hefty deposit, so that sugar-coated the pill.'

'I'm so sorry,' Clem mumbled.

'Not your fault. Very definitely not your fault,' Chad replied, watching her closely. 'Listen, we'll do this together,' he said, taking her hand and squeezing it. 'I can tell you're going to be better at this than you think. You just need to trust your instincts. Whatever you want to do, I'll make it happen for you. That's my job.' He winked at her. 'It's going to be fine.'

'Yeah?' she asked hopefully.

'Yeah,' he nodded. 'In the meantime, you should probably take the rest of the day off. You look exhausted and we don't need to start today.'

'I am pretty tired,' she admitted. 'I had no idea what I was walking into.'

Chad shook his head and for a moment she could see his eyes – hazel brown and sympathetic – before his fringe resettled over them. '*This* probably isn't the half of it. But don't worry, you've got me on your side now. The Golden Fox will protect you.'

She laughed, so grateful for his generosity and laid-back manner.

They got up and she walked him to the door.

'I'll come back at ten tomorrow, OK? We can get started then,' he said, kissing her easily on the cheek as if she'd known him for years.

'OK, thanks. I really mean it.'

He winked and started down the steps.

'Oh, Chad!' she called, remembering something, and he turned back to her. 'What's . . . what's his name? Beaulieu's I mean?'

This time it was Chad who laughed. 'Ah! He told me you'd ask me that.' He walked back up the steps to her and took her hand again, squeezing it comfortingly. 'And he told me it's more than my job's worth to tell you. I can't get fired for you twice.'

'Oh.' Of course he couldn't. Did that mean that all of them – Signora Benuto, Stefano, Alberto and God only knew who else – had been told to keep it from her, too? She tried to smile. He'd thought of everything. 'It doesn't matter.'

'It *shouldn't*. But it obviously does.' He tipped his head to the side, his eyes amused and sympathetic all at once. '*Ciao, bella. E benvenuto a Italia.*'

Chapter Twenty-One

The wind was against her, trying to blow her back and over as she pounded up the narrow path, but she wouldn't stop. The urge to run was stronger here than she'd ever felt before. She had to purge, exhaust, distract herself to the point of collapse every evening. It was the only way she could sleep. To be so close to him here, and yet still so far, there had been nights when she'd thought she was going to go out of her mind.

She knew that sooner or later she would have to leave the headland and go into the port. It had been six days now and she already knew where every twist and turn of these narrow, labyrinthine paths – which she'd first spied from her bridge – led to. She knew how to get to the different beaches, the castle, the park, the lighthouse, and she was running out of track. She was going to need more space soon, more mileage, but there were risks attached to that, risks she didn't feel ready to take. This was a small place.

She rounded the corner and felt the wind lift her hair, as it always did when she came to the sea's edge. The white lighthouse stood staunchly at the furthermost tip and she allowed herself to slow to a walk, hands on hips as she tried to catch her breath before she collapsed on the bench outside the deserted café.

She checked the sign again, even though she knew its message by heart: the café would reopen on Monday 3 May. Next week. She would need a new route by then. She needed to be alone on her runs. They were her only refuge, her sanctuary, the place she could go to inside herself after a day spent poring over swatches and illustrations with Chad.

That was going well at least. He had broken the project down into bite-size chunks for her and they were making good progress on the library, the first room they had decided to tackle – their 'starter' room.

In spite of her declarations that she couldn't clad the entire house in leather, that was pretty much what she was doing in there: firstly, it guaranteed a hefty order in quickly to Alderton Hide, which meant they could get everyone working at capacity again. Secondly, it was a library, and a library more than any other room was all about leather: no one ever stocked paperbacks in these rooms. Somewhere – in Florence probably – an antiquarian bookseller had been tasked with sourcing a mile of books, and would be hunting high and low for precious first editions and grandly gilted leather-bound classics. Leather shelves therefore, in a soft mossy-green, made perfect sense, and they were currently tossing up ideas for words or quotes to be embossed in the front-facing fascias. That had been Clem's idea, and she'd been pretty pleased with it. She smiled as she thought back to her idea of her favourite line of all time, a Winnie-the-Pooh quote, written when he'd eaten too much 'hunny' and got stuck in the door of Rabbit's 'howse': 'Well then, would you be so kind as to find a sustaining book such as would comfort a wedged bear in great tightness?' She and Tom had always loved that line – their father's deep, *lento* voice had been particularly well suited to the rhythms of A.A. Milne's writing – and she and Chad had laughed like drains at the thought of printing it across the front of this grand leather-clad library. It had been the first of many bonding exercises between them.

They were laying down a chestnut leather floor in there, too. The existing wooden strip floor, upon inspection, had been found to be too rotten to save, and Clem had come up with the idea of laying leather tiles on the floor in parquet-style bricks, rather than the more usual stitched squares, arranging them in a herringbone pattern. It was classic but with a twist, would be quieter, warmer, and layer up the luxurious subtle scent of leather in the room. Chad had loved it and seemed impressed by her outside-the-box thinking.

He, in turn, had sourced some wall lights, and they were choosing between a naturalistic bronze oak-leaf design, or a modernist chrome tubular design looped with a sling of chunky mariner's rope – she couldn't quite decide yet on how contemporary or classic to take the scheme; Clem's instinct was that a woman like Fleur would prefer the more classical design, but remembering the Swimmer's modish tailoring, she knew contemporary was the way to go for him. Knowing nothing about the dynamics of their relationship, she wasn't sure which one to follow.

They had agreed, however, on a set of club chairs and sofas with discreet, shallow pin-button backs and softly curved arms that Clem thought should be upholstered in a lustrous silk tweed, and which Chad was currently sourcing.

All in all, it had turned into a surprisingly productive week and she had spent her evenings, before her runs, formulating the shelving and floor dimensions and spec to send through to the office which, in turn, responded only with technical questions. No banter, no concern; just simmering, silent hostility that all their fates rested upon her.

She watched the sun descend to its watery bed, changing the colour palette from blues and greens to pinks and reds, aware that she should start heading back. There was little dusk here, and though she was becoming well-acquainted with the paths, there was practically no lighting along them and she didn't want to negotiate them in the dark. The walls of the private estates on either side were high and indistinguishable, with ivy growing along them, and her best landmarks were the bridges that occasionally straddled the paths, connecting one part of an inland garden to its coastal access. No vehicle was narrow enough to get down here and the clusters of steps meant scooters and bikes were useless, too. Anything that couldn't be carried in a suitcase had to come on to the headland by sea access – all the properties had one. The one exception, that she had seen – quite unsurprisingly – was the lighthouse café, which had a specially adapted micro-van fitted with caterpillar tracks to transport ice creams, glasses and whatnot along the paths.

Clem got up and eased herself into a jog. It was still warm, even at eight o'clock in the evening, and she'd need to have a cool shower to bring her temperature down before Signora Benuto brought her dinner through at nine.

She had rapidly become accustomed to eating alone. She usually Skyped Stella or flicked through the swatch books and websites Chad left with her. For one thing, it stopped her worrying about when the Swimmer was going to arrive. This was obviously all part of his game – keeping her on tenterhooks for his arrival – but she couldn't sustain that level of anxiety. Busy was best.

She made her way back along a different path, moving easily, her breath coming evenly. She could talk, sing if she wanted; her body knew these rigours and rhythms too well. After twenty minutes she passed by the gate to the house with a ferocious-sounding dog, then under the bridge with the oval plaque in the middle, and she knew that meant she had to take the next right.

The path rose in a hump before her and she pumped her arms harder in a burst of effort, sidestepping a broken drain and leaping athletically over a puddle that had formed from the neighbour's overzealous sprinkler system. She took the right turn, where the path began to drop down again, and sped up, always preferring to finish her run on a sprint. She could, if she was feeling lazy, end the run just ahead and go through the house's main entrance on the right, but she never did. The gate that led directly to 'her' part of the garden was just further down, after a turn on the left, and crossing under the bridge was like crossing a finish line. She preferred the extra privacy. She had no idea what, if at all, Signora Benuto was reporting back to her employer, but the fact that he still hadn't liaised with her directly, even though he was in constant contact with Chad, Stefano and Signora Benuto, had the effect of keeping her on edge. The settings of their 'relationship' were so undefined.

Ahead, she could see a man and boy walking up the hill towards her – the first non-estate people she'd seen since arriving here – and she slowed her pace. The path was so narrow they would have to drop back into single file to pass each other.

They were talking animatedly, a football in the boy's hands, a bucket in the man's. The boy was almost chest-height to his father, and when he said something to make him laugh, the father reached down and mussed the boy's hair affectionately. Clem tried to remember 'good evening' in Italian.

They drew closer and she saw that they were both dark-haired, rangy and blessed with the smooth, even dark tan that comes from living in a sunny climate. Clem slowed to a walking pace, her ponytail no longer bouncing manically across her shoulders, and her eyes met theirs as they prepared to pass, the father hanging back to let the boy walk in front.

No!

She dropped her eyes quickly, looking down at the paving stones as they moved past her.

'*Buonasera*,' the boy said politely, looking up at her.

'*Grazie*,' the father followed up, a question mark in his voice and eyes. Clem turned almost to the wall, away from them, the sound of her own blood rushing in torrents in her ears.

They were behind her now, but she could hear only one set of footsteps continuing onwards. Small ones, light ones. Then they stopped, too. She broke into a run, arms pumping, breathing erratic, her ponytail swinging in full revolutions around the back of her head. No style, just power; no grace, just acceleration.

She was around the corner in seconds, her hand on the left wall and opening the gate. She leapt into the garden and closed the door behind her, throwing closed the bolt. She heard footsteps sound on the path, big ones, heavy ones, getting closer. They stopped and she heard breathing on the other side of the wooden gate.

She held her breath. No. No. No. No. No.

Time stopped. Seasons changed. Years rolled back.

Or so it felt.

Then the footsteps moved away again, becoming fainter, disappearing around the corner and continuing along the path to the lighthouse.

She exhaled with a sob, her heart pounding at three times the rate it had hit on the run. She bent double, her hands on her knees, trying to control herself. But she was far beyond that. She tried walking but her legs wouldn't support her. She leaned against the wall, but the effort even of that was too much. Survival instinct took over. Her body folded three times and, with violent efficiency, she turned and threw up in the bushes.

The shower didn't help. The run had already happened. She couldn't understand a word on the TV. She couldn't ring Stella and talk to her about it. She couldn't even get drunk – there was no fridge in the folly and she didn't fancy waking Signora Benuto at this time of night.

It was gone eleven but she was still shaken up. Sleep was a distant promise tonight, she already knew. She walked to the window and looked out at the twinkling light of the glamorous Cinque Terre towns on the far side of the bay. Life continued. It always did, but that was far from comforting to her tonight.

Her eyes rose to the sky. The moon was full and the sky practically clear, only long wispy clouds that looked like they could be threaded through a needle, drifting parallel to the horizon and casting bright shadows on the deep, dappled cove below her. The sea was calm tonight, calmer than it had been at any point since she'd arrived, and she watched it gently buffeting the basalt rocks with a soothing 'shush', like a mother pushing a cradle.

Even from this distance, in this light, the water looked clear and cold. Numbing.

She blinked slowly at the thought. Then, pulling a striped mohair jumper on over her knickers, she jogged down the stairs and settled the door on the latch behind her. She had seen the dirt track from the folly to the beach; it was steep in some places and overgrown in others, but she picked her way down carelessly, barefoot, almost enjoying the sweet sharp scrape of brambles against her flesh. The tangible pain felt more bearable than the one buried deep inside her, like an ache she couldn't cup, an itch she couldn't scratch.

She was down within minutes, and she stepped out of her clothes, gasping as she immersed her feet in the shocking, almost icy water. It would be another two months before the sea heated to a comfortable temperature, but tonight, comfortable was precisely what she didn't want. Defiantly, she stepped in deeper, her feet trying to grip onto the bald, slippery stones. Her body tightened and contracted in defence, and she gasped, almost crying out as the water welcomed her with viscous fingers.

Slowly, she dropped her weight forward, sliding through the water like a cat till her shoulders were submerged. She dived under, wanting to freeze her head most of all and stop the thoughts and memories that were hardest to escape. She surfaced with a sob, but went under again. And again. And again.

Eventually, it worked. Eventually she couldn't feel anything but a distanced buzz, and she tipped her head back and floated with a moonbeam on the heavy sea. Peace, of sorts.

A boat was speeding across the bay, she could hear the engines underwater, but she took no heed. If Portofino was known to the world, this cove neighbouring it was invitation only. She drifted, listening to the underwater crackle of microscopic sealife, wondering for once what lay beneath her, not ahead.

But the drone grew louder. Obtrusive. Unavoidable. She lifted her head and saw the boat heading towards her. She kicked away hurriedly, not because she was in danger of being hit, but because she was in danger of being seen. Though the light from the boat hadn't reached her, the night sky was bright, toplighting the dark sea. She ducked underwater and swam to the shallows, perching crouched on a rock on the opposite side of the cove just as Stefano cut the engine and the Riva drifted in to the jetty.

She stayed perfectly still.

Another figure, who'd been standing by the front seat, turned to talk to him and she inhaled sharply as she recognized the Swimmer's angular lines. She couldn't hear what they were saying, but Stefano was nodding and restarted the engines. The Swimmer's actions were hard to make out from across the water – he was in silhouette to her – but it looked like he had taken off his jacket and was now sliding off his tie. It was late. He must be desperate to sleep.

She kept still, waiting for him to disembark, her heart pounding as she savoured the sight of him from her hiding place. He stepped up out of the boat, but it was a moment before she realized his silhouette was facing her, not away. Then in the next instant he had thrown his arms above his head and dived in – cleanly, sharply – and was swimming, fully clothed, straight towards her.

Stefano carefully reversed the boat out of the bay and, within seconds, its elegant shape had disappeared around the headland, headed for the port. Clem looked back at the

Swimmer, panicked by his actions. He was only 50 metres from her, and she tried to glide deeper into the shadows, but the moon was on super-strength and no friend to her tonight. There was no chance he hadn't seen her.

He stopped just out of reach in front of her, his hair slicked back, the lower half of his face submerged so that she could see only his eyes. Those damned gleaming eyes that made a prisoner of her in the water, in the dark, in a crowded hotel lobby in the middle of the day.

'How did you know I was here?' she asked, her voice scarcely more than a whisper.

'I brought you here, remember?'

Stop. She couldn't take the games. Not tonight. 'I mean . . . here.'

His eyes read hers. 'Who else would be swimming in these temperatures at this time of night?'

She blinked at him. 'You're ruining your clothes.' Her voice cracked as the low temperatures and exhaustion, the stress and games caught up with her.

'A small price to pay.' He looked at her, concern filling his face as he saw her trembling. He intuitively understood it wasn't from the cold. 'Are you OK?'

She shook her head. 'Where have you been?'

'Here. Every night.'

'But—'

'I saw you arrive.' She remembered the movement at the window. 'I was trying to let you settle. I thought you might run again.'

He didn't know that she couldn't, that she was tethered here for reasons beyond him and that if she ran it would be for reasons beyond him. But she didn't want to run from him any more. She was lost anyway, and there was only one safety she knew.

She glided over to him, her feet resting delicately on his as he balanced on the rock, and she felt him tense at the touch of her bare body pressing against his, the water moving them together in gentle rhythm, gentle friction. His eyes locked on hers as she ran her hands up his arms and shoulders to the back of his neck. She could see how much he wanted her, he had proved it over and over; his eyes had told her everything from the start. But she knew there was still only one way to start this.

'Tell me your name,' she whispered.

Chapter Twenty-Two

She watched him sleep, wondering how it was he could look even more beautiful when his eyes were hooded from her. She couldn't stop looking at him, devouring him rapaciously as he slept deeply beside her, a look of utter calm on his features. He was lying on his back, one arm bent behind his head, and she took in the silky light brown hair of his armpits, the pale underside of his arm, the swell of his biceps, soft for now, the muscular ridges over his stomach, the hint of his ribs below his chest.

She leaned over and lightly kissed his nipple, unable to stop herself, able to still taste the salt on his skin. His clothes, sodden and torn from where he'd pulled them off, were in a ragged heap on the floor; hers were still on the beach. She looked up at him, startled to find him watching her back.

They blinked at each other as last night's memories replayed between them. She didn't feel shy, but words were lost to her in his gaze. She had been right to fear this, right to succumb to it. All the pain that had lodged in her over the past week had been dissipated in his arms. She could feel gravity losing its hold on her as he drew her into his orbit, his world, his bed, his body. She felt delirious, almost happy.

In one swift movement, he reached over and pulled her up, settling her on his stomach so that she nearly covered the length of him. Their bodies matched, moulding together perfectly. He clasped her head with his hands and raised his own to kiss her, his stomach rock solid beneath hers. 'Good morning.'

'Hi,' she breathed, not wanting him to stop.

He obliged, kissing her again. 'Sleep well?'

Clem nodded. Being so close to those eyes, seeing the lust, humour and tenderness dancing through them all at once, she wanted to dive in and play. Now that she'd started, she didn't want to stop.

'Are you hungry?'

She almost shivered. His accent gave the words an edge Freddie Haycock, Josh or Jake could never muster. 'Not for food,' she murmured, pushing herself up to kiss him again.

He groaned as she opened her legs around him, straddling his hips, and in the next instant, he rolled her in one fluid movement onto her back, pinning her beneath him. She arched up into him as he kissed her neck, her collarbone, her breasts, before finding her mouth again, his hands covering hers, and sliding her arms back above her head. She moaned, both helpless and helpless with desire.

'Clem, Clem,' he murmured, his eyes blackened with lust. 'I think you will be the undoing of me.'

She laughed, hooking her ankles around him and keeping him as tightly pinned to her as she was to him. So long as they never had to leave this room, everything would be OK.

'Gabriel.'

Chad looked up at her in surprise as she dropped her bag

on the cobbles and sat down in the chair beside him. A white Americano coffee was already waiting for her.

He shifted position and regarded her carefully, taking in her loose-limbed movements and flushed skin, the provocative look in her eyes. 'I see,' he murmured, a slow, hesitant grin beginning to climb over his face. 'So then things just became—'

'A lot less complicated? Yes.' She sipped her coffee, looking at him across the rim. 'But discretion is the better part of valour. Please keep it to yourself. I'm only telling you because we're working so closely together.'

'Well, I'm glad you told me,' he nodded, beaming broadly now. He looked out to sea. 'Wow!'

Clem giggled, looking around them with an ease that would have been unthinkable twenty-four hours earlier. She felt protected, cocooned now, as if her heart had been bubble-wrapped and anything that tried to get in would simply bounce off her. 'Any joy with the tweeds?'

'Joy?' he repeated, amused by her newly buoyant vocabulary. 'Sure. Check this out.' He opened up the iPad and brought up some images, flicking from page to page slowly. 'I've got samples being couriered over for these ones,' he said, pointing to a honey tweed with blue vertical thread, and a mossy green with a red thread. 'Should be here this arvo.'

Clem rolled her eyes at the Australianism – put on for her benefit – as she watched a photogenic couple jog across the piazzetta from the castle and into the near corner that would take them inland. Did Gabriel run? He must do. He exuded athleticism, a low-key but sharp strength and stamina that he'd proved time and again over the last thirty-two hours. She checked her watch. He would be back at ten tonight. Twelve hours to go. She could hardly bear it.

'Oh my God, look at you!' Chad chuckled. 'You're grinning like a crazy woman.'

'Am I? Sorry.'

'You're a goner, you know that, right?'

Clem bit her lip, trying to contain her delight. She'd been a goner long before she'd ever kissed him. Long before she'd known his name. He'd captured her that night at the Electric, that night . . .

Her smile disappeared. Fleur. She'd forgotten all about her. That day in Claridge's he had said he'd end it with her there and then, but had it just been a line? This girl had, after all, attended a meeting for remodelling his house and boat, which was hardly something she would do if their relationship was just a casual thing. Then again, he'd got Clem doing exactly the same thing, remodelling his house and boat to *her* vision, before she'd even known his name. How many other women did he have, all thinking they were number one in his life? Stella and Tom had been right that day when they'd landed the contract – she never usually cared if they had girlfriends, but she felt flattened by the thought now.

She tried to push the thoughts out of her mind, looking around them. It was early May and high season was just beginning, but the port was already almost at capacity, with tourists taking photos of themselves down by the water's edge, and the outside tables of the cafés and bars all taken. She watched in a new subdued silence as awnings were steadily rolled out, parasols put up; the sun was making its way over the hills behind them and throwing beams like bombs into the port.

Not that the white-hot glare was a problem for Clem. She was already incognito in her Tom Ford shades – the khaki green ones – worn with flip-flops and an easy grey-marl drop-waist minidress. No leather today. As Chad had said, it was getting too hot.

She watched a three-legged dog trot across the square, scaring off the pigeons that were pecking fishy remnants on the slipway.

'Are you seeing anyone, Chad?' she asked.

'Engaged actually. My fiancée lives in Rome.'

She tried to imagine him as a groom. Today he was wearing pale purple jeans, a white linen shirt and a grey v-necked cardigan. She didn't see him in morning suit or black tie. 'Rome? But then what are you doing here?'

'Gotta go where the work is.' He shrugged. 'I get back often enough and most weekends.'

'She must miss you.'

'She's a busy girl. She's got her own things going on.'

'Is she Aussie as well?'

'Native Roman. We met when I did up her father's place.'

Clem smiled. 'What's her name?'

'Fiammetta.'

'Beautiful.'

'Yeah, she is. Most beautiful thing you've ever seen. She's like one of their statues come to life.'

'I'm really happy for you, Chad.'

He looked across at her and patted her hand. 'I'm really happy for you. I thought you were the saddest girl I'd ever seen when we met last week.'

She tried to smile it off. 'I've had a lot going on.' Understatement of the *century*.

'Well, I'm glad things have turned out right. Now you can spend all Gabriel's money without any concerns at all.'

That did make her laugh. 'Exactly.'

Her phone beeped and she knew without looking at it that it was Stella. She hadn't picked up her messages at all yesterday, which was tantamount to placing an obituary in *The Times*.

'WTF? What's going on? Text back NOW or calling Interpol.'

She rolled her eyes and tapped back as Chad asked for the bill.

'NOW.'

'Hafuckingha. Was worried!'

'Don't be. All good here.'

'Good how?'

Clem paused. *'I know his name.'*

*'*screaming*'*

'I can hear you from here.'

'Good?'

'Too good.'

'No such thing. Jealous!'

'We'll see.'

'STOP that. Enjoy him. Is three-month limit in place?'

'Hopefully.'

'Hopefully? Hopefully not then.'

The waiter came over with the bill and Chad paid. Clem could see the uniformed driver, Luigi, walking towards them.

'Gotta go.'

'Call me later. Insist.'

'Fine x'

She rose and picked up her bag. They were driving down to the boatyard today – the wind had picked up and the water was too rough for an hour-long journey – to start consulting together on the interior spec. It was much more

Clem's forte and she was looking forward to it. Most boats were fitted out with marine leather finishes, as it was water-proofed and easy to keep clean from the twin corrosives of salt and sandy rain. She had been mugging up on the very latest technologies the week before she'd flown out, and had a file full of ideas, but she still needed Chad's input for areas like the bathrooms and entertaining salons. 'I'm just going to the loo,' she said. 'I'll meet you in the car in a minute.'

'Sure thing.'

Clem wove her way through the tables to the dark, cool building behind them. The door was heavy and she pushed it open with her shoulder, pausing for a moment to see where the toilet signs were. Several tables had been dressed with tablecloths and cutlery, but only the waiters were indoors, one with his back to her, pouring frascati into carafes.

The ceilings were barrelled, suggesting the café had once been either a wine store or boat house, and the walls were lined with sepia-toned photos of the port back in the Fifties.

She saw the universal silhouette of a woman painted on a far wall, and walked towards it, the image of Gabriel and Fleur kissing in the dark, swimming before her eyes, a buzz in her brain.

'Clem?'

Clem stopped and turned. A woman with big, round brown eyes and a plump mouth was staring at her in aston-ishment. She was standing in a doorway, a bunch of files in her arms and a biro in her hair.

'Ch . . .' Clem stammered. 'Chiara? What are you doing here?'

'I am asking you the very same question!' Chiara

laughed, dropping the files on the nearest table and walking over to her. She rested her hands on Clem's arms, her eyes travelling up and down her with undisguised amazement. 'You are exactly the same.'

Look, no shadow, Clem thought. 'And you. You haven't changed a bit.' That wasn't quite true. The last time they had seen each other, Chiara had been as round as a pudding with a frizz problem. Now, she looked like she had been whittled by a potter, with shapely calves contouring into tiny ankles, a tight waist splaying into soft hips. 'You don't look a day over twenty.'

'You are too polite,' Chiara admonished disbelievingly. 'When did you come here? Just today?'

Clem hesitated. 'Last week actually.'

'Last . . .?'

'I'm so sorry. I was going to call, but I've just been snowed under with work since I arrived. I had no idea what I was getting myself into.'

Chiara smiled, less certainly. 'You are doing the advertising in Portofino?'

Clem remembered her last letter and how she'd told her about the job before last. 'No, no. I work for my brother now. He has a leather business. We're doing up a house on the headland.'

Chiara considered for a moment. 'Villa ai Cedri? The Frenchman's house?'

'That's right.'

'There has been much talk about it in the village. I . . . I cannot believe that it is you.' Chiara held her hands out, smiling.

'I know! I know.' Clem nodded, not quite able to meet her eyes. She knew it was unforgivable that she hadn't called; that Chiara's wasn't the first place at which she had stopped. But it was too hard. How was she supposed to just walk – of her own accord – smack back into her past? 'What are you doing here? You don't own this too now, do you?'

'No. But I do their books. It is my other job.' She frowned. 'I think I told you this in my letters, no?'

'Yes, I remember.'

'You must come to dinner. You know you must. Tomorrow night?'

The door swung open, a hiss of warm air and outside chatter rushing in. Chad stepped inside. 'Everything OK?'

'Yes, absolutely,' Clem managed. 'I just ran into Chiara here.'

'Oh, you know each other?' Chad asked, wandering over and giving her an easy kiss on the cheek. 'Hi, doll. How are you?'

'*Bene*, Chad.' She smiled.

'How do you two know each other then?' he asked.

'Oh we . . . we go way back,' Clem murmured.

'Yeah?' He looked between the two of them.

'We are pen pals,' Chiara explained. 'Since school.'

'No shit!' Chad exclaimed, laughing in surprise. 'Since school? You two must have really hit it off!'

'Something like that,' Clem nodded.

Her eyes met Chiara's and the two of them lapsed into silence. Both their smiles had gone.

Chapter Twenty-Three

It was no good. She couldn't pretend. It had been pointless thinking that Gabriel was the answer, the way to put space between her and her past when it had been thrust in her face twice in three days. It was more than she could handle; she was rattled and completely on edge as ghosts came alive all around her.

She watched as the boat drew nearer, the sound of the motor so distinctive to her now, her feet drumming the soil smooth beneath her as she jogged nervously on the spot. She could see him clearly in the moonlight, his face turned towards the lamp-lit folly, his eyes scanning it for signs of movement inside, looking for her.

It was five to ten. He was good to his word.

A lump formed in her throat at the thought of what he'd think and feel when he saw that she'd not been true to hers. Nothing but a smile she'd promised. She could see him loosening his tie, handing his briefcase to Stefano, then the two men diverging as the skipper continued up the steps to the house and Gabriel turned into the gardens. The lights were still on and she kept her eyes on him as he moved through the pools of light from one to the next, chain links that brought him closer to her.

He walked quickly over the bridge, not looking down at

the path at all, his focus solely on the folly that was now ahead and coming into view. She crouched down, watching as he half-walked, half-ran down the meandering path, cutting the corners to save time and get to her faster. She saw him pause at the door before turning the handle and letting himself in.

The lights were on inside and she saw him, through one of the porthole windows, stand at the bottom of the stairs, taking in the empty room. He ran up the steps lightly, easily, and she saw his head and shoulders through the top window, the freeze of his body as he took in the empty, made-up bed.

Then he was running back down, turning round and round in the folly, looking for her, even though there was nowhere for her to hide inside. The front door flung open and his silhouette filled the doorway, urgency in his movements, tension in his limbs. She saw his desperation, even from this distance, and the shock of it made her lose her balance, falling back onto the dry earth, her feet slipping on the shallow soil and sending rivulets of mud and stone skittering down the bank.

The sound reached his ear and he turned towards her.

Clem froze. There was good tree cover here, it was why she had chosen it – it was the only watch point where she could see him clearly from the cove, through the gardens, all the way to the folly, and not be seen herself.

But he had seen her. Or sensed her.

In an instant he was running up the bank, his arms like pistons, powering him up the dirt track towards her with a speed that was terrifying. She scrambled back up the bank, feeling panic rise. This wasn't part of her plan. She was already tired from her earlier run, another exhausting run where she'd tried to pound the feelings out of her. She'd wanted only for him to see her gone, to understand it had been a mistake and to leave again. He wasn't supposed to do this.

She ran without knowing where she was running to. It was dark and there were no lights up here in this part of the garden, but her eyes had become attuned to the dimness and she ran fleetly, as desperate to escape as he was to catch. She understood vaguely the shape of the garden, knowing its boundaries from the paths that encircled it in loops and twists, and she knew that soon the walls would scoop her back down from the top, taking her beneath the trees towards the level of the house. If she could just get back to the folly and lock the door . . .

He was gaining. She could hear him behind her, though he hadn't said a word, hadn't called her name, hadn't asked her to stop.

She saw a faint light ahead, a sign that she was tracking back towards the main part of the garden, and she headed towards it. The dirt path had disappeared altogether now, lost somewhere in the shadows behind her, and she was running ankle-deep through flowers, fragile heavy-headed flowers that snapped beneath her feet and left her footprints there like arrows.

There was a short drop, five feet or so, from the edge of the flowerbed to the path, coming out just by the bridge, and she jumped it, landing like a cat in her trainers.

She straightened up, but in the next moment he had landed beside her, his hands instantly pinioning her arms to her body as he pushed her against the wall by the bottom of the steps, trapping her.

Neither of them said a word; they couldn't, their chests were heaving with the effort of breathing and recovering.

She stared up at him, giddy from the night air and disoriented by his sudden proximity as he bore down on her with silent fury. God, he was gorgeous. How could she have run from him? How could she have fooled herself that she wouldn't share him if that was the only way to have him? How could she have thought he wasn't enough?

She saw that his shirt was torn, his clothes muddied and covered with grass stains.

'You . . . you've ruined your clothes,' she panted as he stared at her darkly, trying to get his breath back.

'Small . . . price to pay,' he replied, his voice deep and strained, his accent thicker than she remembered.

She waited for the question to come – Why? – but part of her already knew he wouldn't ask. He would chase her, he would keep chasing her, but only so far. She had to give too. It was how they were. Their thing. *Them.*

'Fleur,' she said finally, her breathing returning to normal.

He paused fractionally as understanding hit and relief eased his features. 'Yes.'

'Pretty name.' Clem angled her head. 'She's a pretty girl.'

He nodded. 'She is. She's my assistant.'

The words floored her. 'What?'

'She slapped me as soon as the door closed that night in the Electric. I had to give her a pay rise on the spot.'

'You mean—'

'I was using her to make you jealous, yes.'

Clem felt her muscles soften involuntarily beneath his grip. 'Oh.'

'I had to give her another pay rise to go along with it at Claridge's.' He shrugged, his hands loosening slightly around her arms, more confident that she wouldn't run now. 'Small price to pay.'

A tiny smile hovered around the edge of her lips at the echo and she tried to lean into him, she wanted him to kiss her, but his hands on her arms kept her pressed back, close but not close enough. He hadn't forgiven her for running from him yet, for making him believe for four whole minutes that it was over. She could feel the heat rising off him and she closed her eyes, trying to smell him, inhale his scent.

He released her arms. She opened her eyes as he caught the hem of her top and pulled it over her head in one seamless movement, so that she was in just her bra. With one step he reached around her, unhooking it and throwing it over the side of the bridge where it sprawled on the footpath below.

She laughed with shock to be so suddenly half naked in the night, the sound dying in her throat as she saw the look in his eyes. Then his hands were on her waist, lifting her and she wrapped her legs around him as he carried her to the top of the steps beside them, pushing her down, her back arching with the tiny bridge's curve, the stone cold and hard against her skin.

He kissed her urgently, the scare she'd given him transposing into an angry passion now as he undressed them both. She kept up, her hunger matching his, because she had felt it, too. The difference was, she was still running scared.

'I want to show you something,' Gabriel said, wrapping his shirt around her and rolling the cuffs up to free her hands, seemingly forgetting all about her running clothes which they'd left strewn by the steps, her bra still lying under the bridge – just like her clothes abandoned on the beach. Little monuments to the passion that rocked them both.

He held her hand in his and led her through the gardens, walking slightly ahead of her in just his trousers, the midnight moon catching the glint of sweat on his back and making it shine. Clem lagged back, enjoying watching him move as much as she liked watching him sleep. Everything about him was magnificent, the way his muscles rose and fell beneath the surface of his skin in rolling waves, the feeling of his hand covering hers, how a solitary tendril of his hair curling at the nape of his neck left her itching to tuck it in.

She felt soothed again. Settled once more. A bedtime routine for grown-ups.

They walked past the still pool and the ripening kitchen garden; past the lemon trees and under the jasmines that scented the night and decorated the days.

'How long have you had this house?' she asked, stroking the back of his hand with her thumb.

He looked back at her. 'Five months.'

'How can you afford it?'

He paused. 'That is your way of asking what I do?' He smiled.

She shrugged.

'My family is wealthy. We own a grand cru vineyard in Champagne. I work for them.'

'Oh.'

They had reached the main house and he stopped by the door, pulling her in for a kiss. 'Do you like champagne?' he murmured.

She could only nod.

'Good.'

They walked through the hall in their bare feet and up the stairs, not a creak giving them away. He led her to the bedroom in the south tower, where the ivy-fresco'd ceiling swirled to a point and a four-poster bed was the only furniture in the room. She walked towards it and sat down, looking back at him leaning against the wall, watching her.

'Why do you live here when you've got so little furniture around you?' she asked.

'Because you're here,' he replied. 'I usually stay at the Splendido.'

She bit her lip, watching him. The simplicity of his answers was disarming after so many weeks and months of game-playing.

'I thought I was never going to see you again,' she said, giving a shrug so big that his shirt slipped off her shoulders a little. 'After the christening I mean.'

He shook his head as if the idea was absurd. 'I had to find a way to make our lives collide properly. It took time to set up.'

'Why . . .' She cleared her throat. 'Why did you want me so much? I mean, you didn't know me. I was just another girl on the street.'

He frowned, as though her words made no sense to him, even though she knew he was fluent in French, English and most probably Italian, too. 'My Portobello girl,' he said, looking down at the floor, drawing the words out slowly, as if they were soothing to say. He lifted his eyes to hers. 'When I think about you in the day, when I am working, what I see is you on that golden bike in the rain.' He cracked a small, amused smile. 'The way you laughed and shouted at me for being in your way, even though *you* were in the wrong . . . that hat and the glimpse of your eyes beneath it . . . You took the breath from me. I chased after you all the way to your friend's flat. You were fire. The deal was done.'

She didn't know what to say. No one had ever spoken about her like this before. 'Where had you been going?'

'To a dinner at a house in Elgin Crescent. I was late.' He smiled. 'You made me later still.' He shook his head and Clem could see he'd been in trouble for it.

He crossed the room and picked up a large gift-wrapped box. 'But here – this is what I wanted to give you.'

He sat on the bed next to her, watching her face as she pulled out the rose-pink jumpsuit and . . . oh God! Her mother's Birkin! '*You* bought these?' she gasped. 'But how? You weren't there. I would have seen you. Or Fleur,' she added.

He watched her closely, his eyes roaming her face. 'I sent someone else from my office – I couldn't send Fleur after the way you'd reacted at the hotel.'

'But how did you even know about it?'

'I saw you handing out the flyers at the christening. You were so secretive about it, it raised my interest. Besides, you had changed your pattern completely, working late every night, not going out—'

'Did you *actually* have me followed?'

He shrugged. 'In my life, people are very often vetted. It is not a malicious thing. Did you even notice?'

She shook her head. She had to admit she hadn't.

'I was trying to find a way in with you.' His eyes glittered. 'Especially as you were so determined to make it difficult for me. Not *even* asking my name . . .' He shook his head, an amused smile on his lips; she knew no other woman had ever tested him like her.

'You weren't invited to that christening, were you?' It was more of a statement than a question.

He grinned. 'People never ask, it's extraordinary.'

'So that family has got christening photos with a complete stranger in them.' She giggled, knowing full well why no one had questioned who he was: they wouldn't dare risk him leaving. His very presence would have felt heaven-sent.

'When the tweet about the sale came, I told the girl to buy the finale item and the bag. My mother has some Birkins, so I know a little about them.' His words were modest, but Clem had a feeling he was more of a connoisseur than he was letting on – a cultured Frenchman from a grand cru champagne house was bound to have more than a passing acquaintance with the Hermès icon. 'And for you to have come into possession of a Shooting Star model? I thought it must be . . . significant. Was I right?'

Clem looked down at the Birkin in her hands, securing the straps together the way her mother always did. Not just a bag.

'Yes,' she whispered. 'You were.'

Chapter Twenty-Four

Clem stood by the door, the umbrella bouncing softly in her hand as raindrops trampolined on it, water rushing through the downpipe beside her and emerging in torrents at the other end. Her shoes – leather-soled – were soaked, but she hadn't noticed. She was staring at the doorbell, summoning the strength to push it. She'd been there for nearly ten minutes already.

The door opened and Chiara reached her arm out, taking her by the hand.

'I've been watching you on the CCTV. We have it for guests,' Chiara pointed to a small camera overhead. 'It's OK. It's just us tonight . . . Come in.'

Clem walked into the corridor. She had arrived at the back door, which was directly accessible from the footpath into the port. Entering through the front meant walking along the road itself, a bad idea in these conditions.

She tried, unsuccessfully, to collapse the umbrella, but Chiara took it from her in quiet understanding.

'You are OK?' she asked, looping her arm through Clem's.

Clem looked down at her and nodded as Chiara led them down the back staircase, towards the kitchen.

'Rafa has Luca tonight. I thought we should talk, just the

two of us. I have made Braciole alla Livornese. I remember it was your favourite, no?'

Clem hadn't eaten it since her last visit here, but she nodded again and tried to smile.

They stepped into the kitchen and she shivered. Nothing had changed. The place looked exactly the same as it did ten years ago – the cream walls, terracotta floor, glazed orange crockery on open shelves, thin lace blinds, all locally made, hanging at the windows. Even the back-door key, she saw, still hung from the same hook.

'Drink this,' Chiara said, pouring a glass of Soave and handing it to her.

'Sorry, sorry,' Clem mumbled. 'I'll be fine in a minute.'

'Is OK. It was always going to be hard.'

Clem necked the drink, wincing as it burned her throat, and held out the glass for another. Chiara refilled it for her, then went over to a pot on the range and began stirring, looking back at her carefully, assessing her.

'Does anyone know?' she asked quietly.

Clem shook her head vehemently. 'No one. I never told a soul.' She swallowed hard. 'You?'

'No.' They lapsed into their own thoughts, how both their lives had been irrevocably changed by the secret they had kept.

'The letters . . .'

'They kept me going.' Clem looked at her gratefully. 'You don't know what they meant to me.' Clem took another sip of wine, the edge beginning to round off her now. 'I was so sorry to hear about your mother. I know how close you were. She was an incredible woman.'

Chiara sighed heavily, looking back into the simmering pot. 'It is very difficult still. I miss her every day. Little things, you know? Maybe a nice comment from a guest in the book that would make her proud, or . . . or Luca coming first in his spelling test.'

'He must miss her, too.'

Chiara nodded. 'Yes. It has been bad for him. They adored each other.'

Clem watched as Chiara crossed the kitchen and snapped some basil leaves from a plant on the windowsill, tearing them up in her hands and checking their aroma. She was wearing a white apron with two small blue-painted hand-prints splayed across the front pouch pocket. 'Luca, 2.10.06' had been written in spidery writing beneath.

'I'm sorry about you and Rafa, too. I really am. You were together a long time.'

'Yes . . .'

'You look exhausted,' Clem said, seeing the bags under Chiara's eyes, the undercurrent of weariness in her move-ments.

Chiara sighed and smiled. 'Since Rafa left, it has been almost impossible to do it on my own.'

'Can't you sell? You'd get an absolute fortune for this plot. You could move back to Florence and have the career you always wanted.'

'I cannot. Mama left a third share of the hotel to Rafa.'

Clem looked at her in surprise. 'What?'

'I don't blame her. She thought we were going to marry; we had been together a long time, eight years.' Chiara shrugged. 'He was like a son to her after Papa died; he did so much to keep the hotel happy.'

'But you've still got the majority share surely? You could still sell.'

'The other third is in Luca's name, held in trust until he is eighteen.'

'Oh, Chiara! I don't know what to say.'

Chiara shrugged, coming back over with the wine bottle and refilling it for them both. 'It is a mess. We don't have the money to do the repairs or decoration so we cannot charge more money for the rooms; and without more money coming in, we cannot afford the repairs. It is a – how you say?'

'Vicious circle.' Clem nodded. 'Yes, I can see that.'

'I try to make extra money with the accounting, but I am so busy with the hotel all day, and we have to make the season as long as possible . . .' She sighed. 'The days are not long.'

'Not long enough, no.' Clem bit her lip. Her problem was always the opposite – they were too long. She tried moving the subject to something happier. 'Are you seeing anyone new?'

Chiara rolled her eyes. 'No! Where would be the time? And how would I meet anyone new? It is a small town here. Everybody knows everybody.'

'You said in your letter that Rafa has a new girlfriend, though.'

'Sure.'

'Are you . . . OK with that?'

Chiara hesitated. 'It was sore, for sure, but we were not romantic for a long time before we broke out.'

'Broke up.'

Chiara giggled. 'My English.'

'Hey, your English is a lot better than my Italian. I'm really struggling to get my ear in again.'

'Maybe not a surprise. You have tried to forget it.' Chiara patted her hand in understanding. 'I think Rafa stayed so long only because of Mama. She was sick and—'

'Oh God! You don't think he hung around, knowing she'd put him in her will do you?'

'No!' Chiara's tone made them both jump. 'He is not that man.'

'Sorry.'

'You are not the first to say it,' Chiara said, trying to smile and soften the words. 'But I know, in my heart, it was as much a surprise to him as to me. He is good. It is hard between us at the moment, for sure, but it will be OK in the end. For Luca it will be OK.'

'They're close?' Clem traced the grain of the wooden table with her eyes.

'Devoted.' Chiara tipped her head down, trying to catch Clem's eyes. 'And you? You have a boyfriend? I bet you do!'

Clem smiled. She couldn't not. After the fright she'd given him last night, Gabriel had taken the day off again, ruthlessly eradicating her doubts and fears, making her fall deeper and deeper. 'There is someone,' she nodded.

'It is serious, I can tell,' Chiara said, watching her closely.

'Maybe.'

'Do you love him?'

Clem inhaled sharply. 'Trying not to.' She bit her lip.

'Trying?' Chiara echoed, frowning.

Clem met her eyes, tears filling them, and she took another deep breath, trying to stay in control, trying so hard.

'Oh, I see,' she said sadly, squeezing Clem's hand tightly in her own.

She was the only person in the world who really did.

Two hours later, dinner had burned but the cellar had been relieved of three bottles of wine and the world had been put to rights. They were sitting on the balcony outside the main reception, the rain smattering the faded yellow and white striped awning above them, their feet resting on the metal balustrade, their eyes out to sea.

To the far right, almost out of sight, Clem could just make out the subdued lights that dotted the upper gardens of Villa ai Cedri, where last night Gabriel had chased her, caught her and made love to her. Just the memory of it made her skin tingle.

He wasn't there tonight. She had told him about her dinner plans with Chiara and he had taken the opportunity to fly back to France for forty-eight hours. The thought of him not just over the sea, but a country away, made her feel hollow inside, frightening her all over again that she could feel so deeply already. Her three-month rule had never felt so flimsy or unenforceable.

The rain had brought a strong wind with it – or maybe it was the other way round – and they watched as a sleek double-masted yacht that had dropped anchor just outside the port that afternoon, rocked slowly on the whipped-up waves. It was only the beginning of May, but this yacht was just the first of many that would moor here in the coming months, the size of the boats in inverse proportion to the size of the tiny port.

That almost seemed to be the point. The sleeker, bigger and faster the boats, cars and visitors became, the more Portofino seemed to revel in its slow, small, faded grandeur. The harbourside buildings weren't added on to or rebuilt in the pan-modernistic style of the international rich. The paintwork hadn't been revised to a fashionable, sludgy palette – windows and doors remained stubbornly dark green or dark brown – and some of the buildings had paint flaking off them, revealing bare plaster beneath or all but losing the fanciful embellishments imbued by trompe l'oeil trickery.

It was exactly as it had been in the Fifties – that was its unique appeal. Everyone got to imagine they were Audrey Hepburn or Cary Grant when they were here because it was as unchanged as when they had stepped over the cobbles. It was one of the few places left in the world where time had stood still and where old-school glamour could still be found.

Everyone aspired to come here, which was why it was so horribly ironic that Chiara couldn't make the hotel turn a profit. The hotel – well, its sun terraces over the road – stood right on the water on the first cove out of the port, just a three-minute walk away. It was the only such property in the Portofino area that wasn't run as a private residence and the plot alone was worth tens of millions. But Chiara couldn't sell. She wanted to do it up, but she couldn't raise the capital through her revenue stream, because the facilities weren't smart enough to charge more. And she couldn't earn more because there weren't enough hours in the day (Clem had clocked the files sitting on the kitchen table, ready for her to work on through the night). Poor Chiara was damned if she did, damned if she didn't, locked in a cycle of too much work and not enough sleep.

She had given Clem a tour earlier, walking her through the bald, basic bedrooms with beds as hard as tables and pillows with all the stuffing of a teenager's bra. Most of the guests only booked with her because of the hotel's exclusive private beach and the tiered terraces that gave a stunning panoramic view of the sea and the entrance to the port.

Chiara had grand plans for the place in principle – or

rather, Rafa had – wanting to convert one of the basement stores into a spa and open a cocktail bar on the roof. But they were pipe dreams when she couldn't even afford to replace the single glazing in the windows.

Or . . .

Clem sat up suddenly, tipping her chair forward so that it came to rest on all four legs again.

Chiara looked across at her, her sensuous face dreamy and relaxed for once as the wine spirited her worries away for a night. 'What? What is it?' She smiled.

'I'm not sure,' Clem frowned. 'I think I might just have had an idea.'

Chiara arched a thick but beautifully shaped eyebrow.

Clem turned to face her, wondering how to begin. 'Just . . . just before I came out here, I came into some money.' She shook her head. 'Well, no, not came into. I made it. Quite a lot of it. I mean, not enough to do all the things you want to do, but it would allow you to upgrade – to a four star at least.'

Chiara pushed her chair forward and frowned. 'Clem, no. I could not let you do that.'

'Just wait, hear me out. The money wasn't ever supposed to be for me. I can't spend it. I made it for my brother but he doesn't want it. In fact, he refuses to touch it. And . . .' She took a deep breath, her mind racing. 'And he's not going to need it now anyway, as what I'm doing out here is far bigger than we'd realized.' She smiled at Chiara. 'You can have it. I want you to have it.'

Chiara shook her head, but Clem was used to drinking far more than her hostess, and her thoughts were clearer, her wits sharper. 'Yes. Look, I can help advise you, and you already know Chad. I'm sure he'd help.'

'He is one of the most famous interior designers in Italy. I could never afford him.'

Clem tipped her head to the side. 'He's a good guy. And frankly, with what he's being paid to assist at Villa ai Cedri, he doesn't need the money. I reckon he'd be good for it.'

'You are so kind, Clem, but I cannot accept.'

Clem slid off her chair and crouched down beside Chiara, looking up at her. 'After what you did for me all those years ago? I'm not asking you, Chiara. I insist. You have no choice. We both know I am in your debt.'

Chapter Twenty-Five

'What?' Stella screeched down her ear, making Clem lose her balance. 'So you're telling me that now you're doing a villa, a boat *and* a hotel? Jesus Christ, Clem, for the girl who never did anything but drink vodka under the desk and hide out in the Hummingbird, you've sure grown yourself a work ethic out there.'

Clem hopped on to her other foot. She was standing in the middle of the long room, waiting for Chad to arrive with the specialist painters who were going to be starting work on the frescoes on the exteriors of the villa. 'I'm not physically painting the walls or making the curtains, Stell. I'm consulting. Outsourcing.'

'Oooh, get you. A consultant.' Clem rolled her eyes as Stella rolled off some 'la di dahs'. 'Well, just so long as it doesn't mean you're out there even longer.'

'No reason why it should. It's all going fairly tickety-boo so far. The hardest part is actually deciding on all the different schemes and getting down to the nuts and bolts of what we need and where. We need to get the orders in for the products and materials as soon as possible, as most of them are on six- to eight-week delivery schedules, some a bit more. But I reckon I'll be done and out of here by the end of August, give or take a week.'

'Oh do you?' Stella's tone showed she wasn't so convinced. 'And what about luvaboy?'

'What do you mean?'

'Well, I take it you realize that the end of August is over *three months* away?'

'So?'

'Well, either you're going to have to dump your boss before he's paid you – awkward! – or you're going to have to break your own rule.'

Clem was silent for a moment. Could she manage without Gabriel out here? He was her buffer, her safety, her escape. 'Things are different out here. I'm trying not to project. I'm just taking each day as it comes.'

'Project? Have you swallowed some sort of self-help manual?' Stella demanded suspiciously.

'Nope.'

'You were intercepted by the Scientologists at the airport?'

'I was not.' Clem laughed. 'I'm just concentrating on living in the moment.'

'Oh my God! You're Shirley MacLaine's love child!' Stella hollered.

'Well, that would be preferable to being my mother's.' Clem giggled, jumping from one wood strip to another.

'Talking of the wicked witch, any word?'

'I've sent the bag back, but there's been no response. Tom's spoken to me only once since I've been here, and I've tried ringing home, but no one picked up. They're obviously all still sulking with me.'

'Mmm, well, I haven't seen your folks about, now that you mention it. Although, of course, your mother always crosses the street when she sees me.'

The sound of a door opening and voices in the hallway made Clem look up. 'Oh, Chad's here, I've got to go.'

'All right. Keep me posted. But no more new jobs, OK? Please remember I live vicariously through you, and I'm flipping exhausted right now.'

Clem grinned. 'Deal. Laters.'

She clicked off as Chad appeared round the corner, a vision in narrow white linen shorts that clung to his muscular legs, and a blue striped seersucker jacket.

She grinned at the sight of him. 'Hey. We're twins.' She too was in white shorts, albeit teeny ones, camel ankle boots and a striped matelot T-shirt, her hair pulled back in a floppy ponytail.

'In your dreams, sweetheart.' He laughed, kissing her on both cheeks. 'Sorry we're late. I got stuck on a call with Tissus d'Hélène. There's a delay on the Thibaut wallpaper you liked for the third guest suite and I don't think we can afford to wait. We might have to go back to the drawing board on that one.'

Clem wrinkled her nose. 'Oh, bummer. That was the glade print wasn't it? I really liked the idea of making that room like a garden bower. It's got that lovely magnolia tree that taps at the window.'

'We'll think of something else,' Chad said, leading her outside, where a man was standing with his back to them, examining a section of the wall. 'In the meantime, I want you to meet Rafaello Vicenzo. He's the only remaining painter in the entire district who specializes in trompe l'oeils. It's a dying art, sadly.'

Clem stopped dead in her tracks as the man turned round, his own movements stiffening as he saw her.

He walked towards her, his face as set as if it were a stone mask. She remembered the heaviness of his brow bone and the thick, straight eyebrows that lay across it, his chocolate-brown eyes with lashes as long and thick as hers, the pale matte fullness of his lips, how pretty he looked when he scowled. Brooding had suited him, too, she remembered.

She swallowed. 'Hello, Rafa.'

Chad looked at her in surprise, before realization struck. 'Oh, of course. Chiara's your friend.'

Clem nodded. It wasn't how they'd met, but it didn't matter.

'It was you the other day.' His accent was thick and rolling, like a dark, ominous thundercloud.

'Yes.' She could feel herself beginning to tremble.

He gestured vaguely at the cliff-top estate around them. 'You are working here.'

'That's right.' Only Chad knew about her and Gabriel. She had kept his name a secret even from Chiara – she didn't want it to be openly known in the port but she didn't want *him* to know most of all.

They fell quiet, Clem inhibited and withdrawn, Chad shifting uncomfortably as he took in the atmosphere.

'OK, well, then that's all . . . good,' he said, rubbing his hands together uncertainly as he looked between the two of them. 'Like I said, Raf's going to start on the exterior. We've gone over the colour scheme you chose and where you want the fanlights to be reinstated above the windows. The scaffolding's coming today, right?'

Rafa nodded, but his eyes were trained on Clem.

'Great. Super. Well then, we won't hold you up. I'll come and check on you in a bit, make sure you're happy with everything.'

Chad put a hand on Clem's elbow, moving to steer her

away, but the sound of glass shattering made them all start. They ran round to the side of the house, where a young boy was standing, pale and immobile, looking back at them all. He looked like Bambi, all chocolate-brown eyes and skinny legs, hazelnut-coloured hair flopping over his forehead like a forelock. A football, punctured now, was lying on a bed of glass just inside one of the French doors of Clem's office.

'*Lo siento,*' he stammered as Rafa advanced towards him, his jaw thrust forward in fury as he admonished him in rapid Italian.

'Don't! It's OK,' Clem cried, arms outstretched as she rushed over beside them. 'Really. It's fine.'

Rafa took a reluctant step back. She was, after all, the boss.

Clem looked down at the boy staring up at her, the boy she'd passed just days ago on the path. He looked like he might cry and she knew he was scared of her; knew he thought she was the rich lady going to demand the window be replaced. She crouched down to his level and saw he had the same eyes as his father. 'You must be Luca.'

He blinked at her uncomprehendingly. She looked up at Rafa, wanting him to translate for her. 'He speaks English,' he scowled. 'He is just in panic.'

Clem looked back at the child. 'I've heard *so* much about you, Luca. I'm . . . I'm Clem.'

Slowly, the boy put out his hand, on his best behaviour, trying to make amends for the broken window. She looked at it – such a grown-up gesture from such a small child – and took it in her own. 'A pleasure to meet you.'

'A pleasure to meet you,' he echoed in a voice that was as wobbly as his legs.

She stood up again and Rafa came to stand behind Luca, his hand on the boy's shoulder.

'I will pay for the repairs,' he said, his voice even surlier than before.

'You don't need to do that,' she said. 'Breakages are part and parcel of a job this size.'

He blinked once, his eyes dark and hooded. 'I insist.' And then he turned and walked Luca away.

Clem and Chad watched them go, waiting for them to disappear from sight.

'Anything you want to tell me?' Chad asked quietly, turning to face her.

'Nope,' Clem replied, trying to look surprised by his question.

'You seemed a bit . . . tense with him.'

'Yeah, 'cause he's a guy who's really in touch with his feminine side.' Clem forced a laugh, but she wasn't fooling anyone.

'You'd tell me if you had a problem working with him.'

'Chad, you said he's the only guy in the area who does what he does, right?'

'Yeah.'

'So then there's no problem. It's fine.'

'Cle—' he frowned.

'Chad, we just need to get this job done and get it done right. Because the sooner it's done, the sooner I can get back to my own life, all right?' Her voice was all over the octave, skipping notes, flat and sharp all at once.

He nodded, jamming his hands into his shorts pockets. 'Sure.'

'OK then. Now I'm going to find a dustpan and brush and clear this glass up before someone walks through it.' And she walked back into the house, arms swinging, chin in the air. Her heart somewhere in her boots.

*

Clem dropped her head in her hands, her fingers tonging her hair in tight twists. She had been staring at the plans for hours now, but the day had been a write-off. She'd achieved nothing. She couldn't think straight. The thick plastic sheeting she'd secured at the broken window would keep the wind and rain out, but it rustled noisily in the breeze and she was distinctly aware of Rafa just the other side, his body darkly silhouetted as he moved back and forth and around it, working on the far wall.

She could hear Luca was still with him, intermittently passing brushes or refreshing the water, but mainly kicking the ball whenever he could, the slow-puncture making it bounce lower and lower. They chattered non-stop together, Rafa's voice low – not animated exactly, but certainly more tonal as the boy laughed and teased and told jokes in his high singsong voice, running around him all the while. They had a keepy-uppy competition at one point, not knowing she was sitting there just feet away, their bodies cast in dark relief against the white plastic as they kicked the ball with honed skill and a shared boyish delight.

'Hey.'

She looked up with surprise. Gabriel was leaning in the doorway, his briefcase by his feet, his tie hanging loose around his neck.

'What are you doing here so early?' she cried at the sight of him. He was never home before ten.

'I cancelled the rest of my meetings. The only thing I can think about is you.'

She jumped up and ran over to him, throwing her arms tightly around his neck, burrowing her face in the silky pima cotton of his shirt. She was safe again.

'Are you OK?'

She nodded, not lifting her head. 'I am now.'

He clasped her face with his hands and drew her back to look at her, his eyes scanning her like a computer, wanting to decode her. He bent his head and kissed her, his hands sliding down her back as she moulded herself into him.

'Let's go upstairs,' he murmured.

She nodded. It was the best remedy she knew for escaping herself.

Outside the wind caused the sheeting to crackle again. Gabriel looked up and saw the makeshift window.

'What happened?' He frowned.

'Oh, it was just an accident earlier. We were going to replace them anyway,' she lied, her eyes and ears suddenly straining for a clue as to Rafa's and Luca's whereabouts as she remembered them again. Where were they? Everything was silent outside now, but they had been there just moments earlier. They would have heard every word.

She didn't have time to think about it, though. In the next instant, Gabriel lifted her suddenly, hoisting her over his shoulder, and she laughed out loud in surprise, smacking him on the back. 'Put me down!' she shrieked. 'Stop it! You can't do that!'

'I think you'll find I can,' he demurred, even taking the time to slowly bend down and pick up his briefcase.

Clem laughed and kicked her ankles, trying to get free. When she looked up she saw Rafa standing by the far set of windows, watching them. She went limp at his expression and felt a tremor of fear ripple through her as Gabriel ferried her away, seduction the only thing on his mind, survival the only thing on hers.

Chapter Twenty-Six

Summer took hold. Within a month the skies were tented blue every day, the sea soaking up the sun's warmth for her, as she and Gabriel swam in the cove at night, revelling in the pleasure and pain they found there, the place where they had begun.

The days finally had a rhythm to them, and a soundtrack, too, as an army of workmen banged, tapped, chipped and whistled around the house, Chad furiously debating thread counts with her, the drone of V8s in the bay every evening telling her that her man was back.

She and Chiara had started running together, too. She had never let anyone keep up with her before – not even Stella – but Chiara had the answers to her questions. For Chiara, she was prepared to slow down.

Today, though, she was alone. She ran down the paths she now knew so well. She was becoming recognizable to the locals, too, who enjoyed walking to the lighthouse and watching the sun set, nodding to her as she jogged politely on the spot, allowing them to pass, all of them working up to a '*buonasera*'.

She took the right turn down through the winding paths of the castle gardens, even though it was quicker and easier to go over the top – to do that was to miss the point. She ran on her toes, grabbing onto the handrails on the sharper turns, stretching between uneven steps and flying over broken slabs, and she felt her colour rise and the sweat begin to spread between her shoulder blades as the temperatures stayed above seventy, even at eight o'clock at night.

She emerged from the gates of the overgrown park with an athletic leap, arms outstretched, hair flying as she landed lightly on the cobbles of the harbour, startling the fishermen winding in the nets. She smiled at them and ran past without stopping, not noticing how they paused to watch her go.

The piazzetta was busy again after the afternoon lull, with visitors milling around the water – some eating gelatos, most admiring the yachts that sat on the privileged silken waters – and she dodged them gracefully, arms pumping lightly, her lean legs long and strong in her runners' shorts. Her skin had begun to tan lightly in the sun, even though she spent no time lying in it, and her reflection in the mirror every morning (when she bothered to look) was glowing.

She passed the cafés, their parasols down now; passed the restaurants with their evening specials marked up on the blackboards; passed the waiters standing hovering, smiles ready for the early birds who would make the first sittings of the night.

She disappeared up the ramp in the furthest left corner and ran bouncily up the shallow steps between the tall, narrow houses with starfish-embossed railings and waxy-white potted gardenias. Ahead were the steep steps that would take her up off the road and onto the raised footpath – the home straight – and she geared herself to race up and down them three times, a last burst of anaerobic power before she eased down to the hotel.

She turned the corner of the wall, taking the deep breath she would need to blast her up the steps, when everything suddenly flashed into fast forward and she found herself flying towards the stone steps, simultaneously aware, in her peripheral vision, of a man leaning against a girl leaning against the wall.

She landed heavily on her front, her arms only just breaking her fall, and feeling the skin on her bare knees graze and bleed. She looked up angrily.

The long strap of a red patent handbag was tangled around her feet, but the girl it belonged to seemed unconcerned, one foot propped against the wall, her skirt pushed up her thigh.

'For fuck's sake,' Clem muttered furiously from the step, incensed further by the girl's lack of apology, before noticing her companion staring down at her.

Her stomach twisted. To her relief, he had avoided her for over three weeks now, seemingly only working outside her office walls when she was in Viareggio with Chad, and disappearing into the maze of scaffolding that clad the house like an exo-skeleton the rest of the time. Only the occasional sight of Luca, kicking his ball on the terraces, told her he was in there, somewhere.

Rafa reached out a hand, the gesture gallant but reluctant as she saw the hostility in his eyes; she recoiled, balling herself away from him and scrambling up the steps, her hands like paws on the cold stone as she got herself out of there.

She was at Chiara's in a minute when it should have taken her two, her chest heaving so hard she started coughing, her hands pressing against the wall.

Dammit. Dammit.

She paced the footpath agitatedly, her hands on her hips, trying to calm down, shaking her head as if she had a wasp in her ear.

'*Ciao.*'

She looked up to find Luca peering through the back door, watching her.

'. . . *Ciao*, Luca,' she managed back, straightening up and finding a smile.

He held the door open for her and she followed him in, noticing how upright he was when he walked. He seemed tall for his age and nowhere near as little as he'd seemed to her that first day when he'd smashed the window and shrunk into himself. Her kindness that day appeared to have won his trust, too, and they had begun to share shy smiles through the windows.

'I saw your goal today,' she said in rusty Italian as he automatically paused to let some guests pass on the stairs. 'It was really good.'

'Thank you,' he said, replying in English. Chiara insisted upon it, she knew.

She listened to the sound of his bare feet on the tiled floor. 'Who's your favourite player? Lionel Messi?' she asked provocatively, a teasing tone in her voice. She didn't know much about football but she did know Messi was Argentinian.

'No!' Luca shook his head sternly, a frown creasing the peached smoothness of his flawless skin. 'Ronaldo!'

'Ah! Of course!' Clem chuckled.

Chiara looked up at the sound of their laughter, just as the two of them walked in to the small family kitchen. She was sitting at the table, a small glass of Rioja in front of her, her ledgers spread out left, right and centre.

'Oh, is it time?' she said, looking up at the clock on the wall and starting to gather everything into piles. They had planned to go through the ideas for the dining room tonight. At the moment the hotel only offered half board, with a buffet breakfast and no room-service option. It suited Chiara that way as it meant she didn't have to deal with the three-headed monster of daily changing menus, fresh food ordering or temperamental staff.

But Clem was on her case about it. The fact that the hotel was languishing wasn't just because the décor was out-dated, it was because they weren't offering the amenities discerning modern guests expected. They had the space, and Clem was adamant Chiara had to do it if she was going to get that coveted fourth star.

'Relax,' Clem said, waving her to sit down again, as she poured herself a glass of water from the tap and glugged it. 'There's no rush.'

'But I have not even started dinner.'

Clem wiped her mouth with the back of her hand, taking in how pale Chiara looked again. 'I'll do it. I'm sure I can manage. What were you planning to cook?'

'Lasagne.'

Clem's face fell. Oh. She watched Luca take a yo-yo from his pocket and begin to expertly swirl it around his hands.

'You have not made it before?' Chiara asked, watching her.

She hadn't made anything before, unless boiled penne and a tipped-out jar of ragu counted? 'No, but I'll give it a go,' she said brightly. 'It's actually on my "To Do" list for this year. That and learning to drive. I mean, how hard can it be, right?'

Chiara frowned. 'Do you know how to make a roux for the béchamel?'

'You what?'

Chiara laughed, getting up. 'Is OK, Clem. I like the offer, but I will make it. Is quicker.'

'Oh, Chiara,' Clem moaned, dropping her head. 'I feel so useless. And you've got so much to do.'

'I will show you,' the smallest, highest voice in the room piped up.

Clem and Chiara looked over at Luca. He was spinning and threading the yo-yo between his two hands now. It looked impressive and exceptionally cool.

'He can cook lasagne?' Clem asked Chiara in disbelief. It was one thing him speaking English, out-playing Rafa at football and being an expert on a yo-yo, but he cooked too?

Chiara nodded and laughed. 'He is very good.' She shrugged. 'I taught him four years ago when he was six. Family recipe. We are famous for it in the port.'

'Seriously?' Clem looked at him in wonder, amazed that he had done in six years what she hadn't managed in almost thirty.

'Only if you want.' He gave a lackadaisical shrug and went back to his yo-yo.

'Well . . . I suppose we could give it a go,' she said tentatively, a smile spreading across her face as her eyes met his and she saw devilment there.

They made a great team, meeting somewhere in the middle with her Italian and his English as she chopped, he fried, she poured, he stirred, the two of them powdered white from the brief flour fight that had ensued during the making of the roux (he'd started it!). Every second of it went into the memory bank. She would know how to make lasagne for ever now, she would never forget a moment of this lesson; another acquired skill to knock off her resolutions list.

The timer beeped and they crouched down in front of the oven together, staring in through the glass at the golden bubbling cheese-topped dish.

'Looks ready to me,' Clem said, but deferring to the boss. Luca nodded. 'Me, too.'

They pulled it out and let it cool for a moment. Luca had set the table at the opposite end to Chiara's paperwork, and Clem had made a salad; garlic bread lay warm, sliced and wrapped in a cloth. The perfect family supper was ready. They were good to go.

'*Bella,*' Chiara beamed, pushing her books away and smiling at them both as they brought over the dish and Clem started serving. She felt giddy with triumph as the rich sauce oozed and the smells of Parmigiana and nutmeg fragranced the steamy kitchen, the evening's earlier upset completely forgotten, although her knees still stung.

'*Santé,*' Chiara smiled, raising her glass to the cooks.

Clem and Luca, who had his own small glass of red wine, echoed. 'Or, as we say in England, bottoms up,' Clem smiled at Luca.

Luca giggled at the mention of bottoms – his English was good enough to know that word. 'Guests first, please,' he said, motioning for Clem to begin.

She smiled at his extraordinary manners and took a bite. Just wait till she told her father she could cook. He'd be delighted.

There was silence as she chewed, her hosts waiting eagerly for her response. She began to chew more slowly, her eyes scanning the dish. What . . .?

'Oh! I didn't know lasagne was so . . . spicy, out here,'

Clem managed, waving her hand like a fan in front of her mouth and reaching for her wineglass. She downed it in one, but it was no good, her mouth was on fire. 'Wow! I mean it's really . . .' She exhaled through her puffed-out cheeks. 'Wow! Really hot. We have it, uh, much milder in England.'

Chiara's eyes narrowed as she hastily took a bite. Luca was watching from over the rim of his glass.

Seconds later, Chiara's fork clattered to her plate.

'Luca!' she shrieked, reaching for the water jug and splashily pouring herself a glass.

'What's going on?' Clem asked, her cutlery poised above the plate in nervous trepidation.

'He has put hot chilli powder in instead of nutmeg!' Chiara gasped, gulping down the water and pouring some more, all the while hissing at Luca in a rapid, colloquial Italian that Clem had no chance of keeping up with.

Her eyes met his over the rim of his glass – devilment indeed – and she began to laugh. Really laugh. So hard she had to push her chair back and put her hand against her stomach. It was just the kind of thing she'd done as a child, making her mother tut and Tom shout.

Luca joined in, delighted that their guest's response meant he was more likely to get away with it – even Chiara had to smile.

'Salad, anyone?' she asked finally, her dignified stoicism making Clem and Luca laugh so hard that they didn't notice the visitor standing by the door, watching them all.

Chiara saw him first, addressing him in Italian as she explained what had gone on. Clem's laughter died as Chiara took Rafa by the elbow and led him over.

'Clem, I would like you to meet Rafa.'

Clem tried to smile. Chiara didn't know they knew each other already. She had never known. It had been the one thing, the only thing, Clem had never told her: the final secret. 'We . . . we already met. At the house.'

Chiara's hand dropped. 'Oh yes, of course.' She shook her head vaguely and an awkward silence followed as Rafa felt no need, as usual, to make small talk.

'You have eaten?' Chiara asked him, speaking in English again as a courtesy to Clem, and holding up a plate.

Rafa nodded. 'Yes.' His eyes fell to Clem's bare, scraped knees and she hurriedly swung her legs beneath the table.

Clem tossed the salad and put extra heaps onto Luca's plate. 'Garlic bread?' she asked in a low voice, just the two of them again.

The boy nodded, quieter now that Rafa was here, but sharing a secret, conspiratorial look with her.

'Well, thank you for coming over,' Chiara said, walking away with a sigh and reaching over the windowsill. 'It is the bathroom in room fourteen. There's a cracked tile letting in water to the back.' She handed him a single white square tile.

He took it from her, his features softening slightly. 'Everything is up there?'

'Yes. I moved the guests to room nine instead.'

'Sea view.'

She shrugged. 'There was no other room free.'

Rafa looked back at the others – Clem was watching Luca watching them, a heartbreaking expression on his face – and ruffled the boy's hair roughly as he passed.

Chiara sank back against the worktop as his footsteps disappeared up the stairs.

'Are you OK?' Clem asked, getting up with her plate and

joining her as Luca tore huge chunks off the bread and topped it with tomato from the salad.

'Sure,' Chiara shrugged again, but the sadness emanated from her like a radioactive glow. 'I just . . .' She looked at Luca. 'I just miss him being around. It feels so big here, just us two surrounded by all these strangers every day.'

Clem rubbed her arm. 'I'm so sorry.'

'Every day it becomes more normal,' she said, and Clem could see she was trying to be brave. 'It gets easier.'

'It can't be serious with this new girl, can it?' From the looks of her earlier, she was barely twenty.

Chiara's eyes flickered towards Luca again, her voice lower still. 'I don't know. I don't care, not like that. I don't want him back. I just . . .'

'Don't like him being gone?' Clem offered. 'That's loneliness, its normal. You were together a long time.'

'Yes.'

'We just have to find you a new man.' Clem smiled, winking at her, trying to josh her along. 'Best cure I know for a broken heart. Honestly, works for me every time.'

Chiara rolled her eyes and shook her head, a sad smile on her lips. 'But does it work *really*?' she asked, doubt firing every word. And patting Clem's arm, she walked over to the sink to start on the washing up.

Chapter Twenty Seven

'OK, so these are the prelim sketches for the salons we discussed last week,' Chad said, sliding an artist's A3 pad over the seats to her. They were en route to the boatyard for another meeting with the naval architects and stuck in traffic that was tailing back from an accident in one of the tunnels further on.

Clem looked them over – one for the master en suite, the master bedroom, dressing room and principal lounge – loving the way Chad's illustrations gave her thoughts shape. She wasn't short of ideas, but it wasn't always easy for her to visualize how everything could hang together. She'd spent that last meeting trying to articulate her ideas for a roughed-up luxury for the yacht, wanting to get away from the sleek lines that everyone always did for boats, and falteringly coming up instead with underlit marble in the bathrooms with the edges left stubbly, rather than polished smooth, and the use of coloured semi-precious stones like amethyst and pink topaz for the bar, dining tables and cabinets. It had a strong mineral feeling that she thought would complement the boat's aquatic environment, but she'd worried it might come across as a white witch's wet dream or a teenage girl's stab at fairyland.

She needn't have worried. In Chad's hands, it had a

refined opulence that befitted the grandeur and financial investment such a boat involved: he'd in-filled the walls with his own suggestion of oyster linen, and a huge clipped rabbit-fur rug was shown on the floor, set into a tulip-wood surround. 'Actually a totally practical idea because everyone gets cold feet on a boat, it doesn't matter how grand it is,' he said factually. 'And, of course, they're barefoot all the time, so it won't be worn bald from shoes in ten minutes.'

The car started rolling forwards again, inching into another mile-long tunnel and blocking out the sun.

'I love it,' Clem murmured, automatically switching on an overhead light. 'Especially how the palette's so muted and all the colour just comes from natural, organic things like the stone, you know?'

Chad watched her. 'You know, you're really good at this, Clem. I can't believe you haven't had any formal training.'

She swatted his arm without looking up at him, scrutinizing the colour key he'd painted at the corner.

'I mean it. I'm pretty damn pleased you're not staying on in Italy, I can tell you. I don't fancy the competition.' He checked his list. 'Oh, and we still need to decide on the walls for the green suite in the house by the way. I hope you've been thinking about that? We need to place an order soon or it'll delay the finish date.'

'I keep forgetting. I'll put it on my list to do next.'

She fished her notepad out of her bag and scribbled, 'Green suite – walls', across the top. The list filled seven pages, and most of the time it gave her a headache just looking at it. She could fill every single minute of the day with work if she chose to: coming up with ideas, research and sourcing materials, making decisions for even the tiniest details in the house – which directions would the beds face? Where should the sockets go? What wattage should the lights be? – as well as collaborating on the boat (there was a crazy amount of rules and regulations to comply with, in addition to making it look pretty). And as for the hotel, well, bringing that on board had been a mistake, she thought now, with Chiara resisting everything she suggested. Lack of funds clearly wasn't the real reason the hotel was languishing. Not to mention the fact that she never, ever got a full night's sleep with Gabriel next to her, and the fatigue was beginning to tell. In fact, she'd been so busy, she hadn't even spoken to Stella in almost a week, which was an absolute first in the history of their friendship.

'Did you decide on the woven leather for the headboard in the left attic room?' Chad asked her, drawing a line through his own notes.

'Um, yeah . . . the burnt orange with the black accent in the classic tight weave. Anything bigger and it'll just get caught on fingers and begin to stretch.'

'OK, I'll send off that order to Simon later then, I've got the dimensions somewhere. And I'm going to need to get Gabriel to sign off on these invoices,' Chad said, rifling through another file of papers.

'That's fine. Give them to me. He'll be back from Paris in two days.'

Her phone rang and she picked it up. 'Hello?'

'Bunny? Is that you?'

'*Dad*?'

Chad sat back in the seat at the change in her voice, sliding further away to give her a little privacy.

'How . . . how are you?' she asked, turning to look out

the window and facing only her reflection in the dark walls instead.

'Well,' She heard him take in a deep breath. 'I have to be honest, darling, it's been a rotten few weeks. We've been rather low.'

Clem squeezed her eyes shut. She had done that to them. *She* had. 'I'm so sorry, Daddy.' How many times could she say it? 'Did you get the bag?'

'Yes, we did. Your mother is very grateful.'

'I didn't know if you were away. I tried calling a couple of times but . . . Hello? Dad? Are you still there?'

She pulled the phone and checked the signal strength. No bars.

'Dammit!' she cursed, putting the phone back on the seat where she could see it. She craned her neck to see whether she could see any light at the end of the tunnel, but everything ahead was resolutely dark. 'Bloody tunnels.'

'You can call back when we come out the other end,' Chad said helpfully.

'Oh, can I? Gee thanks, Mr Technology, I didn't realize!' she quipped sarcastically, slumping slightly in her seat and wondering what it was her father had been ringing to say. Come home, all's forgiven? Was Tom going to ring, too? Had there been a family council and she'd been voted back in now that the Birkin was safely back in her mother's possession and she'd proved her regret over and over? Or was she still out in the cold, with just a silk-clad secret to keep her warm?

It was late when Stefano dropped her back at the house. Luigi had taken Chad on to Rome for a dinner date with Fiammetta, and Stefano had picked her up from the boatyard with the Riva, speeding her across the bay under the dark sky. There was no moon tonight.

Signora Benuto had left dinner prepared for her, but Clem felt too tired to eat it. She wandered through the house like a spectre, her hands brushing over the freshly primed windowsills, her feet treading lightly over the dusty, sanded floors, cotton shrouds hanging limply over chairs, the plastic window rustling noisily in the breeze; power tools left silent under workbenches and ladders propped against the walls. The house had been steadily and completely colonized by the building works and Gabriel had formally moved into the folly with her. Almost all the preparations had been completed now and the basic team of workmen was getting ready to assimilate the various specialists who would be coming in over the next few months to take the project into its next phase.

She wandered into her office and sat down at her desk, switching on the table lamp and pulling the swatch books closer. She thumbed through the pages of each book slowly, growing steadily more tired, resigned and uninspired, worn down by the bombardment of taste and beauty that had filled her days for five long weeks. One by one she discarded the books, finding nothing in them that moved her.

After more than an hour, she gave up, turning off the light and walking back through the shadowy house. The workmen would be back here in seven hours, their careless cacophony dragging her from sleep. She wandered upstairs to the so-called green suite and stood by the door, staring in at the walls that had been taken back to bare plaster, hoping for inspiration.

There was no bed in here, no furniture at all, and it was easy to appreciate the grand dimensions of the room with its triple-aspect status. One of the windows was still open, the bloomy magnolia tree poking one fragrant tendril through, and she walked across to close it, leaning down to smell the blossom.

Her eye caught on something on the wall beside the window and she stepped closer to examine it. It was a pencil line, drawn lightly and faintly in a falling swirl. She tried following it with her eyes, squinting as it ran into the dark, but the moon gave only as much light as a crack beneath a door and the lines escaped from view, undeciphered. She looked around and saw a workman's site lamp on the floor. She ran over to it and turned it on, drenching the room in a falling white light so bright that she had to blink several times. When she could finally focus, what she saw made her catch her breath.

Feather-light pencilmarks were sketched all over the plaster walls, depicting blossom trees and a rose garden rendered with a gossamer touch. It was masterly and refined, romantic, poetic and haunting, utterly exquisite even just in HB. She turned a full circle in slow wonderment. How long had it been here? It seemed too even and complete to be of any age.

Her eye caught sight of something darker, just below the windowsill and she bent down. It was out of place, a separate motif – naïve, almost cartoonish – drawn with a thicker, heavier pencil. It was a picture of a crest.

'Real Madrid.'

She laughed softly, her fingers tracing over Luca's crude pencil marks and running over the indentations where he'd even signed his name.

And where Luca went . . .

She stood back again and took in the mural with new knowledge, fresh perspective. Never in a million years would she have guessed.

Chapter Twenty-Eight

The phone buzzed insistently under her pillow – there was no bedside table – and she grappled for it without opening her eyes.

'Yeah?' she mumbled, already expecting Stella's shrieks in her ear.

'It's Chiara.'

Clem's eyes opened. What time was it? She fumbled under the pillow for her watch.

'Hi, Chiara,' she said, surprise cutting through the sleep in her voice. She found the watch and peered at it. 8.04. 'What's up?'

'I am in panic. I need your help.'

Clem pushed herself to sitting, her hair falling in a tangle over her face as she rubbed her eyes with the heels of her hands. 'Anything, you know that.'

'You must have Luca today.'

'Huh? What?' Alarm cut through the sleep in her voice instead.

'Please, Clem. I must go to Bologna, my aunt is very sick. I cannot take Luca with me.'

'But . . . but what about Rafa? He usually has Luca at the house with him anyway.'

'He is in Firenze today.'

'What? All day?'

'Yes.'

'Is there no one else? A friend from school?'

'It is high season, Clem. Everyone is busy and school is finished.'

'Oh God, I don't know, Chiara. I'm . . . I'm really not good with kids. Anyone will tell you that.'

'Clem!' Chiara shouted. 'Seriously? You tell this to *me*?'

Clem bit her lip. 'Sorry, sorry. Of course I'll have him.'

Chiara breathed a big sigh. 'Good. Thank you. I shall send him over in an hour.'

'All right then. But what should I, you know. . . *do* with him?'

There was silence.

'Chiara? Are you there?'

The dial tone beeped in her ear and she let the phone drop onto the pillow.

'Oh God.'

Much to the workmen's amusement and Chad's hilarity, she was frantic in the garden when Luca arrived, forty-five minutes later.

'*Ciao*,' he called out as he trotted down the main path, his football under his arm, as she stepped back to admire her work.

'Hey, Luca,' she smiled, breathless from her exertions. 'I thought we could play.'

He stopped and took in the efforts she'd made: white electrical tape on the grass marking out a football pitch and box; lengths of bleached eucalyptus from the log store delineating goals. She had set it up in the rose garden, the first level below the house and the only area with a lawn flat enough to play.

'OK.' He shrugged, jumping down from the terrace to join her, letting the ball drop to his feet. 'Shall we throw the money?'

Clem frowned, puzzled for a moment before realizing what he meant, then she rooted around in her jeans shorts' pocket for a coin. 'Heads or tails?' she asked, patting her head and bottom by way of interpretation.

Naturally, he chose the bottom. Clem flipped the coin – it was tails.

'You go first,' he said with a small bow, rolling the ball towards her.

'Thanks,' she preened, finding his Latin courtesy charming.

'You need all help you can have.' He grinned.

'Oh *do* I?' she laughed, amused by his cheekiness. 'We'll see about that,' she said, rolling her foot over the top of the ball in an attempt at a dummy before kicking it. But before she could even swing her leg back, he had nipped forward, his skinny leg moving like a switchblade – in, out, back, forth – the ball seemingly magnetically attached to his foot as he sped towards the opposite goal and booted it in with a slice.

The workmen on the scaffolding cheered. Clem glared up at them, then back at him, her foot planted on the floor with a stomp. 'It's like that, is it?' she asked, pulling a fierce face.

Luca wandered back, tapping the ball aimlessly from foot to foot, his eyes meeting hers and finding devilment there.

He thrashed her, of course. 32–4. Even when the plasterers and carpenters joined in, no one could get the ball off him. He was like a mini tornado, a whirling dervish, too small, too agile and too skilled to catch.

'Urgh,' Clem groaned an hour later, collapsing on the

grass, her arms and legs stretched out. 'I give up. You win, do you hear me? You win!'

Luca chuckled and came next to her, sitting on top of the ball and rolling on it gently, the tendons in his brown, skinny legs lengthening and stretching like elastic bands beneath his skin.

'You make me feel old,' she grumbled, peering at him out of one eye, enjoying the feeling of the sun on her skin.

He nodded, not disputing it. She was old, of course, in his eyes.

Clem propped herself up on her elbow. 'What do you fancy doing next then? We could swim.' She motioned towards the green pool, lying like liquid jade several terraces above.

Luca wrinkled his nose. 'I like the sea.'

'Well, let's swim in the sea then.' She shrugged, sat up and looked out at the horizon. It was pin-sharp, not a crescent of white to be seen anywhere. 'There are some rock pools in the cove down here.'

An idea came to her.

'Or . . . do you like boats?' She knew Stefano was kicking around somewhere as he had been due to take her to Viareggio today, before Chiara had called and she'd been forced to cancel.

Luca nodded eagerly.

'Rivas?' She said the word in a slow teasing voice, like treacle spinning from a jar, knowing it had the same fantasy factor as Ferrari, Ducati, Ronaldo . . . She saw the anticipation move through him, his little body becoming alert and watchful, waiting for her smile.

She smiled, ideas beginning to tumble one on top of the other as she unlocked the key to the day ahead. 'Well, OK then. I'll get some food from the kitchen and some towels. Why don't you see if you can get a bucket from one of the workmen?'

'Why do we need a bucket?' Luca asked, perplexed.

'For treasure, Luca.' She winked. 'Every pirate has to have their own treasure!'

They were on the water within twenty minutes. She had led a charge through the kitchen, scooping up bread and bottles of water in front of Signora Benuto's disapproving eyes, smashed and grabbed from the folly and performed a quick change into her bikini.

Luca had found a grey bucket, decorated inside with pink plaster tidemarks, and brought his ball along for good measure. Stefano, bemused by the drastic change in itinerary, put the boat into reverse and slid them smoothly out of the cove, turning right at the headland.

Clem hadn't seen the coastline on this side yet. She was accustomed now to the town-dotted vagaries of the sweeping bay that served as her commute to Viareggio two days a week, but the only sight she'd had of this side had been sitting up on the cliffs by the lighthouse. It was wilder and more exposed over here, looking out as it did towards open water, with the cliffs behind rising in vertical straits, huge boulders piled up in some places, in others, jagged and gigantic wedges that had sheared away from the cliffs.

She looked across at Luca. He was sitting beside her, the ball on his lap, his feet in the bucket, his face upturned to the sun. He could have been sleeping, such was the peace on his face. The wind, as they skimmed across the water, blew the hair back from his face, and she thought he looked younger again, younger than he would want to be seen anyway, with his cheeky grins and cocksure trickery. He looked happy.

The shoreline began to pull inland sharply, like a skirt being hemmed, and Stefano bore the boat towards it, cutting the speed, his eyes scanning the landscape above and checking the depth below. Clem and Luca both stood up as they motored slowly in, keen to see where they were.

It meant nothing to Clem, of course, she didn't have a clue, but Luca seemed to recognize it, pointing eagerly to the far left, where a single dead tree stood like a monument alone on the rocks. It was blackened and charred, with the bare sculptural silhouette that was the calling card of a lightning strike, the boulder it stood on long since cleaved from the cliffs, with a narrow choppy channel of water between.

Stefano took the boat over to it, catching Clem's wink and asking Luca to perch on the prow and check for rocks for him. Clem, behind his narrow back, quickly threw the paste jewels and pearls that she had hurriedly broken up in her bedroom into the water. She winced as they landed with tiny 'plops' and sank without trace. This was an expensive game: the pearls – albeit fake – had been from a long-roped Chanel necklace (bought in a sale, admittedly) and the brightly coloured paste jewels came from a horribly expensive Erickson Beamon bracelet. She'd bought them both telling herself they were 'investments', but if this wasn't an investment – enchanting a child for a day – what was?

Luca watched, transfixed, as the anchor chain slithered to the seabed. Clem pulled off her T-shirt and stepped onto the bathing deck at the back. 'Last one in is a—'

But the water was already closing over Luca's feet.

Dammit. He'd beaten her again.

They dived like dolphins, searching for the jewels until they filled the bucket; and afterwards, when they had no more breath and their ears hurt, they floated like otters, their tummies and heads bobbing out of the water as Luca told her about school and the worst teachers (Signor Giordano on account of his BO). He told her he wanted to be a painter if he couldn't be a professional footballer, that he was allergic to feathers and couldn't stand butter or girls.

Clem listened, transfixed, grateful for the saltwater bearing her up without any effort on her part. He was fully formed, three-dimensional, a whole person in miniature. Funny, charming, interesting. Not scary at all.

They climbed out once their skin had wrinkled (Clem won that game, the only one) and dried out on the Tiffany blue-leather deck, feeling the water bead, sizzle and dissipate on their backs. And when they were dry, she spread Marmite on the focaccia and let him break the foil on her treasured KitKats, just like an English boy.

She slept after a while, worn out by their games, drowsy from the picnic and lulled by the rocking motion. When she awoke, Luca was sitting on the front of the boat, his legs dangling over the sides, his feet sinking into the water with the gentle swell of the waves. He was gazing up at the tree, his eyes still and dark upon it.

'What you looking at?' she asked, crawling over beside him. Stefano was reading a book on the bench seat.

'That is the wishing tree.'

'*Wishing* tree?'

He looked at her sharply, hearing the doubt in her voice. 'It is famous here. If you can touch it, your wish will come true.'

'Oh.' Clem looked back at it, trying to hide her scepticism.

It looked very dead and unprepossessing from where she was sitting. 'Is that why you wanted to come here?'

He nodded. 'I thought it was impossible to reach. The rock is so high and there is nothing to hold.'

'Mmm.' The crag rose at least three metres from the water. 'You'd need ropes to get up it, I'd imagine.'

'Or swim to the front.'

'Huh?'

Luca pointed. 'There is a smaller rock at the front you could climb on. You cannot see it from the land. That is how they did it.'

'Who?'

'The people whose wishes came real.'

Clem stared at him. 'Do you have a wish, Luca?'

He looked at her and nodded, his small face so serious now, the cheeky grin gone for once.

'Can you tell me?'

'It will not come real,' he said, shaking his head gravely.

'Ah yes, of course,' she murmured, her eyes resting on him as he looked back at it, his focus intense and unwavering. She envied him his certainty, his belief that getting to the rock was the only obstacle. She would climb it herself if she thought it would work, but she'd lost her childhood innocence long ago. She no longer inhabited a world where wishes came true.

It was a stunning sunset, the sky flaming with fiery tendrils that reached from one side of the horizon to the other. Stefano docked with his usual finesse, the boat nudging the jetty's fenders gently as Clem and Luca jumped off, carrying the bucket and ball between them.

They trudged up the steps, tired out from the twin efforts

of basking and bathing, their skin tight from too much sun. The lights were already on in the garden, the workmen had all gone for the day and the house was shut up and still, with just one light flickering by an upstairs window.

A silhouetted figure was pacing and Clem felt herself tense as she saw they'd been spotted. Rafa was down the stairs and at the door in the time it took them to cross the lawns, the makeshift football pitch still there with its wobbly lines and disjointed goals.

'Where have you been?' he demanded in a low voice that vibrated with anger, his cheeks swarthy with stubble and heat.

'Out on the boat,' Clem replied, taken aback by his aggression.

'It is late. It is dark. Nobody knew where you had gone.'

Clem didn't know what to say. It hadn't occurred to her that they had a curfew.

'I have been here for two hours.'

'I'm sorry, I didn't know. Chiara asked me to look after him.' She rested her hand on Luca's shoulder and looked down at him. 'We had fun.' So much.

'Was ire . . .' He stumbled, struggling with the English. 'Irresponsibile!'

'Irresponsible,' she said quietly. 'I was trying to help.' She squeezed Luca's shoulder lightly and took her hand off him. Rafa reached out and took him, his hands either side of the boy's face, as though checking for injuries.

The gesture was rude, offensive, but she said nothing, knowing that he was being deliberately provocative. She needed to get him on side.

'I saw your drawing in the bedroom,' she said carefully, her eyes flicking up and behind him to the green suite. 'It's beautiful. Is it of anywhere in particular?'

'Is not supposed to be kept. Or seen,' he snapped. 'I just scribbled it in my lunch break.'

'Scribbled? Well, I'd like to keep it,' she said. 'I wondered if you would paint it in.'

Rafa fell still, his jaw twitching slightly, like a cornered animal choosing between fight or flight. She could almost see the dilemma prowling through him.

'Please. We'd pay you obviously.'

His eyes blazed and she sensed she'd said the wrong thing, though whether it was the reference to 'we' or payment, she couldn't be sure.

'I will think about it,' he said finally. 'But I make no promise.' He spoke the words with violence, his eyes flashing, and he turned Luca away, marching the boy up towards the gate.

Luca turned his head and smiled at her – sadly, apologetically – his small hand raised in a wave.

Clem raised hers back in silent acknowledgement of what had been, for one day at least.

Chapter Twenty Nine

The door was open when Clem got back to the folly, and she knew Signora Benuto would be changing the sheets or bringing coffee.

'*Ciao*, signora,' she called up the stairs, hearing movement in the bedroom above. 'It's just me.'

She placed her salted T-shirt (which had dried stiff) and towel on the small radiator, pulling her hair from the topknot that already had more hair hanging down than up.

'Heck of a view you've got up there, babe.'

Clem whirled round in surprise. Stella was standing on the stairs, looking limp and worn out, wearing an orange gypsy skirt and red T-shirt.

'Stell!' Clem cried joyously, bounding up the steps and wrapping her friend in a tight hug. 'What are you *doing* here?'

Stella couldn't hold her gaze, looking instead out of the round window that looked back towards the port. 'Duh! Thought I'd come and check up on you, seeing as you're so completely bollocks at calling me these days.'

Clem hung her head in shame to see her friend's evident hurt. 'I've been pants, I know. I'll totally understand if you've come here to dump me as your best friend.'

It was supposed to be a joke, but instead Stella jerked her

chin in the air. 'I haven't made up my mind yet.' She
pouted, staring at her own hand brushing away non-
existent dust from the windowsill.

Clem narrowed her eyes. Something was up. 'Drink?'

Stella shook her head. Now Clem knew something was
wrong.

'Where've you been? I've been here for ages,' Stella said.

'Not you, too!' Clem groaned. 'I was looking after
Luca for Chiara today. Obviously if I'd known you were
coming . . .'

'You? Babysitting? Now that I'd like to see.' Stella walked
down the stairs, her eyes taking in the room as if she'd just
walked in.

Clem watched her. 'Like it? I think they should have little
round houses on Portobello. At the very least I'm going to
paint the outside of the flat in stripes when we get back.
Start a trend . . .'

Stella didn't even smile.

'Babe, what is it?' Clem sighed. 'You don't seem yourself.
Are you hungry? I don't have any crisps or anything I'm
afraid, but I've—'

'Me and Oscar broke up.'

Clem gawped at her. Stella had come all the way here
because of that? Usually they broke up with a guy every
other week and it didn't even warrant a walk around the
block. 'Stell, I'm so sorry. What happened?'

Stella looked away again, trailing her hand against the
wall as she wandered around the room, aiming – Clem
knew – for nonchalance. She shrugged.

'You got wasted and copped off with someone else?'
Clem offered.

No reply.

'He did?'

Still nothing.

''Cos, you know, if that's made you realize how much you like him, well, it's not insurmountable. I always say—'

'It's nothing like that,' Stella murmured, and then Clem knew.

'Oh God, you're pregnant.'

Stella kept her eyes to the ground. 'Bummer, right?'

'N–n–n–no,' Clem managed, her voice cracked, as if it had been split by an axe. 'It's a . . . it's a surprise obviously.'

'Tell me about it.'

Clem looked across at her. Stella was gnawing on a hang-nail, looking out to sea, and Clem could see from how high her shoulders were that she was trying not to cry.

'Oh, Stell,' she said, walking towards her friend and hug-ging her again, making the tears topple. 'When did you find out?'

'Ten days ago.'

'Ten *days*?' Clem echoed. 'But why didn't you tell me the very second you knew?'

'Because . . . because . . .' She shrugged haplessly.

'I would have come straight back.'

'Yeah, and if I'd seen you, I'd just have wanted to drink vodka and I can't. I can't do *anything*. Can't drink, can't smoke, can't eat prawns, can't go cycling, can't—'

'You don't have a bike,' Clem said, correcting her. 'And you haven't eaten prawns ever since you tried reheating that three-day-old curry and were sick in bed for a week.'

'Well, I know *that*, but . . . ugh!' Stella exclaimed, stomp-ing off and bashing a cushion back into shape on the sofa. 'It would be nice to have the option. I'm a spontaneous girl. You never know what I might do next.'

'That's true, we never do,' Clem said obediently, desperately trying to manage her own see-sawing emotions. She had a feeling she knew what was coming next. 'What was Oscar's response?'

There was a short pause. Confirmation. 'He hasn't exactly had one.'

'You dumped him without telling him?' Clem said, planting a hand on her hip.

'Well, of course I did! He's hardly signed up for a kid, has he? We've just been fooling around. It was never meant to be anything serious.'

'Not meant to be, no. But you've been glued together for four months now. It's more than a fling, babe.'

'Listen, just because you can't get past twelve weeks doesn't mean we're going to walk down the aisle simply because we've got to sixteen,' Stella rebutted.

'You're hardly kids,' Clem said, ignoring Stella's arguments. 'Thirty's looming on the horizon, and I already know you don't like the cut of its jib.'

'Where are you going with this?' Stella asked suspiciously, grabbing another cushion and threatening it with a closed fist.

'You need to tell him. You need to talk it through together.'

Stella broke their stare with a blink. 'What I need is just to get on with it.'

It? Clem felt pressure building on her chest, as if someone was kneeling on her. 'Stell, look . . . It's a massive decision; it's not something you can rush into.'

'I don't want a kid, Clem.' Stella's voice was stony and flat, as if she was trying to stick to a script while she punched the dangling cushion.

'Don't you, though? *Really*?' Clem questioned her, remembering Stella's panic at the christening. 'I think you'd be a great mum, for what it's worth.'

Stella threw the cushion down and was quiet for a long while, her shoulders up by her ears again. 'Fuck's sake. I can't believe you're trying to talk me into it. *You* of all people. You hate kids.'

'*Hate*'s a bit strong. I'm just not a natural. And I'm not trying to talk you into anything. I just think you should let it all settle in your head for a few days. You don't have to decide right this instant.'

They lapsed into fretful silence, Clem desperately trying to find the right words. 'Just try to imagine where you'd like your life to be five years from now. Please God don't be led by me. You're chasing something that I'm not.' It was painful to say. She didn't want to lose her pub buddy, but she'd always known the path she had to take was, by definition, a solitary one. 'You need to talk to Oscar. He's nuts about you. You're the one who keeps holding things back. I mean, maybe this was written in the stars. What if he's the one?'

Stella sniffed contemptuously, wiping her nose with the back of her hand. 'Babe, we are modern girls. Neither one of us believes in that crap.'

Clem fell still. 'No. No, I guess not.'

Stella yawned. 'Damn, I'm so bloody tired all the time.'

'Go upstairs and lie down. I'll get Signora Benuto to bring over some supper. You look wiped out.'

'You sure?' Stella asked, already wandering back to the stairs.

'Of course. Have you booked into a hotel anywhere?'

'No, I . . .' Stella grimaced. 'Sorry, I wasn't really thinking it all through. I just had to see you. Couldn't go another day—'

'I'm glad. You'd have been ripped off. You can stay here with me. We can share the bed.'

'What about Gabriel?'

'It's fine. He's in Paris for a few days.'

'Good,' Stella said, climbing the stairs. 'At least he shouldn't hear me snore from there.'

Clem looked alarmed. 'You snore?'

'Like a bear, baby.' Stella sighed, a tiny amused smile curling her lips. 'Like a fricking bear.'

She lay in bed, the round wagon-wheel windows open, one ear automatically listening out for the sound of the V8 over the waves, even though Gabriel wasn't due back from Paris till the following night. She was trying to sleep but could only manage fitful naps – Stella's news lodged in her mind – before being jerked out of sleep by full body spasms, her heart hammering in her chest, her head spinning with all the changes. Beside her, Stella was snoring; she'd been sleeping solidly since Clem had sent her up to bed earlier – relieved of the weight of her secret now that she'd burdened Clem with it.

Clem thought she heard a sound outside and turned her head towards the stairs, waiting for it to materialize into footsteps and a turn of the latch, but nothing came. Her ear tuned back into the splashing, smashing of the waves and she drifted off again.

When she awoke, the moon was up and she was misted with a sheen of sweat, her legs tangled in the thin cotton sheet. It was the middle of the night now, the lights in the gardens long since turned off, the coast blotted out as if it had been smothered with a coat.

Clem sat up, sensing a change. Stella was sleeping more soundly beside her now, a small smile on her face.

A gust whipped around the room, making Clem shiver, and she realized the wind had picked up. The day had been sticky and still, leaching energy and conversation, but now thick, rolling clouds were gathering like armies in the skies, marching past the moon in tangled formations. A sudden crack of light, as if the sky was splitting open, sent the world into negative image – white was black, black was white – and she realized that was what had woken her.

She got up and walked to the window, watching as the waves steadily reared, row upon row, showing their bellies and beginning to snarl and froth. She looked left, towards Chiara's. She already knew what the storm would look like from there. Was Chiara watching, too, as she worked through the night again, sitting at her kitchen table with ledgers spread around her while the sky flashed? And what about Luca? Every child loved an electric storm, didn't they? Or was he scared? No, she thought, probably nothing scared him, except maybe his wish not coming true, whatever that was.

A sound downstairs, not more than a sigh, made her turn. Gabriel?

She walked down on tiptoes, finding him asleep in his suit on the sofa, his long legs hanging over the edge. She curled up in the lemon chair beside him and rested her head on the arm, gazing at him as he slept. He was just so beautiful to look at; she thought she would never tire of it. He was the ultimate escape; sometimes she felt as though she could climb inside him and hide. He was her oblivion. She felt shielded by him, protected – as she needed to be.

Her eyes roamed the length of him – his expression was

benign, his fingers unfurled, no tension in his legs or brow. She extended a leg, nudging his foot lightly with hers, and he stirred, groaning lightly before blinking slowly into the gloom. He noticed her curled up in the armchair and smiled, pushing himself up to sitting and stretching out his back.

'What are you doing down here?' he asked, his accent always thicker at night, his shirt rumpled.

'I was about to ask you the same thing.' She smiled.

'I came up to bed but saw that you have company.'

'Stella came out and surprised me.'

'So did I, but I didn't think I should surprise her by joining you.' He smiled, a wicked gleam in his eyes.

'I'm sorry, it's not fair that you should have to sleep down here.'

'It is one night,' he said wryly. 'I will survive. I am not so spoiled as you think,' he said, jokingly cricking his neck. 'Is she OK? Was it an emergency?'

'You could say that; she's pregnant,' Clem whispered. 'She needed to talk.'

Gabriel frowned. 'Of course. It is very serious. What will she do?'

'I'm trying to persuade her to keep it. I think she wants to but . . .' she wrinkled her nose. 'I think she's frightened. The father doesn't know yet and he might not want a baby. It wasn't planned.'

He watched her keenly. 'She's lucky to have you as a friend,' he murmured, reaching out to clasp her by the wrist and pulling her onto his lap. He tilted his face to kiss her as his hands slowly brushed up her waist, one hand cupping her breast as another combed through her hair. 'I like to see this side to you.'

'What side?' she whispered, closing her eyes as he kissed her neck, beginning to lose herself in him again.

'Maternal.'

She stiffened, her eyes open as his lips met hers. '*I'm* not the maternal type, Gabriel.'

He chuckled softly. 'You can't fool me. I've seen you playing with the little boy here sometimes. He makes you laugh . . . It makes me think what you would be like if, one day, we had a son.'

She pulled back abruptly. 'That's not an option.'

'Not now maybe, I agree – I want to keep you to myself a bit longer – but in a few years . . .'

'No. I'm never having children.'

He stopped kissing her and met her eyes. 'And you have just made that decision all by yourself? No thought of what I might want?' he asked after a long pause.

'I made that decision a long time ago, long before I ever met you.'

'But why?' he asked, incredulous.

'Because I wouldn't be any good.'

'Of course you—'

'Trust me. I'm never going to change my mind on this.'

'I don't understand.' He frowned as she got up off his lap, pulling down her T-shirt in jerky, agitated movements.

'You don't need to.'

'Well, were you ever going to tell me?' he asked, a throb of anger in his voice at her casual flippancy.

'We've been together six weeks, Gabriel,' she said impatiently. 'I didn't think it was a discussion we needed to have right now.'

She saw the muscle clench in his jaw and she shifted her weight, anxious suddenly that she'd been too vehement in her proclamations. This could be a deal-breaker – it very probably was – but that didn't mean she could be without him now, not while she was still out here. She changed tack. 'I'm sorry, I . . . I'm just a bit freaked out because of Stella. It's a lot to take in. It's going to change my life as much as hers. We're inseparable back home.'

'You are not students any more,' Gabriel muttered. 'Or maybe you didn't notice you are nearly thirty? You think being the party girl is going to make you happy ten, fifteen years from now?'

Clem bit her lip. She'd heard all this before – from Tom, her parents, Freddie and Josh; even Simon had said much the same thing. 'I'm going back to bed. We're both tired,' she replied evasively.

She turned and walked up the stairs with his eyes on her back, her own eyes falling on the heaving, moonlit sea beyond the windows. Being sequestered here on this tiny peninsula had made it easy to pretend up until now, as they played house together and made love in the folly. But reality was already blinking over the horizon, like a distant ship, and their fairytale existence here was as fragile as a dream.

Chapter Thirty

'Oh God, you're never coming back, are you?' Stella drawled, sitting in front of Clem and dangling her toes in the turquoise water of the hotel pool, the roofs of the pink-speckled port far below them. 'I mean, who in their right mind would leave this?'

Clem grinned. 'Lucky for you, then, that we both know I'm not in my right mind.'

She had woken to find Gabriel already gone – a note on the table telling her he'd taken his usual room at the Splendido for the next two nights, until Stella left. When she'd called him, he had been cool, although he hadn't rebuffed her suggestion that she and Stella join him there and make the most of the facilities for the day before heading down to the port later for window-shopping, drinks and dinner. It was a welcome respite from the dust and noise back at the house, and Stella really needed to rest.

Clem lay back on the lounger and looked around at the poolside scene. All around them, honeymooners lounged elegantly in Heidi Klein bikinis and Manuel Canovas sarongs, sipping pink drinks and talking in hushed tones. She and Stella broke the mould somewhat; Clem fiddled with her tiny Isabel Marant bikini, pretty sure no one had ever worn tie-dye in the Splendido before, and as for Stella in her yellow crocheted swimsuit, her wild hair pinned up with clasps decorated with silk butterflies . . . it was as if she'd bottled Portobello – eclectic, irreverent, ballsy – and drenched herself in it. Clem watched as Stella flicked quickly through the pages of her Paris *Vogue*, as though the biggest dilemma in her life was choosing which dress to wear to dinner. There was no sign of her condition yet, but she had slept for almost twelve hours and when she had woken, she was in a bright mood. Clem wondered whether her words had had an impact?

She looked across at Gabriel, who was lying on the bed beside her. He looked obscenely good in his powder-blue Orlebar Brown trunks, and she knew most of the women round the pool were eyeing him up behind their shades. He was reading reports on his iPad, looking sterner than she was used to seeing him, and she squeezed his hand, liking the way his features automatically softened at the sight of her, before he remembered her arrogance and frowned again.

'I'm sorry,' Clem whispered. 'I was a cow. I should never have tried to hold a conversation in the middle of the night. Sleep's all I'm fit for at night.'

He was silent for a few moments and she knew he was thinking that wasn't all she was fit for at night. But this wasn't the time for jokes.

'I wasn't saying I want them now,' he murmured, keeping the conversation deliberately oblique lest Stella should overhear. 'But it was a shock that you wouldn't even discuss it.'

'I know. It's just way too early for that conversation, that's all . . . Forgive me?' He could hear her pout, even if he wouldn't look at her. He raised an eyebrow a fraction of an inch and she knew she had him. She rolled onto his stomach, deliberately and carelessly crushing his newspaper between them as every set of eyes swivelled towards them. 'I'll make it up to you, I promise,' she said, her parted lips kissing his. She pulled back onto her hands and knees like a cat. 'Our first fight,' she said as though it was as sexy as their first kiss, a gleam in her eyes as she backed off the lounger, watching the way his eyes travelled rapaciously up and down her body.

With a teasing wink and deliberately not readjusting her bikini bottoms to cover her more modestly, she joined Stella by the poolside, slipping her legs silkily into the water.

'Do you really have to go tomorrow?' she asked after a while, when it became apparent Stella couldn't be distracted from the fashion spread on the new sports luxe.

Stella sighed as she was drawn back into the present. 'I can't ask Mercy to cover for me on the stall for longer than this weekend. She's got a day job, too.'

'But I've missed you so much. I just wish you could stay longer.'

Stella looked around them and laughed. 'Yeah. Me, too.'

'Have you thought any more about what we talked about?'

Stella snorted. 'Like I've got *other* things on my mind,' she quipped sarcastically, before wincing. 'Sorry. I'm so desperate for a ciggie, it's making me a bitch.'

'It's OK. You slept well at least.'

'Honestly? It's like I fall into a coma every night. I thought you only got that kind of oblivion after half a bottle of vodka.'

Clem smiled. 'Your colour's better, too. I bet you're going to be one of those really annoying people who just looks amazing when they're pregnant.'

Stella shot her a sharp look.

Clem shrugged. 'What?'

'Stop it! I know what you're doing.'

'What am I doing?'

'Selling me this baby.'

Clem bit her lip. 'I just think you'd be great, that's all,' she said after a moment, her voice tiny so that no one, Gabriel included, could overhear. 'And I'd get to be an aunty. I'd help you. And Mercy . . . she could be your nanny! She used to be one, you know.'

Stella looked down at the port, shaking her head. 'Fuck's sake. And to think I thought you were going to be my ally.'

'I am *always* your ally,' Clem said, gripping her arm and squeezing it. 'I'll support you no matter what you decide. I just don't want to see you make a mistake. A termination is a huge thing. You've got to be able to live with it.'

Stella looked across at her, her eyes narrowed. 'Have you had one then?'

Clem's hand dropped. 'N–no.'

'No?'

'No.'

Stella held her stare for a moment before looking back at the port.

'Just speak to Oscar.'

'Maybe.'

They fell silent, their legs swishing in small kicks, watching as a woman in a white Chanel bikini glided past, the water creasing in smooth ripples around her as if it was liquid gold.

'Shit, you will come back, won't you?' Stella asked, genuine doubt bending her voice. 'You won't become one of *them*?'

Clem looked down at her tie-dye bikini and the small gold hoop piercing her belly button. 'What do you think? I'm just gatecrashing the party.'

Stella laughed, the sound dying in her throat as she saw Gabriel walk to the far end of the pool and raise his arms above his head for a dive. 'Holy mother . . .' she mumbled.

They watched him, Clem reminded of his dive off the boat that first night in the cove, fully clothed, swimming towards her in the dark.

'Promise me you'll never chuck him,' Stella said, watching as he sliced sharply through the water and cut up a length in a few, precise strokes. 'It's actually good for my health just looking at him.'

Clem giggled as Gabriel effortlessly touched the far end and turned, his eyes on Clem as he took another breath and slipped underwater, heading towards her like a torpedo.

'OMFG,' Stella whispered. 'How can you stay so calm with *him* coming after you? Do you have no pulse, woman?'

But before Clem could reply, Gabriel's hand had closed around her ankle and, in one swift move, he'd pulled her into the water. She surfaced with a laugh, accidentally splashing Chanel woman on her serene way back, as she tried and failed to escape Gabriel's arms.

'I've got you.' He grinned.

'For now, maybe,' Clem quipped, squealing loudly as he dug his fingers into her waist, tickling her tortuously.

Stella looked on at the playfight, bemused, her keen eyes missing nothing, before picking up her magazine again with a weary sigh.

The lights danced on the water like playful fireflies, the piazzetta's resident three-legged dog snoozing by one of the small lobster boats that had been pulled up onto the cobbles.

'I don't think I've ever seen so much taupe cashmere or designer trainers gathered together in one place before,' Stella hissed, looking around at the diners seated at the neighbouring tables. She, herself, was obeying no such dogma, wearing a leopard-print chiffon kaftan and turquoise bangles that she'd bartered for one of her tops with a trader friend at the market.

'It is a thing,' Clem nodded, trying to look over the specials while her eyes scanned the small square. Chiara was joining them for dinner and Clem felt inexplicably bound up with nerves at the thought of introducing the two women who knew her best in the world.

Stella leaned closer, her eyes darting over to Gabriel quickly, but he was scanning the wine list. 'Gatecrasher are you?' she murmured, her eyes pointedly moving over Clem's beige lace shorts and ivory silk blouse. 'Hmm, not so much methinks.'

Clem gasped, as though insulted that her Portobello-ness should be questioned, and swung out a leg, showing off her perilously high, pale pink suede heels with studded ankle straps. Then she rattled the punky pyramid-coned leather cuff that Gabriel had given her 'as a small gift' for good measure.

'That's *Hermès*,' Stella replied with an arched eyebrow and a wicked smile on her lips, and Clem knew her friend was accusing her of being assimilated into the good taste crowd.

'Oh crap, that's her. I just know it is. Why didn't you say she's like a freaking mermaid?' Stella murmured, pushing her hair back and taking a deep breath. Clem followed her gaze over to Chiara, who looked stunning in a strapless beige maxi dress embellished with blue mosaic swirls.

'Hey, *ciao*.' Clem smiled, standing up to greet her and kissing her warmly on each cheek.

'*Ciao*.' Chiara smiled, pushing her hair back off her shoulder.

'Chiara, this is Gabriel,' Clem said, touching Gabriel's arm lightly. They shook hands and she was relieved to see Gabriel was polite but seemingly unmoved by Chiara's tender beauty.

'It is a pleasure.' Chiara smiled, equally as polite back.

'And this is Stella, my partner in all crimes.'

'Totally *love* your dress,' Stella said by way of introduction. 'Who's it by?'

Chiara laughed, somewhat taken aback by the unorthodox greeting, and shrugged. 'I'm not sure.'

'D'you mind if I . . .?' Stella asked, indicating to look at the label in the back.

Clem rolled her eyes as Chiara turned – astonishment on her face – for Stella.

Stella nodded wisely as she saw the label. 'Yup, I know them. Brazilian. Coming through quickly. Harvey Nics and Selfridges are stocking them now.'

Clem shook her head and indicated for them all to sit. 'You'll get used to it. Every event is catalogued in Stella's memory according to what people wear. Trust me, this is a great compliment.'

The waiter came over to take their wine order, squeezing Chiara's shoulder in friendly recognition as he passed. Gabriel ordered as the girls leaned in to chat.

'So, what's it like living in paradise then?' Stella asked.

Chiara smiled. 'It doesn't seem like paradise when you live here all the time. It is just normal.'

'I don't think I've ever been anywhere so pretty. All these distressed colours and cute balconies.'

'It is so small, though. Only five hundred and thirty people live here full-time.'

'*Really?*' Stella grimaced. 'God that's . . . that's probably fewer than live on the Portobello Road, don't you think, Clem?'

Clem shrugged. 'Maybe, I don't know.'

'Tch, you'd go mad, babes. Way too small for you. I mean, if you estimate that only half of those are men and half of them are either under twenty or over sixty.' She shook her head. 'With your twelve-week rule, you wouldn't get past more than a few years before running out.'

Clem looked nervously at Gabriel, who was still talking to the wine waiter about the top notes of a merlot, then she glared back at Stella to shut up.

'What is the twelve-week rule?' Chiara asked.

'Nothing,' Stella said quickly, realizing she'd overstepped the mark. 'Ignore me. I'm . . . I'm trying to quit smoking and it's making me ratty.'

Chiara placed her hand on Clem's. 'By the way, I want to say thank you for looking after Luca yesterday. He had such a good time. He could not stop talking about the games you played. And you took him to the wishing tree on the boat? It is his favourite place!'

'Yeah? That was more luck than judgement,' Clem said modestly, aware that Gabriel had rejoined the conversation and that it would only add weight to his comments last night.

'Well, he loved it.'

Clem nodded non-committally, but Chiara continued to stare. 'So, I wanted to ask . . . maybe you would think to have him again. My aunt is very sick; she had a – how you say? – a strike?'

'A stroke? Oh, I'm so sorry.'

'She is eighty-three.' Chiara shrugged. 'But my family, we think we can look after her at home.'

'Well, that's wonderful.'

'My day is Tuesday.'

'That's cool, I'll have him for you next Tuesday. No worries,' Clem replied, emboldened by yesterday's success.

'No, I mean . . . it is all the Tuesdays.'

Clem blinked. 'You mean you're going to Bologna every Tuesday? And you want me to . . .?'

Chiara nodded. 'Please, Clem. There is no one else I can ask and I cannot afford the nanny. Rafa is away and it would not be good for Luca to see her so sick.'

'No, no of course not,' Clem said quickly, wanting to ask where it was that Rafa was disappearing to every Tuesday.

'He really likes you,' Chiara said quietly.

Clem met her gaze. 'I really like him.'

'So that is a yes?' she asked, her big brown eyes wide with hope.

Clem shrugged. What else could she say? 'Sure. Why not?'

She saw Stella smirk and sit back in her seat, satisfied that if the lack of a party scene didn't send her screaming back to London, a summer of babysitting would.

The waiter came over with the wine and began pouring, but Stella put her hand over her glass.

'I promise, it is very good this wine,' Chiara said encouragingly. 'The vineyard is only thirty miles from here.'

'It's not that; I just can't drink anything for a while,' Stella said, looking over at Clem with a delighted smile. 'Y'see, I'm having a baby.'

Chapter Thirty-One

Clem stood at the window, watching Luca show off his 'keepy-uppy' skills to the workmen, who were taking a break. He was past fifty already, trying to break his record of eighty-four, his tongue poking through his bright-white teeth in concentration.

She smiled to see him hold the group of grown men in his thrall. She wasn't scared of him any more. He was no longer *A Child*; he was Luca, footballer and trickster extraordinaire, and they had quickly forged a bond based precisely on those attributes. She had even begun to look forward to their Tuesday adventures now – they had had four more since Stella had returned home – having diving competitions in the cove and shootouts with the plasterers at lunch; he took her up the mud tracks that ran through the steep woods at the back of the port, showing her the best olive trees to scrump, the best place to sit and watch the dolphins (after which the Romans had named the port), the massive water tank with its rotten, rusted, half-broken lid, where the local children liked to throw stones. He had, at her bidding, acquired a taste for marmalade; while she had, at his, acquired a taste for black olive spread; and they both had an addiction for the almond cornetti from the bakery on the back street. Their days were long and too often they lost track of time, but Rafa said nothing now when she returned Luca, exhausted, to him at the hotel. His scowl said enough.

A collective, consoling moan brought her attention back to the antics in the garden. Seventy-six. The men were patting Luca on the back and scruffing his hair. Rafa wasn't among them. He couldn't afford to stop for breaks, not now that he'd agreed to work on the mural in the green room, or rather the garden suite as it had become known.

Liaising only with Chad, who knew better than to ask why he was being used as a go-between, he had agreed to paint it in as a spring garden, with pale mists and light buds and lone songbirds hidden in the leaves. Clem messaged back, through Chad, that she didn't want anything too bright or ripe, she wanted a scheme that had a wispy, tentative, almost melancholy beauty, a mood that was about promise and suggestion; a room like an early morning.

In the evenings, before Gabriel came home, Clem would stand in the room alone and try to decipher where he'd worked, her eyes searching for some new added depth and shade or layered light, as he slowly brought the pencil sketch into a three-dimensional dreamscape.

It was slow going as he was still reinstating the trompe l'oeils on the exterior – a huge job in itself and too specialized to delegate: the pitfall, as well as the advantage, of being a one-man band – but Clem had noticed the colour washes only built up on the days when she was safely out of the house in Viareggio. Another slight directed at her.

She walked back to her desk, trying to push it out of her mind. She had bigger concerns than that to dwell upon today. She flicked through the iPad once more, chewing on her lip nervously as she swotted up – again – on the technical details. The library was ready and waiting to be clad in its new skins, the first shipment of which – the leather shelf-sleeves – had just arrived and Chad was out on the drive, checking through the inventory.

Adrenaline shot through her in cold, chilling bursts. This was it, the first day in this warped, inverted summer where everything came back to Alderton Hide. It was the nub of why she was officially here, everything else that was swirling around her – Gabriel, the house, the boat, the small matter of walking among her own ghosts – peripheral to the one simple fact that this was all for Tom.

It had been one thing playing at being the designer with colour charts and wallpaper swatches, getting Chad to draw up her ideas in his intricate Slade-quality watercolour illustrations. He had been right, she did have an instinct for it, and in spite of her misgivings, she had slipped into the role easily, surprising herself most of all, almost every day of the past two months that she'd been here. They were steadily honing the house to her vision, building it back up after months of picking at its bones; but from this point, this day, onwards, the work was technical, intricate, artisanal, skilled. Every single leather fascia had been quality-checked back at the factory for grains and stains, then custom-dyed, hand-cut and hand-stitched. But if a single measurement was out by even half an inch, if the leather wrinkled or bubbled, if the hot glue seeped and stained through the seams, if the tens of thousands of pounds' worth of bespoke work was ruined in any way . . . it was on her.

She started pacing, feeling nauseous with nerves. Instinct told her to stall. She was in charge when she had no right to be, when she had never asked to be. Gabriel had simply had his agenda, while Tom had his own.

She wanted to hear her father's voice. He would be able

to calm her down with one of his impassioned soliloquies on his newest culinary discoveries. She had rung home several times since their aborted phone call in the tunnel, but it had always gone to voicemail and she'd been left wondering whether she'd been premature in thinking forgiveness had been granted with the safe return of the Birkin. Certainly she hadn't heard hide nor hair from Tom.

She dialled the number and walked to the window, staring out at the gardens, the phone to her ear, her fingers drumming her thigh nervously. It went to voicemail again.

She stabbed disconnect with a furious finger. 'For God's sake, Dad! Just pick up!'

'They're away again.'

Clem whirled on her heel, her jaw dropping open in horror at the sight of Tom standing in the doorway – horror that he was actually there; horror at the state of him. He had lost weight – a lot of weight – and his shirt bagged loosely around his chest while his jeans were a size too big. It made him seem taller, his eyes bigger. And he had cheekbones now, too, sharp ones that seemed hard and out of place on such a wholesome, soft face. 'Thought I should probably look in,' he mumbled with ridiculous understatement, his head jerking towards the shipment on the drive.

'Tom!' she cried. 'You look awful.'

'Thanks.'

She carried on staring at him in open dismay. 'What the hell's happened?'

'I'm fine.'

'You don't look it! There's only half of you left.'

'Well, my better half then, hopefully.' He walked towards her, his tic fidgeting madly in his left cheek. He stopped a couple of feet away. 'I was really shitty to you, Clem.'

'No!' she shook her head manically, fretting at the sight of him. 'No, you weren't. I deserved all of it. I was totally selfish, a complete loser.'

'I pretty much blackmailed you, Clem,' he said quietly, his cheeks stained a mottled pink. He swallowed and looked down. 'I was so angry . . .'

'As you had every right to be! You almost lost everything because of me.' Her voice faltered. 'I couldn't see past my own needs. I jeopardized everything, all because Josh was talking to another girl? When I look back, I can hardly believe it. I was . . .' She shrugged. 'Pathetic.'

Tom watched her. 'You look amazing.'

'Do I?' she asked, surprised, looking down at her khaki silk cargo shorts and charcoal vest, sunglasses pushed back in her ponytailed hair and feather lariats swinging at her neck.

'In fact, you actually look happy,' he said, indicating her bright, hopeful eyes.

'Well, I am now *you're* talking to me again. I felt like I'd lost my right arm.'

He blinked, his eyes suddenly watery. 'Me, too.'

Clem threw her arms around him, hardly able to bear the sadness in his face. It had been so long since she'd seen her happy-go-lucky brother. 'Oh, Tom! I've missed you so much. I've got so much to tell you.'

'And me you.'

Clem pulled away and looked back at him. Something in his voice told her his news wasn't as uplifting as hers. 'You first.'

'Well, you can probably guess,' he mumbled, one foot shuffling at the dust that had collected on the parquet floor. 'Clover dumped me.'

'*She* dumped *you*?' Clem answered incredulously.

Tom nodded.

'But why?'

He looked down, his lips drawing into a thin pale line. He was quiet for a long time, then he shrugged, looking more like ten than thirty, and it reminded her of Luca's face that first day on the boat as he stared at the wishing tree: both of them boys with wishes that weren't coming true.

'Obviously, I took the flat off the market once we'd signed the contract for this job, as there was no need to sell it any more—'

'Exactly.'

'Well, she took it badly. Said it was a clear sign I wasn't ready to commit to her, that I never would.'

'But . . . but you selling the flat was never about you committing to her anyway. She said that herself. It was a clear-cut case of releasing equity into the business. Even *I* understood that.'

'I think she hoped—'

'Oh I *know* she hoped!' Clem couldn't help herself from saying.

He was quiet for a second. 'On top of that, I've been doing crazy hours at the office, what with this job becoming so much bigger than we first realized. I just needed to stabilize the business, you know?'

'I so do!' Clem said loyally, clutching his arm.

'She just . . . flipped.' He shrugged again. 'Said she needed time to think.'

'When was this?'

'A couple of weeks ago.' He shifted weight uncomfortably and Clem knew there was more. She tipped her head to the side, waiting for it as Tom sighed. 'I think there might be someone else.'

Clem's eyes narrowed. 'Who?'

He shrugged. 'She didn't say; just that she knew someone who was only too ready to give her what she wanted if I wouldn't.'

Clem listened carefully, a lot less convinced by Clover's rhetoric than her brother. There were less territorial Middle Eastern states than Clover. It was a bluff and she knew it. Clover was banking on him falling apart without her, which, given the state of him, he clearly was, so that when they reunited, it would be with the proposal she craved, and some mythical rival hovering in the shadows had been calculated to get him moving sooner rather than later.

'Coming out here was totally the best thing you could have done,' she said, rubbing his arm. 'The change of scene will help give you perspective and the sunshine will make you feel better.'

He shrugged his eyebrows doubtfully. 'I was nervous about not overseeing the work myself anyway.'

'Control freak,' she teased.

He looked at her, an anxious look in his eyes. 'How's it going with Gabriel?'

Clem paused. 'As you predicted.'

He winced apologetically. 'I . . . I was wasted.'

'But right. Let's face it, it was pretty obvious what was going to happen.'

They were quiet for a moment and she knew he was worrying about the implications on the commission if – and when – the relationship foundered.

'How's Stella? Showing yet?' she asked quickly.

'She was showing before she was pregnant!' Tom chuckled.

'She said the morning sickness has really kicked in now.' Clem sighed. 'I hate not being around for her.'

'Listen, if there's one thing Stella's used to, it's throwing up in the morning,' Tom replied with his trademark grin. 'Besides, Mercy's looking after her. She's helping out on the stall a lot; the days are too long out there for Stella at the moment, especially when she's face first in a bucket.'

'Nicely put. Sensitive, bro.'

He grinned, kicking the floor again. 'I apologized to Mercy, by the way. Clover twisted everything so much that . . . Well, anyway, I gave her a pay rise to make up for it. We're mates now, although she doesn't do the "cleaning in her bra thing" with me.'

'Probably just as well,' Clem giggled.

He jabbed a thumb to his chest. 'Listen, *I* know where the thermostat is. I make sure it's turned down.'

They laughed as the sound of Chad leading the workmen through the house interrupted them.

'Where are you staying?' she asked, wishing she could have her brother all to her herself for a bit longer, but there was no spare room in the folly, and she could hardly ask Gabriel to move back to the Splendido again.

'A little hotel in Santa Margherita, it's basic but fine. It was all I could get at such short notice.'

'Um, talking of hotels . . . I take it you got my message about helping Chiara with her hotel, too?' She felt nervous bringing it up, and unsure about telling him it was being funded with the money from the flash sale. Technically he had rejected it all, but passions had cooled since then. Had he changed his mind? Did he assume it was still his? She could never explain why she was gifting such a colossal sum to her pen pal and she didn't want to bring all that up now and risk souring their reconciliation.

'Yes, Simon mentioned it. I haven't seen any orders come in yet, though.'

Clem rolled her eyes. 'Ugh, that's because she's a *nightmare* to work with! She won't commit to anything. I think, deep down, she actually wants the hotel to fail. She's struggling to keep up as it is, even without all these big changes.' She wrinkled her nose. 'Her heart's just not in it.'

'Well, you'll have to introduce us. Stella said she's great. It'll be nice to meet her at last. I don't know how I never met her the first time.'

'You were in Argentina on your gap year when she came over, remember?'

'Oh yeah.' He smiled at her fondly. 'It amazes me that you two have kept in contact all this time. My pen pal went AWOL on me. Shame, really, as he was a good bloke. D'you remember him? We got on like a house on fire.'

Clem gave a tiny nod, a quiet fear beginning to creep up her nervous system.

Tom looked pensive as the memory took hold. 'Actually, I ought to see if he's still in the area while I'm here. I hadn't thought about that. I mean, he lived in the next village and I bet everyone knows everyone here, don't they?'

'Pretty much,' she murmured.

'Tch, what was his name?' he mused, frowning. 'Agh. It's on the tip of my tongue.'

'Rafa.' Her voice was tiny.

'That's it!' Tom said, clicking his fingers. 'Rafaello Vicenzo. Of course! How could I forget?'

Chapter Thirty-Two

Clem hovered nervously at her desk, pushing paper around like it was a deck of tarot cards. From beyond the closed door in the library, she could hear Tom's calm voice issuing precise instructions to the team. He and Chad had taken to each other immediately – no surprise there as they shared a mutual appreciation of rugby, firm handshakes and cold beers – and Clem had slunk away on the pretext of selecting bedcovers for the boat's bedrooms.

She got up and walked the length of the end room, once, twice, three times, wringing her hands and squeezing her eyes shut in long, slow blinks. It was bad enough *her* being back here, hiding in plain sight. But Tom's presence was the final clue – should anyone be looking – that could unravel her secret.

There was only one thing she could think of to do.

She opened the doors behind the desk and stepped out onto the terrace, looking up into the scaffolding. It wasn't Tuesday, so Rafa wasn't in Florence. She knew he was in there somewhere.

She walked around the building, ducking low as she passed the library windows, so that Tom wouldn't see her. She stepped down into the gardens to look up at the higher levels. There were more carpenters and plasterers than she could shake a stick at, but no sign of Rafa anywhere.

'Claudio,' she called up to the nearest workman, waving her arms to get his attention. She dropped her voice to a stage whisper. 'Have you seen Rafa?'

The old man, as dusty as if he'd walked through a flour cloud, grinned and pointed up to the corner bedroom. The garden suite? Today? He *must* be worried about deadlines.

She nodded her thanks and ran through to the front hall, jogging up the stairs as soundlessly and quickly as she could.

She stopped at the bedroom door. Rafa was painting on the far wall, his back to her, headphones on. He was barefoot, wearing just his jeans, his khaki T-shirt lightly stuffed into his back pocket and hanging out like a magician's scarf. He was holding a long-stemmed brush in his right hand, dabbing at something with tiny, precise brushstrokes, the small muscles in his back tightening with the movements. He looked as though he'd been cold cast in bronze. She watched as he took a step back to assess the work, his face coming slightly into profile as he angled his head, and her breath caught at the sight of him – immersed, passionate, lost.

She tossed her head, immediately throwing the thoughts out, and walked over to him. She tapped his shoulder lightly, but the touch startled him – the combination of music and painting clearly took him somewhere beyond this room – and he turned with agile ferocity, grabbing her by the arm before she could say a word.

His grip was tight, his fingers pressing hard into her skin and pulling her up onto her toes, but not a sound escaped her. His face was inches from hers, and in the shock of her silent approach, he hadn't yet composed his features into the customary snarl that he reserved for her. What she saw . . .

She felt her heart hammering beneath her ribs, like a dove beating against a cage. Seconds passed as neither one stirred, the moment tight, frictional and airless.

It was Clem who pulled away first, falling back into space and safety. 'I didn't mean to startle you,' she said in a quiet voice.

He took a step back, too, widening the breach between them further, hostility restored. 'What do you want?'

'You have to go.'

'What?' The crack in his voice betrayed an emotion that surprised them both, and within a second, the scowl was back.

'You can't stay here today.'

'Why?'

She inhaled deeply. 'Tom's here. He arrived half an hour ago.'

Rafa paled. 'He—?'

'Is in the house, yes. He's in the library.'

Rafa looked at the ground, then back up at her.

She shrugged. 'I'm as surprised as you. I had no idea he was coming. He's overseeing the work in the library.'

Without a word, Rafa turned his back to her, reaching for the paints sitting on the table beside him. She watched as he screwed the lids on the squeezed, crumpled tubes, pulling his T-shirt out of his pocket and throwing it on, not caring that it was inside out.

'Ah, Clem, there you are!' Tom's voice made them both jump. 'Chad needs—'

Rafa turned with the same surprise as he had at her interruption.

'*Rafa?*' Tom laughed delightedly, standing stock still in disbelief before crossing the room in three strides and throwing out a beefy hand – the only part of him that hadn't lost weight – slapping the Italian heartily on the other shoulder. 'I don't believe it! We were only just talking about you! Weren't we, Clem?'

He looked back at his sister, who nodded mutely.

'Tom, it's good to see you,' Rafa said, breaking into a devastating smile he'd kept well hidden from her. Clem looked away, tortured by the sight of it.

'What brings you here?' Tom asked, jamming his hands into his jeans pockets.

Rafa opened his arms and gestured to the mural on the walls.

'No shit!' Tom beamed, impressed. He couldn't fail to be. It was already stunning and it wasn't even half finished. 'I *remember* you were thinking about going to art college. Clem, did you know Rafa was doing this?'

'Uh, no I . . . well, Chad does all the uh . . . liaising. I'm mainly stuck in the office looking at books.'

Tom turned back to Rafa. 'God, I can't believe this. I'm here half an hour and I run into an old friend from what, ten years—?'

'Eleven,' Rafa corrected him.

'Eleven years ago! Amazing.' Tom shook his head, his famous smile back on his face for the time being at least. 'Are you still living in the area?'

Rafa shrugged a 'yes'.

'Me, too. I've not moved from our neck of the woods either, I'm still just down the road from my parents' place, where you stayed with us. We've both got it too good, haven't we?'

Rafa nodded, his eyes firmly off Clem.

'Well, this certainly calls for a celebration! Dinner, tonight, all of us – I insist,' Tom declared, reaching an arm out and hooking Clem. 'We must catch up properly.'

Clem felt her lungs begin to pinch. 'Uh, well . . .' Her mind raced. 'Gabriel and I already had dinner plans.'

She saw Rafa's expression at the sound of Gabriel's name, and remembered the look on his face at the window as he'd seen them together that day. She'd been careful not to be caught twice, but it made no difference. He had only needed to see once to know that they were lovers.

Tom narrowed his eyes thoughtfully. 'Actually, that might be ideal. It's going to be a bit awkward meeting him again as your fella and not just as the client.' Tom rolled his eyes at Rafa as he mussed her hair, just like their father always did. 'A group dinner's probably the best way to go about it. I'll see if Chad's free; he seems a gregarious bloke and it'll be good to get a full debrief on the job. How many's that?' He counted the names on his fingers. 'Five, hmm . . . Oh, let's get your friend Chiara along, too.'

Clem flashed a look at Rafa at the mention of Chiara's name, while Tom held out his hands. 'It's perfect!' her brother cheered.

Clem tried but failed to smile. It wasn't perfect. It wasn't anything approaching perfect. It was about as far from perfect as it was possible to get.

Clem tossed her hair nervously over her shoulder as she walked up the approach to the Splendido, her stomach in knots at the prospect of the evening ahead. She wished Gabriel could have come home earlier and walked over with her, his hand clasped reassuringly around hers, his adoration the bullet-proof armour she needed against Rafa's glare, but with such short notice and several hundred miles to commute, he would have to meet her there.

She knew she was lucky he was even doing that. The surprise in his voice when she'd mentioned the arrangement told her he was less than thrilled at the prospect of dinner with his interior designer, one of his tradesmen and the local girl who ran a three-star hotel. Only the presence of Tom, she knew, had caused him to agree to come. Both men had to renegotiate their brief relationship to each other, but Gabriel, in particular, had rather more groundwork to put in after his targeted pursuit of Clem.

She walked through the doors and into the mahogany lobby, the air-conditioning a welcome relief from the simmering evening temperatures. She felt a light mist of perspiration all over her body and regretted her choice of outfit.

Chiara and Rafa were already there, standing in silence and looking awkward amidst the giant urns of flowers that were taller than they were. Chiara looked beautiful in a sea-green silk dress that glossed her curves, her dark caramel-coloured skin so shiny it could have been buffed, her long, almost-black hair gleaming beneath the light. Her enormous brown eyes flitted over the tablecloths, the light fittings and the colour of the menus – she looked as nervous as Clem, but for very different reasons: this wasn't the Portofino she called home.

Rafa, beside her, was wearing a white shirt and black trousers. He should have looked like a waiter, but there was nothing in his demeanour that suggested an eagerness to either serve or please. His body was stiff, his muscles hulked, as though he was ready to fight, and restlessness radiated from him like sound waves as he rhythmically clenched and unclenched his fists. They made a stunning couple.

'Hi,' Clem smiled at them and they turned, just as Chad walked in behind her.

'Evening all,' he said, kissing Clem lightly on both cheeks, and then Chiara. 'You ladies look especially beautiful tonight.'

Rafa glowered, staying defiantly silent. Chivalry wasn't his thing.

Clem fidgeted awkwardly, the rose suede jumpsuit seeming too edgy suddenly, too urban, next to Chiara's simple riviera glamour. She fiddled with the press stud on her cuff, her eyes meeting Rafa's as she looked back up. He looked away.

'So, who are we waiting for?' Chad asked. He was looking as striking as ever, in a raspberry pink linen suit with grey shirt. 'Hey, we're co-ordinating.'

'Just waiting on Tom and Gabriel,' Clem said, trying to keep her voice steady. 'Tom's staying in Santa Margherita, so he's probably just a few minutes behind us. And Gabriel said he'd be here as soon as he can be. He was in Turin today.'

'Well then, let's wait for them in the piano bar.' Chad smiled, gesturing for the ladies to lead and clearly most at ease in the super-deluxe hotel. They walked through into a room decorated with hand-painted murals, and Clem saw Rafa squinting as he studied the workmanship with a professional eye. Chad ordered a bottle of champagne, the rest of the small group's conversation muted by the grand surroundings and the new social roles they were occupying tonight, where everyone was equal.

'So, who's got Luca tonight?' Clem asked Chiara after a heavy pause.

'My friend Maria Cantara; she owns the *alimentaria*. She always takes him for me.'

'Except on Tuesdays,' Clem joked.

Chiara hesitated. 'Yes. Except then.'

They fell silent again.

'Have you been here before?' Clem asked, watching as a jeroboam of Krug was carried past them on a silver tray to the terrace outside.

'The rooms here start from seven hundred and fifty euros a night,' Rafa said with enough snap to make her blush. 'So, no.'

'Sorry I'm late,' Tom panted, jogging over to them and looking rangy in a pair of red chinos and a linen shirt. 'A van carrying chickens had overturned on the road. There were chickens everywhere, all jumping for their lives over the wall into the sea.' He pulled an 'oh dear' face, holding court already.

Everyone laughed and he kissed Clem and shook hands warmly with the two men.

Clem slipped her arm around Chiara's. 'Tom, after a ten-year delay, I'd like you *finally* to meet Chiara, my pen pal.'

'A pleasure,' Tom said, shaking her hand lightly as though she might break. She did look tiny beside him.

Chiara smiled and Clem thought she couldn't possibly know how beautiful she looked as her eyes sparkled under his gaze. Clem looked discreetly at Rafa, who was watching them both with an inscrutable expression. She felt the knots in her stomach tighten further as she realized he couldn't even pretend to be civil to her, not even to appear polite.

'Well, this is quite something, isn't it?' Tom said, stepping back and gesturing to the four of them. 'All four pen pals reunited after almost a decade.'

'You guys were pen pals, too?' Chad asked the two men in disbelief. 'My God, is this some kind of club?'

Tom laughed and shrugged. 'It's not actually that unlikely. Our schools were twinned and ran an exchange programme. D'you do that in Oz?'

Chad shook his head. 'Everywhere's too far away from us.'

'Well, in the sixth form we all got to stay with each other for a week. We came out here at Easter time, then these guys came back to us early summer.'

Clem and Chiara nodded.

'Of course, we got lucky with these chaps, but some people had absolute shockers. You know, living with a goat and eating curds for a week.' Chad roared with laughter. 'Don't get me wrong, it cut both ways. There was one Italian guy who came over – I think his parents owned one of the houses up there by the castle: big place, sea views – and he ended up staying in a council flat overlooking the bins and eating nothing but KFC.'

'I did not know that you and Rafa were pen pals,' Chiara said, smiling at Tom.

'Well, we weren't really – not for very long,' Tom replied. 'We stopped writing pretty much as soon as we'd done the trips. Typical blokes, just doing the bare minimum.' He chuckled.

Clem looked down at the lie. She knew Tom was being gallant. She remembered how disappointed he'd been when Rafa had suddenly broken off communication between them. They'd actually kept writing for over a year after the exchange trips.

'You never mentioned it,' Chiara said questioningly to Clem.

'No?' Clem tried not to chew her lip. 'I guess it just never really . . . crossed my mind. I mean, you and Rafa weren't together back then and you hadn't met Tom.'

345

'But when Rafa and I got together . . . it was a big connection, no?'

Clem swallowed. She still remembered the day she'd received Chiara's letter telling her she'd met and fallen in love with Rafa, an 'older' boy with a ladykiller reputation in the next town. 'Um . . .' She shrugged.

'So you two are . . . you're married, are you?' Tom enquired, looking at Rafa.

'No, no,' Chiara said quickly, blushing. 'We never . . . I mean, we are not together any more.'

'Oh, sorry to hear that,' Tom nodded, taking a sip of his drink and leaning back against the bar, his eyes moving slowly between the former lovers.

Rafa looked around the room in defiant silence. He was the only one of the group not making an effort, or if he was, the only effort he was making was stopping himself from marching out of there.

A waiter came over to them. 'Your table is ready now.'

Chad and Tom looked at each other. 'Shall we sit? The view's great and we can wait for Gabriel out there,' Chad said.

'Sure,' Tom agreed, and the small party wandered across the lobby, through the dining room and out onto the terrace.

The lights from the port below twinkled like fairy lights, the slow swell of the sea visible only in the blade of moonlight that fell across the inky water like a sabre. They sat down in a boy-girl-boy arrangement around the blush linen-covered circular table, Chad and Tom each holding out chairs for Chiara and Clem. Clem closed her eyes as the night breeze blew softly on her face like a lover's breath. Where was Gabriel?

Chad sat on her right, the chair on her other side left

empty for Gabriel. Chiara sat to the right of Chad, Rafa to the right of her and Tom to the right of him. They settled into small talk, Tom and Chad leading the conversation and flitting around everything from the supercars in the car park, to the area's draconian building restrictions, to the deep-draught boats currently moored in the port.

As the champagne began to flow, the mood settled, with everyone laughing more easily. Tom started regaling them with anecdotes about working on the cattle ranch in his gap year and how it had led to him setting up Alderton Hide on his return.

'You were lucky to find out your passion so young,' Chiara said.

'Didn't you? Clem told me your family has owned the hotel for decades.'

Chiara shrugged. 'Five generations. I always knew as a child it was what I would do, but that is not the same as what I wanted to do.'

'And what do you want to do?'

She gave a nervous smile. 'Accountant . . . Don't laugh!' she admonished as she saw the laughter sprint through Tom's eyes. 'I am good at maths. I do freelance work on the side.'

'On the *side*? Wow! Do you ever sleep?'

Chiara laughed, a low throaty sound that made Rafa look across at her sharply. But she didn't notice. 'Not really, no. But I am used to it. I have done it for a long time now.' She shrugged, and Clem tried to imagine her friend, surrounded by towers of dusty books, working through the night, while she'd partied the decade away, her only self-improvement being when she remembered to exfoliate in the shower.

'If you want to be an accountant, shouldn't you be in a

city like Genoa or Florence? Surely there's only a limited supply of work here?'

'I cannot leave.' She said it simply, a plain, unemotional fact.

'Because of the hotel?'

'Yes.'

The table fell silent.

'That's . . . that's a real shame that you can't live your life the way you want to,' Tom said, his voice low, the look in his eyes . . . what? Sad? Concerned?

Chiara shrugged and reached for her glass, aware suddenly of the group's collective scrutiny and pity. 'It is how it is. I am quite happy.'

'If a little tired.' Tom raised a grin.

'Yes,' she nodded gratefully as the tone lightened again.

'Well, it beats me how you managed to squeeze in the time to teach Clem to cook as well.' Tom looked across at her and winked. 'Stella kept me up to date.' He looked back at Chiara. 'It must have taken days surely? Teams of chefs drafted in, all doped up on tranquillizers.'

'Tranquillizers?' Chiara frowned, not quite understanding.

'To cope with the stress of Clem burning water.'

Everyone laughed, even Clem, and *even* Rafa. 'Ha, bloody ha.' She grinned, shaking her head and rolling her eyes. 'I'll have you know I've done a lot of growing up since I've been out here. I make my own bed every morning, I brush my hair, I even wear underwear now—'

'Come again?' Chad interjected.

'Don't ask.' Tom sighed. 'She was notorious.'

'And now I can cook.'

'One thing,' Tom specified.

'One very difficult, cool thing that happens to be your favourite meal.' She stuck her tongue out at him, and Chiara and Chad laughed. Rafa was watching their teasing with vague amusement, though the only sign of it was in the expression in his eyes, still a closely guarded secret.

'So what's next then in your dramatic reinvention of yourself?' Tom asked, lacing the words with irony. 'Learning to dress yourself?'

Clem gasped in mock outrage, spreading her arms wide and gesturing to the flawless-looking jumpsuit.

'All right, I'll give you that.' Tom laughed. 'You've got that down pat. It does look amazing.'

Her eyes met his at the loaded words. The jumpsuit, after all, had been the proverbial straw. He winked at her. She was truly forgiven.

'I've still got to learn to drive,' she said happily, nestling back in the chair. 'That's on my "To Do" list. It is a bit pathetic not being able to drive at my age.'

'You should do that while you're here,' Chad said, snapping a breadstick. 'This coast road is pretty quiet, and if you're going to learn clutch control anywhere, it'll be on these hills at the back. Is there anyone in the port who does lessons?' he asked Chiara and Rafa.

Chiara shook her head. 'No. But there is a man in Santa Margherita, only ten minutes away.'

'Well, I'll think about it. It's not like I've got much free time,' Clem said non-committally, dipping some focaccia in oil. The way her life was progressing, she might be better off learning to drive a boat first.

Chiara sat forward in her seat, her eyes bright. 'Rafa can teach you.'

'*What?*' Clem almost dropped the bread in her lap, but

she was too shocked to worry about hydrogenated fats on suede.

Rafa leaned in to Chiara and spoke hurriedly – and angrily – to her in Italian, his voice a low growl. Neither Clem nor Tom could understand, but Chad could.

'Don't worry about that. The schedule's fine, I don't see it being a problem,' Chad interrupted them. 'We're on target. Half an hour here or there isn't going to mess things up.'

Rafa looked back at him with studied blankness, his jaw tight, the brief, light-hearted glimmer in his eyes gone again. He slumped in his chair and looked out to sea, his unhappiness at the suggestion blatantly clear.

Clem gave an uneasy laugh. 'Honestly, its fine,' she mumbled. 'I probably won't—'

'No,' Chiara said firmly, slapping Rafa on the arm. 'It is the very least he can do after you gave him the extra work at the house. The money was very much needed.'

Rafa shot her a fierce look to be quiet – the two of them like an old married couple – and she lapsed into a tense silence.

Clem looked away, embarrassed, as Tom and Chad caught each other's eyes, both baffled by Rafa's evident unhappiness with the plan.

A well-cut shadow fell upon them and they all looked up to see Gabriel standing beside the table, a polite smile stretched thinly across his handsome face. 'I am sorry I am late,' he apologized, his gaze coming to rest on Clem's face. 'I hope I have not missed much?' There was an expression in his eyes she couldn't quite read.

Clem felt Chiara's, Tom's and Rafa's stares as his hand lightly, intimately, brushed over her hair while he took his seat beside her. She shook her head and forced a smile back, still shaken by the depths of Rafa's animosity towards her.

'No,' she managed, picking up her menu. 'You're just in time. We were, uh, j–just getting ready to order. Is there anything you'd particularly recommend?'

'Why don't I streamline the process and order on everyone's behalf?' Gabriel smiled, more genuinely now. 'I know the food very well here and the chef always does a few specials for me that aren't on the menu.'

'That sounds great,' Tom said.

'I'm in,' Chad echoed, placing his menu back on the table.

'I prefer to order my own choice,' Rafa said.

Gabriel looked up at him, pinning him with a cold stare, before turning to Chiara. 'How about you Chiara? Are you happy for me to order for you?'

She nodded. 'Of course,' she replied politely.

'So that's settled then. Majority rules, I'll order.'

'Hey! What about me?' Clem pouted.

'I already know what you like,' Gabriel smiled, squeezing her hand and making her blush at his blatant intimacy.

He raised his hand for the waiter, who came running, ordering a feast for the entire party in immaculate Italian, without once looking at the menu, but his eyes all the while on Rafa, who was staring back at him with ill-concealed contempt.

Clem stared up at the vaulted ceiling, the crisp white pillow puffed like a balloon around her head. Gabriel was asleep beside her, his shoulders and back exposed above the thin white sheet. Usually, when she couldn't sleep, she just rested her eyes on his face and body, examining the proportions of him in minute detail, as though it would unlock the sexual power he held over her, but it wasn't working tonight. She felt jittery and agitated, squeezing the muscles rhythmically in her legs, trying to wring out the restlessness that made her want to run.

She sighed in frustration and turned onto her side, her eyes falling to the two tight muscles bunched like fists in the small of his back. What was wrong with her? Why couldn't she just sleep? She was taking Tom to the boatyard tomorrow and she needed to be on form for the site visit. It was the most prestigious element of the commission, and it was imperative Tom was impressed.

Clem felt thankful that Chad and her brother had hit it off so well, so quickly. Chad's support had been vital these past few months and Clem had seen how relieved Tom had been as he'd learned how fully Chad had project-managed Clem's ideas in his absence. At least she hadn't been completely free-wheeling out here.

Things couldn't have gone better between Tom and Gabriel either, so it couldn't be that on her mind. The two men – both on their best behaviour for her – had quickly dominated the table, their conversation swinging from the global recession to Six Nations rugby to the American elections to Brioni cashmere, and pretty much everything in between – except Clem; both men appeared to have a tacit agreement that she was off limits that night. They had talked easily and fluidly, navigating a careful, wary path between their fledgling business alliance on the one hand and vague new personal relationship on the other. Clem hadn't realized how nervous she felt about it, until Tom had winked reassuringly at her when Gabriel left the table briefly to take a call, and she'd felt her shoulders drop and spread an inch.

Rafa had continued to be his usual, taciturn self, of course; she didn't expect anything more from him. He despised her and made it plain to everyone. She knew Chad had long since picked up on it, and she'd seen him frowning and looking embarrassed on her behalf on more than one occasion during the evening, but there was no question of firing Rafa, not if Gabriel wanted the frescoes to be re-established, which he did.

Her jiggering body fell still as she thought back to the exchanges between Rafa and Gabriel. She had been so focused on smoothing the path between her brother and her lover that she'd left no space on her emotional hard-drive for anything else. But there had been a hardness in Gabriel's tone whenever Tom had included his old pen pal in the conversation, his smile fading like a spent breeze every time their eyes met. Had he picked up on Rafa's animosity towards her? Had he overheard Rafa's resentful words to Chiara just as he reached the table, the painter's contempt all too clear in his words and face?

She wanted to say yes. She wanted to believe Gabriel had been defending her, putting the smaller, poorer man back in his place. But she knew it wasn't true. Or at least, not the whole truth.

She watched as his ribs spread lightly with every breath, the power in his incredible body dormant now, but she had glimpsed a fraction of his strength earlier. Their love-making had been rougher than usual, almost angry, and he had been on her the moment the door closed, ripping off the jumpsuit with such urgency that it had torn slightly at the seam on the shoulder.

It hadn't just been lust. It had been Gabriel staking his claim. For some reason, she realized, he saw Rafa not as a labourer or an artisan or an equal. But as a rival.

And once he started down that path . . .

Had he . . .? Clem held her breath at the sudden thought and slid her hand underneath the pillow, exhaling with relief as it closed around the silken pouch. It was still there. She had taken extra precautions now that she was sharing her bed on a regular basis and had hidden it inside the lining of the pillowcase, but she couldn't assume that was enough; not now that Gabriel was on alert. She lifted her head and slipped the silk packet out of its hiding place. Rolling over smoothly, she reached down over the side of the bed and pushed it under the mattress. She looked back at her sleeping lover, but he didn't stir so she lay back, her heart hammering wildly and driving sleep even further away for another night. That didn't matter, though. All that mattered – all that ever mattered – was that the secret was still hers.

Chapter Thirty-Three

The next morning, Clem felt as hellishly tired as she'd feared, but it was only really proved to her when Tom bounded into the folly like an over-excited puppy.

'Why are you so happy?' she mumbled, drawing her knees up to her chest as she sipped coffee from the armchair. She was waiting for the call from Stefano to say the boat was ready.

'Hey! The sun is *shining*, I'm in *Portofino* and I'm just about to ride on a *Riva* in order to go check out a *yacht*.' He grinned, arms outstretched. 'Exactly what isn't there to be happy about?'

Clem arched an eyebrow. She thought people with broken hearts weren't moved by superficialities like those. 'OK, Mr Happy. Well, just to warn you, I'm being a grouch. I slept like shit.'

'You look it . . . damn, this place is cute.'

She watched impassively as he scampered up the stairs, taking in the small, round bedroom dominated by the massive bed. 'Feel free to look around,' she called out sarcastically.

He came back down the steps, every movement fizzing with vim.

'So, you and Gabriel hit it off then,' she remarked lightly, but inwardly dying for his feedback as he started trying to work the TV remote to find a sports channel.

Tom stopped exploring and straightened up thoughtfully. 'Yeah, last night was surprisingly fun. But I don't know whether I *like* him for being so likable, or whether I hate him for it.'

'Huh?'

'Well, this place, that face. He's kind of got it all going on, hasn't he? I really want to hate him just on principle.'

'He's lovely,' Clem said, peering over the top of her cup. He threw a quizzical look at her. 'Lovely? Huh. Interesting word.' He put his hands on his hips. 'You could have chosen – oh, I don't know – perfect?'

Clem blinked slowly. 'Nobody's perfect, bro. Not even me.'

Tom laughed again, and she couldn't help but crack a grin at his ready smiles. It felt good to bask in his energy after all this time, like lying in a sun spot after a winter of blizzards.

Her phone buzzed and she saw the text from Stefano, saying that he was down by the jetty waiting for them. She sighed and drained her coffee, then stood up, tugging down her white shorts and blue striped shirt, which was already untucked. She picked up her iPad. 'Chad's meeting us there; he's going to go on to Rome after. You ready?' she asked, knowing his answer even before it left his lips.

'Sis.' He grinned, loping over to her and throwing a heavy gibbon-like arm around her shoulder. 'I was born ready.'

Boys, Clem thought to herself, as she watched Tom throw his head back, his arms spread across the back bench, his hand subconsciously stroking the leather seats that he'd inspected through slitted eyes as they'd climbed aboard. His reaction was exactly the same as Luca's, and no doubt Gabriel's, too, when he'd first bought the boat – the thrust and guttural roar of the engines, the sleek purity of its lines, it just spoke to something in men, much like Clem's legs and Stella's bosom.

Mario, the owner of the shipbuilders, was there, ready to meet them as they moored on the far side of the bay an hour later, and they climbed onto the powder-blue bikes that everyone used for moving around the giant docks.

Clem let Tom go ahead and stay abreast of Mario whilst he gave her brother the tour he'd given her over two months earlier. She remembered how awed she'd been then by the storeys-high scaffolding, the convex glass roofs vaulted like cathedrals above them.

The yacht was no longer red and rusty-looking, but powdered white with the first basecoats. It was quiet in there today, no banging, drilling or shouting accompanied them, no teams of men in boiler suits and knee pads – all other work had to cease while the hull was being sprayed. Just one air bubble or grain of sawdust and the paint wouldn't take. Chad arrived and Mario went with him into one of the offices to deal with some paperwork, as Clem took Tom over to a separate scaffolded tower, which allowed them to see the profile of the boat from what would be the waterline, rather than having to look up past the belly of the hull. It wasn't stupidly big, not a billionaire's boat with a helipad and a swimming pool, but 30 metres long, with two tiered upper decks and a sharp, elegant prow. It was stunning and as understated as twelve million pounds possibly can be.

'D'you like it?' she asked.

'I love it so much I'm going to keel over.' Tom grinned.

Clem groaned. 'Oh my God, that's awful, Tom! No wonder Clover left y—'

The words were out before she could stop them and she looked at him in dismay. 'That was an idiotic thing to say. I don't know why I said it.'

Tom laughed lightly. 'It's fine, Clem. I'm not going to break, you know.'

She looked at him sceptically. 'No? This time yesterday you looked three days from death.'

'Well, you were right; the sun does make you feel better. I feel different out here already.' He shrugged, his face in profile to her as he scanned the boat's proportions. They were quiet for a while. 'Do you know how much a boat like this costs?'

Clem shrugged. 'Ballpark,' she mumbled.

'He's a big fish, sis.' Tom looked across at her, and she knew what he was really saying: she was out of her league with this one.

'And I'm a big girl,' she replied. 'So you can stop looking at me like that.'

'This level of wealth complicates everything.'

'I don't see why. I'm not interested in his money. Or anyone else's.'

'Just because you don't care about the money doesn't mean it won't affect your relationship. This boat is only a toy to Gabriel and it's worth more than we'll probably ever earn. You're in a whole other world with him and I just don't want to see you get hurt, that's all.'

She gave a small, dismissive laugh. 'As if! No man's ever broken this heart, and they're not going to either.'

She saw Tom's expression. 'What? Don't look so sad. You should be pleased for me.'

'Why?' he shrugged. 'It means you've never been in love. That's sad.'

She rolled her eyes. 'Yeah, because I'm so gutted to have missed out on years of crying into my pillow. No wonder rom-coms are wasted on me.'

'But you do cry into your pillow,' he said quietly. 'I've heard you.'

'I d–d–do not! I'm drunk, you numpty!' she scoffed. 'You know how emotional I get after tequila.'

Tom nodded, but didn't say anything further to contradict her, and she saw that same familiar pity shining from his eyes whenever she was reflected in them.

A sharp whistle made them both jump and they looked down. Chad and Mario were on the ground, looking up at them.

'Want to climb aboard?' Chad called up.

Tom gave a big thumbs-up sign and Clem, relieved by the distraction, began leading him back down the steps.

'Just wait till you see the plans for the amethyst bar and the marble bath,' Clem said quickly over her shoulder to him. 'They rock.'

'Quite literally.' Tom quipped. 'Are you sure she'll float with that much stone inside her?'

'Ha ha.'

Their feet pattered down the metal steps in unison and she heard him clear his throat. 'By the way, I got talking to Chiara about the hotel last night. I said I'd pop in and have a look at the proposals you'd made. You don't mind, do you?'

'Are you kidding? You'd be doing me a favour. I bit off

way more than I could chew with Chiara,' Clem said, turning on the steps to look back up at him. 'But I'm warning you, you're going to be banging your head against a brick wall. She's stubborn as hell. She won't commit to anything.'

'Well, having lived with *you* all my life, I reckon I can probably handle her.'

'Trust me, you can't,' she said, tossing her hair over her shoulder and continuing their descent. She couldn't hear him smiling at her back, but she could feel it. 'Tom, you can't!'

She slammed the car door behind her and looked back in through the window. 'Right, so Luigi'll drop you back at Chiara's and he'll come back for me, yeah?'

Tom nodded. 'This I can't wait to see.'

'It's lasagne, Tom,' Clem quipped. 'Hardly rocket science. Meat and tomato.'

'Yes, but you said there was a secret ingredient.'

A reluctant smile came to Clem's face as she remembered Luca putting the chilli powder in instead. 'Fine. I'll get the shopping and see you back at Chiara's in an hour.'

'I look forward to it.' Tom winked. 'You? Cooking? I'm texting Dad now. He might well catch the next plane out.'

She rolled her eyes and stepped back to let the car pull away, watching them disappear around the sharp bend. Portofino was less than ten minutes away from here and she didn't have long.

She inhaled deeply and looked around her. It was the first time in the three months she'd been here that she had stopped in Santa Margherita, the town that was the backbone to Portofino's pretty face. It was here that the locals did all their shopping, laundry, went to school and caught the train, but she'd only ever been driven through it on the way to the docks, her head down as she worked on her iPad or made calls before the connection became too bad in the tunnels.

The buildings here were in the same palette as the port's – pink, peach, ochre and sand, all with dark green shutters – but they were much larger and more utilitarian, with lots of 1960s blocks with narrow verandas and football flags tied to the railings. There were some smart, over-priced designer boutiques along the promenade, but Clem preferred to amble past the brocante set up on the pavements, miles-long rows of Vespas bracketing it like a picket fence.

She drifted alongside the market stalls as if she were a paper bag caught in the wind, smiling absently at the stall-holders and admiring, without stopping, the local laces and sugar-dusted pastries. Her heart felt lighter in the market here. It wasn't a million miles from Portobello . . .

She sighed, enjoying the time alone. Her days here were so over-scheduled and her nights so short with Gabriel in her bed that it felt almost hedonistic to have some time to herself. It was ironic really that living in the lap of luxury, time and space was what felt most indulgent.

She turned inland, walking into a large square planted with mature orange trees. There was a launderette and a Gulliver supermarket on the far side, a battered lorry parked half on the pavement and its lights flashing as it made a delivery. She walked along, kicking up small dust clouds around her feet and looking into the cafés and kitchens that were filled with the lunch trade. She watched her own bare legs, lost in thought as she walked; they were nut-brown now and super-toned from so much hill-running along the headland and midnight swims in the cove, not to mention keeping up with Gabriel's sexual athleticism.

Not that it was her legs she was seeing – her head was replaying snapshot moments from her time here, the ones that were going to make returning home so unbearable. She flinched as her mind settled on the thought again. The realization she had to go had come to her when she was lying in the dark last night, and it had been the reason sleep had fled for good. But she knew it was the right thing: she wasn't leaving because she had to go, she was leaving because she couldn't stay.

He didn't realize it, but Tom was a neon sign to any interested party – and to Chiara in particular, who was only a hair's breadth away from the full undisclosed truth – about what had happened all those years ago, joining up dots that needed to remain in splendid isolation. She knew Gabriel was on the scent, his hostility towards Rafa barely hidden beneath his manners. But if she was honest with herself, it was getting harder for her to hide the truth, too. Every time she was with him, she felt doors she had long ago welded shut being prised open, chinks of light shining through her and burning down her defences, filling her with light and love and laughter. Her worst fears were being realized: the wall was falling. The longer she stayed, the more her feet were taking root where her heart had long since lived, and she wasn't sure she could trust herself any more.

She resolved to tell everyone at dinner tonight. She had to get the ball rolling, then the news of her departure would steadily gain its own momentum and she would *have* to leave, even when she knew her heart would betray her head and plead, beg, bargain for her to stay.

She turned a corner and heard the sound of children

playing; it was coming from the scuola elementare on the other side of the street. A large, hand-painted banner was fastened to the black metal gates, with 'Scuola Estiva' – summer school – spelled out in rainbow letters.

Summer School? Clem wondered if Chiara knew about it. That would solve all her childcare problems during the holidays, especially now that she wasn't going to have Clem to rely on every Tuesday.

She walked up to the gates, her cheek resting lightly against the bars. It was break time and the playground was full of children running, skipping, playing football. Two teachers were standing by a wall, talking. Clem watched as a little girl came crying over to them, clutching a grazed elbow, and one of the teachers disappeared inside with her, holding her hand. The remaining teacher cast a bored eye around the playground before digging in to her pocket and retrieving her phone. She made a call, looking around at the buzzing activity, before walking round the wall and out of sight.

An angry shout caught her attention. In the far corner, she could see a scuffle breaking out – two boys grappling, their heads locked together in a scrum. A crowd quickly gathered as the boys began to pull apart and a flurry of skinny arms and legs began flailing. The children watching began to chant names, picking sides, choosing a victor from the skirmish. 'Tonio! Tonio!'

She turned away, pulling her phone from her bag and checking the time. Damn, it was later than she'd thought. Luigi would be back for her in half an hour and she'd bought precisely nothing. She began to walk when . . .

She wheeled round, her ears straining to hear it again.

'Luca! Luca!'

Clem ran back to the gates, pressing her face against the bars, trying to see if it was her Luca, Tuesday Luca, the one with devilment in his eyes. There must be hundreds of boys around here called Luca. And yet . . . He was tall for his age, but skinny, and she'd caught sight of the other boy's bulk, if not his face.

Her eyes strained to make out the furious bodies that were now rolling on the ground as the other children – not a single child was left playing now – widened into a large circle around them, their chants growing loud with delight at the fight. She ran up to the next set of bars, trying to get a better view, but it was impossible to see anything through the children's legs. Until a football slowly trickled out through the crowd, forgotten in the melee.

Then she didn't need to see the boys' faces. She knew.

Clem looked around to see whether one of the teachers had come back, but the children were unattended, left to their own, cruel hierarchical devices. Tonio's name was the one gathering fans and growing in strength.

'Hey!' she shouted, rattling the gates, but they were locked and at least 200 metres from the children; not that she would have been heard over them if she'd been two metres away, they were that loud. 'Hey!'

No one turned.

She took a step back and looked up at the gates in desperation; they were at least two metres high, she figured. There was only one thing for it. In an instant, she had thrown her bag across her body and was climbing over the gates and jumping down on the other side. She ran across the playground, wading into the waist-height scrum of kids all jostling for a better view, and picked up the child wrestling with Luca. He was twice Luca's weight and had angry tears silently streaming down his face as he tried to land the punch on Luca that the smaller boy had clearly landed on him. From the looks of things, he was going to have a shiner in the morning. But that was nothing compared to the mess he'd made of Luca. There was an angry graze across his left cheek, where he'd clearly been pushed into the ground, and he was bleeding at both knees and elbows; small mottled patches were already coming up purple, heralding the bruises to come.

'What the bloody hell do you think you're doing, you bully?' she demanded furiously, holding the bigger boy by the scruff of his T-shirt as Luca scrambled to his feet, more frightened by the sight of Clem in the middle of the playground than of his opponent.

The children fell silent, beleaguered by her English as much as her sudden, strange appearance.

'Well? Who's going to explain what's going on?' she asked again, still not clocking the language barrier because she was so mad. At least, not until the children took a step back, began to disperse and Clem saw the errant teacher finally coming back round the corner. Clem watched the teacher freeze in alarm as she took in the situation before racing over.

Good, they could get to the bottom of this now.

'This boy was bullying Luca,' Clem said furiously, letting the boy drop as the woman reached her.

But the teacher didn't appear to be interested in who was bullying who. She was more intent on hurrying the children away and screaming at . . . Clem.

'I'm sorry. I don't know what you're saying. Please slow down,' Clem implored. Her Italian had improved enormously from a standing start three months ago, but she still couldn't keep up if anger or excitement were involved.

Another two teachers ran towards them from the school building, one on a phone, and Clem swallowed hard, getting a sudden sense of how much trouble she was in.

'Now hang on a minute!' Grabbing her by the elbows, they began to hustle her towards the school. 'For God's sake! This isn't what you . . . Luca! Are you OK?' she called, trying to catch sight of him over her shoulder, but one of the other teachers, who was attempting to calm the overexcited children, threw an arm over Luca's shoulder and herded him away from her. 'For God's sake, I was just trying to *help*,' she protested as she was frogmarched into the shadows. But from the set of their jaws and the accusing looks in their eyes, her pleas were falling on deaf ears.

Chapter Thirty-four

'You did *what*?' Stella screeched, forcing Clem to move the phone away from her ear and making even her companion – or rather, guard (although he was armed with only a biro and a packet of cigarettes) – wince; and he was sitting two chairs up.

'I was just breaking up a fight. Honestly, I don't know what the big deal is,' Clem muttered, her eyes on the closed door ten yards ahead of her, behind which voices kept rising. The only bits she'd snatched before the door had closed had been names: Luca's and Chiara's. 'And stop screaming. You've got a condition for God's sake.'

'Clem, I know you're not a natural with kids, but even you must be able to appreciate that a strange foreign woman vaulting the gates and assaulting a ten-year-old because of a playground scuffle is cause for concern. They probably thought you were trying to nick one of them!'

'Hardly,' Clem snorted, slumping lower in the seat.

'Well, obviously *I* know you've got more maternal instincts for your shoes than kids, but they don't,' Stella quipped. 'Have they called the police?'

'Yeah, but they called Chiara to come and get Luca, too. I think she's in there now, trying to sort it out.' She sighed, exasperated. 'I don't know. They won't let me in.'

'Where's Gabriel? I bet he's got scary lawyers who could sort this out.'

'It's not going to come to that! Anyway, I don't want him involved in this. Chiara's the best person to sort this out. She can tell them I do actually know Luca.' She sighed again, worn out by the debacle. 'Cheer me up with your news; how are you feeling? Boobs big?'

'Big?' Stella screeched. 'They've tripled! Mine are making Mercy's look like bee stings.'

'Oscar's happy, though, right?' Clem guffawed.

'Yeah.' Stella laughed down the line. 'Yeah, he really is.'

'Well, I'll be able to see for myself next week.' She braced herself for the response. Phase One was go!

Stella gasped. 'What? You mean you're coming back?'

'Next few days hopefully. Now Tom's out here, he can take over the project – we don't both need to be here – and it'd be better if he stayed here, away from you-know-who for a while.' Even to herself, the alibi sounded convincing.

'And what does Gabriel think? He was the one who lured you out there in the first place.'

'I haven't spoken to him about it yet, but why should he object? This whole job was just a ruse to get me alone, and . . . well, he's got me. It doesn't matter now if we're in Portofino or Portobello.'

'Mmm,' Stella murmured, and Clem could hear the distant rustle of a crisp packet. 'Or maybe you're just pretending you want to come back 'cos the authorities are gonna deport you anyway.'

Clem rolled her eyes as Stella cackled wickedly in her ear, her eyes trained on the silhouetted figures behind the glass door. They had come closer.

The handle of the door turned, the murmur of voices low

now as the meeting on the other side came to a close. 'I'd better go. Looks like they're coming out to tell me my fate.'

'Keep me posted about when you're coming back. I'll get some fresh milk and bread in for you.'

'Sure thing.'

She disconnected and put her phone back in her bag, throwing a sulky look across at the male teacher who was watching her closely, as if she might make a break for it.

The door opened and she looked up as the local guardia came out, putting his hat back on and coming over to her with a stern expression. The headmaster followed after him and . . . Rafa too.

Her mouth dropped open in shock, then closed again in embarrassment. Their eyes met briefly and she looked away, feeling furious and humiliated by his presence. Where was Chiara?

The guardia said something slowly to her, but she was too thrown to keep up and just looked back at him blankly.

'He says you are not allowed to come to the school again,' Rafa said, watching as her cheeks stained a deep, dirty red.

'Yeah, like I'd want to,' she muttered, keeping her eyes off him and staring mutinously at the policeman and headmaster instead.

'They have to hear you say it,' Rafa continued. 'I said you would promise. The headmaster wanted to press charges.'

'For what? I didn't *do* anything,' she protested crossly.

'Trespassing.'

'*Trespassing*?' she echoed, incredulous. 'For Christ's sake! That boy was bullying Luca.'

Rafa refused to be drawn. 'Just say it. Then we can go.'

His voice was quiet and had a calm, faintly pleading tone

that she hadn't heard before. She looked back at him. His usual scowl had gone and his eyes were begging her not to be stubborn – not today, not right now.

'Fine,' she said finally. She looked back at the headmaster. 'I promise not to come near the school again.' She felt ridiculous and made her feelings plain, enunciating the words with exaggerated, sarcastic care.

The teacher and policeman both narrowed their eyes at her tone – which translated perfectly – but before either could react, Rafa quickly spoke to them both in quiet, conciliatory tones, whilst grabbing her by the arm and marching her through the door, out of sight and out of trouble.

Without a word, he part-led, part-dragged her across the playground, and several times she had to jog to keep up with him. His hand was still on her arm, the fingers pressing hard into her flesh, as they had that afternoon two days ago when she'd startled him in the garden suite, and she wondered whether he knew he was hurting her.

He marched her through the gates – now unlocked – and stopped in front of a miniature green three-wheeled truck that looked like the love child of a Reliant Robin and a Piaggio.

'Get in.'

She wanted to laugh; he couldn't possibly be serious. But one look at his face told her that he was – deadly so – and she falteringly opened the door and peered in. An empty hand-crushed can of Coke was sitting on the seat, along with an old copy of *La Repubblica* that had notes written in red biro up the sides. Rafa threw himself into his seat and waited, with an impatient expression, for her to get in; the scowl was coming back as habit won out.

Clem bit her lip and climbed in; her thighs lifted clear off the seat there was so little room to stretch them out. She could actually feel his body heat radiating towards her in the tiny cab, his shoulder just an inch from hers, and she leaned slightly towards the window, away from him. Rafa turned on the ignition and pulled away with a squeal of tyres, not bothering to indicate or use his mirrors. Clem's hand automatically reached for the handle overhead, trying to balance and keep her body from being pressed against his as they swung around the bended, narrow roads out of town and back towards Portofino.

She looked out of the window, trying to concentrate on the rugged majesty of the coastline, but her mind wasn't on the scenery. Every part of her – mind, body and soul – was trapped in this tiny cab with him, his musky smell covering her like invisible smoke, the silence like a bloodied, beating heart throbbing between them.

His driving calmed as they moved further away from Santa Margherita, partly because the twists were too perilous to take at any speed, much less in a vehicle with all the traction and finesse of a shopping trolley. She dropped her hand from the handle and clamped both of them between her knees instead; Rafa looked across at her a couple of times, their eyes meeting fleetingly in looks that neither of them held.

They passed through the little tunnel, past the striped water-lapped folly, then the red-coloured beach huts and sandy beach of Paraggio, which neighboured Chiara's bay – she rolled her lips, anxious to get there and out of the truck. The silence between them felt oppressive, airless and draining, pushing her further when she'd already been pushed enough today. She was at the limits of her emotional endurance and felt ready to snap. She had to see Chiara, Tom . . . friendly faces.

The little yellow hotel hove into view as they rounded the sharp bend and a sigh of relief escaped her, prompting Rafa to glance across at her again. He parked with vehement carelessness astride three spaces in the small car park, and she quickly unbuckled the seat belt, rushing to get out.

She turned to open the door when she felt his hot hand on her arm. She stalled at his touch, but the heavy silence between them remained. She twisted back to face him, though she wouldn't meet his eyes.

'Thank you for your help,' she said quietly, obediently, politely.

But it wasn't gratitude that he wanted. The pressure in his hand increased and she looked up at him, bewildered.

His eyes were shining with barely suppressed emotion, all the defiance and pride he usually wore like a mask was gone. 'You never said why . . .' His voice was thick, every word an agony to get out, and she felt her heart begin to pound like a boxer's fist, the blood pooling to her feet.

'I . . . I couldn't,' she managed, her voice no longer husked but raspy, as if it had been sandpapered. 'I can't.'

'Even *now*? All this time later?' There was anger and disbelief behind his words, the muscles in his arms solid with tension, the tendons in his forearms straining beneath the self-control this conversation required.

'I'm so sorry,' she whispered, her voice too broken to do the job.

He dropped her arm with a look of disgust, his other arm stretched over the steering wheel as he stared out through the windscreen.

'I–I wanted t—' she tried.

'Just get out.' The words were like bullets, coated with a contempt that was designed to wound, but it was the sight of him, so closed, that pulled the sob from her like a reflex.

Blinded by tears, she reached for the door, grappling with the handle and having to kick it with her feet to force it open. She ran towards the back door, already able to see Tom and Chiara through the glazed window, both sitting by the table, their heads bowed together as Tom patted Chiara's shoulder, her head dropped disconsolately. Clem burst in, turning to push the door shut as if she were trying to keep an intruder out.

But he hadn't followed. He wasn't going anywhere. He was still sitting in the car, his elbows on the steering wheel and his face in his hands.

'Clem! What the hell happened? What did they do to you?' Tom asked in alarm as he took in her blotchy skin and juddering breaths as she struggled to compose herself in front of them.

'It's f–fine,' she managed. 'Just a s–storm in a teacup.'

'It doesn't look it,' Tom said, coming over and placing a hand on her shoulder. 'We only just got the message. Rafa took the call; Chiara and I were on the terraces over the road when the school rang. He just left a note on the table and raced off. We had to wait here for Luca to be dropped back.'

She swallowed. 'Where is he? Where's Luca now?'

As if in answer, a grubby little face emerged from under the table, his dusty, bloodied cheeks streaked clean with tear tracks. His doe eyes blinked at her, just as they had that first day, with the broken window lying smashed on the ground between them.

'Sorry,' he said in a tiny voice. 'I did not want you to be trouble.'

Clem laughed at the comment – no one ever did! –

though she understood his sentiment. 'It's OK, Luca. I'm a toughie. Your teachers don't scare me. I'd do it all over again.' She crouched down to his level. 'Are *you* OK? Did you get your ball back?'

He swallowed and nodded.

'It looked like you landed some big thumps on him.' She pulled a fist with her own hand, to show him what she meant, and he nodded again, his eyes still enormous with apprehension. 'Good.' She smiled and straightened up, holding her hand out for a high-five.

His smile, by return, split his face with relief – a flash of devilment returning – and he dashed out from under the table, ignoring her hand altogether and throwing his arms around her waist.

'Thank you,' he said in a small voice, so that it rumbled against her tummy.

'Any time,' she whispered, roughing his hair lightly with her hand.

Clem looked across at Chiara, who was still sitting at the table, watching them. 'I'm afraid everything that happened meant I didn't actually get round to doing the shopping,' she said apologetically.

'You call getting arrested an *excuse*?' Chiara dead-panned before an infectious smile gave her away. 'Is OK. I have chicken. We can have Milanese.'

'Get in!' Tom rejoiced, prompting a delighted smile from Chiara as she moved over to the cupboard and began rifling through the contents for the ingredients. Clem noticed Tom looking at Chiara's suntanned legs below her orange printed sundress as Luca scooted back across the kitchen to get his ball.

Clem walked over to the sink and let the water run cold

before splashing it on her face a few times. She always looked hellish when she cried. She patted her skin dry and saw through the window that the little green truck had gone. She could guess where to.

It didn't matter. It didn't. This time next week she'd be home and today would be just another memory that she would hide from the light, letting the colours, sounds and smells fade like an old photograph, until nothing remained but a vague, indistinct ache.

Chapter Thirty-Five

It was Tuesday – 'the new Friday night' in her book – and, as usual, she'd got nothing done. Luca had spent the morning trying to teach her football tricks – nutmegs, round-the-worlds and rainbow flicks – although Clem had only come out of it with bruised shins that matched his, and the afternoon session of doing bombs off the rocks had left them both with red bottoms.

'You've broken me. I hope you don't abuse all your babysitters in this way,' Clem teased, sitting down on the small shingly beach as he skimmed stones across the water, using the legendary Alderton method her father had taught her as a girl.

Luca laughed, before scoring a six on the water. He cheered, jumping up and down on the spot, and she rested her chin on her knees to watch him. She could have sworn he'd grown just in the time she'd been out here; his hair was longer and flopped in his eyes, his skin two tones darker after a summer of racing around in shorts and bare feet.

As was hers. She fiddled with her top. She was wearing a yellow bandeau bikini today, trying to even out her tan lines, and she'd tied her hair into a scruffy topknot to get it off her shoulders.

'See if you can get an eight,' she called, watching as he

found a perfectly smooth, thin oval stone, expertly running his long fingers over it and feeling for lumps or ridges that might affect its flight.

'Eleven? Wow!' she shrieked as he ran over for a high-five, before doing a series of cartwheels in a circle. She laughed at his celebrations. He was like a baby woodland creature, all legs, eyes and running instinct. She thought she'd never seen someone so unself-conscious, so free, a little imp who was as at home diving in the water as he was shinning up a tree or haring around the headland paths. Several times, she had heard him from the folly, playing out there in the early evenings, bouncing his ball in front of him as he ambled back from the lighthouse. They were so perfectly at ease with each other now, after a summer of Tuesdays and her standing chatting in their kitchen several evenings a week (on the nights when Gabriel couldn't get back), a glass of wine in hand while Chiara cooked for them all.

'Hey! I bet you can't do a crab,' she said, lying on her back and pushing herself up onto her hands and feet, forming a bridge with her body.

Luca ran to her side, impressed for once, and tried it himself. Sheer determination got him up, but he wasn't as supple as she was and his arms wobbled as he looked across at her, and the two of them giggled upside down, raising the stakes even further by trying to lift a leg in the air.

'Lock your elbows,' she said. 'It'll help.'

She heard the sound of somebody crunching over the stones, but she couldn't see who it was from her position, so she slid back down, rubbing her wrists.

Rafa was coming towards them, Luca's football under his arm from where he'd retrieved it on the lawn on his way down, his expression as inscrutable as ever. Clem scrambled to her feet, looking for a T-shirt to throw on, but it was still wet and drying on the rocks from when it had been splashed by one of Luca's spectacular bombs earlier. She stood awkwardly, wrapping her arms around herself in a way that she never did wandering around in her underwear elsewhere. Even fully dressed she felt exposed under his glare, and she saw him hesitate as he took in her discomfort.

'You're early,' she said. It came out almost as an accusation, and she realized she was as cross with him for cutting into her time with Luca, as for catching her upside down in just her bikini.

'I finished early today.' His voice was a low growl, as though every word spoken to her pained him. Luca dropped out of his position, certain that Rafa must have noticed his new skill by now, and sprang up. Clem watched as Rafa handed him the ball and squeezed the boy's shoulder affectionately. '*Ciao*.'

'*Ciao*,' Luca said casually, leaning against him whilst he spun his football on his index finger.

Clem couldn't help smiling at the bare, masculine exchange, but when she looked back at Rafa, she caught his eyes on her. They hadn't seen each other since their tortured conversation in the green truck last week, and the echoes of it lay strewn between them like bones.

'What is it you do in Florence?' she asked finally, struggling to break the silence that seemed so loud with all the words that drifted unsaid between them.

He stared at her and she could tell from his expression that he wasn't going to answer. He was blanking her as well as avoiding her now.

'Art school,' Luca piped up.

Clem looked down at Luca, then back at Rafa in astonishment.

'Art school?' She frowned. 'But I thought . . . I mean, didn't you do that when—'

'No.' His tone alone was enough to shut the conversation down, but Clem looked at him pensively.

'Well, will you be able to take Luca with you, to Florence?'

'Why would I?' Rafa snapped. 'It's a long way, and the school is no place for children.'

'What I mean is, I'm not going to be here for –' she swallowed, having to take a run-up to the words – 'I'll be going back to London . . . at some point.' She winced at the cop-out, too cowardly to tell him to his face. He would hear about her leaving from someone else and think she simply hadn't been bothered to tell him herself. Not that he would care. 'Who'll look after Luca when Chiara's in Bologna?'

'Why would she go there?' Rafa demanded.

'Well, to care for her aunt, obviously.'

Rafa stared at her as if she was playing a game he didn't understand. 'Her aunt is dead.'

Clem gasped. 'She died?'

'Nine years ago,' Rafa said in a low voice, suspicion clamouring in his eyes.

'What?' Clem whispered, confused by all this conflicting information. 'But then . . .?'

Her eyes fell to Luca who was staring up at her, and she tried to smile at him as comprehension began to dawn and she realized what Chiara had really been doing with her Tuesdays.

She hugged her arms tighter around herself as a sea breeze brushed over her and her skin goosebumped. She gave a small shiver. The wind was warm but she felt cold suddenly. 'Uh, Luca hasn't had dinner yet I'm afraid,' she said finally. 'Signora Benuto usually feeds him in half an hour.'

'I will take care of it,' Rafa muttered, his eyes on her chilled skin. 'What do you say, Luca?'

The boy looked up. '*Grazie*, Clem.'

'In English,' Rafa insisted.

'Thank you.' He sighed, tired out at last. 'It was a good day again.'

'Yes.' She smiled, her voice cracking at the understatement. She wanted to crouch down and hug him to her but she couldn't. 'It was. You practise those crabs, OK? You can't let me be better than you at something.'

Luca looked puzzled, not quite able to keep up, and Rafa translated quickly. Clem listened, rapt at the difference in his voice – when he spoke English it was surly and truculent, but in Italian he sounded animated, teasing, colourful. Then again, it wasn't a language thing. It was just the difference between him talking to her and anyone else, because the discrepancy wasn't just in his voice; it was in his eyes, too. She saw the switch clearly as he looked from Luca back to her, all expression deadening before her eyes. She blinked as he stared at her vacantly for a moment more, before he turned and led the boy up the path on the far side of the beach – the one that would go past her folly and out through the second gate.

She didn't watch them go. It was beyond her. Neither of them knew it, but that was the end of it, this awkward weekly ritual – their last Tuesday was done. She wouldn't see him – either one of them – again. She walked past the jetty and up the steps without a backward glance, holding her breath and counting to ten.

*

The next morning, Clem came out of the *pasticceria*, clutching the brown paper bag she had spent the past twenty minutes queuing for. It was just before lunch and the queue snaked all the way down the lane to the Gucci boutique. She knew better than to come at this time of course; it had been one of Chad's first pieces of local advice to her, and she had spent the summer only ever shopping there first thing in the morning, when the smell of their famous freshly baked olive focaccia drifted down the street. But she was on her farewell lap, doing the 'lasts' of everything that had made her so happy here; she didn't mind joining the tourists today.

It was really happening now. She was leaving here and the more people she told, the more real it became. She had set everything in motion for her departure now, speaking to Gabriel last night – as she had suspected, he was only too happy for them to decamp back to London, saying the commute had become 'draining' – and she had told Chad this morning, who would in turn tell the workmen, who would in turn tell . . .

She pulled out a corner of warm focaccia and began nibbling it. The last person to tell, and the most important, was Chiara. She couldn't afford to let her learn it from someone else, but she felt sick with nerves. She didn't fool herself that it was going to be anything other than a difficult conversation, especially now that she knew what her friend had been doing every Tuesday.

Tourists were everywhere, filling the narrow Via Roma as they swarmed around the smudge-free glass windows of the designer boutiques – Louis Vuitton, Hermès, Pucci, Dior, Missoni, Gucci – cooing at the handbags that cost as much as cars.

Clem, not in the mood for waltzing with strangers, dodged left up a tiny, metre-wide lane. Isolotto it was called, on account of its being so isolated from the bustle of the square and in every other way. On the other side of the buildings that flanked it were the most prestigious brands in the world, but here at the back was a warren of narrow footpaths, as small as capillaries, feeding off the port's famous public face and leading to the homes of the families who had lived here for generations. They had to have done. Even a broom cupboard here would be far out of reach of local wages on the open market.

Lines of washing reached from one side of the lane to the other, and rugs were hanging over the sides of the balconies, airing in the sun. A woman was throwing a bucket of soapy water down the drains and two elderly men were sitting at a table in companionable silence.

Clem nodded as she walked past, an intruder in their private den. Not a tourist, but not quite a local either. The sound of shouting made her look up, and she could just see a girl in one of the dark apartments, her back to Clem, gesticulating vigorously to someone further out of sight.

She popped another morsel of focaccia in her mouth and exited the lane a few moments later, stepping back into the bright sunlight and bustle of the piazzetta. The three-legged dog was chasing some ducks on the cobbles and every table along the waterfront was occupied. The port was at capacity, full to overflowing, like the azure blue water that lapped quietly just an inch or so below the pavements.

Clem hooked a left, but she didn't take her usual shortcut up the steps to the footpath above the road. Instead she followed the contours of the port, walking slowly, trying to take everything in and commit it to memory. This would be the food that would sustain her.

She passed the jeweller's, which glowed like an ice cave, mineral-white walls interspersed with rough floating shelves and glittering with treasures. She passed the bar with low-slung leather banquettes and rich young hipsters defying convention – eating mussels and drinking beer. She passed the gelateria with the grand chandelier and the antique mirrors, where coffee was served in tiny cups, sculpted like shells, and the ice cream cones were dipped in chocolate.

A group of school children were crowded around the glass counter, marvelling at the myriad flavours, and she looked at them, a vague smile on her face as she passed.

She stopped and retraced her steps.

Through the glass, she could see Chiara sitting at one of the tables. She was in profile to Clem, her hair pulled up in a high ponytail that curved into the nape of her neck and wearing one of the dolce vita sundresses that looked so good on her and positively ridiculous on Clem: it was pink with a red paisley print, and it had a square-fronted halterneck that emphasized both her soft cleavage and smooth back.

Clem took a deep breath. Serendipity. It was now or never.

She pushed her way through the school group and was emerging when a man set two ice creams in glass bowls on the table before sitting down; Chiara's smile grew further, her beauty increasing tenfold. Clem stopped, stunned, as she watched how their legs angled together, though not touching, their foreheads only centimetres apart on the table as they leaned in to eat off long-handled spoons, eyes connecting briefly before being torn away modestly, only for the sequence to be repeated seconds later. It was stunningly obvious what was happening.

Clem didn't need to see the man's face to know who her companion was. She would know the back of her brother's head anywhere.

'Clem!' Chiara cried happily, catching sight of her reflection in the mirrors.

Clem raised her hand mutely.

'Join us!' Chiara said, rising slightly from the table, and Clem could see from the way Tom moved that all he actually wanted to do was dive into her cleavage.

Clem wandered over. 'Hi.'

'Hey!' Tom said, draping an arm over the back of his chair as he twisted to face her. 'Fancy seeing you here.'

'Yes, fancy. Why are you hiding away in here?'

'Have you seen the crowds?' He pulled back a chair for her to sit down. 'Join us. Want some?' he asked, holding out his spoon.

'No, thanks. I'm good,' she said, rustling her bag of bread. 'So what are you doing *here*?'

'I'm afraid I'm still in full tourist mode.' Tom shrugged. 'And it was too gorgeous to spend the day in the kitchen looking over floor plans. I'd forgotten how beautiful it is here.'

'Ah, you wouldn't feel so sure in January, when the wind is strong and the rain is like ice. It can be bitter here,' Chiara said.

'That's nothing. You should see London,' Tom replied.

'I'd love to.' She sighed. 'It has been so long since I visited.'

'Yeah?' Tom asked, forgetting to eat. 'You should come over.'

'I would like that.' Chiara nodded, her big eyes on his. 'I love big cities. I think it's a reaction to living here all my life.' She rolled her eyes. 'So small.'

'Why haven't you left then?' Tom's tone was earnest, his gaze intent, and Clem wondered whether they even remembered she was there.

Chiara smiled. 'There's a certain little boy who calls this home.'

'Don't you think Luca would like London?'

'Don't be ridiculous,' Clem spluttered, interrupting before Chiara could answer. 'He's a wild little thing, clambering over rocks and swimming in the sea. You couldn't take him away from all this and put him in a *city*.'

'I wasn't suggesting he live in a favela,' Tom said wryly.

Clem sat back again, embarrassed, and watched a waiter set down two ice creams at the next table. She was overreacting, but they were talking about London. This was her in. She took a deep breath. 'Well, while we're on the topic, I thought you both should know I'm going back later this week,' Clem said casually, twisting a paper napkin in her hands, out of sight.

'But I've only just got here. Was it something I said?' Tom asked, laughing in surprise.

'I've spoken to Gabriel about it and he's actually happier being based in London than here; it's a bugger getting back to the peninsula every night. And with you here to oversee the projects now, there's no need for me to stay.' Clem watched him surreptitiously look across at Chiara.

'There is every need,' Chiara said sternly, making them all jump.

Clem looked up at her. 'But—'

'No buts,' Chiara said, her colour rising. 'You cannot leave. Not . . . not yet,' she added, glancing quickly at Tom. 'It is my cousin's wedding in a few weeks. Luca is ringbearer. You must come.'

Her cousin's wedding? Clem flicked a look over at Tom before coming back to her friend. 'Whilst that would be lovely,' she said quietly, her eyes lasered to Chiara's, 'you know I must go.'

'*I* know that you must not. I will not allow it. You owe me this at least.' Chiara rose from the chair imperiously, the sweet, exhausted, selfless, deferential woman Clem knew was gone. She looked down at Clem sternly. 'If you leave now, just like this, I will never speak to you again.'

Clem stared at her, open-mouthed and speechless. She had expected Chiara's disappointment but she hadn't expected this response. 'Chiara—' she pleaded.

'Never, Clem.' And with a flick of her skirts, Chiara turned and literally flounced out of the gelateria.

Tom watched her go in dismay, before leaning in on his elbows and staring his sister down. '*What* was that about? What does she mean, you owe her?'

'Oh great, you're cross with me, too. I'm straight back to the good old days,' Clem muttered, slumping back in her chair, but trembling slightly. That had gone as badly as it possibly could have done.

'Don't change the subject,' he demanded. 'Tell me what's going on, Clem. I'm not stupid. There's something going on between you two. I permanently feel like I've just walked in on the end of a confidential discussion.'

'Well then maybe you should respect our privacy,' Clem huffed. 'I've known Chiara a long time, and we share a bond that doesn't need to be articulated or explained.'

'She's your school *pen pal*. Very few people find a lifelong friend in theirs,' Tom said sceptically.

'Well, I did, so just drop it, yeah?' Clem said, getting up from the table.

'Oh, so now you're off, too,' he said. 'That's great.'

'Yeah. You were right, Tom,' she said sarcastically, patting him on the shoulder. 'It was something you said.'

Chapter Thirty-Six

Clem crouched down low as she lit the thick stubby beeswax candles she had found in a cupboard in the kitchen. The workmen had disconnected the electricity supply for twenty-four hours while they fitted the state-of-the-art security system that had its own control room, and even Signora Benuto had left the premises overnight.

The villa was at a curious stage, like a beautiful woman half-dressed for a big night out – her face painted, underpinned in her lingerie, but with only her shoes on. All of the rooms were primed and prepped for their new skins – some were merely awaiting the hand-painted wallpaper panels to line the walls, others the new floor. None had their soft furnishings yet: curtains, blinds, chairs and bed drapes were all being made in Florence and weren't due for another two to three weeks, while the Alderton Hide leather finishes were being flown in on a weekly basis.

Clem sat cross-legged on the floor and looked up at the walls around her, flickering in the candlelight. There was no moon tonight and the garden scene delicately etched on the plaster was as shadowy and enigmatic as the one outside. She felt her breathing slow as she took in its depths, peering through the branches into dark hollows and beyond the blossom to misty nooks. There was something indefinable about it that soothed her and drew her in like a warm memory.

From her spot on the floor, she glimpsed the one flaw, the idiosyncrasy that interrupted the dream-like perfection of the scheme, and she crawled over to it on all fours. Crouched below the windowsill, she could still see Luca's crest beneath the watercolour washes, though it was fainter now and only visible to an eye that was searching for it. Running her fingers over it, she vaguely wondered how happy it would make the small boy to know that his mark remained in the grand house.

A sound made her start and she looked over to the doorway. Rafa was coming down the hall, brushes in one hand, a workman's lamp in the other and headphones hanging around his neck. He stopped at the sight of her.

'I did not know anyone was here. I will go,' he said, turning to leave.

'No, wait! I . . . I'll go. If you need to work, I'll get out of your way,' she said, clambering to her feet.

He walked slowly into the room, laying his brushes on the trestle table, making no further effort to acknowledge her.

'. . . It's so beautiful, you must be pleased with it,' she said quietly after a moment.

He shot her a look – frowning to find her still there – but didn't reply.

'You really must take photographs of it when it's finished . . . for your book.'

'What book?' he asked, his back still to her.

'To showcase your work. You know, for new commissions.'

He snorted dismissively. 'Here we go by reputation, not *books*.'

'Oh.' She looked around the room, feeling small and inadequate in his presence, as always, knowing that was how he wanted her to feel. She watched him as he kept his back firmly to her, wanting to ask him why he hated her with such vehemence, why he couldn't stand to even look at her, why he couldn't forgive her after all these years? 'Raf—'

'You are going, yes? Or shall I?' he demanded curtly.

She stopped, chastened, and nodded as he put on his headphones and turned away from her.

'What's going on in here?' a voice asked.

Clem looked over and saw Gabriel standing in the doorway, watching them. Rafa – his music audible even from across the room – didn't hear as he had his back to them both.

'Rafa's come to get on with the mural. I was just getting out of his way,' she replied with forced brightness, managing a smile as she walked briskly towards him. 'Have you had a good day?' she asked, trying to nudge him back out into the hall.

Gabriel ignored her question and remained where he was. 'What is going on in here?' he asked more loudly, determined to be heard.

Rafa turned this time and stopped as he saw Gabriel in the doorway. He turned off his iPod and pulled off his headphones. '*Buonasera*,' he said in a low voice that was polite but unfriendly.

Gabriel stared at him stonily. 'Do you have a problem working with Miss Alderton?' Oh, God. Clem closed her eyes. Gabriel had overheard them this time.

Rafa was still. 'No,' he said after an age.

'Because every time I find you talking to her, she looks close to tears and you look close to a fight.'

The room fell silent again, Clem standing like a statue between the two men.

'I have no problem working with her,' Rafa finally repeated.

'Good,' Gabriel replied abruptly, 'because I don't like to see my girlfriend upset. You understand that, I'm sure.'

Clem looked at Gabriel. The comment seemed pointed, but Rafa simply nodded.

'She is rare, this woman,' Gabriel said. 'I think you know that too.'

This time, Rafa didn't move, not even to be polite. There was a long silence as both men squared up, the deference of employee to boss plainly gone.

Clem heard the change in Gabriel's breathing. 'Whereas I can get a painter anywhere. There is a renowned specialist in Florence, I hear. But I could get someone from Bolivia, if that was what I wanted. It would really be very easy.'

Rafa looked incandescent at the thinly veiled threat but Clem knew, from what Chiara had told her, that he needed this job. After an age, he nodded again.

'So then, we understand each other,' Gabriel replied in a more leisurely voice, his eyes scanning the mural with evident disinterest. 'This is the last time there will be a problem.' He looked back at Rafa, his eyes chillingly cold, before reaching for Clem's hand and leading her out of the room after him.

'Was that really necessary, Gabriel? You didn't need to humiliate him like that,' she whispered, trying to catch up with his long, haughty strides.

'I simply treated him with the same disdain he shows you. Maybe now he'll think twice.'

'But it doesn't offend me. That's just his manner,' she

fibbed. 'Besides, I'm tougher than I might look. I can fight my own battles.'

'Why should you have to when you've got me?' Gabriel replied, looking back over his shoulder as he led her down the stairs. 'The message is loud and clear now: he either treats you with respect or he's gone.'

'But he's the only person in the area who specializes in this kind of—'

'That is irrelevant. He needs to know his place.'

They were at the bottom of the staircase now, standing in the hallway opposite the front door. Gabriel rested one foot on the step above as he turned to face her, his hands resting on the giant oak corbel. 'You think I am blind?'

Clem felt her heart lose rhythm. What did he know? She couldn't shake the fear that he knew more than he was showing.

'I think you're over-reacting to some perceived slights that *I* don't even notice,' she lied. 'Besides, they need the money so badly. Please, just leave him be, for Chiara's sake if nothing else. Please.'

He looked down at her hand as she placed it on his chest, one finger sliding through the placket, her nail grazing his skin lightly. He looked back at her, knowing her ruse, but liking it too much to make her stop. He took her wrist and pulled her to him, kissing her – staking his claim again, she knew.

'So that's a yes?'

He shrugged, his mood appeased now. 'What does it really matter when we're leaving this weekend anyway?'

Clem inhaled nervously and bit her lip. He took in her expression and his face fell. 'What now?' He sighed, taking a step back.

'It turns out I can't go just yet after all.'

Gabriel frowned, his displeasure evident. 'Why not?'

'There's some wedding Chiara wants me to stay for, a family thing.'

'Why must *you* go to that?'

'I don't know – because she's my friend and she's asked me to?' She shrugged. 'It doesn't really matter, does it? It's only a few extra weeks away, and as long as I'm back in London in good time to help Stella get ready for the baby . . .' She looked up at him with pleading eyes.

'A few more weeks and then we will be gone?'

She nodded. 'We'll be gone, I promise.' Gone from here. Gone from him.

'I shall hold you to it,' he murmured, his eyes travelling over her with the lust their kisses always awakened.

'Thank you.' She smiled, kissing him lightly again to seal the deal.

She pulled away, more reassured. 'What?' she asked as he continued to gaze at her, his eyes dotting over her like tracks in the snow.

'Nothing.'

'That look is not nothing.'

'No?'

'No.'

He pinned her still with his eyes – as only he could – looking suddenly serious as he reached into his pocket and pulled out a small box. He opened it, his eyes on her the whole time. She swallowed as she saw the ring inside. 'I didn't think I could wait too long. You're a flight risk, Miss Alderton,' he joked, but there was no joking in his eyes.

'What is it?' she mumbled, looking at it glistening in the box, reaching out one finger and stroking it tentatively.

'A chocolate diamond flanked with aquamarines,' he said in a low voice. 'But that's not what you really mean.' He tilted her chin with the crook of his finger, so that she was forced to look at him. 'What do you want it to be?'

She blinked at him as they stared at each other – words wouldn't come; thoughts wouldn't form. Everything was a blank. She was too stunned, too surprised by this. She'd thought the biggest news tonight would be telling him she had to stay here until the wedding was over. But this . . .

What would she choose? Right hand? Left hand? Massive life decisions represented by a simple cosmetic detail.

'Then it's a cocktail ring,' he murmured finally as the silence stretched out and he saw how she had stalled somewhere deep inside herself.

She exhaled involuntarily, her muscles softening as he took the ring out of the box and gently pushed it onto the ring finger of her right hand. It looked sensational against her deep tan, and she laughed suddenly with delight as she held it up to the flickering light. 'It's so beautiful,' she gasped.

'It is on you.'

She held her hand up at different angles. 'I've never even heard of a chocolate diamond before.'

'They're hard to come by,' he murmured, raising her hand to his lips and kissing it again. 'But I knew I had to find something extraordinary for you. You're not a white diamonds kind of girl.'

She looked over at him, hearing the pale shade of sorrow in his voice. 'I'm sorry that, that I'm . . .'

'Not ready?' he finished for her. He looked at her for a long moment. 'It is maybe too early. I just wanted you to be sure how serious I am.' He kissed her hand again. 'And for you to know, you will have to surrender to me eventually.'

A shiver ran over her, but she hid it with a toss of her hair as he leaned in to kiss her once again, this time tenderly, his jealousies forgotten. She closed her eyes and tried to forget, too, but it was impossible when her past was standing just metres away, upstairs in the bedroom.

Chad knocked as he entered the office. 'Knock, knock,' he said loudly.

Clem stirred from her sleep on the sofa, her left cheek pink from where it had been resting on her arms.

'Ay ay! Had a sleepover, did you?' Chad's eyes twinkled as she blearily lifted her head. She was wearing Gabriel's shirt and boxers.

'Ugh, what time is it?' she mumbled, oblivious. The sun was streaming through the windows in blades of light; outside she could hear the boards along the scaffolding trembling as heavy-booted workmen stomped around on them. She blinked hard twice, remembering how she and Gabriel had been too lazy to go back to the folly in the middle of the night.

Chad perched on the back of the gold sofa, looking down at her, his arms crossed, his eyes watchful. 'I thought you should know we've had word the leather floor's been passed through customs and it'll be here later.'

'Oh, right. Great.' She yawned. 'I can't wait to see how it looks. Have you told Tom?'

'I did, yeah.'

'Is he here?' Oh God, had her brother seen her sleeping on the job?

'No. I stopped in at Chiara's on the way over. He wanted to talk through some plans for the new dining room.'

'Has he convinced her to go for it then?' Clem asked, astonished, and not just to hear that Tom was already at

Chiara's place. He was known for never tabling meetings before 10 a.m. back home.

'It appears so.'

'Right.' Clem felt vaguely deflated by the news that Tom had succeeded where she had failed.

She swung her legs round and stood up, the clothes hanging off her slender body as if she'd been shrunk in the night.

Chad's eyes ran up and down her – he was happily engaged, but not so loved up that he couldn't see the immediate appeal of a woman wearing her man's clothes. 'You might want to get changed before your appointment. That's a pretty full-on statement you're giving there.'

'What appointment?' Clem frowned, rubbing her face vigorously in her hands. Damn, she was tired.

'Your driving lesson.'

'*What?*' Her hands dropped away. 'Since when did I agree to have a driving lesson?'

'Since dinner at the Splendido.'

'That was weeks ago! And I think I made it very plain that I wasn't interested in learning to drive out here.'

Chad gave a non-committal shrug. 'Well, obviously not.'

'Who organized this?' Clem demanded just as she remembered the way Chiara had insisted Rafa help her out. She groaned. One good deed for another. 'Well, *he* made it very plain that he would rather drink paint than teach me to drive,' she added.

'Who's he?' Chad asked innocently.

'You know perfectly well who, Chad! Rafa. Stop being so obtuse. It's too early for this shit.'

'Wow! You're grouchy in the morning. Such bad language!' A small bemused smile played upon Chad's lips.

'Besides, I don't understand. Why would Rafa rather drink paint than teach you to drive? Don't you think you're over-reacting?'

'He *hates* me, Chad,' she hissed, remembering how he'd blanked her the night before, the anger it had ignited in Gabriel. 'I am not spending time alone with him shouting orders at me.'

'He does not hate you.'

'Oh come on! You've seen what he's like around me. He can scarcely look at me,' she raged, glaring at him.

'Nor you him, I've noticed.'

'What?'

He watched as his words blindsided her, leaving her flapping at him helplessly. 'There's some weird aura between you two,' he said calmly.

'No there isn't. I don't have an aura. I don't even wear perfume.'

'Yeah. There is. I thought it that first day I introduced you.'

'Bully for you,' she muttered, turning away from him and walking over to the desk, checking her diary.

Chad sighed, watching her. 'It's all clear till eleven. I already checked. You've got an hour. Well, forty-five minutes by the time you get dressed and out of here.'

Clem turned and glared at him. 'I'm not going.'

'Fine,' Chad shrugged. 'You tell him then.'

'*You* tell him! You bloody well set it up.'

'No, I didn't.'

'Ugh, Chad! It has to have been you and Chiara. You are the only other person who knows my diary. God, you're doing my head in and I've only just woken up.'

'Which is why you need to get a shift on. He'll be here

any minute,' he said, checking his watch. 'Go on, hurry up. Unless you want him to see you looking like *that*.'

Clem looked down at herself and knew there was no way she could let Rafa see her like this. She looked so post-coital she may as well still have a neck blush. 'Fuck's sake,' she muttered, throwing him furious looks as she ran from the office.

She was running down the long room – she was going to have to use the back door and sprint along the footpaths rather than the garden if she didn't want the rest of the workforce to see her either – when she came to an abrupt stop.

Slowly, she turned and looked back.

Rafa was leaning against the wall, his arms crossed and his colour up. From his body language alone she could tell he'd heard every word.

Oh God, where was that paint? she wondered as she looked into his blacker-than-black eyes. She'd drink it herself.

Chapter Thirty-Seven

Clem sat with her hands between her knees, trying not to jig. She had hurriedly thrown on a pair of white denim cut-offs with a slouchy grey T-shirt and had piled on so many long pendant necklaces she actually jingled as she walked. Rafa had gone on ahead whilst she'd been getting changed, telling Chad she should meet him by the car park behind the port, and now they were sitting in the little green comedy truck as Rafa pointed out the accelerator and brake pedals, the indicators, the horn, the windscreen wipers and so many other gadgets she felt she may as well be in a Bond car.

'You understand?' he asked, without a hint of a smile. He could have been mugging her, such was the hostility in his face – she was just relieved Gabriel couldn't see them now; he'd fire Rafa on the spot. Still, he might get off on a technicality. They weren't working now and she wasn't his boss in here, so he could behave as he liked.

She nodded. 'I turn it on, put my foot on the clutch, release the brake and—'

'In gear first. Put the truck in gear and then release the brake.'

'OK. Foot on the clutch, move the gear stick, release brake, off I go.'

'Check mirrors, off you go,' he corrected.

Clem bit down the impulse to argue that *he* never used his mirrors. But they'd been here ten minutes already and hadn't even turned on the ignition yet. Rafa seemed to care about his truck the way most men cared about Maseratis.

'So, shall I . . .?' she asked, reaching for the ignition questioningly.

Rafa hesitated, clearly nervous, before nodding. 'Just go slow.'

She turned the key in the ignition and the old engine jump-started on; Clem couldn't quite stifle a giggle as the cab vibrated on its wobbly suspension and she saw her thighs begin to jiggle. The random thought of Stella in here, jiggling, wandered into her head and made her laugh out loud. She felt Rafa glaring at her and tried to stop, but that only made the laughter increase in intensity – it was just like being back at school and getting the giggles in assembly – and it was all over when the image of Stella and Mercy jiggling in just their bras drifted into her mind. She put her face in her hands as the tears began to fall.

Rafa reached across her furiously and switched off the ignition. 'What is so funny?' he demanded, which only served to make her laugh even harder.

'I'm sorry, I'm so sorry,' she managed finally, wiping her eyes and throwing her head back on the headrest. 'I'm sorry. It must . . . it must be nerves. Sorry.' She sighed and looked across at him, trying to look serious. 'I'm sorry.'

He looked at her and then away. 'Go again,' he muttered.

She turned on the ignition and quickly disguised her laugh as a cough, as the engine made them both vibrate again. What was it he'd said? Clutch, gear, gas?

She pressed her foot down on the clutch and moved the gearstick.

'Wrong gear. Further over,' Rafa said, watching as she tried to move the car from third into first gear. But she had taken her foot off the clutch and the engine protested loudly, screeching as metal jammed against metal.

Clem, in panic, took her hands and feet away from the moving parts of the car, and the truck shuddered and stalled. Oh dear.

She looked across at Rafa nervously. He had closed his eyes and tipped his head back against the headrest, obviously praying for strength.

'This clearly isn't a very good idea,' she murmured. 'We should probably stop before I do some damage.'

He opened his eyes and turned to face her. 'Just go again.'

She turned to open the cab door.

'What are you doing?' he demanded.

'I'm going.'

'I meant go again. Do the . . . truck again. Turn it on.' He looked frustrated that he wasn't making himself clear, and he rubbed his face in his hands. Clem noticed how very tired he looked. Girlfriend keeping him up? He was wearing the same T-shirt she'd seen him in last night.

She turned on the ignition again and, this time, didn't laugh. She depressed the clutch, found first and slowly – as though she were atop the Matterhorn on a silver tray – released the brake.

'You didn't check your mirrors,' he murmured, even though they were parked against a wall and facing into a tiny, deserted square. 'But just keep going!' he added quickly as he saw her go to move back a step and risk stalling the engine again. Slowly, they eased forward. 'Gas.'

Clem tapped a foot to the accelerator and the little truck began to move over the cobbles.

'Follow the road,' he said, pointing to the only road in and out of the village. 'And keep right . . . Mind the scooters!'

She clipped a scooter with the wing mirror as they passed.

'What . . . what did I do? Shall I stop?' she asked, panicking, her knuckles white from gripping the steering wheel so hard.

Rafa, who was watching the scooters fall one on top of the other like dominoes in the rear-view mirror, shook his head. 'Just keep going,' he murmured.

She wanted to look across at him – she was sure she'd heard a smile in his voice – but she didn't dare take her eyes off the road.

'More gas,' he said as the road began to incline, and Clem hesitantly moved up to 15 kph.

'Is it OK? Am I doing it right?' she asked, her words threaded together by nerves, her chin practically resting on the steering wheel.

There was a short pause. 'You're doing fine.' She thought he was looking at her but she couldn't be sure. The sea was on her right now and she was quite convinced she might accidentally drive into it. 'Try to move up to twenty.'

'*Gear?*'

'Kilometros an hour.' Now she *knew* he was looking and laughing at her.

She breathed out through a little nervous 'o' as they sped up – just. The road was winding on the way back to Santa Margherita, and she took the corners as if the truck were in heels.

'What was that?' she breathed anxiously, her eyes flitting to the wing mirrors. 'I thought I saw something.'

Rafa twisted round and saw an orange Lamborghini sitting restlessly on their tail, bobbing left intermittently, as though it intended to overtake on one of the chicanes at any moment. It had no doubt joined them as they'd passed the Splendido half a mile back, and it looked like *it* was going to stall. It had probably never moved so slowly before. 'Is OK. Is nothing,' Rafa said calmly, facing the front again, his right arm laid along the open window. 'There is left turn coming up. Use the indicator.'

Clem switched on the windscreen wipers. 'Oh! Shit!' she hissed.

Rafa chuckled – a surprisingly soft sound that couldn't have surprised her more if he'd started tap-dancing on the bonnet. 'Other side.'

Clem indicated left, braking for the full quarter-mile it took to get to the turning and almost inducing a stress-fuelled heart attack in the Lamborghini driver behind. Rafa had turned his face to the window, away from her, and begun laughing into his hand.

The road climbed a steep but fairly wide hill, and Clem used most of it, like a novice skier traversing the slopes, as she pressed harder on the gas, trying to get the little old truck up it. She was almost holding her breath, leaning forward in her seat to help bring the weight forward as they crested the hill, and when she finally thought it was safe enough to glance across at Rafa, she saw his shoulders shaking hard.

'Stop laughing at me!' she cried, half laughing, too. She'd have liked to slap him on the arm, but she didn't dare take a hand off the wheel. 'Where am I going?'

He pointed, unable to speak, to a large parking area in front of a community park on their right. A rusty barbecue was set up with four or five trestle tables clustered around it, a basketball court behind and some outdoor ping-pong tables. Cruising into the parking spot in first gear, she brought the truck to an abrupt halt – no mean feat given that it had scarcely been moving beforehand.

She cut the engine and almost fell upon the steering wheel with relief. 'I did it,' she whispered, resting her cheek on the top of it and looking across at Rafa, who had brought himself under control now that she could see him again.

'You did,' he nodded, a glimmer of laughter still in his eyes.

She turned away, wanting to see where they were. The slope was gentle here and the views out to sea magnificent. She could just make out the tip of the lighthouse on the headland; the dense, clipped topiaries of the exclusive estates over there were in sharp contrast to the short stubby olive groves here, bent over like old men, their branches tangled together and throwing down dappled shade as chickens pecked at the ground. In contrast to the smart, shabby-chic striped properties in the port, the buildings in the hills were ramshackle and, in some cases, practically bolted together. In one, a tree was growing through the middle of a roof of an outbuilding, and everywhere were sweetly scented jasmine hedges, rangy and unclipped, their delicate blossoms shimmying in the sea breeze.

'It's so wild up here,' she mused. 'I love it.'

There was a short silence and she felt them both re-member themselves and their roles again.

'Wait here,' Rafa said shortly. 'I come straight back.'

He jumped out of the cab and jogged across the road, into a wild, untended garden. The house it belonged to was low-built, made from a dark grey stone, with a raised deck area at the front and brown, broken shutters at the window.

She watched as he disappeared inside. Was this where he lived now? She had assumed he lived, if not in the port itself, then in Santa Margherita still, his home town. It was bigger, younger, vibier over there. She leaned across the passenger seat, trying to see past the lemon trees growing out front, but their branches were heavy with fruit and hanging low. Curiosity getting the better of her, she followed suit.

She walked up the path, unaware that she had started to tiptoe, the grasses in the garden brushing against her bare knees; she saw a football lying inert by the jasmine hedge, but she didn't stop. Her eyes were on the small house. A wind chime hung at one of the windows, revolving slowly, and she could hear the sound of running water coming from within. A shower? So he hadn't come home last night; he'd gone on to his girlfriend's after working at the villa. The realization flattened her, even though she was guilty of the same crime herself.

She pushed open the outer door, which was covered with a mesh mosquito frame, and stepped into the cool, dark few square metres that passed as a kitchen. It was clean and functional, with mainly grey melamine and rough wood surfaces, clearly patched together on an 'as needed' basis. A glass was sitting in the sink and there was a box of Coronas on top of the old white, humming fridge.

She walked through into the sitting room. It was much the same as the kitchen – spare, bald, impersonal – only a pair of jeans strewn across the sofa gave any indication that someone actually lived here.

No, that wasn't quite true. On the windowsill, she saw a single wooden-framed photograph. She walked over to it. Luca was sitting on Rafa's shoulders, Chiara leaning against him, her arms around his waist, with one hand on Luca's leg as she gazed contentedly at the camera.

Clem stared, frozen, at the photo that was testament to the happy family they'd been. From the looks of Luca, the photo could only have been taken in the past year or two, yet she could see a vivid change in them all now, even Luca. In the photo, they all looked peaceful and unaware of the sadness that was coming their way. Seeing the boy on his father's shoulders, their faces stacked together, the resemblance between them was startling: they shared the same liquid chocolate eyes, proud mouths and scruffy hair.

A sound behind her made her turn and she saw Rafa coming out of the bedroom, pulling a clean, faded navy T-shirt over his head. He stopped dead at the sight of her in the house, holding the photograph. She saw the way his muscles tensed. It was easy to – his skin was damp from the hasty shower and his T-shirt was gripping onto his stomach, in no hurry to fall. She tried really hard not to look. Really, really hard.

'I–I didn't mean to snoop,' she said in a small voice, putting the photo back down again with nervous hands. 'It's a lovely picture.'

She looked up again to find Rafa still immobile, silence the faithful companion that sat between them at all times, like an obedient dog.

'Rafa, please,' she whispered. 'Don't . . . don't look at me like that.'

'You think I hate you,' he said, echoing her earlier rant at Chad.

'Yes.' She shrugged haplessly, before shaking her head lightly. 'I don't know . . . I just know you don't want me here.'

'*I* don't want *you* here? You were the one who ran when you saw me.'

She remembered her violent reaction to seeing him and Luca that evening on the path.

'That was shock. I didn't expect to see you.'

'How? This is a small village. You knew I lived here.'

'I knew you *once* lived here. You could have moved away for all I knew.'

'You knew through Chiara's letters that I still lived here,' he argued with almost leisurely certainty, his voice low and calm.

'Yes, but then you broke up . . .' she mumbled weakly. He watched her looking around the room, her gaze anxious and flitting, unable to settle on anything, least of all him. 'Did you . . . did you know I knew her?' She tried to hold his gaze.

He went perfectly still, and for a second she thought he wasn't going to answer again. 'Not until two years ago.'

Two years ago? That was when his relationship with Chiara had begun to unravel 'And did you tell her you . . . knew me?'

He inhaled sharply, his head tipping back with the movement. 'No.'

'Why not?'

He shrugged. 'It was the past. Dead.' He lobbed the word at her like a grenade, letting it explode between them.

She froze in the blast, her body trembling from the direct hit, and turned to leave.

'Why did you come back?'

She looked back at him. 'I had no choice. I was trying to help Tom. I came here for him, not to . . . not to complicate your life.'

He gave a short, bitter snort, planting his hands on his hips and finally, inadvertently, dislodging the T-shirt to hide the rest of his stomach. '*Now* you worry about complicating my life . . .' he muttered, his handsome face juggling pain and pride all at once. 'Well, thank you for the concern, but my life is very uncomplicated, very simple: I am a single man and enjoying it.' The memory of the blonde against the wall shimmered between them like a hologram and Clem looked away. She couldn't say what she wanted to, so what was the point in saying anything?

A muffled bang outside made them both turn and Clem's eyes widened with horror; the sound was unmistakeable. Rafa, paralysed for a moment, sprinted through the kitchen and out into the garden. By the time Clem caught up with him on the pavement, he had sunk to sitting on his heels, his hands in his hair.

A hundred yards down the hill, black smoke was puffing in plumes into the blue sky from the crumpled bonnet of the green comedy truck, the stoic tree it was resting against marginally less upright than it had been for the last fifty years. Paint was streaked all over the back from upturned pots so that it looked more like a Pollock than a Piaggio.

'Oh *shit*,' she whispered. 'Handbrake.'

Chapter Thirty-Eight

'Gorgeous!' Clem smiled as soon as Stella picked up. 'Got your looks for sure.'

'You got it then,' Stella chuckled. 'She looks like a jelly-bean, doesn't she? I don't know how those people can tell jack-shit from looking on those scans. Oscar thought her leg was a willy.'

'Her? Does that mean you found out the sex?'

'Nah. Oscar's convinced it's a boy, but I'm betting it's a pink one.'

'Well, as long as it's one *or* the other, I won't mind either way. How are you feeling?'

Stella yawned. 'Knackered. Not getting much sleep. She's really beginning to kick now.'

'Still taking your folic acid I hope?'

'Yes, Mum,' Stella replied. 'Anyway, what are you doing? You sound like you're shovelling bricks.'

'Thanks! I'm actually just walking over to Chiara's for supper. Gabriel's away tonight.'

There was a short pause and then the sound of humming down the line. 'Happy Birthday'?

'You know full well it's not my birthday till November,' Clem pouted.

'Not that, you daft nana! It's your three-month birthday. You and Hot Lips.'

What?

'Stop that! I can hear you panicking from here. It's fine. It's good. You can do this,' Stella instructed bossily, rustling open some crisps. 'If I can have a baby, you can go past your twelve-week rule. I'm not going to be a grown-up on my own. You're doing it with me.'

Clem gave a small, indistinct sound that Stella decided to take as concurrence.

'Next week, you and me are going on some sort of adulthood course. I need to get my shit together before this baby comes.'

'About that . . .'

Stella stopped munching.

'I'm afraid it's going to be another few weeks before I can come home after all.'

'Oh Cl–e–m!' Stella whined. 'I knew this would happen! Why'd you get my hopes up like that? I'm an emotional wreck as it is! My hormones are all over the place.'

'I'm sorry. I thought that with Tom being here I could get away.'

'So why can't you then?'

Clem remembered Chiara's face in the gelateria. 'There's just stuff that I need to finish before I go.'

Stella tutted. 'Well, just so long as you're bloody well back before Christmas. You do know you're my birth partner, right?'

'*What?* But what about Oscar?'

'Ozzie?' Stella laughed. 'Listen, I love him to pieces, I really do, but the boy has a phobia about jelly, for Christ's sake. He'll be as much comfort to me in there as . . . as your mother!'

Both women shuddered. 'Talking of which, have you

seen my folks recently? They're *never* at home when I try calling.'

'Hmm, come to think of it, I haven't. And I did pass the house last night on my way to preggers yoga. The place looked empty – all the lights were off and it was after nine by then.'

'Probably playing bridge,' Clem replied, knowing her parents' social diary by heart, just as something knocked against the back of her knees suddenly, causing them to give. She yelped before turning in alarm. Luca was grinning back at her from the steps above, his football rolling by her feet.

'You monkey!' she shrieked, picking it up. 'Stell, I've gotta go. I'm under attack.'

'Huh?' It was the best sound she could manage with a mouth full of crisps.

'Nothing to worry about. I'll call tomorrow.'

She pressed disconnect and held the ball out as Luca jumped down the steps three at a time towards her. 'You've been up at the lighthouse again.' She grinned, taking in his wind-tangled hair. The same thing happened to hers up there, too. 'Why do you like it up there so much? It's a pretty long walk.'

Luca gave a little shrug. 'Bianca gives me ice cream that must be finished by the end of the day.'

'Oh, does she?' Clem grinned. 'Maybe I'll start going up there myself then.'

'No!' Luca looked worried. 'She say it for the local children only.'

'Oh fine then.' Clem winked at him. 'Well, I was actually just on my way to your house; maybe there's some ice cream over there,' she said, putting her arm over his shoulder and squeezing it. 'You can be my bodyguard.'

They started down the steps together, walking into the shade of the park and following the dusty winding tracks that would lead down to the fishing boats. But where they would usually be joking around, Luca seemed quiet and distracted. She frowned, glancing down at him frequently as they shuffled along in silence.

'Is everything OK, Luca?' she asked, resting a hand on his shoulder.

He shrugged.

'You just seem a bit quiet today, that's all.'

He shrugged again, and she bit her lip, nervous about pushing him on it. Was it that bully at school again?

'All right, but just remember I got in trouble with the *police* for you! I'm always on your side, OK? You can tell me anything.'

He looked up at her, a more interested smile on his face, and she grinned back, ruffling his hair as they walked across the crowded piazzetta.

On the footpath on the far side of the port, she finally managed to engage him in a fierce competition of racing back to the hotel without stepping on the cracks, and they hopped and skittered along like crazy people, barging each other with their elbows until he finally dazzled her with his elfin smile again. Clem thought she might burst with pride that she had turned his mood around. *She* had!

Luca got to the finish line first, entering the passcode on the guest entrance as Clem caught up, disputing his win.

'I saw you cheat.' She grinned. 'You definitely ran over the last four.'

'No! Was only two!' Luca contradicted as he skipped down the stairs, before realizing he'd just dropped himself in it. They both laughed, throwing the ball between them, like basketball players, down the corridor. Clem dummied a bounce pass before doing an overhead shot that sailed over him into the kitchen.

Luca ran after it.

Clem followed him a moment later and almost tripped straight over him. Luca was standing stock-still, only inches into the room, the ball still bouncing lightly by the fridge on the far wall.

'H–hi!' Tom managed, straightening up from the kitchen table.

Clem blinked in shock as she watched Chiara slide off the table beneath him, smoothing her hair and rumpled dress, her lips the colour of crushed raspberries.

'*Ciao*, Luca,' she murmured.

The boy didn't reply. Clem automatically placed a hand to his shoulder. His small body felt rigid and tight.

Tom cleared his throat. 'Good day at school, buddy?' he asked, summoning up one of his gap-toothed grins. Usually Tom could charm the devil, but there was a heavy silence as Luca stayed quiet. Clem couldn't see his face, but she could feel, beneath her hand, that he was holding his breath, that every muscle in his body had set as hard as concrete. Then he turned and fled the room in a movement so fluid and quick that he was gone before she could even react.

'Luca!' Clem cried, spinning around.

'Leave him,' Chiara said calmly.

'Shit!' Tom said under his breath, raking a hand through his hair and looking back at Chiara worriedly.

Clem glared at him and he shrugged, helplessly. 'It wasn't on purpose, sis. We just lost . . . track of time.'

Clem rolled her eyes, but she knew it could have been worse. A lot worse.

She looked across at Chiara, who had her back to them and was smoothing her hair with her hands. Clem saw the way Tom watched her, worried about her reaction, worried she might call it all a mistake.

'I'm so sorry,' he murmured, walking up behind her and sliding his hands up her arms. 'It was all my fault.'

Chiara sank back into his chest. 'No.' She wrapped her arms around herself till her hands found his. 'He had to find out at some point.'

'Yes, but of all the ways to introduce me as your new boyfriend to your son, that wasn't ideal.'

Chiara turned and stared up at him. 'But Luca is not my son, Tom.'

Tom took a half step back in surprise, his hands dropping hers. *'What?'*

Clem almost keeled over with shock.

'Luca is not my son,' Chiara said in a quiet voice.

Only the almost-empty bottle of wine in the middle of the table stopped the scene from looking like a council of war – fingers threading, knuckles blanched, expressions tense and anxious all at once, as Chiara and Tom looked at one another reassuringly while they waited for Rafa to arrive.

Clem emptied her glass and hurriedly poured herself another. Her drinking had tailed off hugely in the past few months since she'd been with Gabriel, and she was down to a respectable glass per night. The upside had been bright eyes and more energy, but the downside was her alcohol tolerance had dropped sharply, and she could already feel the third glass beginning to dull her senses.

Her stomach was in knots. Chiara had followed after Luca and spoken to him in his room at length, while Tom had stirred the risotto and Clem started on the wine.

They heard the guests' back door slam shut and they both looked up, listening to the footsteps coming down the hall. A moment later, Rafa filled the doorway, his surly expression suggesting he'd had more exciting plans than this for tonight.

'Raf,' Tom said, simultaneously tasting the risotto off the wooden spoon and holding up a hand in far-off greeting. 'Thanks for coming, mate.'

'*Prego*,' Rafa murmured, managing, if not quite a smile, certainly to enliven the light in his eyes. He scarcely looked at Clem, his anger at her still palpable for crumpling his truck – and more besides.

'Here, have some wine,' Tom said, walking over and pouring him a glass. There was a momentary hesitation, as both men took in their roles – Tom, the host; Rafa, the guest – in this, the very hotel where Rafa had been man of the house for the best part of a decade and still part-owned.

Tom cleared his throat awkwardly and they nodded a toast. 'Chin chin,' Tom mumbled.

Chiara, hearing their voices, came back into the kitchen. Tom met her eyes, the question in them not needing to be articulated. 'He'll be OK,' she said quietly. '*Ciao*, Raf.'

Rafa looked between them, alert. 'Is Luca? What is wrong?'

'It's nothing,' Chiara said calmly. 'Just a confusion. Please, sit,' Chiara said to Rafa, gesturing for him to join Clem.

Tom came over, too, and the three of them noisily scraped their chairs into position around the table.

'Thank you both for coming,' Chiara said quietly, clearly leading the discussion. 'There is something very important I wanted to talk to you about.'

Clem lunged for her glass and gulped down the remnants. She was scarcely over the shock of Chiara's last bombshell. What the hell was coming now?

Clem felt Tom's eyes on her, and the weight of that look, the one he reserved for her alone and which had been curiously absent out here since she'd been proving herself as an independent, fully-functioning adult. She wiped her mouth with the back of her hand, her gaze skippy and restless, like a horse about to buck.

'Clem, you . . . you obviously know about me and Tom—'

'Well, if I didn't before, I sure do now,' Clem drawled.

'What?' Rafa frowned, trying to catch up, looking between them all as if they were keeping a secret from him – which they were.

Chiara looked across at him directly. 'Tom and me . . .'

Clem winced. She wanted to correct her to say 'I', but didn't. Damn, she was more like her mother than she cared to admit.

'. . . we are together.'

Everyone fell still, as the words settled like pieces of a jigsaw on the table between them. From the rapid flicker of Rafa's eyes, Clem watched him trying to piece the picture together. She watched the small pulsing bulge at his jaw, saw how he had inhaled deeply but not yet let it go again.

Rafa looked up at Chiara, pointedly not looking at Tom, as though it wasn't safe and he didn't quite trust himself. 'You only just met,' he said in Italian, a voice so quiet that Clem and Tom could scarcely hear it.

'I know,' Chiara nodded. Then she shrugged. 'It was instant.'

Clem's eyes swivelled between them. She wasn't sure why *she* had to be here. She had guessed at what was happening long before today; she'd picked up on the chemistry that first night, during dinner at the Splendido. This was a love triangle, not a square.

She reached for the bottle again and emptied the contents into her glass.

'Don't you think you've had enough?' Tom asked, a rebuke in his voice.

Clem hesitated, thinking back to the events of the past thirty-six hours. 'No,' she said, defiantly taking a large swig and then immediately ruining her hard-drinking image with a loud hiccup.

'We are in love,' Chiara said quietly, her eyes tender and apologetic on Rafa's. This time, Clem felt her brother's stare swing like a compass needle towards Chiara, the woman he loved, the woman Clem sensed he loved more in three weeks than he had loved Clover in five years.

Tom cleared his throat again. 'Raf, I . . . I don't want this to undermine our friendship, mate. My understanding was that you broke up long before I arrived.'

Rafa couldn't meet his eyes; hostility shimmered around him like a heat haze.

'Neither of us was even looking for this. We're as surprised as anybody,' Tom continued.

Not quite, Clem thought to herself. Not as surprised as the little boy in the next room. Her eyes glanced at the wall that separated them.

Rafa said nothing, his jaw grinding slightly from side to side, as though he was massaging his fist under the table, getting ready for the killer punch. Clem saw the muscle spasm in Tom's cheek, his childhood stress tic, and felt a familiar protective rush course through her.

'Oh, don't get too worked up about it, Tom,' Clem said

too quickly, too rashly. 'Rafa moved on long ago. He's already got a girlfriend. Gorgeous, she is. Not to mention . . . young.'

Rafa's glare was upon her like flames over petrol, furious and fast, beating her back.

'What would *you* know about any of it?' he growled. 'You? You just look for the rich man.'

Clem couldn't reply – the hatred he directed at her almost seemed to be a living, breathing thing that he nurtured inside himself.

'Stop!' Chiara interrupted, smoothing her hands between them both. 'This will not help anybody. We did not ask you to come for this. We are here for Luca.'

'Luca?' Rafa and Clem echoed in unison, both looking back at her. What did he have to do with it?

Tom's head had snapped up at the boy's name, too.

Chiara met his gaze, both of them visibly softening as their eyes rested on each other. 'Tom must return to London soon' – she took a deep breath – 'and I want to go with him.'

Silence fell on them, flattening them all. In an instant, Rafa had gone completely white, even his dark lips appeared pale.

Somewhere – not on a conscious level – Clem could see this was news to Tom, too; a whimsical suggestion made more in hope than expectation that had suddenly come to pass, a dream that was coming true. But that didn't make it OK. Even her beloved brother's happiness couldn't come before Luca's.

'We've already discussed this,' Clem hissed to them both, instantly on the attack. 'You can't take that boy away from *here* – the middle of fucking paradise – and just drop him in the middle of a city.'

'You discussed this? Without me?' Rafa butted in, his voice ominously quiet, his eyes burning at Chiara. The wine was forgotten and the council of war reconvened.

'No. No.' Chiara shook her head, staying calm. 'Because Luca is not coming. He will stay here.'

This time it was Clem who paled. '*What?* You're just going to leave him here?'

'Please. I am not *just* going to do anything. I have spent much time thinking about what is best, and it is best he stays here – for the moment. Here he is surrounded by people who know and love him. He is at school, he has friends here and he will be with Rafa.'

'That is it? This is how you tell me you are going? This is how you tell me you are leaving me with the child?' Rafa asked, his colour returning after the initial shock.

Chiara looked at him. 'You love him, Rafa.'

'Yes!' he agreed vehemently. 'But that does not mean my life is . . . is fit for this. I live in a small house, I work crazy hours . . .' He looked desperate, as panic-stricken as Clem felt.

Chiara looked across at her calmly. 'Clem, you have spent very much time with him this summer. Maybe you would consider to stay, too?'

'*You* know that I can't do that,' Clem whispered, transmitting urgent, desperate messages with her eyes.

But Chiara wouldn't play ball. They had an audience and she was using it, both of them knowing Clem was gagged. 'Why? When you stop to think, there is not really a reason to leave. You have a beautiful home here, a man who loves you, and Luca talks about you with very much affection. It would only be for a few weeks to begin with, but *if* I decide to stay in London, then that is when we can decide if he joins me there.'

'And I get no say in this?' Rafa raged. 'I just get told he will live with me and then he won't?'

'You get every say. He loves you like a father. But he is my brother, not my child, and I have looked after him and taken care of him every one of the days in the eight years since Mama died. I gave up my own life in Firenze and my career hopes to come back here for him, because I love him with all my heart. But it has come at great cost to me. I have been sad for very long and now . . .' Her glance flickered back to Tom, and once there couldn't wrest free again. 'This is my chance for happiness. I love Tom and I want to be with him.' She looked back at Clem, her expression tender, affectionate and utterly implacable. 'I would not even consider this if I did not believe Luca would be safe, protected and loved by you both.'

'Why do you include her?' Rafa roared. 'She is a stranger.'

'Not any more. Not after this summer,' Chiara said, her eyes on Clem as they communicated without words, their tangled past twisting into the present, too, keeping pace with them both, keeping them connected.

'Well, it will not work, your plan,' Rafa hissed. 'She is already going. I heard her. They cannot wait to leave.'

Clem gasped at his words. He'd been listening that night?

He nodded, leaning in to her, his eyes on the ring glittering on her right hand. 'Not a white diamonds girl?' he snarled, standing up with such force that his chair went flying back, clattering noisily to the floor as he stormed from the room.

The back door slammed behind him and Clem stared at her hands miserably, shaking from the blitzkrieg. 'When are you going?' she asked after a few minutes, defeated. She knew when Chiara had made up her mind; and she also knew what Luca's response was going to be, if this afternoon's was anything to go by.

'After the wedding. Luca goes back to school a few days later and he will be so busy he will not miss me so much as he thinks. He will only be home to sleep and eat. Anyway, Rafa is his world.' She reached her hands out to Clem's, her face low to the table, trying to catch Clem's eye. 'Please, it would just be a few weeks more for you, Clem. Surely, after everything, you can give me that? Is it really so dreadful to stay?'

'You know perfectly well what it is you're asking of me . . .' Clem whispered.

'I do,' Chiara nodded soberly. 'And I *still* believe it is the best. For all of us.'

Us – the very word was inclusive, implying their shared, overlapping lives, how they were as linked as sisters.

Overwhelmed by all of this, Clem got up and walked to the back door in silence.

'Clem?' Tom asked, looking concerned.

But she shook her head. She didn't want to talk any more – she'd had too much to drink and was feeling dangerously emotional; she didn't trust her own tongue. She pulled the door shut behind her and leaned against the wall, breathing in the night air. She walked slowly through the garden, trying to take in the bombshells that had fallen on her in the course of one afternoon. She had spent the last ten years trying to outrun her past, but it had well and truly captured her now, gathering her in its sticky claws and refusing to release its grip, no matter how much she struggled to get away again.

She opened the gate and stepped onto the road just as a scooter blasted round the corner, its lights dazzling her. She pressed herself against the rough wall in fright as the Vespa passed. She couldn't see who it was over the headlights, but she could guess. The blonde hair streaming from the passenger riding pillion was a dead giveaway.

'You are awake.' Gabriel's voice was soft in the dark, like fur brushing over her skin.

'No, I'm not,' she whispered from her position, lying on her back and staring at the ceiling. She wished she could brush her fingers against the smooth silk envelope that had always kept her going during her most difficult moments, but she couldn't. It was hidden beneath a hard and heavy mattress – away from Gabriel and Signora Benuto but, crucially, away from her, too.

'You are. I can tell.' She could tell that he was smiling. She felt the mattress dip as he shifted position to face her, and she knew he had planted his head on his hand and was looking down at her. 'You are a truly dreadful sleeper. If I had known this before, it might have changed things between us.'

She turned to look at him and his mouth swooped down on hers. 'Got you,' he murmured.

She smiled and turned onto her side, facing him, nestling down into the pillow and closing her eyes again.

'Do you want to talk about it?'

'How can I? I'm still sleeping,' she mumbled.

'Maybe I shall use that to my advantage.'

Somewhere further down on her thigh, she felt his fingers beginning to tiptoe over her skin, and her muscles contracted involuntarily, her body instantly waking up to his touch without hesitation. His fingers stopped their march.

'Is it me? Us?'

Her eyes opened. 'No. You're everything.'

Slowly, after a pause, his fingers continued their walk over her hipbones. 'Good.'

Clem blinked into the dark, feeling more awake than ever, and not just because of where his hands were now. She'd told him the truth, no word of a lie. He was everything.

But it was never going to be enough.

Chapter Thirty-Nine

Clem fidgeted in her seat and tried not to stare. The benches were hard and narrow and her knees pressed up against the back of the pew in front. The church was almost full now – the pews filling from the front to the back (although she'd made a beeline for the back row as ever) and she had a prime view of the backs of everyone's heads. Surprisingly, she recognized many of them and had been gratified by the number of greetings by name she had received as she approached the church. She certainly wasn't unknown in the port, even though she'd kept herself to herself for the most part, and she wondered if Chiara and the workmen talked about her? If they did, it would seem to be positive, given all the smiles she received.

She smoothed the fabric of her dress across her thighs – a three-quarter-length, simple, faded coral linen number with a deep scooped back, which she'd picked up in the port. She had twisted some chunky beaded necklaces around one wrist and was wearing her hair up, messily, to show off her long feather drop earrings. Simple leather flip-flops and her skinny-fit khaki biker jacket completed the look. No one else looked like her, but she didn't stand out in a wrong way, she didn't think.

She kept her eyes moving. Tom and Chiara were sitting

further towards the front, but she hadn't joined them – their happiness was slightly more than she could bear, their hands clasped on the bench between them as they spoke in trailing whispers, their eyes doing most of the talking.

Gabriel was coming later. He had some dratted meeting in Rome that couldn't be cancelled, but he'd promised to get back in time for the dinner; she'd smiled and told him she was a big girl, but she wished he was here now. She felt conspicuous sitting alone, especially when . . .

No. She made herself shift position again, smiling as she remembered Stella wanting to light up at the christening, six months ago, back in March – the last time she'd been in a church. She missed her friend more every day, hating that she was absent from this, the biggest journey of her life. Not that Stella was stranded without her presence. Mercy had started picking up the threads during Clem's prolonged absence, especially now that Clem had rung with the news that she wasn't returning until November at the earliest. Stella's baby was due Christmas week – she quite literally couldn't keep holding on for Clem.

No one could, it seemed. Not Stella, not Chiara any more – she was taking her life back – not even Gabriel. Since that night in the villa when he'd given her the ring, every look he gave her was loaded, searching for commitment.

She looked down at her hand and gazed at the stunning ring sparkling on it – the cocktail ring that could have been so much more, something significant rather than just pretty. If she'd only worn it on her left hand, not her right . . . Slowly, she pulled the ring off her ring finger and slid it onto the other hand, examining how it looked and felt. See? Not so hard. Not so different. So why couldn't she do it? She splayed her fingers wide and held her hand up a little higher, letting it catch the light. Chad had almost died when he'd caught sight of it weighing down her hand, although she'd told Tom it was just a costume piece she'd bought herself. For some reason, she knew him knowing it was real and from Gabriel and on her *right* hand would prompt another of his concerned looks.

Her hand reached for the football, which was rolling away from her slightly on the bench, and she sighed rest-lessly, waiting for the action to begin. Her eyes tracked the last guests coming in – an elderly couple – following them as they moved to the only spaces left, down near the front. They waited in the aisle as people shuffled along the pews and then sat down, nodding their heads and smiling grate-fully, saying a few words to the beautiful young couple beside them.

Her eyes lingered where they wanted to, at last, studying the girl with crystalline precision – taking in her profile (cute but not beautiful on account of her snub nose), eye-catching hair (which on inspection was too-blonde with two-inch-deep dark roots), figure (knockout, depressingly, from what she could see) and woeful dress sense (a red polka-dot prom dress that was a poor pastiche of Dolce & Gabbana's Sicilian iconography). She was the kind of woman other women hated and men dribbled over. No wonder Rafa was hooked.

She hadn't seen him since that night in Chiara's kitchen – he'd gone AWOL immediately afterwards for a couple of weeks, not turning up at work and almost driving Chad to a breakdown; Gabriel would have had him fired on the spot if he'd known, but she'd begged Chad to keep it quiet from him. Chiara had had no idea where Rafa was either, until he'd just walked back into the kitchen again one night last week as though nothing had happened.

Clem watched as Rafa leaned in, a smile on his lips, saying something to the older couple that made them all laugh, his arm resting casually on his girlfriend's shoulder as she looked up at him with an adoration that, if it was matched by passion . . . Clem felt her stomach tighten. In the five months she'd been here, he hadn't even smiled at her, not once, and the prospect had never been more remote.

A commotion at the enormous carved wooden doors made him turn, but he didn't see her. The bride was here and Clem twisted in her seat to see her. She had her camera ready in her hand and was on her feet slightly too early, ready for the shot. She would only get one chance as the bridal party passed her pew.

The bride sailed in like a yacht into harbour, shrouded in a cloud of tulle, her face bent to the ground like a tulip. Clem bit her lip, camera to her eye, her finger ready to press down the moment they came into view.

Then there he was, looking cleaner than she'd ever seen him – Chiara must have scoured him with a wire brush; Clem could have sworn he'd lost his tan he looked so pale. He was wearing a light blue linen shirt and taupe linen shorts, his brown eyes enormous, the way they always were when he was anxious, as he carried the velvet cushion and, atop it, the two rings loosely threaded together by a silk ribbon. He was biting his lip, and Clem could see how hard he was trying not to drop them or step on the bride's dress. She could picture Chiara this morning as she dressed him, reminding him with quiet urgency to keep clean, not play football until after the service, not overtake the bride, not drop the rings . . .

He looked across at her – finding her exactly where she'd told him she'd be – a darting, almost frightened movement, and she pressed the button, capturing the moment. She smiled at him, grabbing the ball beside her to show him it was safe, and a tiny, relieved smile softened his face before he disappeared from view down the aisle.

Clem immediately scrolled back through the memory card, looking at the pictures. She'd taken four but there was one that stood out. It was almost haunting, his doe eyes too big in his face. He looked scared and she winced at the thought of how much bigger those eyes would grow when Chiara told him her news tomorrow.

If she told him. It had been bad enough with Rafa going missing in action, but Luca had begun playing up too – thrown by Rafa's sudden absence, refusing to even acknowledge Tom, much less talk to him, defying Chiara, climbing out of his window at night, scarcely touching his food – and Clem knew Chiara was wavering. That had no doubt been Rafa's intention, especially after he'd outed Clem's determination to leave, slashing the success ratio of Chiara's grand plan by half. But even now that she was staying – she had to tell Gabriel by tomorrow, even though every time she tried, the words tripped her up – what consolation would it be to Luca to hear that he was getting Clem instead of Chiara? She didn't fool herself that she was anything more than a vaguely interesting babysitter.

Clem watched as Luca stepped forward with the rings, holding the cushion aloft with trembling arms. As he walked back to his seat, he glanced over at Rafa; Clem looked over, too, and saw the pride written on his profile, the reassuring nod and wink he gave as Luca looked for his approval. Clem felt a flutter in her stomach at the brief but touching exchange, one of so many she'd witnessed this summer. Maybe Rafa would step up after all, no matter how angry he might be at Chiara's first-ever act of selfishness?

But then his girlfriend's delicate hand snaked up the nape of his neck, her fingers burrowing into his dark hair, making him move his head slightly, liking it. He turned to face her, kissing her lingeringly on the lips, everyone else forgotten. '. . . *I am a single man and enjoying it . . .*'

Clem knew then that simply 'hoping' wasn't good enough. Luca deserved more than that. She couldn't stay. But how could she possibly leave?

Clem sat on the old stone wall and watched as the bride and groom were showered with rose petals that didn't touch the ground but were lifted up instead by the wind and carried out to sea in a long and winding ribbon. The wind had picked up just as the weathergirl had predicted this morning, and although the sky was still blue, the area's notorious winds had gathered in strength just in the time they'd been in the church, and purple clouds were blossoming on the horizon.

Clem smiled as the bride's veil was lifted like a steeple by the tugging winds and her full skirt filled with air, making everyone laugh. She was a beautiful girl, with shoulder-length nearly black hair and a petite figure; Clem even thought she could spot the family resemblance as Chiara swept her up in a delighted hug, chattering excitedly. In fact, with her lilac silk dress and upswept hair, Chiara was perilously close to upstaging her cousin, her eyes backlit, a flush in her cheeks.

Everyone was in high spirits, laughing and greeting each other with wide smiles and even wider arms. Clem wished Gabriel would hurry up and arrive; she felt like a spare part standing on the sidelines. Even Tom, who had only been here a few weeks, looked more at home than her, although of course he was actively currying favour with Chiara's extended family.

Clem, feeling alone with only a football for company, turned away, pretending to take in the view instead. The yellow-striped church was at the top of the hill of the castle peninsula and had a commanding view of the area. She could see pinprick-sized people eating leisurely lunches on their roof terraces, their tablecloths flapping sporadically in the gusts, while those on their boats began scurrying about the decks as the water beneath them eased into a slow and heavy swell. A storm was definitely coming.

She felt a small nudge in her ribs and turned round. Luca was standing beside her, looking at her with a beleaguered expression. 'You look sad.'

'Do I?' she bluffed and gave a small half shrug. 'Sorry.'

'You want to get married, too.'

She gave a little laugh. Was that what he thought? 'No, not really. That's never been my thing.'

'I thought all grown-ups wanted to be married.' He pulled himself up and sat on the wall, his skinny legs dangling from beneath his smart shorts. She could see a deep yellowing bruise on his shin – no doubt incurred from a particularly fearless tackle. She held out his ball and he gave that scampish, endearing grin she knew so well now as he took it from her and hugged it to him like a teddy bear.

'Will you get married when you grow up?' she asked, clutching her jacket tighter around her shoulders as the wind flew at her.

Luca pulled a retching face – universal to little boys the world over – and she burst out laughing. 'I'll take that as a "no" shall I?' She chuckled.

'Rafa says he will not be marry so I won't.'

Clem cleared her throat, not sure what to say. 'And do you want to be just like him when you grow up?' she asked after a moment.

Luca nodded, spinning the ball between his middle fingers like a basketball player.

They both heard his name called and looked back towards the church. The photographs were being taken before the weather turned completely. He gave a weary sigh and she knew exactly how he felt: being on best behaviour was exhausting.

'You're on,' she said. 'I'll look after this for you. *Again*,' she groaned, rolling her eyes as she took the ball from him.

He grinned and shuffled off, as she spun the ball between her fingers while she watched him go, being enfolded into the big, bustling group of his family. She watched as plump, sun-weathered, gnarled hands patted his head and ruffled his hair; thick, arthritic legs shuffling to make a space he could nestle into.

'You never got over it, did you?' said Tom. He was leaning against the wall to her right, his hands in his trouser pockets and his sand linen blazer slung over his shoulder.

'Hey! Got over what?'

There was a complicated pause before he said the words, as though he was scared of saying them out loud. 'The abortion.'

A vacuum opened up between them, swallowing time and space. She felt instant and intense pressure on her chest and she looked quickly away. Words weren't even close to coming out of her throat.

There was a pause and she could feel Tom assessing her, nodding. 'Mum didn't tell me either, so don't give her a hard time. It was just a hunch.'

Clem blinked in rapid succession, angling her face into the wind and willing it to whip the tears from her eyes. 'Hell of a conclusion to come to, then.'

'Not really. Whenever I see you with Luca you're different with him, you seem *more* you, somehow. You're happier when he's around, always playing and laughing about.'

'And from that you came to the conclusion that I had had an abortion?'

Tom was undeterred by her sarcasm. 'I've seen the way you look at him. I think that when you look at him, you see what you gave up. I think you see him as the little boy you never had.'

'He's just a cute, funny little kid,' she muttered, her voice thick and cloddish.

'Yeah, he is, he's great. And he obviously adores you, too.'

'You've got this all wrong.'

'I don't think so.' He shook his head slowly. 'It's the only thing that makes sense of everything – the non-stop party-ing, refusing to let a relationship ever get serious, your blasted twelve-week rule. And when Stella told me you'd talked her out of having an abortion—'

'I didn't talk her out of anything,' Clem snapped. 'She made her own choice.'

'You told her she'd make a great mum,' Tom said.

'That's because she will.'

'So will you . . . so *would* you.'

His words wrapped themselves around her, but she twisted free. 'Let's not fool ourselves, Tom,' she said sharply. 'We both know what I am, and "Mum" ain't it. Luca's a sweet little boy and Chiara's my friend, but there's no great mystery to it. She's overworked and worn out, so I've babysat a few times. End of. It doesn't mean I could replace

Chiara in his eyes, and it doesn't get you off the hook for taking her away from him.' She stared at him fiercely, breathless from the effort it had taken to say those words, just as Chiara skipped over, the wind blowing her dress against her like a second skin and robbing the breath from Tom's body.

'Hi.' She smiled, slipping her arm through Tom's and standing on tiptoe to kiss him on the temple. She faltered as she noticed Clem's closed expression, the turgid body language between the two siblings.

'What's—?' she began, but Tom shook his head and she lapsed into silence.

Clem turned away from them and looked out to sea, watching the white horses beginning to dance in the bay, her body hunched over the football in her arms as she struggled to keep down the anger, the panic, the overwhelming dismay that threatened to subsume her every single moment of the night and day. A cheer erupted behind them as the photographer got his shots, and she startled at the roar, as if it was the crack of a shotgun, dropping the ball by Tom's feet.

Chiara reached out to her. 'Clem, you are shaking.'

But Clem pulled back, out of reach. 'No. I'm not.'

'Clem—'

'Leave it! All right? Just leave it!' Clem shouted, her hands held up as she edged away from Chiara and Tom's concern. 'Just back off!'

They watched her, open-mouthed, as she walked backwards, away from them, her slitted eyes on them as if they were holding knives. Then she turned and ran, past the guests all mingling and chatting, some of them taking in her tears as she darted past, her dress gathered in her hand. She saw Rafa's head jerk up, his eyes trained upon her as if she was a target, but she didn't stop; his contempt was the last thing she needed.

She was at breaking point, she couldn't take any more – of the lies, the false smiles, the pretending . . . She ran past the church and beyond it, through the cemetery behind, where marble monuments of fat-cheeked angels and beatific saints towered over urns filled with silk flowers, her flip-flops scattering stones on the neat gravel paths.

At the back she came to a gate and she passed through it into a narrow, high-walled nook with another gate that led back out to the peninsula paths. It was locked, but she was out of the wind here, and she leant against the wall, her eyes raised to heaven, tears streaming silently down her cheeks. She would lie and protest and stare the truth down until the last breath left her body, but Tom had been right: she did look at Luca and see what she'd given up. His every smile wounded her even as it healed her at the same moment; he undid her and put her back together again all in the whip of his hair or the devilish flash of his eyes. He was everything she had given up, but she couldn't undo the past. What was done was done and wholly irreversible.

Beneath the whistle of the wind, she heard the sound of footsteps approaching and she tensed, pushing herself back so that the walls crowded round her on three sides. No! She didn't want to talk.

Rafa rounded the corner, stopping abruptly as he took in her distress, his eyes covering her face as if she was a map that he alone could read. And then in the next instant he was moving towards her, his expression telling her he didn't want to talk either.

Chapter Forty

Clem watched, seated, as the bride and groom danced the tarantella, their first dance. She knew he was looking again. She could feel his stare all the way across the room; she could still feel his touch on her skin, his breath on her cheek. She brought her hand to her neck, still tingling from where he'd kissed it, her eyes sliding over to him once more. She knew she shouldn't, that it had been a massive mistake and just about the most dangerous thing she could have done, but she couldn't stop herself. He was her opium.

He didn't move, not a muscle betrayed her effect on him. His expression was as inscrutable as ever; anyone looking between them would think he was wholly unmoved by her, but she knew differently. The anger was still there – it had still been there even as he'd cried her name – but now she knew that wasn't *all* that was there.

Beside him, his girlfriend was constantly touching him – stroking his hand on the table, fiddling with the tuft of hair at the nape of his neck, stroking the lapel on his narrow black suit – but he was completely still, as immobile as if he'd been painted into the scene, his eyes never leaving Clem.

His girlfriend turned his face towards her, saying something – probably lewd, judging by her body language – before kissing him with an open mouth, one hand disappearing under the table.

Clem looked away, her heart pounding erratically as jealousy stampeded through her. She turned back to the table, forcing herself to pursue a grammatically incorrect conversation with one of Chiara's elderly uncles, while all around them couples flooded the dance floor, the formalities over.

The chair to her left was empty. Gabriel still hadn't arrived, in spite of his promise, but Clem was grateful for his absence now. After the post-ceremony cocktails, everyone had moved onto wine and now liqueurs, becoming steadily more uninhibited, and she would be able to leave shortly without appearing rude. She needed to get away from here. She needed to regroup – remind herself of all the very valid reasons why nothing had actually changed . . .

'Dance with me.'

It wasn't a request. Rafa was standing in front of her, his hand held out, and she took it wordlessly, her resolve eviscerated, just like that. She walked into his arms until his mouth was by her ear again, his hand closed around hers. Her back was bare and she felt his fingers splay across her skin, his cheek brushing her hair lightly as they covered the floor, each step perfect thanks to his strong lead, completely in rhythm, not a word spoken by either of them; just the sound of their breathing between them.

She felt his lips by her ear and her skin responded first, with goosebumps that ran over her skin in shivers. 'Don't leave.'

The words were more like a wish carried to her by the beat of angels' wings, the summer's hostilities burned out; this afternoon's lust sated, for now, and all the passions that had clamoured between them like an entourage, pacified. She looked up at him and saw in his eyes what had been there over a decade earlier, what had been hidden there all along – she wasn't the only one good at keeping secrets. She had to tell him.

'Clem—'

But it wasn't his voice she heard. She turned. Gabriel was standing beside them, hands in his pockets and a dangerous dance in his eyes. 'You didn't hear me?'

She shook her head, mute, her arms falling away from Rafa, although he kept his hand on the small of her back: a possessive gesture that Gabriel didn't miss. He stared at Rafa with a heart-stopping coldness. There was war in his demeanour and Clem felt Rafa's arm stiffen behind her. He wasn't going to back down.

Time became elastic as neither man flinched. She watched Gabriel's eyes travel over them both, taking in the truth that none of them had dared speak, but that he had sensed running beneath their feet like a spring. Then Gabriel moved towards them, a trace of a smile on his face growing as he came closer. He stopped, inches from them both, and Clem felt Rafa's fingers curl tighter around her waist. He wouldn't let her go. Not again.

Except it wasn't Rafa that Gabriel was looking at now; it was Clem. He leaned down, so close Clem thought he was going to kiss her and gently, he picked up her left hand, holding it before the three of them so that they could see the ring glistening there. He brought it to his lips, victory in his eyes.

Clem's mouth formed a shocked 'o'.

'Clem, you make me the happiest man.'

'Gabriel, I—'

She looked up at Rafa, wanting to explain, to tell him everything, all of it, *why*. But it was already too late. Neither man had said a single word to the other, but Gabriel had won. Rafa turned on his heel, walking straight back to the table where his friends were starting to get rowdy. His girlfriend – a quizzical expression on her pretty face – draped herself around him, one hand languidly stroking his tie as he picked up a shot of limoncello and downed it.

Clem didn't dare watch, and not just because Gabriel was watching *her*. She looked at the ground, trembling at how close she'd come to giving up and letting go at last of the secret that so completely defined her. His arm around her had undone all that. But she was out in the cold again, away from his touch, and reality was reasserting itself: no matter what, the lie had to go on.

'You were punishing me for being so late,' Gabriel murmured, stroking her cheek with his finger. 'I understand.'

She glanced at him. He didn't really believe she'd been flirting to spite him, did he?

'Come, I want to show you off,' Gabriel murmured, taking her hands in his and leading her into the crowd again. She trailed after him, her body unresponsive to his touch for the first time as he held her close, leading her round the dance floor with finesse, but never positioning her so that she could see Rafa's table.

The songs segued from one to the next, but Gabriel kept her dancing, his fingers stroking the ring as though it was lucky as he held her hand. Clem didn't notice. She didn't feel anything. She'd thought she'd found refuge in their passion this summer, but it was nothing compared to the intimacy between her and Rafa as he'd pushed her up against the wall, and she couldn't pretend otherwise. Not any more. As much as Gabriel really was everything – the perfect man in every way – the one thing he couldn't be was *Rafa*.

'Clem?'

She looked down blankly to find Luca staring up at her.

'H–hey, Luca? Are you having fun?' She took in his wan pallor. 'You look tired. Are you OK?'

'I know it's not true.'

'What's not?' She frowned, crouching down so that she could hear him better over the music. Gabriel wouldn't let go of her other hand.

'That you're leaving.' He blinked at her, his face pale and stony.

'What? Who told you that?'

Luca pointed back to Rafa, who was standing talking with a group, one hand stuffed in his pocket, the other gripping a beer bottle that he was swigging quickly. As though sensing their scrutiny, he turned his face to theirs, his expression black and sour. Clem could see he was drunk.

She looked back at Gabriel. He was still oblivious to her newest change in plans. She'd been planning to tell him tonight, hoping a few drinks would sugar-coat the pill (as he would see it, especially now).

'Of course she's leaving,' Gabriel said brusquely, answering for her. 'Summer's over and we'll be back in London by next weekend.'

Clem glared at him. Gabriel might not have the full facts, but to be so tactless to a little boy . . .

Luca took a step back, his eyes wide, his ball tucked under his arm as always, as much a comforter to him as the silk envelope was to her.

'Hey, hey, Luca . . .' Clem soothed him, trying to reach his hand. But he was too fast for her, darting away through the crowded floor and out of sight. 'Luca!' she called, trying to run after him, but Gabriel held on firmly to her hand.

'Ignore him. He just wants attention,' Gabriel said, pulling her back up to standing.

'What would you know about it?' she demanded, pulling away from him angrily, just as Tom came over, a wild look in his eyes and raking his hands through his hair. 'Oh Christ, what's happened?' she asked. She knew that look too well.

Tom groaned as he looked around the room, clearly searching for someone. 'I've completely cocked up.' He grimaced.

'How?' she asked distractedly, her eyes scanning the crowd for Luca. She wasn't especially interested in hearing about Tom offending some maiden aunt right now.

'Luca overheard me telling Chad about Chiara moving to London.'

'*What?*'

'I know! I'm a bloody idiot, but I just didn't see him standing there. There were so many people and—'

'Does Chiara know?'

Tom nodded. 'She's looking for him, too, she's in an awful state. We really need to explain things to him properly. I don't suppose you've seen him recently?'

'Yes! He was . . . he was . . .' Clem whispered, her eyes growing wide with apprehension as Luca's words echoed in her head.

'He was just here,' Gabriel said, stepping forward and pointing in the direction he had run.

Chiara appeared around one of the pillars, breathless,

fear rising like a moon in her face. 'I can't find him,' she panted. 'Maria Cantara said she thought she saw him going outside but . . . but the storm.' Her eyes travelled to the windows, and the sight of a cypress tree being bent low by the wind. 'No. No! He knows better than to go out alone in these weathers.'

Rafa stormed over. 'What is going on? Why do you look like that?' he demanded of Chiara.

'We can't find Luca,' she replied in a timid voice.

'Why does he need finding? It is a wedding. He will be play—'

Tom cleared his throat; their burgeoning friendship had been firmly grounded by the revelation of his and Chiara's affair. 'He found out Chiara's leaving.'

'*Che?*' Rafa paled, his eyes sliding towards Clem as he suddenly understood why the boy had come over asking questions, wanting reassurances that couldn't be given and receiving answers fuelled by jealousy, anger and drink. 'Who saw him last?'

'We did,' Clem said, Gabriel's hand on her shoulder. 'Just a few minutes ago.'

'Where did he go?' Chiara asked, her voice high with panic.

Clem pointed and they all looked at the dance floor behind them and then beyond it, to the tall double doors.

'He's probably under a table or in the loos,' Tom said firmly, as outside the wind howled wolfishly, the cypress tapping against the window as if it wanted to be allowed in, rain flying past the glass like poison darts. No one would willingly step out into that.

Surely?

*

441

The men took charge, organizing a search party and heading out into the storm in groups, as Chiara sat down and wrote a list of the places he liked to play, the names of his best friends ... Clem sat, silent and wretched, already knowing most of the answers and knowing they wouldn't help. So he liked to kick his ball against the wall opposite the fishing boats, so what? So he played hide and seek in the top levels of the park around the castle walls, so what? So he often went exploring up the back track, playing near the huge water tank with its rusted, half-collapsed roof, so bloody what? He wasn't going to be found in any of those places. She could feel it.

She stood up, unable to bear the inactivity a moment longer. She had to do something, make it up to him. Luca needed her. He had come to her needing the support Chiara had asked her to give in her absence and she'd failed. Chiara hadn't even gone and she'd already failed him! The men had been adamant the women must stay here with the other children, but Clem didn't belong here. She wasn't one of them. She wouldn't be missed.

She ran from the room and stepped into the storm, the wind whipping around her like a jester. It was almost dusk and the sky was a majestic rippling red, the black clouds rolling and rumbling with menace. She ran to the wall and looked down at the port – lights flickered across the piazzetta but it was deserted, the outdoor tables covered beneath rain canopies like plastic conservatories. She could hear the bells ringing on the masts of the smaller vessels as they bobbed and jigged on the rough waters.

Her heart lurched. Luca was out in this somewhere, and there was only forty minutes, at most, before it would be too dark to search in these conditions. Rafa, Tom and

Gabriel were searching for him together, their tightly plaited jealousies cast aside for now, and she knew if anyone would find him, *they* would – she'd seen the desolation on Rafa's face as he'd understood what had happened.

She looked out into the storm. Where was he? She paced in circles, her dress flapping loudly about her legs, as the minutes passed and still no one called to say he'd been found. Where was he? *Where?*

She stopped abruptly as she suddenly remembered bumping into him on the path the other week – the day they'd later discovered Tom and Chiara in the kitchen. He had seemed unusually quiet and subdued that afternoon, *before that*, she recalled. Had he already sensed there was something growing between Tom and Chiara before he'd seen it for himself, with his own eyes? Had he known that his family was changing again? Rafa and Chiara had split up, and Rafa had a new partner; but Chiara now, too? Did he know his family was going to be torn apart for ever?

She felt her pulse quicken as the thoughts came fast and sure. He had been up at the lighthouse back then and he must be there now. Clem ran. She gathered her wet skirts in her hand and pulled them up past her knees, so that she could run more easily.

Her long legs were strong and she felt her fitness help her as she ran against the wind. But something was niggling her . . . something . . .

And then it came to her: it hadn't been closing time when she'd seen him that day. Sunset had been a couple of hours off and therefore the prospect of free ice cream, too. She began to slow, less certain. It was hardly likely that a ten-year-old boy would walk a mile just for the view? Had he wanted to be alone, to think? She tried to imagine him sitting there on the bench as he looked out to sea and watched the waves crash on the splintered granite slabs—

She stopped abruptly, her eyes wide with horror. Oh please God, no. No!

She felt terror grip her like an icy hand and she couldn't move. Her brain began working at lightning speed, making other connections and discarding them, trying to come up with alternative, plausible ideas, but she knew, she knew . . . Slowly, she turned back the way she had come, her eyes unseeing of the ivy-walled paths she'd already run through for half a mile. It made perfect sense. That was why he went to the lighthouse. He could see it from there; it was the best vantage point for miles around. He was there for the view, but not to think; he was there to wish.

She began running again, back the way she'd come, her arms like pistons, propelling her with a speed she'd never known. Every second counted. She couldn't stop, couldn't slow. Because he wasn't lost any more, he was in danger. There was only one way to get to it – she'd seen that for herself that day on the Riva. And that meant he was in the water.

Chapter Forty-One

Clem ran blindly. She had never come over this way on foot before, only ever on the boat, and the ground was rough and uneven, the scrub scratching her bare legs. Only instinct told her which way to head, and soon she saw the heaving horizon of the mass of grey water that lay between here and the wishing tree.

'Luca!' she screamed, but the wind threw her screams straight back over her. She kept running, slipping in places and having to use her hands to keep her going. She couldn't see the tree yet, and it was rapidly darkening, but she could make out the shallow sweep of the mile-long bay and the roar of the sea bashing itself against the rocks. She would have to get to the cliffs and then turn right, looking both for the tree and a way down at the same time.

The water looked inky and mercurial, only the white froth clearly visible in the dusk.

'Luca!'

She thought she could see the tree ahead, its scarified branches reaching into the storm-filled sky like tongs, not a single bit of it moving as the wind howled and flattened the grasses and full-canopied firs nearby. It's very stillness was eerie amidst so much fury and chaos.

Oh please, God, let him be there – and not there at the

same time. She wanted to find him, but please not in the water, please . . .

She scrambled down the cliff-face recklessly. It wasn't a sheer drop like at the lighthouse, but a tumbledown pile of boulders and mud banks, creating a stepping-stone effect with five-metre drops.

'Luca!' she screamed, feeling her vocal cords strain as she battled to be heard against the wind. 'Luca!'

She stopped suddenly, as alert as a lioness on the hunt. What was that?

She gasped and turned, trying to locate it. Then she heard it again.

'I'm coming, Luca!' she screamed. 'Hold on!'

She was almost down at the water now, but still 100 metres along from the Wishing Tree rock, and she scrambled over the landslips, gravity no longer on her side and driving her down. Ahead of her was a huge two-metre boulder that she couldn't possibly get over, so she had to navigate her way around it, cursing furiously as she lost precious time, her feet slipping as the mud crumbled beneath her and her body strained to remain connected to the giant rock.

She clawed her way round the boulder and, as she rounded its belly, stopped with sudden fright. Directly in front of her, a metre below, the black sea swelled, quietly threatening. There was a 30-metre gap between the boulder she was standing on and the next one, the one nearest the Wishing Tree, and if she wanted to stay on dry land, she was going to have to go back up and inland again.

She looked into the darkness, frantically trying to focus. Where was he? Everything was moving; the sky was a deep indigo now and the moon had yet to switch on its beams.

Then she saw something, the tiny bob of something round in the water, pale, milky arms stretched wide and clinging to the front of the rock as the water pulled, splashed and smashed against him, enticing him, forcing and demanding he get in.

'Luca!' she screamed.

'Clem! Stop!'

What? She turned. Tom was far above her, atop the cliffs, and she saw the swing of torch beams like lasers over the grass.

'He's in the water, Tom!' she screamed, just as Gabriel caught up with him and saw her beside the water. She could see the change in his expression even from where she was.

'I'm coming! I have rope!' Gabriel shouted, running down the slope at an angle that didn't even seem possible.

Relief flooded through her. Rope? Oh thank God!

'Stay there, Clem! Promise me!' Gabriel shouted. 'Promise me!'

'I promise!' she shouted back. She turned towards the threshing water. 'Hold on, Luca! Help is coming!' She squinted. 'Luca? *Luca!*'

But he was gone.

She let the blackness claim her, the shocking cold jolting her body as she tried to make herself move, a tiny pinprick cutting against the huge rolling body of the Mediterranean. She stayed under for as long as she could – she could keep a straighter line underwater, away from the splash and froth on the surface – but sooner or later she had to come up for air, to breathe. She had to see him. She had to tell him. She would stay this time and she would never leave.

She gasped – her lungs screaming for air – as she surfaced, close to the rock. She had covered a good distance, but she could feel the water pulling her towards the rocks like a gravity field, and she knew that she would feel her bones break and snap as water and rock met over her.

Her limbs were beginning to feel leaden and her dress was weighing her down. It was no good, she couldn't stay on the surface while she was wearing it. She dived down quickly, letting it float up and over her head, until it was off and she was all but naked – lighter in the water, but colder, too.

She resurfaced with a frantic gasp and trod water, turning desperately in a circle, trying to find him. It had been at least a minute since she'd seen him.

'Luca!' she cried, just as a wave hit her in the face and she began choking. The water was so salty she felt her stomach contract, but still she kept searching for a splash or bubble or break that would show her where he was.

Somewhere high above she could hear Luca's name being called. And . . . and hers too. She knew what this would be doing to Tom, watching her in this water, but she couldn't think about him. Luca was all she could keep in her head.

Then her eyes caught a movement. Beyond the rock. It was only a flash – it could have been a fish's tail slapping against the surface, a piece of driftwood carried in by the storm, but she moved towards it immediately. It was all she had.

She dived down into the deep, where light wouldn't have penetrated even in the middle of the day. The pressure in her ears began to build, but she kept going down, her arms reaching in front of her in huge arcs, feeling for a slip of silky flesh in the vast aching space of the sea.

Then her hand touched something. Skin on skin – the primal touch she had known once before. She grabbed it and kicked up powerfully, holding Luca's inert body against her own and streamlining their progress through the water. She was almost out of breath; her lungs and ears felt like they were bleeding, but she had to get to the surface.

They broke through the sea's skin like a bullet and hands grabbed them, pulling them roughly, nails scratching as they scrabbled for grip and tenure, then her skin freezing as air replaced water, and the sweet stinging roughness of the barnacled rock cut into her. Coughing and retching, she dropped onto all fours, her body spent. She lifted her head and saw Rafa kneeling over Luca, giving him heart massage. In the force of the waves, his clothes had been ripped from him and his body looked tiny and soft upon the mammoth black rock. She thought about his enormous eyes, which managed to hold so much fear and yet so much mischief; she thought of how quickly he moved and the skill those small feet possessed when there was a ball beside them; she thought of his gappy grin and the way he stuck his tongue out when he was concentrating . . .

Gabriel and Tom pulled themselves out of the water, weak, both of them, from the effort of punching through the waves that had avalanched over them, stopping dead at the too still, silent sight on the dry rock. Clem was shaking her head, tears skimming down her face in sheets, her entire body convulsed with terror.

Gabriel fell to his knees and threw his arms around her, trying to warm her up, his hands rubbing hard over her frozen arms.

'No, no,' she moaned as Luca remained motionless. If he

died she would jump straight back into the water. She couldn't live without him. She had tried and it had been half a life.

'He'll be OK,' Gabriel murmured quietly, his eyes also on the still child.

'My boy, my boy . . .' she whispered, her stare fixed on Luca as if it had been anchored with weights.

Rafa sat back suddenly on his heels and she gasped, every muscle in her body bunched and taut. Why was he stopping? He couldn't give u—

Luca coughed, his shoulders heaving once, twice, and then up came the green saltwater he had swallowed, forcing him to twist on the rock, his body contorted, the veins on his neck bulging blue.

Rafa sobbed, covering his face with his hands as Luca brought up more and more water, crying from the effort as the corrosive salts tore against his throat. He fell back against the rock, weak, his eyes blinking rapidly, his breath ragged, and Rafa gently moulded him into the recovery position, grabbing Tom's jacket to place over him. Someone covered her too with . . . something; she didn't know what, she didn't know who. Every fibre of her being was focused on Luca. He was alive. She crawled towards him in weakened lumbering movements, her knees bleeding against the rough rock.

In the distance, the thrum of a helicopter could be heard and she could make out a solitary light in the sky. She placed her hand on his arm, and the tangible feeling of her skin on his once more felt almost violent, as if her heart was exploding in her chest, emotions tearing through her like poisons, making her fold and cry, love mixed with pain. The only way she'd ever known it.

She was shaking uncontrollably, barely aware of Gabriel beside her, or that his hands on her shoulders were now still and heavy and calm.

Luca moved, breaking the contact, and her eyes flew open.

'No, Luca, you must stay still,' Tom said, trying to hold the boy back as he wriggled free from the hands and clothes that were trying to protect him. Rafa – curled into himself, his face hidden in his hands – looked up.

But Luca had proved his dexterity many times before now and, in a moment, he was flat on his tummy, his arm reaching out to the black, rigid tree that stood above them, unmoved by the storm, unmoved by them. Luca's fingertips brushed the smooth bark and he closed his eyes.

'What's he doing?' Rafa asked desperately, bewilderment and terror jumping in his eyes, on high alert again, as though he expected Luca to jump back into the water.

Clem looked at him, her tears falling harder so that she could barely see. 'He's wishing.'

'Wishing for what?' he cried.

She could scarcely get the words out. 'For a family.'

Chapter Forty-Two

Her eyelids fluttered lightly, her vision blurred, and she tried to move, still drowsy and heavy-headed from the blunt-edged oblivion that had claimed her. She hadn't slept, she had simply dropped away into a fathomless black hole where there was no pain, no light, no horror, no yesterday.

'Luca!' she gasped, sitting bolt upright in the bed she'd been sleeping in and sending her heart rate rocketing.

'He's OK. They kept him in hospital overnight for observation,' Gabriel said, turning from his position by the window. The sunlight beyond the window backlit him, and she could see his silhouette through the fine cotton of his pale blue shirt. 'They'll let him out today.'

Clem looked at him, bewildered. She had no recollection of what had happened after Luca had been airlifted to hospital and she was surprised to find herself in bed, in their room.

Outside the folly, the day looked crisp and clear, blown through, making a mockery of the memories of the night before.

'How are you feeling?' he asked, watching as she pushed away the duvet a little. She was surprised to find it was one of three layered on top of her. 'You couldn't stop shivering last night. The doctor said you had mild hypothermia.'

'Oh.'

'Your colour has improved.'

Clem lay back on the pillows, wondering why he was staying at the window, so far away from her. She sensed a change between them. He seemed distant somehow, newly reserved as he fiddled with his cuffs. She tried to remember the minutiae of the previous day's events – the argument they had been on the verge of having the moment before Luca's disappearance – but so much had happened since then, and only one thing mattered: Luca was safe.

'Is everything all right, Gabriel?'

He looked straight at her. 'After what happened last night? How can it be?'

He turned away again, one hand on the wall, and she watched his back expand and narrow with slow, deep breaths. He had nearly lost her. It had been traumatic for him, too. She had defied him and dived into the black water even as he'd begged her not to; she had disregarded his heart for hers, and she would do it all over again in a heart-beat if needs be. As far as she was concerned, there wasn't even a choice.

'What you said . . .'

She watched him impassively. What had she said?

He turned back again, leaning against the wall. 'At least now I understand.'

She didn't reply; it was hard to focus on his words. The lingering chill of the midnight water had begun to creep up on her again and she pulled the duvet back around her shoulders. Whenever she closed her eyes for a fraction too long, she saw the black murk of the churning depths again, Luca's thin arm a milky glow in the gloom. The fear of losing him clung to her still, an odourless stench that drenched her with horror and made her heart quake.

'I can actually see it now: the resemblance. He's got your nose and bones.' He shook his head. 'Tom's smile. And he does that thing with his tongue when he's concentrating – like you.'

'Gabriel, what are you talking about?'

He looked back at her in astonishment, as though he hadn't counted upon this response. 'Are you really going to deny it? Even after you said the words yourself?'

A new fear was filling her, and it was every bit as terrifying as the black water. 'What did I say?'

Gabriel stared at her for a long, drawn-out moment, his adoration for her still spelled out on his features, though the purity had gone, his feelings clouded now by what he had learned. 'You said he was your boy. Clem, I know that Luca is your son.'

A silent, violent sob escaped her. Hearing the words spoken out loud – for the first time in her life – was like bringing a sledgehammer down onto a frozen pond, and she didn't know whether the deep cracks splintering through her were pleasure or pain. Relief, terror, isolation, years of conditioning – all of it collided inside her as if she were inside a rolling car, being thrown and tossed, crumpled, battered . . . broken down.

He looked away, tormented by the anguish he saw in her. 'I know you were young,' he managed, his voice heavy with torment and what this meant for them.

Her breath came in silent hiccups, sudden and snatched, unpredictable, unreliable. 'Yes.'

'Eighteen.'

'Yes.'

He dropped his head. 'Too young.'

She bit her lip, feeling the same rush of anger she'd felt

when she'd heard those words more than ten years earlier. 'Well, my mother certainly thought so.'

Her sarcasm changed the tone, the pace. 'But you didn't.'

'Of course I did! But I didn't want an abortion either. I knew who I was, even at eighteen. I knew what I could and couldn't live with.'

'Yet you could live with leaving your child to be raised by another family? In another country? You could live with *that*?' he asked in disbelief, and she knew he thought she was a monster.

'Just.' She swallowed hard as the familiar pressure at her temples began to build. 'Because I knew it was the best thing for him.'

Gabriel shook his head, deplored by her actions, confounded by the decisions she'd made, the secret she'd kept. 'Why *here*? Why did you bring him all the way out here to be raised as an Italian child, to speak a different language? Why didn't you at least keep him in England where you—?'

'Because none of it was planned, Gabriel!' she screamed, enraged by his cool logic, his superior judgement. 'Because he was born six weeks early, OK? I had to come out here for my exchange trip, because I had to behave as normal. No one fucking knew! No one!'

'You said your mother—'

'My mother knew jack-shit! She gave me an ultimatum: have an abortion or get out. She thought I did it!'

'But . . . how could you hide something like that?'

'Oh! What? You think it's so hard? You'd be *amazed* what teenage girls can get away with. Baggy clothes, puppy fat . . . I barely had a bump, my muscles were so tight. It was almost easy!'

He stared at her, his eyes darting over her face, trying to

455

keep up with the story that took a twist with every answer. 'But Chiara . . .? If she was your pen pal, why would she take Luca for you? She would hardly have known you. It doesn't make sense.'

Clem fell silent. 'It does when you know her. She's the best person I've ever met.'

Clem sank back into the pillow, her voice lower as she stepped back into the memories. 'There was a storm that night, too, just like last night's. She had heard the gate banging and she went to investigate; she found me moments after Luca was born. She was amazing, completely calm – well, after a couple of minutes anyway. She took total control of the situation. I was . . .' She shrugged, unable to condense the feelings down to one word. 'Delirious. Frightened that it had happened so early, and so far from home, but so happy, too. He was strong, I could sense it immediately, even though he was so small.' She blinked, looking down at her empty cupped hands. 'So small.'

A beat pulsed. 'What did Chiara do?'

Clem looked up at him, as though pulled from a trance. 'She gave him to her mother.'

The words clanged around the room as if they had bells attached. She was monstrous again.

'You handed them Luca and they took him? Just like that?'

'No! Not just like that! They spent the week begging me to take him back with me . . .' Her voice faded. 'But there was no way I could go back home with a baby in my arms. I'd have had no home for him. My mother had made it perfectly clear that she wasn't prepared to start on the babysitting rotas just yet. She would have thrown me out on the streets.' She began to sob, decade-old anger choking her even now.

Gabriel walked to the foot of the bed in silence. 'Why did Chiara's parents keep him? They could have put him up for adoption for you.'

'Because they wanted me to have a way back to him. They were good people; they made the mistake of thinking I was good, too.' Her eyes flicked towards him, dully. 'They believed I would come back for him when I could.' She was quiet for a long moment. 'They weren't entirely selfless; Chiara's an only child. Her parents had tried for years to have another baby, but Rosa kept miscarrying. She was older; they'd given up trying . . .' Clem shrugged. 'They decided to say he was an orphan of their cousins' and they were raising him.' Her voice broke and she raised her hand to her mouth, trying desperately to keep control. 'I knew they would love him . . . I named him and nursed him for as long as I was there . . . I didn't sleep at all that week. I couldn't bear to close my eyes and lose a minute with him.' Her voice cracked again and her lungs gasped for air with the same urgency as they had when she'd broken the surface of the water the night before. 'Chiara wrote to me all the time, keeping me informed of every milestone: when he first walked, his first word, his favourite toy . . . She sent pictures.' She thought of the letters in the silk envelope, which had sustained her for all these years.

'But you never saw Luca yourself? Not once, in all that time?'

She shook her head vehemently. 'I couldn't take the risk. Leaving him behind was the hardest thing I've ever done in my life.' The tears fell harder again and her entire body contracted as the sobs heaved her body like waves in a storm. 'I thought I was going to die. Rosa gave me a tranquillizer to help me get on the plane. She had bad arthritis so . . . There wasn't a day when I didn't think of him.'

Gabriel sat on the bed beside her, his warm hands finding hers as he tried to understand. 'Why didn't you go back for him?'

She stared up at him through blinded eyes. 'How could I? It sounds so easy in principle, but in reality . . . Rosa was his mother by then, Chiara his sister, this was his home. He didn't speak any English . . . He was happy here. How could I take him away from all that just because I wanted him with me?'

'But what you must have gone through . . .'

'It was the right thing for him.' Clem sobbed. 'That was all that mattered.'

'My darling,' Gabriel murmured, pulling her into him so that her face was buried in his neck, soaking his skin with warm tears. He stroked her hair as she wept, her shoulders trembling beneath his jaw. Finally, he pulled back, tipping her head up to his. 'I'm so sorry I forced you back here.'

'I'm not.' She blinked, her eyes refilling instantly every time, the tears streaming down her cheeks. 'Even as I said no to Tom, part of me knew I would go. I was so frightened, but at the same time, just the thought of it made me feel alive again. As soon as the thought was planted, I couldn't hold back any more. I told myself I'd be able to cope with it, that it was worth the risk.' She closed her eyes. 'I fell apart when I saw him for the first time. I felt as though he could tell, as if he could see right through me.'

Gabriel rubbed her hand, watching her closely. 'But he didn't.'

She shook her head. 'I was so terrified of him to begin with.' A tiny, disbelieving laugh escaped her as she thought back to their first meetings. 'I could hardly speak to him. But . . . but then I got to know him' – her voice was as soft as fur – 'and I fell in love with him all over again.'

'And you're prepared to leave him *again*?'

It would have been kinder to punch her, and she squeezed her eyes shut, her face scrunched tight with pain. 'I have to.' She wept. 'If there's one thing being here has shown me, it's that I *did* do the right thing. He's had a much better life here than I could have given him. He's happy! But the longer I stay here, the more I run the risk of him finding out who I really am. I have to go, Gabriel, for his sake.'

Gabriel nodded. 'We can leave tonight if you wish.'

Clem stiffened, a small vein of disgust opening somewhere inside her that he'd answered too quickly, was too ready to whisk her away from her child and restore her as his alone.

But it wasn't just that. He knew everything now, but he still didn't understand. It wasn't just Luca he was competing with.

'No . . .' she faltered.

'You want to wait a few days to make sure he is OK?'

She couldn't reply. She stared up at him through full eyes again. She may have broken her twelve-week rule for him, but it hadn't meant anything after all; it really was just an arbitrary number that had kept things tidy, neatly glossing over the messy truth that no one else would ever be enough. Her heart had never been in danger of being broken by him, or by any of the others, simply because her heart wasn't hers to give.

Gabriel recoiled in understanding as she remained silent. 'But the ring – you changed hands?'

'That was a misunderstanding, I'm sorry,' she whispered. 'I never intended for you to think it meant more.'

He blinked at her, fear running through the eyes that had made a prisoner of her for a while. 'The passion between us—'

'It's amazing, I know. But it always is. That's all it ever is. It's what I do. It's how I . . .'

'Hide?' He got up from the bed, pacing to the window, anger suddenly prowling through his body like a cat in the night.

She swallowed, remembering Chiara's words that night in the kitchen when they'd been washing up; how she'd seen through Clem's bluff of using one man to get over another. '. . . cope. It's how I cope. It's just a game; it's not . . . it's not . . .' She couldn't say it.

'Not love?' he finished for her. 'No! How can it be when you're still in love with *him*?'

The room echoed with silence. They both knew to whom he was referring, but that wasn't what had caught Clem's attention.

Still?

'How did you know that I ever loved him?' she asked, pale.

He turned his face away, a twitchy, irritated gesture loaded with pride. 'I am right, aren't I?' he demanded, ignoring her question.

She knew he had been suspicious of Rafa's antagonistic behaviour towards her – didn't they always say the line between love and hate is a thin one? – but there was no way Gabriel could know about her past with him. Chiara had never known, so it wasn't in the letters she had hidden so carefully in the mattress. But if he knew that they had had a past . . .

She met his stare and his eyes narrowed in recognition of the truth. 'I know exactly what he is to you . . . and to Luca.'

Clem's jaw dropped. 'Gabriel—'

'Does he know?'

'No.'

'No?'

She scented the threat in his tone. 'He was back here by the time I found out.' She pushed the covers away, climbing onto her knees. 'Gabriel, please, you can't tell him.'

'Does Chiara know? She was in on the secret. You kept it from him together?'

Clem shook her head vehemently. 'No, she never knew. She only met him a few years after Luca was born. She never knew that I knew him.'

'And it never occurred to her? How could she not see the resemblance? It is so obvious!'

'Why? Because they have brown hair and brown eyes? This is Italy, Gabriel! And who would have looked for it anyway? Why would she have ever considered *I* might have met him? He was my brother's pen pal; it all happened a year before I even met her.'

'How convenient.'

'Convenient?' Clem replied shrilly. 'Do you know what it did to me when I got her letter saying she'd met him? Do you have any idea what it was like knowing that, not only was my son here, but they were going to marry? But how could I tell her, after everything she'd done for me?'

He looked at her as if he were studying a butterfly – beguiled by her beauty, baffled by her purpose. 'You know he hates you.'

The words hit their mark and she slumped back on her heels. 'I know.'

'And you will settle for that?' he whispered, incredulous. He rushed at her suddenly, grabbing her by the shoulder. '*I* love you! Why is that not enough? I can give you everything.'

Clem shook her head helplessly, crying again as her hair stuck to her wet cheeks. Gabriel released her, a look of disgust on his face. 'You would rather have his hate than my love.'

She juddered, trying to catch her breath – out of words, out of explanations. She had spent ten years living a lie, covering the fatal cracks within her and trying to build a life on shifting sands. She gave a tiny nod.

'Say it!' he shouted.

'Y–yes.'

Silence fell like snow as he rose from the bed in disdain. Her lack of pride had gifted him his, at least. 'Then we are done here.' His voice was quiet. Final. 'There is nothing I can do. You are determined to suffer because it is all you know. You will never be happy.'

'Gabr—'

A familiar sound – so familiar – outside startled them both and they turned to look towards the open windows.

No! Her heart pounding against her ribs, Clem threw the bedcovers off and ran to the nearest one, looking back up the path towards the garden gate.

Tom turned back, looking up to face her at the window, his eyes red-rimmed, his face full of sorrow as he pressed his palms to his temples. By his feet was a posy of flowers from Chiara's garden, and a football bouncing slowly down the path – the calling cards of a broken family who'd come in thanks. And left in tears.

PORTOBELLO

Chapter Forty-Three

'You're a mum.'

Stella's voice was as weak as Clem's colour and Clem couldn't meet her eyes. She hadn't met anyone's for nine hours now – not since Tom's had joined hers in despair as Chiara, Rafa and Luca's door had remained defiantly shut to them both. She hadn't closed them, either. Sleep wouldn't come, and she'd spent the entire flight home staring at the haunting image of Luca coming down the aisle, her handsome, nervous little boy looking over to *her* – for the first time in both their lives – for encouragement. Her tears were constant, merely coming at variable speeds, and Tom squeezed her hand as a fresh batch splashed onto the rough, wooden, slightly sticky table.

It was lunchtime and Charlie's Café was rammed – Clem hadn't been able to face going straight home – although Stella, in her excitement, had arrived early and bagged the last table. A converted, whitewashed chapel with the original church chairs and a sunny courtyard outside, it was the perfect back-to-Blighty hangout, with colourful pictures of Portobello hanging on the walls and high tea behind the counters. On the table, a large teapot, three flapjacks and several bags of ready-salted crisps – 'welcome home' presents – lay untouched between them all, and even Stella wasn't eyeing them up. One look at Clem and the story Tom had told swiped her appetite clean away.

'A mum,' Stella echoed in utter disbelief, as though she'd been told Clem was an alien and had come to obliterate planet earth.

'Yes, I'm a . . . I'm a . . .' Her voice, even to her own ears, sounded strange and disconnected, and she could feel Stella's and Tom's stares joining up, like a cat's cradle, weaving them tightly together with mutual concern.

'You poor, poor darling,' Stella whispered desperately, batting Tom's hand off Clem's and replacing it with her own. It was warmer, Tom's cool with his own shock. Forced to choose, Chiara had chosen Luca over him. 'Why don't you try calling Rafa? He's probably had a bit of time to . . . you know, calm down. Take stock.'

'What? Of the fact that the boy he loves like a son really is his son?' Clem said sarcastically. 'I think it might take more than a day to absorb *that* one.'

Stella winced.

'Anyway, if you knew how much he hated me before all this even came out . . .' Clem's voice trailed away again.

'You're always saying how much he hates you—'

'That's because he *does*! I'm not imagining it, Stell. I'm not being sensitive. He treated me with contempt at every encounter. He didn't smile at me – not once – during the entire bloody summer.' It was true. Even as she'd clung to him, and he to her, their bodies intertwined as one, he hadn't let go of the anger, resentful of the hold she still had over him after all these years. And even if it had meant to him what it had to her, it was irrelevant now. It wouldn't have survived this.

'But why should he hate you so much?'

'Pride? I never told him why we broke up.' She shrugged. 'I just stopped writing.'

Stella looked dubious. 'That's a pretty long time to hold a grudge for what was effectively just a fling.'

Clem shook her head. 'It was way more than that. We had made plans. He was going to transfer his art degree from Florence to the Ruskin. We wanted to be together. *Properly.*' Her voice tremored. Didn't they see? It was supposed to have been for ever. 'But then I found out I was pregnant and . . .' She shrugged. 'Everything changed. I confided in Mum. We'd always shared everything and I knew she'd know what to do.' Her voice became tiny. 'I couldn't believe it when she gave me an ultimatum.'

'Ultimatum?' Stella echoed.

Clem looked up at her. 'Have an abortion or get out,' she replied flatly.

Stella and Tom were silent.

'Why didn't you tell Rafa? Surely he would have w—'

'What? Wanted to give up his studies, his home, his future – to scrape together a living supporting us? He was nineteen! He wasn't any more ready for a baby than I was. He would have thought I'd tricked him or trapped him . . .' She threw her hands in the air despondently. 'It would only have messed up both our lives.'

'So you just pretended to have the abortion?' Stella asked, the horror on her face the same as it had been on Gabriel and Tom's. 'You went through all that *alone*?'

Clem slumped over the table, her forehead only inches from it as she tried to breathe through the wave of agony that broke over her again without warning. Tom's and Stella's hands both reached out, as though trying to hold her up or pull her back, but she didn't notice their efforts.

Breathing hurt. Moving hurt. Thinking hurt – living without Luca – hurt.

Her blood ran cold again as she wondered what Chiara was telling him about her. How was she recounting to him the story of how his mother had got on a plane and left for home without him? In her dreams and daydreams over the intervening years, when she had fantasized about Luca being told about his English mother, and their subsequent reunion, she had known that Chiara would be her ally – articulating Clem's distress and anguish, how she'd not left his side even for a moment in the few days they'd had together, how she'd crammed a lifetime of love into those mere hours . . . But that was before Chiara had found out that the man she'd loved for so many years was Luca's father. It wasn't only Luca and Rafa who'd been deceived by Clem, but Chiara herself too. So what was she telling him now?

'You've got to stop blaming yourself, Clem,' Tom said quietly. 'You were eighteen.'

'Plenty of girls are good mothers at eighteen,' she replied flatly. It was no excuse.

'Yes, but you weren't given that opportunity. Our mother made sure you had no chance of bringing up that baby alone.' A foreign note of bitterness soured his words and Clem looked up at him. 'Just when you needed her most, she threatened to withdraw everything: love, security, your family, a home.' He shook his head. 'If anyone's to blame for all this, it's *her.*'

Clem frowned. She had never once heard Tom utter a word against their mother before. Not once.

'No wonder you hated her,' Stella said quietly.

Clem looked ahead at her best friend, her head spinning

from the sudden change in direction of the blame game. 'I
. . . I didn't hate her.'

'No?' Tom cocked an eyebrow disbelievingly. 'Well, you
bloody well should have hated her. I would have done.' He
stared back at her angrily. 'In fact, I'm glad you threw everything back in her face, including that fucking bag.' He
shook his head as context gave Clem's actions a new meaning. 'She only gave it to you to salve her conscience, to buy
your forgiveness for what she made you do. She's got no
fucking idea of the devastation she's wreaked. I'm amazed
you were as civi—' He stopped speaking abruptly, and both
girls looked at him. 'Hang on a minute! If she thinks you
had the abortion then . . . she doesn't know she's a grand-
mother.' Tom's voice was quiet, menacing. Clem watched
his hand ball into a fist. 'She needs to know what she's
done.'

'What? No!' Clem blanched.

'Tom,' Stella said in a warning tone, watching Clem
closely.

'Why not? Everybody else knows now. The secret's out.
At the very least she should know the damage she's caused;
the number of lives she's fucked up because of her precious
reputation.' His lips pulled into a tight sneer and Clem
knew he was thinking of Chiara and his own loss. He
looked across at his sister. 'You have to confront her with
the consequences of her actions.'

'Or what?' Stella asked, leaning in towards him as she
picked up on the implied threat.

'Or I will. I mean it. She's not getting away with this.'

'Tom, this is all too much, can't you see?' Stella said in a
quiet voice. 'It's too soon. Clem needs time to come to terms

with what's happened. It's hardly appropriate to start charging around, throwing accusations about.'

'But it's *her* fault,' Tom roared, causing several people to turn and stare.

'I'm not saying it isn't. I just don't think now's the ti—'

'Tom's right.' Stella and Tom turned as one as Clem stood up, her cheeks unnaturally pink and her eyes too bright. 'She needs to know.'

'What are you going to do?' Stella asked in alarm, her arms instantly wrapping around her belly as her blood pressure rocketed and the baby kicked.

'Tell her the truth.'

'I'll come with you,' Tom and Stella said as one, rising from their seats.

Clem silenced them both with a look and they shrank back. This was between mother and daughter.

Or rather, two mothers.

Clem waited until the bell's echoes were absorbed into the thick walls and silence rang out again, before crouching down and peering in through the letterbox. Inside, everything in the smart hallway was still. The small hillock of letters and junk mail that had built up just inside the door had finally over-balanced, so that a few were scattered across the floor, one or two pizza delivery flyers even making it as far as the finely tapered legs of the console table. On top of the console, Clem saw the dendrobium orchids her mother tended with such fastidious care, drooping and yellowed, and the blue Hermès ashtray that usually held her parents' car keys was empty. Lulu's lead was also missing from its hook.

Clem straightened up, turning back to look along the

residential street, as though she expected her parents to come walking down it towards her. But it was quiet. She found her own set of keys in her bag and let herself in.

Even just three steps in, she could detect the air was musty and she knew the doors and windows hadn't been opened for a couple of weeks at least. Hesitantly, she closed the door behind her and looked around. The hall looked different again at standing height, although the strange sense of desertion was still the same. On the stairs to her left was her mother's paisley Etro shawl, a present from her father the Christmas before last; it was draped over the banister, as though waiting to be taken upstairs by the next person passing. Clem's fingers touched it softly as she passed, the movement triggering the release of a trace of her mother's scent; Clem was surprised by the depth of emotion – misplaced nostalgia? – that crashed over her from that one tiny gesture.

She inhaled sharply, holding on to her rage, and continued down the hall, not bothering to check herself anxiously in the mirror as she usually did. There was no one here who cared today. The breakfast room was bright, even though it was an overcast day, and there were still a few flaky crumbs from a croissant on the pale green tablecloth at the round table. Clem frowned to see them there. Her mother was fiercely proud of her well-kept home and crumbs were unheard of. There may as well have been a stack of porn on the table as *crumbs.* One of the chairs was still pushed away from the table, left at a distracting angle, as though someone had got up in a hurry, and a copy of *The Times* had been left behind, folded in half in her father's usual way. It was dated 14 September. Today was 6 October.

She felt a shiver of concern creep up on her at the confirmation that her parents weren't just out; they were gone.

Clem noticed that the giant ferns in the conservatory were chestnut brown and papery, a filled copper watering can standing beside them – so near yet so far. She picked it up and sprinkled water over the parched leaves, watching as the potted earth soaked up the water as quickly as she could pour it.

When the can was empty and a half-inch of water slowly puddled in the shallow overflow dish, she walked through to the kitchen and stared with her mother's keen scrutiny at the bare worktops. Not a coffee ring or dice of shallot could be seen anywhere. She walked over to the sink and found nothing inside it, no solitary teacup stained with a tidemark, no saucer that may once have held a croissant. Where were they this time? Another cruise?

Clem walked upstairs, anticipating the squeaks on the treads even before her feet touched them. She had grown up in this house and the only secret it held from her was the whereabouts of her parents.

On the walls were the pretty watercolours her father had judiciously bought at various mid-level auctions in the Cotswolds and at brocantes on their annual holidays to Burgundy each summer, and as she stepped onto the wide landing, her eyes fell to the large square mahogany table cluttered with sepia-toned photos of her and Tom as children. The resemblance between the two of them had been more apparent when they were young, and both still boasted the same plump skin and bright eyes, but that wasn't what she saw as she took in their baby selves now, and she had to place a hand on the wall to steady herself until she felt she could move again.

She stopped by the door of her old bedroom. It was years since she had looked in – years, actually, since she'd last come upstairs. She had made a conscious and deliberate decision long ago never to use the private quarters of the house, to reject the intimacy it implied and to make a point instead of only moving through the house like a first-time guest, setting her mother on edge, pushing her back. Clem was surprised to see the same blue-striped wallpaper pasted to the walls, although the Nirvana posters had long since come down, leaving faded patches behind, like memento mori hinting at the girl who'd once lived there, the girl she'd once been – the family they'd once been.

On the bedside table, where her multi-stacking CD player had taken pride of place, was now an antique hand-painted water carafe and a vase of flowers that looked like they'd been burned, tiny specks of ash peppering the wooden surface like teardrops. On the floor was a small oval rug in muted hues, a far cry from the garish-coloured rag-roll rug she'd bought in the market for £5 when she was fifteen. The room's overall effect was odd, as though her mother had been conflicted in both wanting to hold on to her teenage daughter but sanitize her taste, too, for occasional guests.

She opened the wardrobe and the bare hangers rattled lightly on the wooden bar, some cuffed with lavender sachets. Only a tapestry opera coat was still in there, with a spare duvet folded neatly on the wardrobe floor and a white glossy shoebox pushed into the corner, the lid half-off. She went to close the door when she remembered . . . she hadn't kept shoes in that box.

She crouched down and pushed the lid off fully with her finger, as if she was pushing away a leaf to peer at a ladybird. On the top was a lilac card, covered with a densely glittered number six, and 'Darling Daughter' written in an elaborate script. She didn't need to look inside to remember her father's precise writing – written in sharp black ink with his italic pen – and the joke he'd written about what the fish said when he swam into the wall: 'Dam!' Beneath were some letters from a girl called Hilary, from Birmingham, who she'd corresponded with briefly when she was eleven after they'd done pony club together. She flicked further down the pile: more cards, mostly birthday cards, but some Valentine ones too, all illustrated with twee pictures of bunnies, teddy bears and fat red hearts. She saw a postcard of a Greek island with blue-orbed roofs and thick white walls and remembered the island-hopping holiday she'd taken with her friend Jax the summer before . . . everything. She remembered the freedom she'd felt as she took those first steps to adult independence: sunbathing topless on the rocks, walking over parched fields with a warm bottle of water in the midday sun, perfecting backward dives in salty pools and drinking chilled beer in waterfront bars every night as the local boys clamoured to talk to them. It had been her first – and only – perfect summer, where she'd been free of everything: school, her controlling mother, exams . . . herself. She'd met Rafa seven months later.

She got up and forced herself to walk out of the room without a backward glance. She walked down the landing, looking into Tom's room from the doorway. It had been given much the same treatment as hers – the ugly, teenage idioms removed (posters of butt-naked Pirelli girls and acrylic Chelsea supporter scarves draped across the curtain pole in Tom's case) – in favour of more tasteful pastel landscapes, although his rugby and cross-country trophies were still on the shelves, polished and dusted, and his boyhood bear, Snowball, was still sitting on his pillow. Beside her, on the small return wall to her right, was his pinboard. It looked untouched – invitations to twenty-firsts and school balls that dated all the way back to 2001 yellowed and curling at the edges. There were some photos of him, too, with assorted mates, sporting dreadful hair in almost all of them. She recognized Tommy, with whom he used to catch the bus to school, and Marty, his erstwhile bandmate (their musical ambitions thwarted by Marty's ability to sing like a cat and Tom never having progressed past grade II cello). Lots of Clover, of course. And she caught sight of herself in a photo almost entirely hidden behind the others. She was looking at something to her right, her hair pulled back in a ponytail and wearing hoop earrings and a ridiculously big grin. Tom, no doubt, was pulling a face – he had a peculiarly elastic face that gave him special abilities in that area, which was the only reason he'd ever won all of their staring competitions. She pulled it out carefully, but after years of sitting wedged between everything else, the photos had begun to bond to each other and a whole pile was dislodged and fell to the ground.

'Shit!' she muttered as she crouched down and tried to find the one that had caught her eye. She knew it was vain to be so eager to see an old photo of herself, but she had no recollection of the photo, or even of where it had been taken. She rifled through the mess until she found it. It had stuck to a brochure detailing Harlequins' 2002 home and away fixtures and she had to carefully, and very slowly, peel it back so as not to pull away the top layer of film. It bubbled a little in the middle, but eventually gave – along with her knees as she saw the full picture.

Her mother had taken the photo, she remembered that

immediately. It had been taken on a day trip she'd organized to some Tudor castle in the country – wanting to steep her son's pen pal in some English history – dragging them around rose gardens and long halls haunted with suits of armour. In the picture, they were at the entrance to a maze, Tom goofing around and pointing at the sign that read: 'Beware. Do not enter the maze without a map. Children must be accompanied by an adult at all times.'

But it wasn't her brother that she was smiling at. Rafa was standing on Tom's far side, looking at her with soft eyes and a tentative smile. It was the final image of her, *before*. She had surprised him with her first kiss moments later, utterly fearless and with all the precocity that is the preserve of pretty young girls coming into their prime.

It had been her sliding-doors moment, when she'd had a choice and the choice she'd made had led her to this point: sitting wretched and mute in her parents' empty home, her young son 800 miles away. She hadn't known, in that moment, that her provocative act was going to lead to love; the big one. She'd just fancied him, her big brother's pen pal – the older man, the foreign guy – and had been testing her new-found womanly wiles. She had only been seventeen; she hadn't been chasing love. When that photo was taken, she and Jax had been planning to backpack through India after their A levels that summer; she was waiting to hear whether she'd been offered a place at St Martin's and could finally set out on the path to a career in the fashion industry that she'd dreamt of since she was seven. When that photo had been taken, she'd had so much ambition, drive, purpose and self-confidence, but within the month she was pregnant and it was all gone. All of it.

And ten and a half years later, it still was.

She let the photo drop back onto the pile and got up. There was no point in this, playing with ghosts – seeing Luca's face in her family's; finding Rafa's on a wall – it wouldn't bring them back. The only thing within her power now was to tell her mother the whole truth, to offload and close the circle at long last.

She strode into her parents' room, rigid with anger and tension, flinging the door open, as though she expected to find the two of them eating toast and reading the papers in bed. But the bed, naturally, was neatly made, with hospital corners and plumped-up pillows, her father's leather slippers positioned symmetrically by his armoire.

She instinctively reached for the doorframe as she tried to make sense of what her eyes were showing her: a wheelchair and an unattached drip; a collection of small, white child-proof bottles grouped on her mother's bedside table. But it was the grey, bobbed wig on the dressing table that really took the breath from her, already combed through and just waiting to be put back on.

Chapter Forty-Four

The nurse smiled back at them as she held the door open. Tom reached forward and put a hand to it, nodding in thanks. He hadn't spoken much since Clem had rung him from their parents' house, and they'd ridden the long cab drive over pretty much in silence.

Brother and sister kept their eyes to the floor as they followed the pink-trouser-suited nurse leading them swiftly through the corridors, absently tracking the red, yellow, green and blue lines painted along it and leading variously to X-Ray, Pathology, Oncology and Haematology. Clem realized they were following green for Oncology.

'What can . . . what can you tell us about our mother's condition?' she asked, trying to keep the fear out of her voice.

The nurse turned back again to glance at them, but didn't stop walking. She smiled kindly. 'Your mother was diagnosed with stage four lung cancer in both lungs and has just finished a combined course of chemotherapy and radiotherapy.' She paused. 'I should warn you, it is an aggressive treatment approach. You may be shocked by her appearance.'

Clem felt her muscles tighten, not knowing what that meant she should expect – frankly, she'd have been shocked by her mother's appearance if she'd had a cuff button missing from her blouse or chipped nail varnish.

Tom's hand found hers and they walked together, in step, in unison.

The nurse stopped by a set of double doors. 'Your mother's in here, in isolation at the minute. I'm afraid I'm going to have to ask you to put these on before you can see her. Her immune system has been very compromised by the treatment and we can't risk any infection getting to her.' She held out two all-white suits, with integral gloves, boots and face masks.

Clem's face crumpled at the sight of them – It was that bad? End-of-the-world, apocalyptic bad? – and she put a hand to her mouth to try to stop a cry escaping her. Tom hugged her hard.

'It'll be OK, sis. She'll rally when she sees us. I know she will.'

Clem nodded and they climbed into the suits with shaking limbs. Would their mother even recognize the two of them in these get-ups? Would she recognize the two of them without them?

The nurse, suited up herself now, too, led them through the ward towards a room at the end. A bold yellow sticker was on the door: 'Strictly No Entry to Unauthorised Personnel. Infection-control suits must be worn beyond this point.'

'Please prepare yourselves,' the nurse said, her hand on the door. 'As I said, your mother's been very poorly.'

Slowly she pushed the door open. Another white-suited figure was sitting beside the bed, head bowed, gloves clasped around one small, inert, pale bony hand, which led up to an atrophied arm with wires connected to it. Clem felt the floor drop a foot beneath her. Their mother – always particular about her figure – was so emaciated, her form barely broke the flat skim of the sheets that covered her; her skin had a putrid yellowish tinge, as if she'd been cast from wax, and she looked dessicated, stripped of all moisture, as though there was no longer blood in her veins or water in her tissues, just cold, grey ash.

The cry that came into the room, announcing their arrival, wasn't hers but Tom's, and their father jumped up at the sight of them both.

'Tom! Clem! What are you . . . how did you . . .?' Words failed him as he rushed over, enveloping them both in clumsy, over-sized hugs. He pulled back to look at them both – tanned, fit and healthy from their summer in the sun – and Clem saw exactly how much of a toll their mother's illness had taken on him, too. He had lost a considerable amount of weight, so that his skin hung slack around his jaw, great bags of exhaustion and despair puddling beneath his eyes. His complexion was scarcely better than his beloved wife's, and his eyes were red-rimmed from the silent tears that fell as she slept. 'Thank God you're here.'

'Why didn't you tell us?' Tom demanded, his voice croaky, and Clem knew he was remembering the vicious blame he'd directed at their mother only a few hours earlier.

'She swore me to secrecy, Tom. She was adamant that she didn't want to burden you with a mother living with cancer. She thought you'd fret at every cold, every sneeze . . .'

Tom blinked and Clem could read the fear in his face. 'You make it sound like she's known about this for a while,' Tom said.

Their father paused. 'Eleven years. I don't know if you remember that she had a persistent cough she just couldn't shake.'

Clem looked at him, startled. She remembered it well. She'd been woken up for weeks at a stretch by the sound of her mother coughing through the night and early in the morning; she remembered how bitterly she'd wished her mother would just go and get some antibiotics so that she could get some sleep.

'When she got it checked out, she was referred immediately to an oncologist that same day.'

'But Mum's never smoked!' Tom protested, as though this information alone would mean it couldn't be possible; their mother couldn't possibly be suffering from lung cancer.

His father shook his head. 'No. No, it was just bad luck, Tom. She had stage three and embarked upon a course of radiotherapy. She insisted we tell you we were going on a cruise.'

'The cruises?' Tom echoed. 'You mean, for all these years you've been telling us—'

'No, no, no. It was just that first time that was a lie. You were doing your exams. Your mother didn't want you distracted by her condition. She had her treatment and, blessedly, went into remission. But it gave us the idea to start escaping the worst of the British winters and protect her health.'

'You just said it was stage three, but the nurse told us it was stage four,' Tom said with effort, trying to negotiate now, if not on the origin and undeservedness of the disease, then at least on the severity of it. What was it they said about the seven stages of grief? Denial? Bargaining?

'It is now,' their father said gently, knowing that every word he said was a punch in the guts to his children.

'But that's . . . I mean, that's still OK, right? She's still going to be all right? It's been eleven years and she's clearly beating it,' Tom said, his words tripping over each other as they looked at their mother, who didn't look like she was beating anything. She was sleeping, a tube coming out of her nose, and Clem watched the pulsing numbers on the screen, which even she knew were weak.

'Your mother's a fighter. She's been in remission since the original diagnosis. But this relapse has been very rough . . .' Edmund's voice wavered and he pinched the bridge of his nose for a long moment. 'You have to prepare yourselves – there is no stage five.'

'No . . .?' Clem knew that beneath his mask, Tom's tic would be in full spasm. She wanted her hand to find his, she willed it to, but she couldn't move. Something else was demanding her attention.

Eleven years. Her mother had been diagnosed with cancer eleven years ago. Tears streamed down Clem's face, soaking her mask, as she understood that it hadn't been Clem her mother had worried about coping with a baby – it had been herself.

'You should have told us, Dad,' Tom said, his voice cracking. 'We had the right to know. She's our mum. What if Clem hadn't found the wheelchair and all those pill bottles?'

Edmund frowned. 'But we did tell you. Or rather, your mother did, in the letter.'

'What letter?'

Edmund frowned harder and looked back at his wife before facing them, dropping his voice. 'At Christmas, I finally convinced your mother to write you a letter telling you the truth. I told her she didn't have to send it if she didn't want to, but I could tell she was getting worse. I–I suspected she'd moved into the next stage . . .' He was silent for a moment. 'She didn't show me the letter, but she spent days working on it, even going so far as to burn the drafts she discarded. When she had finally finished, she wrote your name on the envelope, Clem.' He looked imploringly at his daughter. 'Relations between you two have been so poor for so long, you both needed to make peace with each other before . . . before . . .' His voice trembled and Tom put a hand on his arm and squeezed it. 'She left it propped up on the dressing table for a week. I would walk into the bedroom and she'd be sitting on the bed, just staring at it. I knew she wanted you to read it; I just wasn't sure that she'd ever have the courage to send it. And then one day, it wasn't there. When I asked, she told me she'd put it in the Birkin for you, inside the zipped compartment where you always used to put your dolls' dresses. She felt it was safest there.'

Clem looked back at him in dismay. 'I never even opened the bag.'

'But why?'

She shook her head. How could she explain to him that the bag had been her mother's peace offering – or bribe, as she'd seen it – without telling him why her mother had had to make peace? 'It's back at your house now. The letter will still be in there.'

He closed his eyes for a long moment. 'I thought she'd lied about putting the letter in the bag. I couldn't for the life of me understand why you never mentioned it. That's why I arranged that breakfast – I was determined to tell you. But then Tom cancelled and you were so closed, so unhappy already.' Edmund sighed. 'I should have just told you, but as much as I disagreed with your mother's decision, I couldn't bring myself to go against her wishes.'

'But what if she'd died, Dad?' Tom demanded. 'How would you have explained that to us?'

'I thought if she'd been in remission once . . . I thought we still had time.'

They all looked towards the frail figure lying on the bed. It was clear there wouldn't be a remission this time. Portia stirred slightly, her eyelids dragging open heavily, as though they were weighted down. Her head moved fractionally towards their voices.

'Edmund?' Their mother's voice was scarcely more than a whisper, as papery as her skin.

'Mum!' Tom cried, running over and pressing his masked cheek to her hand. 'Mum, we're here.'

'Tom?' The effort it took to say even that word expunged her voice and she rested again, closing her eyes.

Clem felt rooted to the spot, wanting to run to her, but too scared, frightened off by years of conditioning herself to do the opposite.

'Clem?' Her father's voice beside her was rounded with suspended hope, his hand hovering lightly on her shoulder.

Clem, unable to take her eyes off her mother, walked slowly across the room, getting closer to the tiny figure that didn't appear to grow in size with proximity.

'Mum?' Her voice quavered and a tear fell from her lashes onto the cold hand on the bed.

Her mother opened her eyes again, the same eyes she'd given to Clem and which had made so many men, Rafa included, fall at her feet.

'Bunny?'

'I'm here, Mum,' Clem whispered, almost poleaxed to

hear her pet name coming from her mother again after so many years. Whatever had happened, whatever they'd done to each other, they were in time; it wasn't too late. 'I'm so sorry, for everything,' Clem said as she pressed her mother's hand against her cheek, trying to warm it with her own heat.

She felt her mother grip her hand back with her fingers as tightly as she could, though the pressure was feeble. 'It is you who must forgive me, darling. My letter was years too late. I was selfish, only thinking about myself . . . I hurt you both so much . . . But I wasn't coping . . . and . . . he just kept calling, I knew it would stop if I told him about the abortion . . .' her mother said, her voice barely audible, though her eyes blazed intensely at Clem.

Clem rocked at the bombshell, Rafa's enduring anger explained in a breath. He thought she had got rid of their baby.

'Abortion?' Edmund exclaimed in alarm, looking between his wife and daughter.

Clem blinked, trying to take it all in as she realized her mother's letter had been the real gift all along, not the bag. It had given her the apology she'd craved, even though it was too late and couldn't possibly have changed anything.

Except . . .

'You're still in love with him . . .'

Gabriel's bitter words floated through her mind and she realized it had changed one thing: *he* had found the letter when his assistant had bought the bag on his behalf. He'd found it and read it – an unopened letter addressed to her, an unopened letter in which her mother told her she was dying and which he had ignored because it told him about Rafa, too, and that was all that concerned *him*. He had wanted to take her away from everyone – Rafa, Luca, her mother . . . Her instincts had been right after all – he had wanted total possession of her.

'I made so many wrong decisions,' her mother whispered.

'But for the right reasons,' Clem whispered, forcing Gabriel's treachery from her mind and squeezing her mother's hand as much as she dared – it felt like it might break in her clasp. 'You were sick and just trying to cope. And . . . and anyway, you weren't the only one.' She swallowed hard, wondering how to say the words. Clem looked down at her hands intertwined with her mother's. The words that had been bottled up inside her for so long were rising, and the pressure just to hold them back was overwhelming, but was now the right time? She looked at her mother's frail form and knew there might not be another time. It had to be now.

'I made the wrong decision for the right reason, too.' Clem felt sick. What if the shock was too great? Oh God, how could she lessen the enormity of what she had to say?

An idea struck her.

'There's something I want to show you,' Clem said, delving into her bag and pulling out her phone (which the receptionist had insisted was set to aeroplane mode before they could even leave the waiting area). She flicked it open onto the photo that was saved as her wallpaper and turned it round for her parents to see. 'His name is Luca. He lives in Portofino.'

She watched as her parents blinked at the screen, confusion gradually clearing as they recognized her bone structure, Tom's dimples . . .

Open-mouthed, they looked back at her in stunned amazement. Her mother's eyes met hers first, understanding immediately, and in them was relief, regret, delight and pain. How much time they had lost.

'Is that . . .?' Edmund choked, supporting himself with the bed, scarcely able to believe what he was seeing.

Clem nodded, one hand clamped over her mouth as a sob of anguish, love and pride burst out of her like a sunbeam, strong, powerful and dazzling. 'Yes, Daddy. That's your grandson. My son.'

Tom darted round the bed to support his father, who looked like he might fall as the truth finally broke like a wave over their family.

'I'm so proud of you,' Portia whispered, a single tear sliding down her cheek.

'I'm a g–grandfather?' Edmund whispered as Tom rubbed his shoulder, nodding frantically.

'He's amazing, Dad! And so like Clem. Cheeky as hell and always in trouble!'

'We have a grandson? Portia! Can you believe it? I just can't believe it! Look, darling, doesn't he have exactly Clem's—'

But Portia didn't respond. Her eyes had closed, and she was completely and utterly still.

TWO MONTHS LATER

Chapter Forty-Five

'Have you got it?' Clem asked, arms hovering on either side of the tree as she kept the blanket slack.

Tom, who was positioned precariously on an extra-long ladder, three metres above the floor, nodded. He was at full stretch, trying to attach the enormous star to the topmost branch of Claridge's' Christmas tree. It was a composite of five enormous baguette-shaped diamonds – 10 carats each – arranged in a star formation and held in place by a brooch brace on the back, which could then be dismantled and the diamonds sold on individually – unless a passing billionaire should choose to buy the whole thing as the star for *his* Christmas tree, and that was reasonably likely with Claridge's' clientele. The assembled star's full, terrifying value came in at £6 million, and security teams were milling around everywhere. Cartier was taking no chances and neither was Claridge's; once the ladder was removed, the diamond would be impossible to access – even swinging from one of the chandeliers – but there would still be a twenty-four-hour guard on duty by the tree until it was taken down on twelfth night.

Clem looked directly at the diamond, on eye level with £6 million for the first and, she knew, only time in her life. She blinked into its brightness, musing blankly at how easy it would be to simply pluck it like a berry from the branches and walk out. Six million pounds, just like that, a life-changing sum by anyone's reckoning – except hers. Six million, *sixty* million pounds couldn't improve her life. It wasn't money that she lacked or craved.

Below them, Clem could see a cluster of frowning, uni-formed security men huddled over a clipboard, alternately jabbing the page with stubby fingers and pointing to the various doors, entrances and exits that fed off the lobby. Tensions were high enough, even without the diamonds. Alderton Hide and Cartier had only had from 11 p.m. to 6 a.m. to bring in, position and dress the Christmas tree. The unveiling of the Claridge's Christmas tree was one of London's big Christmas triggers – right up there with the switching on of Regent Street's lights and Santa's Grotto at Harrods – and Tom and Clem had worked on it almost exclusively since their sudden return home, both cloaked in their bereavements and desperate not to stop lest they should have time to think, or feel. Chad was overseeing the completion of the Portofino job on their behalf now that they were as unwelcome in Gabriel's house as they were in Chiara, Rafa and Luca's; the project was in the final stage anyway, and it was simply a matter of hanging curtains, paintings and light fittings. Chad, true to his word, had sent them photos on an almost daily basis and everyone, even Simon, was impressed by Clem's vision. Gabriel's verdict hadn't yet come in: he had returned to Paris and no one, not even Signora Benuto, knew when he would be back.

Clem let the blanket sag further between her hands. If those diamonds should fall, there would be a national emer-gency as everyone clamoured to find them in the bushy fronds of the blue spruce.

'There,' Tom whispered, slowly raising his hands up and away from the tree, ready to lurch forward again lest the diamond should wobble, but it stood firm, dazzling as powerfully as the North Star. A relieved and exulted round of applause ricocheted around the room as Tom's tired eyes met Clem's, a triumphant smile on his face.

'Last one down's a ninny.' She winked, throwing the blanket down to the ground like a parachute. She ran down the wide staircase that swept around the tree like a nautilus seashell while Tom shinned noisily down the ladder, beating him only by two seconds. Clem stuck her tongue out as the Claridge's housekeeping and estate teams slapped them both on the back and the smartly suited executive teams shook hands with each other. Everyone was giddy with exhaustion after a full night without sleep and Clem was tempted to book a room in the hotel and be fast asleep in ten minutes rather than have to negotiate the London traffic home. Hourly caffeine had kept them all going, but mostly they'd been galvanized by a desperate desire to see the finished result. The buzz around the confidential project had been immense for weeks. Cartier – having heard the rumours about Alderton Hide's heavy, near-fatal investment in formulating the technology to sew diamonds into leather – had been quick to come in on the project (Perignard who?) and the trade was clamouring to get the first look they'd been denied at Berlin.

'You like?' Tom whispered as they gazed up at it, arms folded across his chest. From down here, the tree seemed immense and hauntingly beautiful.

Clem could only nod. She was too full of emotion to speak just yet.

He looked across at her, knowing her silences were never empty. 'Is it how you imagined?'

'Better. It's beyond imagination.'

'I think it's magnificent,' Tom murmured, his eyes scanning the whistle-thin leather lariats, snow-white and stitched with pave diamonds, which were delicately draped across the branches – 'like tinsel for the rich,' he'd joked. Other lariats had been intricately hole-punched into lacework that was as fine as spider's webs and which wove around and through the tree like the spun sugar of a croquembouche.

Clem herself couldn't stop looking at the hundreds of tiny white solitaire-studded leather boxes that were hanging like baubles from the branch tips. Each one had a small square of hand-made parchment inside, upon which – for a small donation to charity – hotel guests and visitors could write a wish. It was a Christmas Wishing Tree in the middle of Mayfair.

'Ten minutes everyone,' the manager said, indicating that the famous revolving doors, which had been locked for confidentiality and security all night, were going to be released, and the dignitaries and VIPs who called this their London home would be sweeping through once more. He clapped his hands lightly and the works teams efficiently and expertly began to clear away the blankets, sweeping away dropped pine needles, removing the ladders and restoring the gracious art deco lobby to its pristine splendour.

'I'll get Dad to come down,' Tom murmured, fishing for his phone in his jeans pocket and wandering off towards the lifts.

Clem watched him go, leaning against the buttermilk-coloured wall, before realizing, with a small, sudden start, that she was standing in the exact spot where Gabriel had cornered her eight months earlier, on the morning of their meeting last April. Her hand blindly smoothed the wall as her eyes flooded with tears at the memory – not because of Gabriel's seductively relentless, ruthlessly dogged determination to capture her, but because she understood now that it had been the morning when her life had been pitched another curve ball, swerving from its path to angle her back to Italy and the man and boy she'd left behind ten years earlier. Though she hadn't known it at the time, it had all started up again right here, in this very spot that now stood in the shadow of the wishing tree.

She stared at the highly polished floor, counting to one hundred – ten wasn't close to cutting it any more – as the last members of the estate teams disappeared and a slow trickle of well-heeled guests came through the revolving doors. Clem, hiccupping, tried texting Stella, who had promised to be first through the revolving doors at 6 a.m. – although, in truth, she was so large now that she was full term, the doorman would probably have to open a swing door for her instead.

'I'm way ahead of you, babes.'

Clem turned in surprise. Stella was standing behind her, wearing the vintage black and red nurse's cape she had decided upon as her pregnancy cover-up, and an intense expression. Her colour was up and her breathing rapid.

'Oh God,' Clem exclaimed immediately worried and clasping Stella by the arms, trying to gauge her friend's symptoms as she'd been taught in the ante-natal classes. 'You haven't started having contractions, have you? You can't have your baby in the middle of Claridge's lobby. It's not like BA, Stell. They won't give you free rooms for life you know . . .'

Stella simply smiled and hooked her arm through Clem's, wheeling her round to face the tree again.

'What do you think?' Clem whispered nervously, tilting her head to rest against Stella's.

'Stunning,' Stella breathed, clutching her arm tightly. 'I love the look of it as much as the idea.'

'Yeah, me too,' Clem said quietly, pushing one of the leather boxes with her finger so that it swung.

'What's your wish?'

Clem shot her a pained look. 'Don't. You know perfectly well—'

'Yeah, I do,' Stella said quietly, turning her friend another 20 degrees.

Clem felt the breath leave her.

Stella leaned in so that her cheek was almost against Clem's. 'I found him on your doorstep last night; told him you were out on an all-nighter, so he stayed at mine,' she whispered.

Clem opened her mouth, but no words would come.

'Worth the wait, I should say,' Stella whispered, squeezing her arm lovingly before stepping back.

Rafa, who'd been standing beside the bottom step, walked towards her. His tanned skin seemed darker than ever amidst all the pasty British winter complexions, and he was wearing a coat and black jeans, a grey cashmere scarf knotted at his neck in the way that only Italian men – even relatively scruffy ones like him – knew how to carry off. He seemed taller and his hair was longer than she remembered, falling into his eyes, which were hooded and wary upon her, as though *she* had startled *him*.

They stared at each other in the long hanging silence that always came when their eyes met – words would never be enough – but they weren't needed anyway. In the next moment, his hand closed around her wrist, pulling her to him, and his soft, full lips, which had denied her so much over the summer – a smile, a kind word – met hers, pushing her, tasting her, reclaiming her. She could feel traces of his anger still, but also his longing, and she wrapped her arms around his neck, riding the kiss as it told her all she'd ever wanted to know: that he loved her, always had, always would.

He cupped her head, tipping her back, and she looked up at him as he pulled away, as though checking she was real and not still the figure that walked through his dreams. 'I could not lose you again.' His voice was jagged and she saw the same haunted look in his eyes that she recognized in Luca's.

'You never did. I've never loved anyone but you.'

Her words were like electric shocks to him, almost painful to hear, and clasping her face between his hands, he kissed her again, hard then sweetly, his beautiful mouth curling against hers into a delighted smile, a smile that was almost as welcome as his kisses.

Something knocked against her feet and she looked down.

A ball . . .

A jolt of adrenaline arrowed through her as she looked up to find Chiara standing ten feet away, holding Luca's hand. Her hands flew to her mouth to see her beautiful child suddenly so near, and she fell to her knees, wholly unable to stand, as he came slowly towards her. She found the ball though her eyes never left his, and she held it up as he stopped in front of her.

'Is this yours?' she whispered.

Luca nodded but didn't move to take it.

'Am . . .' She swallowed hard as tears filled her eyes. 'Am I?'

He blinked rapidly and she saw the faintest wobble of his bottom lip, her hand shooting out to cup his cheek, desperate to reassure him that he didn't have to decide.

'Yes.' And before she could respond – before she could sigh, gasp or cry – his arms were around her neck, his face burrowed into her shoulder as he tried to hide the tears she could feel hiccupping through him.

'Luca, my Luca,' she whispered into his hair, rubbing his back as he tried to control his sobs, trying to be the big boy. 'My darling child, my precious boy . . . I l–love you . . . so much. Every day I loved you.'

Rafa crouched down next to them, his hand heavy and reassuring on Luca's shoulder as the sobs kept on coming, his other hand in hers, their little family linked at last.

She looked up at Chiara. 'Thank you,' she mouthed to the friend who had schemed so cleverly all summer, constantly throwing her in the path of her son and forcing them to bond, to know each other, to laugh together, making it impossible for her to ever leave again. Chiara had succeeded in giving Clem what Rosa had known she needed all those years ago – a way back.

'Did you see what I made?' Clem whispered when Luca's tears finally began to slow down, turning him gently towards the grand tree. 'It's a wishing tree, just for you.'

He blinked in disbelief and looked at her. 'For me?'

She reached a hand out to the nearest branch and took one of the leather boxes. 'Each box is to be filled with a wish. And *you* must write the first one.' She reached in her jeans pocket for a pen and handed it to him. 'Don't worry, I won't ask you to tell me what you're wishing for this time.' She smiled.

There was a pause as the little boy thought. 'You do not have to.' Luca looked at her. 'You already know.'

'I do?'

He nodded. 'It is the same as yours.'

At his words, the lead lining that had formed inside her ten years earlier melted away, like ice cream in the sun. 'Oh Luca . . .'

Over his shoulder, Clem saw the lift doors open and Tom and her father step out, Tom pushing their mother's wheelchair with adroitness and pride, her hands over her eyes.

'Are you ready, Mu—?' Tom asked, stopping abruptly at the sight in front of the Christmas tree, his eyes immediately scanning the vast space for Chiara. His body softened as he found her gaze already upon him, promises in her smile.

Without another word, Tom stopped their mother's wheelchair in front of them, Edmund looking at Clem for confirmation of what he thought he was seeing. She gave a tiny nod, though her smile said it all, and she stood up, her hands in Rafa's and Luca's. Ready.

'Can I open my eyes yet?' her mother asked, oblivious to the silent conversations whizzing past her.

Clem took a deep breath as Rafa squeezed her hand tightly in his. 'Yes, Mum, you can look now.'

Epilogue

Dear Chiara,

Greetings from Portofino!

So, there's eight sleeps to Christmas and you're not going to believe this, but it snowed here last night! I know, I'm so jammy: my first Christmas here and it will be white. Rafa says it's the first snow here since he was four! It's made everything feel extra-Christmassy, and I was bad enough before. We've all put on weight from the amount of mince pies I've been making (Luca's obsessed) and Rafa got really cross with me because I insisted we drive all the way to Rapallo yesterday for a tree. They did have some smaller ones in Santa Margherita but the shape wasn't good enough and he just doesn't appreciate that you have to get these details right.

Anyway, I really hope the snow stays till you arrive next week. We made a snowman the second we woke up – it was Mediterranean-style with black olives for the eyes and mouth and that Missoni scarf of yours that you left behind. It was so fab. I've enclosed a photo of it for you.

How's work? Massive congrats on your promotion, by the way! Tom told me all about it. Junior exec. in just eighteen months – you must be doing something right! I just hope you're not *working too hard? We've finished all the work on the hotel now. It was definitely the right thing to do, not opening this summer. We stripped everything right back and pretty much started from scratch. I can't wait till you see it. The photos don't do it justice.*

I have to admit I was a bit worried about what to do when the refurb was finished, because with the new management team sorted, it's not like I'm needed for the day-to-day running of the hotel, but Chad came for dinner last week and guess what? He's starting on a palazzo over in Monterosso in the new year, and he wants me to come in on it with him!

It's going to be so good to see you all, we just can't wait. Luca's counting the days. He's really missed Dad since he went back in the autumn, they spent loads of time fishing together, and every time I saw them, they were talking and joking around. They're so alike it's ridiculous.

As for me, I'm massive! Rafa can hardly get his arms around me. The doctor in the port gave Luca a stethoscope and he listens to his sister's heartbeat every night before bed. It's so sweet.

Anyway, must stop nattering or we'll have nothing to tell you when you get here. See you next week, masses of love,

Your sister,

Clem xxxx

P.S. Can you have a word with Stella? She's really convinced that neon is the way to go for midnight mass.

Acknowledgements

In part, the idea for this book was prompted by a trip I took to Italy last May to read at a prestigious literary festival in the spotlit ruins of Ancient Rome. It was one of the most daunting and spectacular nights of my life, and I will never forget it. I would like to offer thanks to Maria Ida, the festival organizer, and my Italian publishers, Newton Compton, for making everything feel so effortless – though I'm sure it can't have been – and for making me feel so welcome, particularly Raffaello Avinzini, Anna Voltaggio and Fiammetta Biancatelli.

It was on this trip that I visited Portofino, researching ideas for a possible book – I know, it was tough – and really fell in love with a country that I had been flirting with for years. But possibly the moment of capitulation happened in San Benedetto del Tronto, where I did a short book tour and was treated to Italian hospitality at its very best. Mimmo Minuto, Cinzia Carboni and Sandra Libbi, I will never forget your kindness and generosity, thank you so much!

A huge debt is owed, as ever, to Amanda Preston, my long-suffering, chic, indomitable agent; to Jenny Geras for steering me so expertly into these deep, calm waters; to Caroline Hogg for taking the helm, and Jeremy Trevathan, Natasha Harding, Wayne Brooks, Katie James and the rest of the team at Pan for their unstinting support.

But as ever, I'm saving the tears for my family. I'd like to thank my parents for the selfless support they gave me last year; my sister (even though she steals my clothes and teaches the children rude jokes); my children, who grow funnier, more delectable and – God help me, hungrier! – by the day, and last, but the opposite of least, my husband Anders, the best man I ever met.

Karen Swan Author Q&A

1) What inspired you to write Christmas at Claridge's?

Each book usually evolves in one way or another from the one preceding it, and in this instance, I wanted to write about a character who was everything that Laura, from *The Perfect Present*, wasn't. Laura was an emotionally vulnerable character looking for safety in mediocrity and her journey was about finding the courage to embrace life again. This time round, I wanted to write about the girl who has it all – the charisma, the looks, the lifestyle, the background. Everybody loves her, but we quickly learn she's vulnerable too. The difference is, her pain is her own fault. Her secret is a very dark one – almost unforgivable really – and the challenge for me was to try to ease the reader past the golden-girl image and encourage them to find a sympathy and understanding for her actions. It's a book about forgiveness.

2) Is the character of Clem based on anyone you know?

No, but out of all my characters, she is the girl I would most like to be myself (her wardrobe, not her life). I really had her worked out in my head very early on. With some characters, it takes almost an entire book before I feel I know them –

Laura in *The Perfect Present* for example, really only came together for me as I wrote the closing scenes – but I saw and understood Clem by the end of the first chapter. She pretty much came to me fully formed.

3) What are your top tips for shopping at Portobello market?

Always go on Fridays as that's when the best stalls are up; carry cash; wear clothes you can change out of easily (most of the stalls share changing facilities that consist of little more than a woman shielding you with a coat!), and try to keep your hands free for rifling through the rails, so preferably carry a bag with a long strap that you can sling over your body.

4) Was there a particular reason for setting part of this book in Italy?

Well, partly I loved the fact that they are iconic locations, evocative the world over, and I know from the emails I get that my readers love being taken on journeys to glamorous places. But the main inspiration was that I started out loving the echo of the names: Portobello–Portofino. They sound so similar and yet are poles apart in terms of lifestyle and aesthetics: Portobello is gritty, urban, cool and young; Portofino is luxurious, sophisticated, European, old-world glamour. I kept thinking about how different the women would be from each place (a train-of-thought hangover from *Christmas at Tiffany's*) and before I knew it, I was trying to come up with a character who could somehow belong to both.

5) How did you become an author?

Mainly due to persuasion, from people who know better than me, to have a go at writing stories! I was a journalist beforehand and had studied English at University, so I suppose becoming an author was a fairly predictable outcome, but it took me a long time to really believe I could think up stories, plots and characters that people would care about. Nothing thrills me more than when readers tell me I made them laugh or cry. It means they believed in the world I gave them on the page.

6) Describe your typical working day

It starts with the school run for my three children, then a walk in the forest with my two dogs, where I really let my mind wander into a lucid, free-thinking state. I'm not always trying to think about the book but that's invariably where my mind ends up – focusing on plot niggles or what scene I have to write that day. I try to be sitting down and writing by 9.30 a.m. – fine, 10 a.m., then – but I'm up again at eleven for my first coffee of the day. I always get up and put the kettle on if I become stuck on something – moving around seems to help physically dislodge ideas that are stuck in my subconscious. I have to collect my daughter from school at 3 p.m.; the school is only a ten-minute drive away, but often I'll be working until 2.49 p.m., desperate to get down just one more word. From then on, I'm just Mummy again until 9.30 a.m. the next morning. OK, 10 a.m., then. Whatever.

7) Do you have any advice for aspiring writers?

Plenty! If you want to write a book, don't talk about it, just do it. Don't wait for inspiration to strike – it never does – the best ideas usually come whilst you're writing something else, so force yourself to sit down and stare at the screen or page until something comes to you; it will, eventually. If an idea surprises you, explore it, go with it – if you're surprised, your readers most likely will be, too. Finally, edit to the point of OCD and ask someone you can trust to be brutally honest, to read it. Kindness is no friend to an author.

8) What do you hope readers will take away from your novels?

Laughter, hope, and the feeling of having been in the company of good friends. All my characters feel like friends to me. I so wish they were real.

9) What does Christmas mean to you?

An obscenely early start, thanks to my over-excited children, cooking the turkey overnight in the Aga, my children wriggling around in the giant stockings I made for each of them for their first Christmas, and a smelly donkey being walked down the nave for the Christingle service on Christmas Eve. This year's was particularly thrilling because, for the first time, the donkey properly lost its temper. No one listened to a word the poor vicar said about baby Jesus. The donkey was the star.

10) Can you tell us a little bit about the book you will be writing next?

It's a summer book based around a group of strangers in a house-share in the Hamptons. My main character has a 'family media' company, cataloguing other peoples' DVDs into short films, their photos into beautiful photo books and so on. Through this, she becomes intimately acquainted with the lives of people who remain strangers to her on the street. One family in particular draws her fascination, and as she trawls through their digital archives, she uncovers a private tragedy. Weaving around that will be a mix of glamour, romance and friendships set to backdrops of beach barbecues, polo parties and tennis tournaments.

Players

by
Karen Swan
ISBN: 978-1-4472-2373-3

Friendships are strong. Lust is stronger . . .

Harry Hunter was everywhere you looked – bearing down from bus billboards, beaming out from the society pages, falling out of nightclubs in the gossip columns, and flirting up a storm on the telly chat-show circuit.

Harry Hunter is the new golden boy of the literary scene. With his books selling by the millions, the paparazzi on his tail and a supermodel on each arm, he seems to have the world at his feet. Women all over the globe adore him but few suspect that his angelic looks hide a darker side, a side that conceals a lifetime of lies and deceit.

Tor, Cress and Kate have been best friends for as long as they can remember. Through all the challenges of marriage, raising children and maintaining their high-flying careers, they have stuck together as a powerful and loyal force to be reckoned with – living proof that twenty-first-century women can have it all, and do. It is only when the captivating Harry comes into their lives that things begin to get complicated, as Tor, Cress and Kate are drawn into Harry's dangerous games.

Prima Donna

by
Karen Swan
ISBN: 978-1-4472-2374-0

**Breaking the rules was what she liked best.
That was her sport. Renegade, rebel, bad girl.
Getting away with it.**

Pia Soto is the sexy, glamorous prima ballerina, the
Brazilian bombshell, who's shaking up the ballet world
with her outrageous behaviour. She's wild and precocious,
and she's a survivor. She's determined that no man will
ever control her destiny. But ruthless financier Will Silk
has Pia in his sights, and he has other ideas . . .

Sophie O'Farrell is Pia's hapless, gawky assistant, the
girl-next-door to Pia's prima donna, always either falling
in love with the wrong man or just falling over. Sophie
sets her own dreams aside to pick up the debris in Pia's
wake, but she's no angel. When a devastating accident
threatens to cut short Pia's illustrious career, Sophie has
to step out of the shadows and face up to the demons
in her own life.

Christmas at
TIFFANY'S
by
Karen Swan

ISBN: 978-0-330-53272-3

**Three cities, three seasons,
one chance to find the life that fits**

Cassie settled down too young, marrying her first serious boyfriend. Now, ten years later, she is betrayed and broken. With her marriage in tatters and no career or home of her own, she needs to work out where she belongs in the world and who she really is.

So begins a year-long trial as Cassie leaves her sheltered life in rural Scotland to stay with each of her best friends in the most glamorous cities in the world: New York, Paris and London. Exchanging the grouse moor and mousy hair for low-carb diets and high-end highlights, Cassie tries on each city for size as she attempts to track down the life she was supposed to have been leading, and with it, the man who was supposed to love her all along.

The Perfect
PRESENT
by
Karen Swan

ISBN: 978-0-330-53273-0

Memories are a gift . . .

Haunted by a past she can't escape, Laura Cunningham
desires nothing more than to keep her world small and
precise – her quiet relationship and growing jewellery
business are all she needs to get by. Until the day when
Rob Blake walks into her studio and commissions a necklace
that will tell his enigmatic wife Cat's life in charms.

As Laura interviews Cat's family, friends and former
lovers, she steps out of her world and into theirs –
a charmed world where weekends are spent in Verbier
and the air is lavender-scented, where friends are
wild, extravagant and jealous, and a big love has to
compete with grand passions.

Hearts are opened, secrets revealed, and as the necklace
begins to fill up with trinkets, Cat's intoxicating life
envelops Laura's own. By the time she has to identify the
final charm, Laura's metamorphosis is almost complete.
But the last story left to tell has the power to change all of
their lives for ever, and Laura is forced to choose between
who she really is and who it is she wants to be.

An extract from *The Perfect Present* follows . . .

Chapter One

Laura looked at the shoes in her hand and knew before the assistant had come back with her size that she would buy them, even if they didn't fit. They were red, and that's all they needed to be. She was almost famous for them around here, and Jack always teased her about it – 'You know what they say – red shoes, no knickers.' Of course, he knew full well she'd be the last person to go knickerless. Maybe that was why he found it so funny. Anyway, she preferred him saying that to his other response, which was to roll his eyes. 'You've got almost fifty pairs!' he'd cried last time before he'd caught sight of her expression and quickly crossed the kitchen to apologize, saying he secretly quite liked that she had a 'signature'.

The shop assistant came back, shaking her head apologetically.

'All I've got left is a thirty-six,' she shrugged. 'We're completely out of thirty-eights, even in the other colourways.'

Laura bit her lip and stalled for a moment as the assistant moved to return the shoe to the display shelf. 'Well . . . I'll take them anyway,' she muttered, looking away as she reached into her bag for her credit card. 'They're such a good price now. There'll be someone I can give them to . . .'

'Okay.' The assistant hesitated, casting a glance at Laura's red patent slip-ons, which she'd polished so hard at the breakfast table that morning that their eyes met in the reflection.

A minute later, she savoured the jangle of the bell on the door as it closed behind her and stood for a moment on the pavement, adjusting to the brightness outside and the change of pace. The day was already limbered up and elastic, the late-November sun pulsing softly in the sky with no real power behind it, local businessmen rushing past with coffees-to-go slopping over the plastic covers and pensioners pushing their shopping carts between the grocer's and the butcher's, tutting over the price of brisket; a few mothers with prams were congregating around the bakery windows, talking each other into jam doughnuts and strong coffee to commiserate over their broken nights.

Laura turned her back on them all – glad their problems weren't hers – and started walking down the street in the opposite direction, swinging the carrier bag in her hand so that it matched the sway of her long, light brown hair across her narrow back. Her studio was in a converted keep, just beyond the old yacht yard, eight minutes away. People tended to have a romantic notion of what it must be like when she told them where she worked, but it wasn't remotely pretty to look at. Tall and ungainly on its stilts, it towered over all the corrugated-panel workshops and dilapidated boat huts on the banks, and her square studio-room atop them looked like it had been bolted on by an architect who'd trained with Lego. The wood was thoroughly rotted, although you wouldn't know to look at it, as it had been freshly painted two summers previously by a student at the sailing club who was after extra cash. She loved it. It felt like home.

She turned off the high street and marched down the shady

grey-cobbled lanes, past the tiny pastel-coloured fishermen's cottages with bushy thatched roofs – which were now mostly second homes for affluent Londoners – and over the concrete slipway to the compacted mud towpath that led down towards her studio. It sat on a hillock in the middle of the estuary. 'St Laura's Mount', Jack called it. The brown water merely slapped at the stilt legs during the high spring tides, but the path over to it was only accessible at low tide, which was why she was enjoying a late start this morning. Strictly speaking, if she really cared about doing a nine-to-five working day, she could have bought a small dinghy to row over in, but she rather liked the idiosyncratic hours it forced upon her. But even more than that – and she could *never* admit this to Jack – she loved the occasional stranding overnight, when her absorption in her work led her to ignore the alarm clock and the path became submerged. After the first 'stranding', she had brought a duvet, pillow and overnight bag to the studio so that she was properly set up for the eventuality, but Jack hated it. He felt it encouraged her – enabled her – to continue working when it was time to stop and come home.

The tide was almost fully out now, and the mudflats looked as glossy as ganache, but Laura didn't stop to watch the avocets and bitterns picking their way weightlessly over them. Their mutual fascination with each other had worn off a while ago and now they existed in apathetic harmony. She walked quickly up the two flights of metal stairs and unlocked the door. Jack was forever telling her they had to up the security on the place. She had thousands of pounds' worth of materials in the studio.

Dumping her handbag on the floor and carefully lifting the too-small shoes out of their box, she placed them on the windowsill. They looked like two blood-spots in the all-white interior. The wide planking floorboards had been painted and overvarnished so that they looked glossy and more expensive than they really were, and it had taken over twenty tester pots and Jack on the edge of a nervous breakdown before she had found the perfect white for the walls. She hadn't wanted it to look cold in the winter, but it did, in spite of her best efforts – there's precious little that can counteract the pervasive grey light that characterizes the Suffolk winter. She had had some blinds run up in sandy-coloured deckchair stripes and that had helped warm things up a bit. It had to – the windows ran round every side of the room so there were lots of them. Jack always used to worry that she was too exposed working up here, with 360-degree views where anyone could see her alone in the creek. But Laura insisted that neither bored teenagers nor avid bird-watchers had any interest in her.

The red flashing light on the answering machine caught her eye and she went over to listen. After several years of working alone with only Radio Four for company, it was still a surprise to realize that people were actively seeking her out and calling her up with commissions. The move from jewellery hobbyist to professional goldsmith had been accidental, when the charm necklace she'd made for Fee's mother had provoked a positive response at the WI. After weeks of ignoring Fee's nagging, well-intentioned demands to set herself up properly, her friend, young as she was, had taken it upon herself to place a formal advert in the *Charrington Echo*. Rather serendipitously, the editor of the *FT* magazine had been holidaying in neighbouring Walberswick at the time and happened to chance upon it whilst waiting for her lunch order in the pub. An hour later she had knocked on

Laura's door and from there it had been but a hop, skip and a jump to the prestigious placement in the *FT* magazine's jewellery pages.

Today there were two messages, both from Fee – now working as her self-appointed PR and manager on the days she wasn't manning reception at the leisure centre. Through squeals and much clapping, she was forwarding appointment dates for three prospective new clients. Yesterday there had been another one, and this was several weeks after the article had come out. Laura scribbled the dates and times in her diary, shaking her head over the fact that the commissions were still coming in. The feature had been about new-generation jewellers, and the box on Laura had been the smallest, squeezed in at the very last minute. She had pretty much dismissed it as soon as she'd seen it because they'd cropped the photo so you couldn't see her shoes, but clearly lots of people hadn't, because the little red light was still happily flashing most mornings when the tide finally let her in.

Laura walked over to the bench and began casting a critical eye over the previous day's work – a necklace that was for a wedding next week. She caught a glimpse of the grey heron beating past the east window, and knew her eleven o'clock appointment had arrived hot on her heels. Good old Grey. He was better than any CCTV system. He stood for hours in the reed bed, only retracting his neck and leaping into flight when one of her customers passed by on the path to the studio. Like the avocets and bitterns, he just ignored her now.

'Hello?' a male voice drifted up questioningly, and she heard his shoes on the patterned metal treads.

'Come up to the top,' Laura called before taking a deep,

calming breath. She slid the unfinished necklace into a drawer and refilled the kettle, somewhat aghast to notice that the limescale had flourished unchecked so that it looked more like a coral reef in there.

'Hello,' the voice said, near now.

She set a smile upon her lips, took a deep breath and turned. 'Hi,' she replied, as a well-dressed man emerged through the doorway.

He stopped where he was, either transfixed or appalled by the sight of her. In keeping with her 'take me as you find me' defiance (and in direct contrast to Fee's 'take me, I'm yours' dress sense), she was sporting a grubby pair of boyfriend jeans that fell so low they exposed the upper curve of her hip bones, and a faded black Armani A/X sweatshirt of Jack's. The only things about her that were shiny were her teeth and the glossy red flats on her feet.

'Ms Cunningham?' he enquired, holding out a hand.

'Laura,' she replied, shaking his hand so lightly that her fingers slipped away just as he squeezed and he was left gripping her fingertips. He looked down at their star-crossed hands and released hers.

He straightened up. 'Robert Blake. You were expecting me?'

In her dreams, maybe.